With their extreme ideas about traditional Ojibway life, the radical Kabatay clan have made enemies in their fight to rid the reserve of Western culture and its religion. Disowned by her family for daring to love the church deacon's eldest son, Jude, Raven Kabatay longs to put an end to the feud started by her mother, brother, and sisters against the Matawapits . . . people she's come to think of as her own since Jude changed her life.

Jude Matawapit suffered a humiliating divorce after his wife left him for another man, but with Raven, he's created a beautiful, new sanctuary after losing his previous one, and his new haven is everything he's ever wanted for himself and his children. Only two things could destroy his pristine bliss: the secret he holds close to his chest, and the vengeance Raven's family wants to exact on the Matawapits. A secret and vengeance that could cost the unlikely lovers their hard-won, much longed for happily ever after.

Renewed
Copyright © 2019 Maggie Blackbird
ISBN: 978-1-4874-2700-9
Cover art by Martine Jardin

Published by eXtasy Books Inc or
Devine Destinies, an imprint of eXtasy Books Inc

Look for us online at:
www.eXtasybooks.com or www.devinedestinies.com

Renewed
Sequel to Sanctified

By

Maggie Blackbird

DEDICATION

For my nephews and nieces: Joshua, Darren, Carly, Lucas, Travis, and Alice.

Thank you to my husband and the Mals for your never-ending love and support.

And additional thank you to my editor, Emmy, my proofer, Bri, cover artist, Martine, and EIC, Jay. Without you four wonderful people, my books would remain "drafts" on my laptop.

CHAPTER ONE: THE BIG CRASH

By eleven o'clock this evening, Jude would learn whether his brother-in-law or a man who despised his family and aimed to rework the reserve into a dictatorship would become chief of Ottertail Lake. Although the rich scent of coffee beckoned him to pick his mug off the desk and sip, the tightness in his gut forced him to rise from the high-back chair.

He slid his hands into his pants pockets and stood at the window. Snow covered the school parking lot. Winter was refusing to call it a day and let spring take over.

The office door opened. Jude didn't have to turn around to see who'd bypassed his secretary — his brother-in-law.

"Did you go to the community center and put an X by my name yet?" A hint of concern lurked in Darryl's question.

"Not yet." Jude leaned against the windowsill.

Carrying a mug full of coffee he'd readied at the side bar, Darryl plopped in the chair facing Jude's desk. "How's Raven doing?"

"Good, but I think she's a little lonely." Jude pushed off the windowsill and sat at his desk.

"Y'mean Clayton still hasn't tried to talk to her?" Darryl asked in disbelief.

Jude shook his head.

"I thought he might've come around when he backed off at the forum."

"She hasn't heard anything from them. None of her family's been around."

"Then I guess they're still on the warpath." The expression

1

on Darryl's face was a man experiencing a migraine head-
ache. "If I don't make chief —"

"You'll win." Jude crossed his fingers beneath the desk,
since he couldn't sign the cross as all Catholics did. Doing so
might unnerve Darryl, and as his campaign manager, Jude's
job was to keep his brother-in-law as relaxed as possible today.

"I dunno, man. Clayton's change in attitude at the forum
really impressed everyone." Darryl drummed his fingers on
the arm of the chair.

"His new face didn't fool me. He only agreed with you
about *if a leader can't take care of his own family, he's not fit to lead*
so clan Kabatay wouldn't come across as jerks for disowning
one of their own." Jude made no attempt to hide his *pfft* of
disgust.

"A lot of people said he seemed sincere."

"He's not any more sincere than a crocodile shedding tears
after downing a live meal."

"Welp, I told Em he has to vote for himself. Did you know
he wasn't gonna?" Darryl finally cracked a half a smile. "I
mean, yeah, he's voting for me for chief and band councilor,
but not voting for himself? Geez."

"Uh . . . that's Emery for you." Leave it to Jude's too-mod-
est little brother to put an X beside everyone else's name on
the electoral roster but his own. "Sometimes he takes fairness
too far."

"I reminded him each vote counts. I said if Clayton gets in,
we're in for a fight. We should get over to the diner. I need to
feel everyone out."

"I imagine it's busier than the four-o-one during rush
hour."

Darryl set aside his mug. "You wouldn't catch me driving
that highway. Way too busy."

"Where's your zoo?" Jude stood and wandered to the coat

tree.

"Outside somewhere. They came down with us in the truck." Darryl stood, not having to bundle up because he'd yet to remove his coat or mukluks. "Em's in the adult ed. wing. He has a lecture to listen to first. I told him to meet us there."

Jude tugged on his thigh-length black leather commuter jacket, the one he'd worn last year when he'd still resided in Thunder Bay. The stylish coat was overdressed for the reserve, but just because he lived in the bush didn't mean he had to resort to plaid and toques like ninety-five percent of the men around here.

"Walking over?" Jude ambled to the door. The school and diner were *downtown*, what everyone referred to as the main part of the reserve.

"Sure. It'll do me good to stretch my legs."

In a few moments, they exited the school. The three dogs converged on them, local strays Emery and Darryl had adopted.

"Hey, Bandit. How ya doing?" Jude petted her black-and-white patched coat while peeking at Darryl. "Have a good smudge when you got up?"

Darryl's lips straightened to a line of trepidation. "All I can do is leave today in Creator's hands. I did the best I could. So did you. You're a great campaign manager."

"And you're gonna make a great chief."

"We'll find out tonight when the last ballot's counted."

Minutes later, they were at the diner and entered to the scent of frying bacon, diesel fuel, and fresh coffee. As predicted, every booth and chair was occupied. The rest of the customers stood, holding their mugs.

"I don't think we'll find a place to sit." Darryl glanced around.

"It's the chief," someone called out.

"The chief!" another hollered.

"Laugh it up, you guys. But we won't know until tonight." Darryl wormed his way through the mob.

Jude followed.

Raven was at the congested main counter, pouring refills into mugs, a pink apron wrapped her tiny waist. Leggings hugged her slim thighs.

"Hey, I'll catch up with you." Screw waiting around for Darryl's answer, not when Raven was in the vicinity.

Jude snuck around the counter and crept up behind her. A laugh sat in his chest. He placed his hands on her waist and leaned in, whispering, "Need any help, gorgeous?"

Raven jumped. The tail of her black braid hit Jude's face. "You scared me. I could've poured coffee all over George's lap." She motioned at the man seated at the counter responsible for the stench of diesel fuel and sans his false teeth.

"Hey, George." Jude nodded. He squeezed Raven's waist. "I know what I'm doing, beautiful. I made sure you were done pouring."

"Just for that, you can start refilling the tables." She fluttered her false lashes and shoved the pot between his still-gloved hands.

"I'm already working." Jude winked.

"Not right now you aren't. So get busy." She poked his chest. Her smile was brighter than April's morning spring sun.

"Only if I'm rewarded after." He snickered and pecked her cheek. "See you later."

"You got it." She picked up two plates from the order window, threw him a flirty waggle of her black brows, and sashayed off.

Jude removed his coat and gloves.

"You vote yet?" George held up his empty mug.

"Not yet." Jude refilled the cups for the people seated at

the stainless-steel counter. "I'm going over on the lunch hour."

As he made his way through the diner, offering refills and listening to the people argue back and forth about who'd get in for band council and who'd become the new chief, the diner door opened. Raven's brother, Clayton, strolled in.

The talking ceased.

Jude filled the last of another customer's mug.

Mirroring a cowboy from one of Jude's favorite old spaghetti westerns, Clayton, flanked by his two uncles, strutted up to the counter. The customers moved aside to give him plenty of room, as if he was a gunman entering a saloon. Clayton grabbed a spare mug and turned it over. So did his uncles.

Jude clutched the coffee pot. The son of a bitch could help himself to the fresh pot on the burner. He sure wasn't filling the jerk's mug.

From the kitchen, Raven came through the swinging doors. She stopped.

"Three Hunter specials," Clayton said in his natural sneer, but there was a hint of warmth present.

"Uh . . . sure." Raven moved around Jude and wiggled her way to one of the tables at the back of the diner.

How could someone, especially a mother, brother, and sisters, renounce their own flesh and blood? Jude shook his head. He strolled over to where Darryl sat. Not that Darryl required Jude's protection. The guy was perfectly capable of defending himself, but if Clayton started anything, Jude would be right there in case the tension ramped from strained to ugly.

****

Darting back into the kitchen, Raven came to a screeching halt to prevent running face-first into the upright deep freezer.

5

Cookie stood at the grill, working on sizzling bacon, flipping sausages, and turning slices of ham. A cast-iron frying pan held a huge helping of diced potatoes, mushrooms, and green onions with his special secret flavoring of spices.

Toast popped from the toaster. Raven scooted to the side counter to begin buttering—anything to keep her racing mind busy and hush her racing heart.

"Hey, hey, hey, why so quiet out there? Did everyone leave?" Cookie laughed at his own joke. "I thought everyone loved my cooking."

Hands shaking, Raven rinsed them under hot water and then grabbed the toast. "Clayton's here."

"Oh . . ." Cookie's perennial cheerfulness faded. "Aww . . . it'll be okay."

Easy to say. Only three weeks had passed after Mom had thrown Raven out of the house and Jude's parents had offered her their spare bedroom.

"We say in the recovery program *first things first,* which means I'm supposed to keep my eye on the job and let Creator handle Clayton." Raven buttered the toast. She wrinkled her nose at her unconvincing resolve.

"C'mon, you'll always have me." Cookie's soothing words were a grateful pat to Raven's heavy shoulders.

She set the four slices of toast on the plates. "What would I do without you?"

Cookie added the food that went with the toast. "We can only change our attitude. And trust Creator it'll work out how it's s'posed to work out."

"I know." Raven scooped two servings of panfries from the frying pan.

Cookie checked two more orders. "You make sure to take the time to go and vote."

"The deacon's taking me when he picks me up after my shift." Raven glanced at the clock on the wall. Two-thirty was when she finished for the day, having arrived at quarter to seven.

"I'm going over at the same time." Cookie added more bacon, ham, and sausages to the grill. He swiveled and retrieved a bowl. "I can give you a lift. Then I'll drop you off at the Matawapits."

"Thanks a bunchies. You're always riding to the rescue. I'll text Mrs. M when I get the chance." Even though Jude's mom had asked Raven to call her Maria, she couldn't bring herself to adhere to the offer. For some reason, they'd always be Deacon Matawapit and his wife. Maybe things might change after . . .

Raven shooed the thought from her head before it went any further. She retrieved the three orders Cookie had readied. "Clayton and my uncles asked for three Hunter's Specials."

When she pushed on the swinging doors, chatter had resumed in the main area, but a smidgen of tension permeated the room.

The corners of Clayton's eyes softened. He never turned away but kept staring at her.

Raven held his gaze and then submerged herself into the crowd. Her heart seemed to beat loud enough to drown out the boisterous gossiping from the customers.

Nothing sat right tonight, kind of like too-tight pants or a shirt buttoned up crooked. Normally, the deacon and Mrs. M retired at ten, but they remained awake, glancing at the phone for the inevitable ring when Jude called from the community center where voting for chief and band council was taking place.

Raven had already cast her ballot. Ignoring her brother's name and putting an X beside Darryl's had left a lump of *fuck!* in her stomach, and the chunk still resided there.

During dinner, she'd forced down the meal, because pushing food around on her plate was an insult to the person who'd cooked. Not eating what Creator offered was also disrespectful to the plants and animals that gave their lives to nourish the two-legged people.

Raven threaded the leather sinew through the deer hide. The fire in the woodstove burned low, not hot enough to produce a sweat, but cozy like a trusted blanket, a toasty blanket she needed right now to quiet her tense muscles.

The deacon's eyes kept opening and closing. He held his prayer book, something he referred to as his Office of Hours he was obliged to recite every day.

Mrs. M had set aside her string of praying beads and kept stealing peeks at the clock. She'd already recited what she called the Rosary prayer. Neither had minded when Raven had smudged. The cedar she'd burned in the abalone bowl a half hour ago continued to scent the small house.

Darryl and Emery were at Jude's, babysitting Noah and Rebekah.

"Do you think he'll text or stop over?" Mrs. M sat in the rocking chair. She kept repeating the same stitch on the doily.

"Text. He'll go straight for the house to tell Darryl and Emery first," the deacon replied in his low, authoritative tone Jude had inherited.

Raven glanced at the clock. Eleven-thirty. Late. She had to be up at quarter to six to open the diner.

The phone rang. Deacon Matawapit retrieved the cordless sitting on the small round table beside his leather recliner. "Hello."

Fingers twitching, Mrs. M set aside her work. So did Raven. She rested the deer hide on her lap but kept the needle, which she rolled around between her thumb and index finger.

"He did? That's excellent." The deacon beamed. "One sec . . ." He covered the mouthpiece. "Darryl's our new chief."

A mixture of disappointment and elation tugged and pushed at Raven's insides. Clayton would be hurting. This was her fault for resigning as his campaign manager and leaving big sister Fawn no choice but to take up the reins. Tonight was a celebration for the Matawapits but a day of defeat for Raven's family — once more.

"He did?" The deacon's grin stretched across his face. He pressed the phone against his ear again. "Emery's in. My youngest made it on his first try. Roy and Jenny also got in."

A ball seemed to stretch and press on Raven's rib cage. Three die-hard Catholics at the leadership table.

The deacon pursed his lips. "I see." He cleared his throat and gazed at Raven. "Clayton made band council."

Another term on band council wasn't what Clayton had desired, but band council held the most power, he'd always told Raven. Councilors voted on decisions made at the table. The chief's job was to chair and only cast a deciding ballot if the vote was split, since their system, under the pathetic Indian Act forced on them by the government, operated under majority instead of consensus, as was tradition.

But Darryl wanted to change the electoral system to the model their ancestors had used. He'd worked on the self-governance project after moving back to Ottertail Lake from Winnipeg.

"I see." He wrote on a piece of paper. "Melvin, Kathy, and Jackie."

Raven strangled the deer hide on her lap. Those three had supported Clayton for chief. Her family had four seats at the leadership table. While Darryl had three.

"Jackie got in because Darryl had to withdraw his name on band council since he won chief." Deacon Matawapit continued speaking to Jude but also stared at Raven and Mrs. M.

"Well . . ." He heaved a heavy breath. "This'll be interesting, err . . ." He stared at Raven. " . . . since, err . . . Clayton has the majority."

Chapter Two: Calm Before the Storm

Jude hung up. Not even the cozy woodstove at his house, a cup of black tea in his hand, or his kids sleeping soundly in their beds could produce a smile. Yes, there was cause to celebrate because his brother-in-law and brother had gotten seats at the leadership table, but four who supported the Kabatays would thwart every suggestion that came from Emery, Roy, and Jenny's mouths.

Clayton's threat from February hovered in Jude's mind. The bastard had said if he got in, this time he'd demand the education portfolio instead of recreation. And the jerk would go after Jude's job, as promised.

"How ugly will it get?" He fingered his lower lip.

"I never sat at the council table before. Will it get out of hand?" Concern loomed in Emery's green eyes.

"Very ugly." Darryl's dark brows hunched. He cast his grim gaze at Jude. "And yeah, it'll get outta hand."

"Great." Jude flopped in the leather recliner. He'd moved here in February to begin anew, but he'd be back in Thunder Bay if Clayton got his coyote paws on the education portfolio.

"What's done is done." Darryl sat forward on the leather sofa, furniture Jude had moved from his once-magnificent house in the city to the reserve. "Roy told me Willie had to work with a split council before. If he can do it, so can I. So can we." He patted Emery's hand. "We both got busy days tomorrow. We should head out."

11

"Clayton's portfolio is recreation. When the council changes over, is it still gonna be recreation?" Jude angled his leg and rested his foot on his knee.

"Don't get ahead of yourself. We're not sworn in until May fifteenth." Darryl stood.

Yeah, a measly month away before Jude's life came crashing down like a house of cards and he might be regulated to The Joker.

****

Jude and the kids should be stopping over pretty quick. Raven needed to speak to him. After last night's election, time alone after her adult education class was imperative. Thank goodness they'd drive to the school together.

The front door opened, then shut.

Rebekah rushed in. Jude's daughter always made a beeline for her grandmother and then sought out Raven. Her latest project was teaching Rebekah how to make a beaded keychain and a dreamcatcher for Jude's truck as a present for his thirty-ninth birthday at the end of May.

With Raven's own birthday in June, figuring out what Jude would get her was like playing twenty questions. Maybe they'd spend her big day with the children and his family or sneak off to Thunder Bay.

As for Jude's birthday, she'd consult Jude's sister, Bridget.

Raven set out the cutlery on the dining room table and rested her hand on her womb. Close to turning thirty-two. If she remained with Jude, she'd never experience children, something she had to think hard about, because when they'd first begun dating, he'd confessed to undergoing a vasectomy last December.

"What's up, good-looking?" Jude poked his head in the dining room and wandered in. "Need help with any homework?"

A glow appeared in Raven's belly. His dimples always did the trick. What a killer smile. Bold red lips. Jet-black hair cropped around his ears and slicked back on top. Dark-brown smooth skin. And shoulders popping to the size of baseballs.

"Care to join me outside for a vape?"

"I'll pass on vaping but will gladly join you outside." Jude winked.

A giggle sat in Raven's throat. "C'mon." She grabbed her vape off the buffet.

Jude opened the sliding door in front of the table that led out onto the screened-in deck.

A slight chill swept inside.

They both hurried through the doorway.

Raven set the e-cigarette between her lips and sucked in the tobacco flavor.

"Oh? You wanna vape first? I don't get a kiss?" Jude arched one thick but neatly groomed eyebrow.

Everything about this man was metrosexual, from the sweater and shirt clinging to his strong upper build to his crisp dress pants. "I gotta ask you something."

"Fire away." Jude drew Raven into his arms. They were almost eye level at his five-eleven to her five-nine.

"Can we go to the camp after class?"

"Sure." Jude traced her cheekbone. "You okay?"

Raven shrugged.

He set his finger under her chin. "Where's my bold, honest girlfriend who speaks her mind?"

"I gotta admit I'm sort of bummed about the election. I know what becoming chief meant to Clayton."

Jude frowned. He glanced away then glanced back. "Yeah . . . that. Well, he's still got a majority at the table."

"He does. But his heart was set on chief."

"It was a full turnout. Even most of the off-reserve

membership mailed in their ballots. The people want Darryl."

She rested her palm on his shoulder.

"I know it's hard." Jude leaned in, rubbing his nose against hers.

Raven couldn't stop the smile forming. Their special northern kiss.

The sliding door opened. Raven peeked around Jude's shoulder.

Rebekah stood in the doorway wearing a grin brighter than her striking blue eyes and shinier than her glossy black hair. "Are you coming inside? I wanna show you my new school project."

"Yes, I was just vaping." Raven held up her e-cigarette. She removed Jude's hands from her waist. "Shall we?"

"Sure." Jude craned his neck. "We'll be right there, baby girl."

"Okay." Rebekah closed the door.

"Now, where were we?" His grin took on a satisfied cat licking a bowl of cream.

"I think we should get inside. I don't want your kids catching us kissing. They're far from ready for that."

"Smart woman."

"Very smart." She couldn't resist giving him another northern kiss. "Supper should be ready."

"Then we'd better not keep them waiting." His hand remained on the small of her back while leading them into the house.

Everyone was seated at the table. Raven took her usual spot beside Jude. The kids sat opposite them. The deacon and Mrs. M always sat at the head and foot.

The family bowed their heads in prayer. Raven's cell phone beeped. Since she never joined them in saying grace, she quietly retrieved the phone from the serving buffet that housed Mrs. M's collection of knickknacks and china.

Her heart almost burst into a sprint. The messenger was Clayton.

She darted through the kitchen entranceway beside the dining room that also faced the lake. While standing at the sink, she slid her thumb across the screen. The message popped up.

Fawn and I are leaving on the plane tomorrow. We're taking Mom to Thunder Bay. Nurse practitioner recommended it. Mom's gotta see a specialist.

Raven set her hand on the sink to steady herself. She furiously typed in . . .

What's going on?

Dunno. She's been sick since last night. Stomach.

Which specialist?

Whichever one's at the hospital.

The hospital?

Raven leaned on the counter.

Will let you know what's going on after we get there. Later.

She typed back a goodbye and held the phone to her mouth.

"Is everything okay?" Jude's breath warmed Raven's ear.

She turned. "Clayton texted me."

"Oh?" Jude's half-smile vanished.

"He—he said Mom's not feeling well and the nurse practitioner set everything up for Mom to go to Thunder Bay for tests."

Concern flooded Jude's eyes. "Oh . . ."

"She . . ." Raven licked her lips. "Before she booted me out, she was complaining about her stomach lots. It started at Christmas. I think it made her angrier than her normal angry."

"We can talk more after class tonight. C'mon. It'll be okay."

Raven let Jude lead her back into the dining room, but her phone remained tight in her hand.

****

Jude pulled up to an all-too-familiar place—Geoff's Camp, a good five clicks outside of the reserve, owned and operated by a guy originally from the Northwest Territories, a big red-headed Irishman who was currently in Mexico, where he always bolted during the season's downtime.

He shifted the gear into park. They didn't have to race home. Emery had volunteered to watch the kids tonight after Jude had texted his little brother, saying he had to speak to Raven and wasn't sure when they'd finish.

Raven cracked open the truck door and got out. Before joining her, Jude retrieved a couple of bottled waters from the small cooler in the backseat. She stood in the headlights, puffing on her e-cigarette.

"I'm sure it'll be okay." Jude winced. Trying to solve everyone's problems, especially his ex-wife's, was what had ended his marriage. Raven needed comfort and support, not answers or a handyman ready to fix her problem.

He cleared his throat. "I'm here for you." Much better. "Need this?" He patted his shoulder.

Raven's bleak stare vanished, and her downturned mouth moved upward. She did rest her head on his shoulder. He draped his arm around her waist and pecked the top of her head.

Her white puffs of breath floated away on the air. He brushed at her arm.

"You're the best," she said quietly.

"No. Not the best. You're teaching me how to be a . . ." He'd almost said *partner*. Were they partners after only seeing each other since February? She was his girlfriend, but the word was more appropriate for people in their teens or twenties. Not two grown adults in their thirties. Perhaps she *was* his partner then.

"I'd say we're both teaching each other." Raven's husky voice was the *kitten-claws scratch* whenever she spoke quietly. "If not for you, I woulda let Clayton hurt Darryl, and hurt Emery, hurt your family . . . all for a diner."

"But you didn't. You did the right thing by standing up to your family. Using another's mistake against them isn't right. Your family's always promoting the Seven Grandfathers teachings. It's about time they started living by them."

"They try . . . they do." Raven tapped her fingers on her hips. "It's Mom. It's always Mom. I'm not sure how to feel."

"Is that what's bothering you?" His lips brushed the smoothness of her silky black hair.

"I told you a million times, she's had it out for me from day one. It's not my fault Dad died when she was pregnant with me. Or that he drank himself to death. I guess me being a drug addict . . . I think whenever she sees me, she sees him."

"It could be something else."

"The recovery program teaches me I'm not supposed to judge others by how I think or how I interpret the world. It teaches us everyone has their own point of view. It's like this one book I read. It was a memoir. The author said in the introduction this was the truth she saw during the events she described, and it might differ from how others involved in the events saw it."

17

"Smart outlook."

Her cell phone beeped. She dug inside her pocket.

Jude stole a sip of his water.

"It's Clayton." Raven gasped. "Mom's stomach pains got so bad they took her to the nursing station."

This wasn't good. An ulcer? Jude could only guess until the doctors in Thunder Bay ran tests to determine what was going on.

"I-I-I don't know what to do." Raven wormed out of Jude's embrace and stuck the vape between her lips.

"What do you mean?" At times of crises, Jude had always taken charge, but this wasn't his place to tell Raven what to do. Being handcuffed to only offering support was a jail sentence.

"I-I don't know if she wants to see me or not. She hates me. She kicked me out." Raven hugged herself.

"Hey. Easy . . ." He drew her back into his arms. "Who's all there?" He petted her hair.

Raven typed away on the phone. "When I did the sweat, I thought—"

"You consulted a higher power you believe in during your sweat. Let's try trusting Him. Okay?"

"I'm going." She raised her chin. "If they wanna keep hating me, they can. But at least I went, even if Mom tells me to get the hell out."

Jude forced a nod when his head ached to shake no. "I'll take you there. Let's go."

****

Raven's heart rattled and shook more than the truck going over the few spots worn away to washboard as they made the trek from Geoff's Camp to the Grassy District, where the nursing station was located. Someone needed to grade the road, and they might as well run the grader over her chest to still her banging heart.

Jude pulled up outside the nursing station.

Vehicles belonging to her brother and sisters and a couple more people were already parked. Just what Raven needed — a family reunion. The nurses had probably called in the emergency medical plane and were preparing to fly Mom out.

The truck engine hummed. Raven grabbed her purse. "I think it's best if you stay here."

"I . . . I . . . understand." Jude reached over and locked his fingers around hers. "I do . . ."

"It's not because I don't want you there. But it'll be easier if it's only me. Maybe they'll react differently if they don't see you."

"They'll know who gave you a ride — one of the terrible Matawapits," Jude said quietly, which told Raven even if he understood, her family's shit behavior still bothered him.

"I know," she murmured. "I wish it could be different. I really do."

When he squeezed her fingers, a smidgen of courage washed away the fear coiling around Raven's ribs. "I should only be a few minutes."

She freed her fingers from his. The unfairness of her family seemed to rake like nails down her back, because her brother and sisters had probably brought their partners for support.

Taking one last vape, Raven forced her feet to make the trek from Jude's midnight-blue four-by-four to the health station.

CHAPTER THREE: HEAVEN IN THE BACKSEAT

Raven held her head high and sashayed into the small reception area of the nursing station to the strong scent of medicine. Beyond the main desk were the section of curtains where patients received medical treatment. Murmurs carried from behind the first one by the window. Whispers belonging to Clayton, Fawn, Lark, and Wren. Mom's groans also drifted to where Raven stood.

Her shaky emotions were a giant wave on the lake, ready to swamp Raven's little boat. She flopped on one of the plastic chairs and clutched her purse to her chest.

A nurse appeared from behind the curtain. Fanny. A non-native who flew up on the usual schedule of two weeks on and one week off. She sat at the desk in front of Raven.

Raven leaned in. "How's my mom?"

"Go on in and see her. Your brother and sisters are here."

"Is she up to seeing anyone?"

"She's in a lot of pain but medicated. We're waiting on the plane. As soon as it arrives, she'll be taken to Thunder Bay. Fawn's accompanying her."

If Mom was sedated, at least she wouldn't holler and cuss. Raven stood and inched to the curtain, licking her lips. Fawn was speaking soothingly to Mom.

Raven pushed through the curtain.

Fawn's sleek eyebrows bunched together. Wren's nose wrinkled. Lark glared. Clayton simply nodded.

"What're you doing here?" Fawn rose and pointed at the curtain. She stormed past Raven.

"I came to see Mom," Raven replied quietly.

Fawn poked her head back inside the curtain. "Let's go."

Mom lay on the hospital bed, moaning, eyes closed, face pale. Her wrinkles were more pronounced. It was hard to believe she was a year younger than the deacon. And even harder to fathom she'd once been the most stunning woman on the reserve. Mom had lost a good fifteen pounds in the three weeks of their estrangement, which was bad news on her already ultra-slim frame.

"Let's go." A low hiss caked Fawn's order.

Raven stuffed her hands into her jacket pockets and followed Fawn past the curtain. They stood between Mom's cubby and the reception area.

"What're you doing here? She doesn't need your bullshit right now." Fawn thrust her finger at the door. "Get going."

Raven shoved her chin at Fawn. "She's still my mom."

"A mom you turned your back on—for a Matawapit." Fawn's upper lip curled into the sneer of a viper ready to strike. "You're not wanted. Go back to the deacon and his precious white woman."

"I didn't choose anyone." Raven refused to stand here and be accused of something she didn't do. "I told Mom she was wrong. I told Clayton he was wrong. You can't win an election by disrespecting another candidate. That's not our way."

"Disrespecting? Darryl Keejik dug his own grave by—"

"He didn't cheat on Emery. Darryl picked up that hooker in Winnipeg when he was twenty-four—before he married Emery, so get off it." Raven shouldn't let her temper surface, but reasoning with her family, she'd get more cooperation from one of the reserve's stray dogs.

"*My* brother had every right to do what he did. Darryl sure hasn't played fair. He tried to turn the whole reserve on us."

Fawn set her hands on her slim hips.

"He did no such thing." Raven gasped. "All he's trying to do is walk the red road."

"If all you're gonna do is defend that family, get out." Again, Fawn pointed at the door.

"Fine." Raven trounced straight to the door with Fawn's thundercloud expression glaring in the reflection off the glass.

Raven shoved the door open and strode out into the cool night air, straight into the headlights from Jude's running truck. She got in, her butt thumping hard on the heated leather seat.

Jude reached over and squeezed her hand.

A lump the size of an onion settled in Raven's throat. She forced the stupid thing downward. If her family didn't want her during such a crucial time for Mom, so be it.

"Wanna take a drive?"

Raven's neck was stiffer than an unoiled hinge, but she managed to nod. She stared out the passenger window.

"Y'know, it's okay to cry."

Tears gathered in Raven's eyes. "I'm not gonna cry for them." Her voice shook.

"They're your family. If my family acted that way, I'd be pretty upset. I'm thankful they accepted us. When Dad and Emery were estranged over Darryl, he was hurting really bad."

Raven turned. "I can't believe your dad did that to his own son."

Jude sighed. "Family can have strong feelings about who we associate with, especially people we don't approve of. But Dad understood he was wrong. If Emery was truly meant to be a priest, I'd be going to his ordination next month. I'm not."

"Would it have been weird?" Raven dug her vape from her purse.

"Nope. I thought good and hard about the permanent

diaconate at one point. I have no regrets I didn't even get past the orientation." Jude chuckled.

"I can't picture you as a deacon like your dad." At least the lump had vanished. Again, Jude had worked his magic, dispelling the terrible ache in Raven's chest.

"Can I?" She held up the vape.

"Go ahead." Jude cracked her window down one-third of the way. "After what happened, you deserve it. It's only vapor."

He released her hand and shifted the gear into drive. "Where to?"

"Anywhere. Far from here."

"Gotcha." He drove away from the nursing station.

After a few minutes, they turned off onto the other road. Soon they'd come upon the junction leading to the Matawapits' house, or they could go straight or hang a right.

"I wanna go to the Treaty Grounds."

"Sounds good in my book." He reached over the console and locked their fingers together again, his thumb massaging the back of her hand. "Whatever you need."

"What I need is to get fucked." Raven sucked on the vape. The nicotine flavor scooted down her throat.

"Funny." Jude chuckled.

A deep breath left Raven's lungs. "I'm serious."

"Uh . . . really?" Jude glanced at her and back to the road.

"Yeah. Why?" She peered at him.

"It's just—honestly?"

"Yeah—honestly."

He cleared his throat. "I assumed most women wanna be held during a . . . tough time."

"Remember, I'm nothing like your ex-wife." Having Jude deep inside her would ease away the queasiness in Raven's stomach, an off-and-on queasiness after meeting Jude and knowing sooner or later she'd have to choose him or her family.

"You sure aren't." Jude expelled a low whistle. "Nothing like her at all."

Raven let go of his hand. She stuck the vape in the cup-holder and worked off the leather jacket Jude had bought during their trip to Thunder Bay. To save time so they could get busy right away, she discarded her mukluks. She might as well remove her clothes, too.

When she unbuttoned her cardigan, Jude sputtered. "Whoa, what're you doing?"

"Undressing."

"Uh, yeah, I see that." He grinned wolfishly. "I . . . I feel guilty being turned on when you're feeling bad."

"I told you. I'm not like other women. They want cuddles? I want dick. Your dick." Raven shucked the cardigan. She unfastened her bra.

"My dick belongs to you."

The headlights bounced off the skeleton remains of sleeping underbrush soon to wake with the coming spring.

Raven wiggled from her leggings. She folded them. All she had left was her panties.

"I gotta admit, I like this way of making you feel better during a tough time." Jude's reply was deeper than his normal authoritative tone, slightly dewy when he grew horny.

He pulled up at the Treaty Grounds. Snow still blanketed the grass area leading to the bleachers and arbor. He turned, smiling.

At her height, scooting into the backseat wouldn't be easy, but Raven managed to get her limbs through the gap between the two front seats. Jude's fingers pinched her bare butt, wiping away the last of the heaviness in Raven's chest.

She plopped on the comfy seats. Thank goodness the club cab was roomy enough to accommodate three full-sized adults comfortably.

The front door opened then closed, followed by the passenger door opening. Jude bared his dimples. He removed his jacket and tossed it in the front. A nip of chilly air scooted into the vehicle. Goosebumps peppered Raven's skin, and she palmed her arms while caressing her calf with her toe.

"No need to fear. I'll warm you up." He doffed his sweater. Next came his tie, since he'd taught class earlier. She didn't think of him as her Mr. Metrosexual for nothing. He worked on the buttons to his dress shirt.

Raven shifted to her back and spread her legs. He was magnificent to look upon. Strong upper build. Strong arms. Flat stomach. He was putting on more muscle again, filling out his bronze skin from playing outdoors whether they went hiking or cross-country skiing on the trails Darryl had made with his snowmobile while dragging three old tires because Emery liked to walk the dogs deep in the bush.

"You have no idea what an invitation you're presenting." Jude peeled off his dress shirt and tossed it in the front seat.

He moved inside the truck but didn't climb all the way in. Instead, he caressed her chilly thighs. The warmth from his palms dispelled the cold air nipping at her bare flesh.

"Mmm . . ." Raven licked the rim of her mouth. "It feels so good."

"You feel good, baby." He kept massaging her inner thighs. His lips grazed the landing strip of her pussy.

His touch lit a fire in Raven's crotch. She always had to watch him. Watch the change in his eyes, the change in his voice, the change in his mouth that always slightly parted, as if in awe. Knowing what she did to him always left excited flutters in her groin.

She set one foot up on the top of the backseat and the other on the driver's, completely open to let him do whatever he wished.

Jude's lips left a trail of sweet kisses on her landing strip, moving farther to the excited heat coming from her clit. Close. The pecks were teasing, meant to coax her to open her cunt to his cock. Or a finger.

"Finger-fuck me," she whispered.

"You got it."

He eased his finger inside, filling her pussy. His breaths steamed her already hot cunt. When he thrust, she tightened her flesh around him. The tension she'd created was enough to coax a sigh from her lips. His groans seemed to draw circles on her belly, they were so pleasurable to hear.

His tongue flicked at her slit. Quivers erupted under her skin. She lifted her hips and humped his mouth with her cunt lips, daring him to dive in and eat. His hot breath gathered around her pussy. She drew in a gulping of air. Waiting. Anticipating.

Finally, he gave her throbbing clit what it needed and ran his tongue around the folds of skin surrounding her hard, sensitive flesh. His licks were deliciously drawn-out, meant to taunt and build tension, and each one did. He was carrying her somewhere else — the special place he always did when he ate her out.

She sighed and rocked her hips in rhythm with his feasting. Each moan from his throat left her shivering with delight, touching her deeply that such a wonderful man could want her so much.

The heat kept building around her clit. His eating was tormenting her beyond all hope. She dug her fingers into his short hair and kept his face buried between her thighs, which she locked about him. How she loved capturing him with her legs, forcing him to stay put and kotow to her demands.

Grinding her pussy against his nibbles, she gasped and moaned, savoring his swirling tongue taunting her wet flesh. He clamped down on her clit and suckled. Raven stiffened. The tension was too much, her tiny hard flesh too sensitive. It almost hurt, but a good, soothing hurt. When she tried to wiggle away, he kept suckling.

The stiffness in her belly unwound to sweet bliss. Her breaths came harder and faster. The tight anticipation was uncoiling, ready to erupt into a savory explosion of bliss.

His licking tongue, his hard breaths from his nostrils dusting the landing strip above her cunt, his finger still fucking her, Raven let the heady pleasure consume her. A rush of elation rode her spine, and she welcomed the heavenly sensations only Jude could produce.

She thrashed and bucked her hips until the explosion dissipated to sweet pleasure that left her cooing. Before she could recover, he was on top of her, the scent of pussy on his heavy breaths. His hard cock, almost bursting with thick, hot cum, plunged into her wet opening.

He fucked her fast and forcefully.

Jude pulled up at his parents' house. At eleven-thirty, the lights were off.

Raven breathed a sigh. Whenever they snuck off after class, the Matawapits kindly went to sleep and didn't wait up for her to arrive home. This always gave her hope that his parents were accepting of their relationship, even though it went against the church rules.

Throughout the drive, Jude had kept one hand on the steering wheel and the other cupped with Raven's.

He lifted her hand and kissed the back. The gentleness of his lips warmed Raven's belly.

"If you need me, text. Okay?" He spoke softly.

"I will."

"I know this is tough. Did you wanna talk about it?"

Raven picked at her leggings. "Same ol'. Same ol'. They gave me the usual shit. Nothing'll change. If Mom had been awake, she probably would've told me to get the fuck out.

Fawn did it for her."

"Remember, Clayton texted you."

"Yeah, he did." Raven bit her lower lip.

"And remember this." Jude shifted. He leaned in. "At the forum, he could've raised a lot of shit when he challenged Darryl. He didn't. When Darryl mentioned how a man protects his family, that it says a lot about him, Clayton agreed. He agreed while he was looking at you. I watched it all. And then he said he had no more questions."

"I cost him the election." She dropped her chin to her chest.

"You didn't cost him anything." Using his finger, he prodded her chin upward.

Jude was right. Clayton had chosen to take the wrong road, not the red road during the election.

"I'm sure he'll keep you informed about your mother," Jude reassured her.

"I hope so. Fawn's going on the medical plane. The rest of them are leaving on the afternoon flight tomorrow." *Except for me.*

****

Jude pulled up at the house, making sure not to park behind Emery's truck so his brother could get out. Late. And Emery had his own schedule to adhere to. He liked getting up early to walk the dogs before tackling his distant education classes for his master's in social services.

The only light came from the living room. Emery was probably watching TV.

Jude quietly entered the house. To balance himself in the dark while removing his boots, he leaned on the bathroom door. If he flipped on the small light, he might alert the kids, who probably had their bedroom doors open by now to catch the heat from the woodstove.

The noise of the TV didn't carry to where Jude stood. He

hung his coat on the hook and wandered across the kitchen to the living room.

"Thanks."

"No problem." Emery stood. He gathered up an empty bag of chips and bowl of dip.

"How were they?" Jude could've smacked his forehead. Always, while he taught the adult education class, he set his cell phone to vibrate and checked his messages afterward, but he'd forgotten to tonight.

He slipped his phone from his pants pocket. Great. One missed call. His ex-wife.

Chapter Four: Run Your Hurt Away

At the school at quarter after eight in the morning, Jude sat at his desk. Charlene resided in Kenora, so they were in the same time zone. She usually didn't see patients until eight-thirty and liked to get to work a half hour earlier to review her paperwork. Now was the perfect time to call.

Hopefully she'd keep whatever she had to say brief. The kids were due to see her this weekend. He called up her number on his contact list and hit *send*.

Charlene answered on the first ring. Not good, if she was eager to speak to him.

"Hey. What's up?"

"Do you have time to video chat?" Her question matched their daughter's little-girl voice.

"Yep. I already have my laptop on."

"Great. See you in a second." She hung up.

Jude turned his laptop to face him and signed in. He sipped his coffee. Her call came up on the screen, and he hit *accept*.

She appeared, blonde hair pinned into a loose bun—what she used to do when they'd been married. She preferred a professional look working as a nurse practitioner. Only a touch of mascara and a tint of lip gloss for makeup.

"How're the kids?" Her words had once been soothing and silken enough to work away every kink in Jude's muscles. Now, it was a reminder of what she'd done to him.

"Good."

She licked her pink lips. "Are they happy about coming this time?"

During Easter, the kids had wanted to remain at the reserve. He'd had to almost bribe them to get on the plane — something he didn't believe in. And during their visit, the kids had called home, begging for him to come and get them. They'd wanted to attend Holy Thursday, Good Friday, the Easter Vigil, and Easter Mass with their grandparents, because they liked watching Grandpa do his *very important stuff* with Father Bennie. And Noah had wanted to help altar serve.

"So far no complaints." He took another sip of his coffee.

"You're looking well. You put on some weight." Her assessment wasn't insulting but flattering, full of pride, because she'd always told him how much she'd loved his body, which was a lie in his book, otherwise she wouldn't have cheated on him with one of his colleagues.

"Life's been good. I regained the fifteen pounds I lost." No thanks to his ex-wife. Her affair had sapped him of his appetite the first year they'd separated.

"I guess it is, if you're seeing someone." Her remark wasn't snide but simply a quiet observation. And she did her usual glancing about instead of facing Jude.

She'd done this the last time she'd asked to video chat. Why bother meeting face to face if she wouldn't stare at the screen?

But he knew the answer. From the start of their university days, whenever something had upset Charlene, and confrontation not being her forte, she talked around her feelings, very much like Mom did.

"Is there something specific you needed to speak to me about?" It was hard for Jude to shuck his natural way of addressing someone, but he did his best to coat his words with thoughtfulness.

While Charlene's gaze bobbed everywhere but on him, he

kept stealing drinks from his mug until it was empty.

"I'm going to get some more coffee while you . . ." *Waste my time.* " . . . think of the best way to tell me what you wanted to speak about." He stood.

She drew in a breath. "Go ahead."

At least irritation hadn't crept into her answer, like it had in the past.

Jude wandered to the sideboard and fiddled about by adding cream and sugar to his coffee. Then he replenished the sugar bowl and refilled the creamer. He stirred the contents in his cup a good fifty times. Finally, he made his way back to the desk and sat.

Please, please let her be ready to speak. I got a busy morning.

Charlene's gaze continued to ramble everywhere. "I'm just going to say it." She moved her hand in a determined straight line. "Tell the kids we'll be staying at a hotel."

Jude squinted. That was fast. "Oookay."

Maybe Stephen Baker, the man he'd introduced to his family, the man he'd given his sister's phone number to, the man who'd taken Bridget out on a date twice, the very man Charlene had the gall to pursue since his sister had been hung up on Adam at the time before marrying him last year, wasn't so perfect after all.

Charlene toyed with her French-manicured nails. "You don't want to know why?"

Nope. "Unless it impacts the kids, your personal life is your personal life."

"It will impact the kids." She again glanced around. "I'm taking a break for the time being."

Yep, there was trouble in what she'd assumed was a perfect paradise—perfect enough for her to run off to Kenora when Jude had confronted her about the affair and had demanded a divorce.

"I see . . . Okay, welp, I guess you'll be telling them?"

"No. No." She shook her head. "I'll simply tell them I want

to stay at a place with a pool for the weekend." Her bright-blue eyes shifted about, eyes their daughter had inherited. "They'll like that."

"They will." He twirled the pen around in his fingers. "Is there anything else?"

Charlene's gaze again traveled around. "I . . . I . . ." She glanced downward. No doubt she was picking at her nails. "I . . ." She heaved a breath. "For the time being, I'm not pursuing the annulment." She bowed her head.

The coffee threatened to unseat itself in Jude's stomach. He sat straighter. "What?"

"Y-you heard me. I need time to think," she said firmly.

Jude looked away. He stuck the tip of the pen into his mouth. But the Catholic Church and God considered them still married. Okay, he could do this — stay cool and ignore the heating of his blood.

"May I ask why?" He made sure not to bark his question, even though sand seemed to coat his tongue.

"I . . . I . . ." She swiped at her pulled-back hair. "I need time to think. That's all."

"Okay." The word came out slowly, methodically.

"There's been talk . . ." She huffed another breath. "Talk about us at church. Talk at Stephen's school."

Naturally there was talk. Stephen Baker was the principal for a Catholic school, as Jude had been before he'd resigned and relocated from Thunder Bay to Ottertail Lake.

"And . . ." Her eyes took on the glassy still water of a pond. "I-I feel like I rushed everything. I-I . . ." She was twisting something in her hands Jude couldn't see.

"I . . . it all happened fast." The spout that took forever to twist open had finally released its rusty grip on her mouth. "Too fast." She swiped at her patted-down hair.

"You — you . . . we . . . you . . . confronted me. We fought. You demanded a divorce. It all . . . I never had time to stop and really think." Her delicate shoulders shook.

"You never listened to me," she murmured in the familiar delicate echo from whenever they'd previously fought and she'd withdrawn in frustration while he'd thrown up his hands in disgust, and she'd fled, accusing him of only hearing what he wanted to hear.

Jude kept gnawing on the pen cap. The muscles of his shoulders tightened. Here they were again—same fight. The same fight they'd had for the duration of their marriage.

"I . . ." He must choose his answer wisely. "Let's take a time out. Okay? We can talk some more tonight."

Charlene's delicate shoulders kept quivering. "Sure."

"Call me tonight. After supper."

"Thank you . . . *Jude*."

The way she'd said his name, a faint whisper on his ear, soft, luxurious, and quietly satisfied. Goosebumps spooked his spine. The same nineteen-year lullaby with Char's head resting on his chest after he'd made love to her.

"Yep. Bye." He punched the *end call* button and snatched his mug, slurping his coffee.

He'd better get these folders to the teacher. He had too much to do. Busy. Busy. He rose and strode from his office, gripping the folders.

"Mr. Matawapit," his secretary called out.

Jude stopped at the second office door and whipped on his heel. "What is it?"

He was close to strangling the folders.

"There's an urgent phone call from—"

Red kept appearing in front of his eyes. Red anger. Red disgust. Red loathing.

"Look . . ." He held up the folders. "Leave any messages on my desk. I'll be right back."

He trounced down the hall, but instead of heading for the math classroom, he steered himself to the adult education wing where he'd find Emery.

The sticky black tar of doom sat in Jude's stomach. He'd never sought help before from his siblings, or anyone else. But the Lord and Raven had taught him holding problems in his head was what had—No, it wasn't his fault Charlene had cheated.

The memories he'd chained behind the iron gate raced like water rushing through a broken dam. He stopped and pressed his hand on the wall, chest rising and falling.

The fight *that* Thanksgiving weekend. Charlene walking out the door—walking out to Stephen, unbeknownst to Jude. Her weekends spent with supposed friends. When he'd picked up Emery at the airport and had encountered Stephen there who'd sputtered that he'd flown in from Kenora to visit his mom who'd relocated to Thunder Bay earlier in the year.

Jude swiped at his face. His heart was a battering ram slamming against his rib cage.

At the airport, he'd invited the bastard to dinner, insisted Stephen come over Saturday night, stating Charlene was going out with friends. He'd introduce Stephen to Emery. The three of them could enjoy a barbecue and some beers. Stephen red-faced and stammering, gulping a *sure*. Charlene deciding she didn't have to go out with friends after all and joining them for dinner. The concern on Emery's face.

Little brother had tried to reach out, knowing something was wrong in the marriage, but Jude had shut Emery down, insisting his marriage was perfect.

Jude palmed his forehead, where sweat seeped from his pores.

Too many weekends spent alone. Stephen always flying in to Thunder Bay to *visit* his mother, so of course Mrs. Baker's devil-in-disguise son had accompanied her to church before he'd flown back to Kenora. And Jude had foolishly greeted the jerk, had told them to join his family for brunch at The

Bistro.

He squeezed his eyes shut. Fumbled his hand along the wall. His feet guided him down the hall, heels clicking quickly on the shiny floor the custodian constantly washed and waxed.

All Jude had to do was keep going straight and he'd be in the adult education wing where Emery was studying.

Jude rocked on his heels. Turning, he bolted for the exit doors and straight into April's chilly air.

His keys hung from his neck strap. He pressed the button to his truck. The vehicle started.

Bandit, Lucky, and Keemooch, Darryl and Emery's dogs, spied him. They bolted straight for him.

His pulsating heart seemed to curl into itself. Two weeks before Christmas, the night he'd removed his wedding band—a beautiful brushed inlay in cobalt he'd proudly worn—he'd waited up for Charlene. She'd come home after midnight.

Keemooch yipped. Jude huddled on his haunches and petted the dogs.

"What's going on?"

Jude froze. The fog of memories swept backward like a rewind button, water receding behind the gates, and the lock to the iron gate turned and clicked shut. He glanced up to Emery's green eyes curiously peering.

Jude cleared his throat. "I forgot something in my truck." He still held the files. "These . . ."

"Are you okay? You look as if you saw a Jesus walking on water." Emery squatted. He petted Lucky and Bandit, who attempted to lick his face.

"I'm . . . I'm fine . . ." Jude almost gripped Keemooch's fur. Hadn't he gone to the adult wing to see his little brother? And now he was wrapping himself back into a tight cocoon, pushing everyone and anyone away, what Charlene had accused him of doing.

"Are you sure?" Emery kept petting the dogs. His look said he wasn't buying the pathetic excuse.

Jude straightened.

Emery turned and pointed. "Your truck's running."

"I . . . I must've hit the button by accident." Jude jangled the keys.

Emery straightened. "What's going on?" His perennial gentle tone seemed to touch Jude's face.

Jude licked his lips. *Stay calm.* "I was . . . I dunno . . . I was going to take a drive. What're you doing out here?"

"I was in class and noticed I forgot my binder. I was on my way to get it." Emery motioned at his own truck parked about ten vehicles down from Jude's.

"Well . . . I don't wanna make you miss any more of your class. Going for your master's is tough work."

"My family's more important than schooling." Emery raised his hand, palm open. "Yours is already warming up. Why don't we get a coffee?"

Jude glanced at the double doors then back to Emery. "Sure."

There was no better place to chat than the church basement, something Dad had taught Jude as a boy. Dad had always said if something was on a person's mind, the best place to seek guidance or bare one's soul was in the safety of God's house.

"See? I'll even put up with your *Coffee Coffee.*" Emery filled the machine with water.

Jude snickered. "You? Seriously? A *Reggie's Donut* man?" He swiped at the fur on his shirt. The dogs had accompanied them in the truck and were now outside running around the church.

They were back in the Grassy District, where Christ the

King and the rectory were located, just off Sucker Road from Mom and Dad's house.

"Sure. Sacrifices must be made when someone needs an ear." Emery readied their mugs and the condiments. Since Jude had purchased a fast-flow coffeemaker for the parish about six years ago, the java was ready in three minutes.

They filled their mugs and left the kitchen for the back of the church where the lift chair was located. The spot was a cozy area where Father Bennie or Dad met with parishioners who needed spiritual guidance or to simply talk.

Jude sat in the armchair he'd used during his first date with Raven, and where he'd first kissed her.

He faced his brother, who sat in the opposite chair. A painting of Mary the Blessed Mother hung on the warm pine wall. Dad had wanted to create a cozy ambience to put parishioners at ease. The light from the table lamp produced a velvety glow. Two small mats were placed beneath each chair.

"Hmm . . ." Jude sipped his coffee. Whatever had turned his soul a deep shade of mourning purple, the color of Lent, had vanished.

"Nope. You're not changing your mind this time. Out with it." For once, Emery spoke determinedly.

CHAPTER FIVE: FIRE AND WATER

"There's nothing to speak about. It's gone." The deep pit of agony had magically floated off somewhere, far from Jude.

"What's gone?"

"The feeling. It's gone."

"Look, something upset you enough to wander outside without a jacket and start your truck. And who're the files for? You can't tell me you went to retrieve them. I'm betting you left your office with them," Emery doggedly continued on. Not quite Dad's authoritative baritone. Closer to Mom's and Charlene's hisses when they were fed up.

Jude tugged at his shirt collar.

"Something's bothering you. That vein, the one on your forehead, it's starting to make an appearance."

Well, it wasn't like Jude looked in a mirror whenever anger simmered beneath his skin. "I see . . ." He drummed his fingers on the chair arm.

"I know we're total opposites." Emery's soothing words touched Jude's cheek, as if Christ Himself was comforting him.

"Too bad the church doesn't ordain married men, or should I say married gay men."

"I'm not bothered I don't qualify. I made my decision, one I'm happy about." Emery tilted the mug and sipped.

"You mourned, though." Two summers ago, Jude had flown up to the reserve at Dad's request after Emery had resigned from seminary and had passed on Mass for two weeks.

"Mourning was important. I had to choose between my husband and the priesthood. I'm aware May's around the corner. In a month, I would've been installed into the presbyterate." A tinge of melancholy attached itself to Emery's reply.

"You're still grieving, aren't you?"

"I wish I could have both, but I can't." By the look in Emery's eyes, Jude was correct.

"You woulda made a heckuva priest. An even better priest than Father Bennie. A better deacon than Dad. Don't tell him I said that." Jude sat up, pointing his finger. A grin bubbled on his mouth.

A trembling smile formed on Emery's lips. "I've been told the same thing by many." His contemplative stare settled on the picture of Mary. "God called me elsewhere." His green-eyed gaze settled on Jude. "Just as He called you elsewhere. You're here. You're settled. You have a girlfriend. Even though you found someone else, it doesn't mean you can't miss what you lost."

"It's not about missing it . . ." Jude cocked his head to the side. "I . . . I got overwhelmed."

"Overwhelmed about what?"

Jude angled his leg and rested his foot on his knee. "We were talking. She told me she wasn't ready to file for an annulment yet, and the way she spoke . . ."

He traced the rim of the mug. Something strange formed in his throat, and he swallowed. "It was the way she spoke when . . . when we were . . . *alone*." He arched his brow so he wouldn't have to elaborate.

"I see." Emery's nod was a small one, barely moving his head. "Did you ever mourn her? Mourn your marriage? You're so much like Dad, and Dad lives in denial."

"Denial." Ugh, this was hard to spit out. "I'm used to solving everyone else's problems. I guess . . . I guess I don't consider my own."

"Sometimes one's so busy assisting others he forgets about himself. Or he does so because he's unsure how to . . ." Emery raised his hand. "Don't go off on me. Okay?"

"I won't."

"I'm saying this as your brother, not a counselor or a *priest*."

They both chuckled.

"Correcting the lives of others can be a way of ignoring our own shortcomings."

Jude fixed his stare. "You're saying I don't like to take a good look at myself or problems I've created?"

"I believe you're great at what you do. It's why you're a leader."

"Leader? I'm not sitting at the leadership table. You are."

"I wouldn't have run if Sadie and Basil didn't nominate me. I can't tell two respected elders *no*."

"But you got in. People voted for you," Jude pointed out.

"It doesn't matter. This'll be my one and only term. Politics isn't something I'm interested in. You, however, are perfect to sit at the table. You were the parish president of the Catholic Men's Association. You were chairman for the pastoral council. You sat on the board at your country club. You ran a school. You're running another school. What you did and do is lead."

"And?"

"Christ taught us to also follow. Following is important. It's how we learn. Maybe He wants you to follow? Follow what you're feeling."

"You mean the divorce?"

"You married her right after you earned your bachelor's degree. You were twenty-two. You started dating the first week of university. You two were a couple for almost two decades."

"I gave her nineteen years of my life." Jude picked at the

chair arm.

"Did you cry?"

The familiar red heat infiltrated Jude's chest. Red heat he'd carried for well over a year. He fisted and unfisted his hand.

"Your body language says you don't want to acknowledge what she did to you."

"Put away your counselor hat." Jude couldn't help his harsh order.

"It's what I'm trained to do. I can't help it." Emery sipped his coffee. "And I hit a nerve, by the tone of your voice. So . . . you didn't cry. You became angry, but you also denied yourself anger. You instead chose a position of *I don't care*."

Man, little brother was too good at his field. "Maybe I did."

"You know you did. Like it or not, pride is a biggie for you."

Jude nibbled on his inner cheek. "My pride . . ." He again picked at the chair arm. "It was Char's biggest bone of contention. She even told me it was."

"I guess what you have to figure out is why you don't like making yourself vulnerable."

"Vulnerable?"

"Mourning makes you vulnerable. Grief makes you vulnerable. Love makes you vulnerable. You loved and lost. She failed to honor her vows and committed adultery. She chose a man you once respected and viewed as a peer. I know if Darryl did that to me, I'd be devastated."

"I'm not . . ." Jude tapped his finger on his thigh and glanced up at Mary staring down at them from the wall. "Fine. I was hurt," he managed to huff out between his glued-together teeth.

"Devastated, perhaps?"

"At the school, I . . . I was thinking about when I removed my wedding band." Jude touched the ring finger on his left hand, a spot that had sat empty for almost a year and a half now. "I wore it . . . I wore it for fifteen years."

"You miss it sometimes, don't you?" Emery reply wasn't a question but a statement.

"Y-Y . . ." *Open your mouth. You can do this.* "Yes." Jude forced the word from between his sealed lips.

"You took pride in wearing your wedding band, didn't you?" Another damned statement instead of a question.

Jude shifted in the chair and nodded.

"You were proud to be a married man."

"I . . . I was." The breath left Jude's lungs where he'd buried the discomfort. "I . . ." He had to overcome the hurdle, finally put the past behind him. Raven deserved a fresh new life. *He* deserved a fresh new life.

"You wanna know what pain sounds like?" Jude whispered.

"What does it sound like?" Emery's question was fingers brushing Jude's hair.

"Cobalt with a brushed inlay meeting granite. It makes a small tinge sound."

"Cobalt with a brushed inlay meeting granite," Emery repeated slowly.

"Yeah." Pain gathered around Jude's rib cage. A rope braiding around his heart. "That's the sound it made when I set my wedding band on the kitchen island."

"I see . . ." his brother said solemnly.

"She . . ." The cushion beneath Jude grew hot. "She cried . . . She cried, and I told her to save it."

"But you wanted to cry with her."

The pain was climbing, rising from Jude's chest, snaking up his windpipe and nesting at the back of his throat. He sat forward and clasped his hands, head bowed. His shoes needed polishing again. They were rich black leather.

"And?"

"I . . . I never cried." Jude lifted his head. "It's sitting in my throat, and I don't want it to happen. I keep swallowing it. I'd rather . . . assess my shoes."

"You have to. It's how we mourn. Mourning is a human emotion. God-given. He wants you to cry. You don't think our Lord wept when your marriage ended?"

"I get it." Jude batted at the air. "Now I even let the Big Guy down."

"No." Emery shook his head. "He wants to cry with you, because He feels your pain. Your pain is His pain. He probably wept before you did. So, if the Lord can weep . . ."

"Y'know, the Indian Residential Schools still affect our people." Jude massaged the back of his neck. "It taught Dad not to cry, to not acknowledge his feelings, to stay silent. Clayton's right. Remember his speech outside of Children and Family Services when the Indigenous Women's Alliance staged the walk for Sheena Keesha? The girl whose father was in prison with Adam?"

Emery nodded.

"Clayton said we, the following generation, inherited our parents' baggage."

"Yes, we did."

"He also said we learn by watching. Clayton's right. I watched Dad. You watched Mom. Bridget . . . she's so headstrong, she must've been adopted."

They both laughed.

The chuckling basted Jude's insides with a sunny yellow color. He reached for his coffee and sipped. The hot liquid rolled down his throat and warmed his stomach.

Emery crossed his legs. "Feeling better?"

"Yep. I forgot to stretch out on the couch, though."

"The couch?"

"Aren't you playing psychiatrist?" Jude snickered.

"No. Not psychiatrist. Priest." It was Emery's turn to laugh. He stood. "I'm going to get a refill. You want one?"

Jude checked the clock on his phone. "I should get back to the school . . ."

"We have one more thing to speak about." Emery reached down and grabbed Jude's mug.

"What's that? I thought we talked about everything?" And the discussion hadn't been as bad as Jude assumed it'd be. Was he comfortable baring his soul? Not really. But he'd made a big step in the right direction.

"Your annulment." Emery vanished. The sound of his boots meeting the floor echoed through the basement.

Jude flopped back in the chair. He'd told Charlene they'd talk tonight, which meant he wouldn't be taking the kids to Mom and Dad's for dinner or see Raven.

"I have no answers," he hollered. "I won't find out until tonight."

A couple of minutes later, Emery returned, carrying the mugs. "Did she give a hint?"

Jude took the mug. "Same ol' bullshit. She's confused. Everything happened too fast. Me catching her. Her leaving. Moving to Kenora and shacking up with Stephen. Y'know." He blew on his coffee.

"I assumed she'd have uncertainties." Emery sat.

"Uncertainties?" Charlene had made her pick.

"Considering she wasn't sure how to deal with problems she believed were occurring in your marriage, she . . ." Emery fingered his mug. "I met Stephen. He seemed like a nice guy. Bridget mentioned he was a great listener and quite understanding."

"Aren't we all romance heroes in the beginning?" Jude couldn't keep the sarcasm from his words.

"Yes, we're on our best behavior when we're first trying to impress someone. And you're making progress. Before, you would've tried to hide your feelings."

Jude flicked his hand.

45

"See. You're doing what you always do. Trying to blow it off."

"I'll admit I'm not looking forward to this convo. I'd rather bring the kids to Mom's and see Raven."

· "I think it'll be a good conversation for you. Maybe you two will finally have the conversation you never had but needed."

Jude didn't need any conversation. He tossed the tea towel over his shoulder while filling up the sink. They really ought to buy a dishwasher. Oh, hell, hire a housecleaner, something he missed because one had come in twice a week when they'd lived in Thunder Bay. At least Mom took care of the after-school cups and plates the kids tended to pile up because they always arrived home starving.

"Dad, when's Mom calling?" Rebekah scurried from the living room to the kitchen.

"I told her to call after supper." He glanced at the clock above the sink. Six-thirty. "Be a good girl and help Dad. You can dry." He removed the tea towel off his shoulder.

"Okay." One thing about Rebekah, she always listened, unlike Noah, who was hooked on gaming.

Jude looked to the living room. Noah had the laptop open. Yep. Gaming. "Turn it off, bud. Dad's expecting a call from Mom, remember?"

"Just one sec." Noah kept staring at the screen, thumbs working away on the controls.

"Off. Now. I won't ask again." Jude submerged the plates in the suds.

"Aww, geez." Noah huffed a breath.

"Don't talk back, or it's to bed early for you."

"Yeah. Yeah." Noah set the laptop on the coffee table. "Can we talk to Mom?"

"Sure. Once I talk to her."

"Here she is." Noah beamed. He carried the laptop into the kitchen and set it on the table.

"Let me answer."

"Too late. Mom," Noah exclaimed. "Guess what I did?"

Charlene's voice filled the house. Jude kept washing the dishes. He'd let the kids visit while he finished up.

"Go ahead," he said to Rebekah.

She tossed aside the tea towel and scurried around the table to join her brother.

Every time Charlene called, the kids perked up, which was normal. Kids needed their mother. Jude scrubbed at the cutlery. No, he wasn't happy about what his children had to face by growing up in a split home, but other kids had survived broken marriages. In time, Noah and Rebekah would adapt.

Ten minutes later, with the last pot put away and the kids still laughing and chattering, Jude fixed himself a tea, although he could sure use a drink. Too bad the reserve was dry. A buddy back in Thunder Bay was enjoying Jude's expensive Scotch.

Giving away his liquor collection was for the best. Raven couldn't drink, and drinking in front of her was unfair and an insult to her sobriety. Not that he drank a lot. He enjoyed the occasional beer. And his Friday night Scotch while relaxing in his former study.

"Okay. Dad's gonna talk to Mom."

Hope lit Noah's eyes.

Jude knew it was because he'd never joined them when they spoke to their mother.

"C'mon. Sit here." Noah dragged one of the chairs over.

"In private."

"Oh . . ." Noah's face fell. He stared at the peeling linoleum floor.

"Hey, you'll see her this weekend." Jude ruffled his son's hair.

"Yeah, without you." Noah stared at the screen, eyes gloomy. "G'night, Mom. I love you."

"I love you, Mom," Rebekah piped in.

Jude held the laptop in one hand and his tea in the other. "Give me about twenty minutes. Okay?"

Noah shrugged. His feet dragged as he rambled back to the living room. Rebekah followed.

Turning nine soon, Noah was old enough to understand divorce and parents not being together. Their split was the only regret Jude had, because their doomed marriage had hurt his children terribly.

With his bedroom off the kitchen, he simply kicked the door shut, set the laptop on the dresser, and sat on the edge of the bed.

"Hey . . ." He held his tea. Boy, if he had to watch his ex-wife look everywhere but at him for ten minutes and then take another ten more minutes to choke out what she had to say, he was hanging up.

"Hi." Charlene held a glass of wine. Hmm, she'd had the occasional glass on holidays and during special dinners or barbecues, but this was the second time she'd drunk while they talked.

"How're the hotel accommodations?"

"Okay, I guess."

"How's Stephen?"

"He's . . . he'll manage."

Looked like Mr. Perfect was hurting. Good enough for him. "The annulment . . ."

"Yes, the annulment. I'm not ready yet. I need time to think. It's . . . We both know it's based on whether the marriage was invalid. Can you say we went into our marriage for the wrong reasons that would deem it invalid?" She spoke in her confident, delicate voice, which used to turn him on. Not anymore. Now he experienced an itch.

"I guess it's something we have to talk about."

"Do . . . you?" She took a large drink.

He wiped his face. "I've had time to think. I can admit I've been assessing my contribution to our failure."

She winced.

"We failed." He shrugged.

"Yes . . . yes, we did." She tipped more wine into her mouth.

Jude sighed. "Please . . . say it." *I don't have all night.* "What you have to say is important to me." *Thank you, Raven and Emery. You're showing me how to consider someone else's feelings instead of taking charge.*

"It . . . it is?" She blinked.

"Sure. Why not? We're talking about our annulment."

"I thought it'd be better if we could meet face to face."

She wanted him to fly out to Kenora? It was his turn to blink.

"Do you have plans for this weekend?" she asked.

"Yes."

"I see . . ." Her eyes narrowed. "Your . . . girlfriend."

He nodded.

"What about the next weekend?"

"Let me check my schedule and I'll get back to you." He wasn't about to make this kind of decision without speaking to Raven. She was a part of his life and deserved to know what was going on.

Chapter Six: So Good to be in Love Again

Two pairs of eyes stared at Jude in the rearview mirror. He returned their stares in the backseat of the truck. Friday evening. They were on their way to Mom and Dad's, where Raven waited. This was Jude's first official date away from the kids.

Sure, Noah and Rebekah enjoyed hanging at their grandparents' and participating in activities Raven set up for them, but the four of them needed their own time. Were the kids ready, though, and Raven? The children understood he wanted to go for dinner alone tonight at the diner, when he'd told them earlier. And Raven had joined them for a couple of dinners at the house. Those had gone extremely well.

When Jude pulled into his parents' driveway, Emery and Darryl's truck was already parked. The dogs bounded up to the vehicle.

"Uncles are here! Hey!" Noah threw open the door and dashed after the dogs.

Rebekah also scrambled to get out.

"Grandma'll be calling you for dinner pretty quick." Jude went inside the house. The hallway allowed him a view through the entryway of the living room.

"Good evening. I'm here to take your guest, Raven Kabatay, on a date — with your permission," he said jokingly.

Dad peeked over his newspaper. He sat in the recliner. "I want her home by ten. And no funny business."

Emery and Darryl, who took up the couch, burst into a fit of laughter.

So did Jude, because Dad rarely joked. Halley's Comet made more returns to Earth than Dad clowned around.

Raven appeared from the secondary hallway that led to the bedrooms and bathroom, in tight jeans hugging her slim thighs and a turtleneck molded to her high breasts.

Jude let out a low wolf whistle.

This earned him more chuckles from the peanut gallery in the living room.

"I don't need to ask if you're ready." He cocked his brow.

Raven sashayed up to him. She peeked in the living room. "I see you have an audience."

"Sure do. Meet the peanut gallery."

"Ten o'clock, you two," Darryl warned them. "Not a minute later, or you're grounded."

"I do have two kids to retrieve." Jude snickered. "I'll be back way before then." He lifted Raven's jacket off the coat tree. "Ready?"

He couldn't help feeling taller than the clouds. It felt so right to retrieve Raven for a date without having to hide. And wait until she saw what he had in store for her.

****

"These are the plans I downloaded." Jude held out the papers.

Raven took them. Her heart seemed to giggle since he'd included her in something *this* important. On their way to the diner, he'd told her he had a special treat for her to see.

She glanced over the plans while munching on the perogies she'd ordered. The houses she was looking at were three bedrooms but nothing like the reserve cribs. These homes ranged from a minimum of eighteen hundred to a maximum of under two thousand square feet.

Each had a master suite with a massive walk-in closet and an elaborate bathroom consisting of a shower, separate tub, and double sinks. There was a dining nook, kitchen with an island and eating bar, and a walk-in pantry. The centered living area had a fireplace. The separate children's wing held a shared bath and walk-in wardrobes. Each house even had a utility and mud room leading from a double stall garage. Off the entryway was a home office where Jude could work. Even the garage had a storage area for a hot water tank and furnace.

"These are really . . . um . . . nice." She shook her head. Jude had referred to the houses as downsized from the place he'd owned in Thunder Bay.

"I'm leaning toward this one." Jude set his finger on the fourth plan. "I like the bonus room over the garage. It'd be great for guests."

"Are you going to install a furnace?"

"I'm thinking good and hard on it." Jude forked a piece of the chicken Alfredo he'd ordered, the diner's dinner special for the night. "I'd have to get propane. Dad and Emery insist it's expensive, but I miss a furnace. I can't get in-floor heating because my hydro would go through the roof."

"You have a fireplace." Raven tapped on the living room sketch of the plan. "Be like everyone else and use wood heat."

"Oh . . . wood heat." Jude waved his fork and then twirled more noodles around the noodles. "I don't think—"

"When are you planning on building the house?"

"Not for at least another spring."

"Then you got one more winter of using wood heat. You'll get used to it."

He grinned and shoveled a helping of noodles between his lips.

"What? Install some ceiling fans. The air will be circulated throughout the house then." She pointed at the plan. "The heat'll get down the hall to the children's rooms. I'd recommend installing a woodstove in the master bedroom. It's more isolated from the main living area."

He kept grinning and swallowed. "Your heart is really set on wood heat, is it?"

"I guess . . ." Dampness seemed to appear on Raven's face. "I guess it doesn't matter what I want. You and the kids'll live there."

"You never know what the future holds . . ." He winked.

Raven's heart almost dropped out of her chest. Yes, their relationship was moving fast, having only gotten together in February, but she swore she'd known Jude for over a year — at least.

"I do have something I need to speak to you about." Jude wiped his mouth and set his knife and fork on his plate.

This didn't sound promising. "What is it?"

"Next week the kids'll be going to Kenora." His words were solemn.

"Yes, they will." And she was looking forward to some alone time.

"I'll be joining them."

Raven pushed away her food.

"It isn't what you think," he quickly added. "She contacted me the other night, needing to talk."

"I see . . ." Raven scratched at her thighs.

"I guess she and Stephen are taking a break." He seemed to be trying not to roll his eyes.

"Wh-what?"

"And she hasn't filed for our annulment. She said she needs time to think. I guess." His jawline twitched.

"You're not happy." This gave Raven hope.

"No, I'm not." He motioned at the two aluminum pots sitting on the table. "Wanna drink our teas?"

"Sure. I'll pour. You . . . talk."

"There's not much to talk about. I won't know any more

until I see her. I tried to get her to speak while we were video chatting, but she's not comfortable talking over the Internet."

"What else is there to talk about?" Raven poured. The panic had vanished, replaced by annoyance. What was that woman's problem? She'd cheated on Jude and now had second thoughts?

"I don't know." Jude took the offered cup. "Thanks."

"No prob." Raven fixed her own cup. "She wants to still be married in the eyes of the church?"

"It's about the validity of the marriage. Annulment isn't a divorce. It's a decision made by the marriage tribunal that the marriage lacked an essential quality or qualities to make it valid. The tribunal examines what led to the marriage and its breakdown. All marriages in the church are considered valid unless proven otherwise."

"I see . . . and her cheating?"

"The tribunal considers four characteristics. The relationship's permanence. Our openness to having children and educating them in the church. It's a relationship of love and trust. And the relationship must be exclusive and faithful. She wasn't faithful, of course."

"It sounds like you have solid grounds to file if she won't. She's got to understand she's disrespecting your spirituality." Raven sipped her tea. "You told me you can't participate in this Mass thing because you're seeing me."

Jude nodded.

"If it's annulled, you'll be able to participate again. Her doing this to you is . . ." *A total bitch move.* "I know how important spirituality is to you. I wish she understood this." Too bad Charlene wasn't around to throw up on.

"I didn't mean to upset you." Jude reached across the table and took her hand.

Raven glanced about. Only a couple of people were at the diner, but each time Jude showed public affection, her heart fluttered.

Two women entered. They were a couple of years older than Raven. She got the usual snotty look from them—the same look every woman cast her way. Well, as the program had taught her, she couldn't make people like her, and the most she could do was engage those who did.

"Did you hear from Clayton?"

The night waitress sauntered over, carrying the pies they'd ordered for dessert.

"Nothing yet." Raven's cell phone dinged. "Speak of the devil." She checked the message.

Clayton, Fawn, Lark, and Wren had gotten rooms at a nearby hotel. Tests would be done. Mom was in the hospital. The doctor wouldn't confirm anything, but based on her symptoms, they were considering gastroesophageal junction cancer.

Cancer . . .

"Oh fuck . . ."

"What is it?" Jude leaned in.

"They're . . . they're testing for stomach cancer."

"What?" Jude's eyes widened.

"Yes. Cancer." Raven shivered. This couldn't be happening. She fought to read the blurred words that kept popping up. "They're gonna do an upper endoscopy. If they find anything suspicious, they're gonna do a biopsy. They're gonna do a CT scan and a test called a barium swallow. After that, she'll have more tests. Maybe even surgery. They're not sure yet.

"My nephew, his girlfriend, and their baby are gonna stay at Mom's to watch the house. Right now, they're at Fawn's."

"Who'll watch Fawn's place?"

"Her husband's there, and one of my other nephews."

"So Fawn's staying in Thunder Bay?"

"They're gonna take turns while Mom's down there.

Fawn's staying the first week. Lark's staying the second week. And if there's a third week, Wren's gonna stay. Clayton after that." *But not me.* "I . . . I . . ."

"Here." Jude handed Raven the truck keys. "Let me get the bill. I'll get our teas to go."

She grabbed the keys.

****

Raven sipped the tea and sucked on the vape. She stood in the headlight beams.

Jude kept his arm around her waist. "Remember, nobody knows yet what it is. It's why the doctors are running tests." He pecked the top of her head.

Dad's confession to Jude inside the church on the March break kept racing through his mind. His father had admitted to a love affair with Raven's mom while they'd attended the Indian Residential School as kids. They'd tried to make their relationship work, but Dad had been too caught up in drinking. Mrs. Kabatay had fled back to the reserve because Dad had been constantly cheating on her while they'd lived in Thunder Bay in some slum house. Dad had blamed himself for Mrs. Kabatay's feud with the family, as well as her marriage to an alcoholic.

There had to be more than what Jude had been told. Mrs. Kabatay was a woman full of venom. She'd taught her kids to hate. And she despised Raven enough to throw out her own flesh and blood in minus sixteen degrees weather, knowing how tight housing was.

He kneaded Raven's arm. She was wearing the beautiful coat he'd bought her. "I'm not trying to solve your problem," he began.

"Jude?"

"Yeah?"

"Don't pussyfoot around me. I'm not your ex-wife. I'm not gonna ream you out for not listening, interfering, or trying to solve my problems. You ever think I don't mind hearing what you have to say?"

Nobody *got* him the way this super-special woman did. "I was going to say have faith. You don't know the outcome yet. They're starting tests tomorrow."

"I know. I know. Everyone in the program would say the same thing."

"Speaking of programs, you got a meeting in ten minutes."

She snuggled up against him. "I'm glad Harvey's chairing tonight."

"I'll see you tomorrow. Okay? I'll swing by the diner with the kids." Yep, that was what he'd do. The first step of the four of them starting to spend time together.

He turned her head so she faced him. He slid his lips over her warm mouth.

"Hurry, Dad. Hurry. I want pan-a-cakes."

"It's pancakes, Becky. Don't be so dumb."

"Daaad, Noah called me dumb."

"Wear it, sista. Haha."

Jude loved his kids, but not on a Saturday morning when they were bickering in the backseat of the truck.

"Dad, I'm old enough to ride in the front now."

"No, you're not. If the airbag goes off, you're toast." Jude glanced in the rearview mirror at his son.

"I'm gonna be nine. I'm old enough."

"Nope. And we're already here." They'd driven to the diner, although they only lived a road over, because they were going to Mom and Dad's afterward so the kids could play outside.

"I'm out first. Haha." Noah slammed his door.

"You always gotta be first. Not fair." Rebekah flung aside

her seat belt and dashed after her brother.

Hauling himself from the vehicle, Jude dragged his feet after the kids. Breakfast should be interesting if the children were more hyper than a hamster tearing round and round on a wheel. He pushed on the diner door. The kids had already claimed a table by the counter.

"Good morning, Miss Kabatay." Noah had replaced his horns with a halo, beaming at Raven as she came through the swinging doors.

Only a couple of old-timers were around at eight in the morning.

"I wasn't expecting you so early." Raven's painted red lips spread into a wide smile. Her hips moved in the familiar wiggle Jude could have watched for hours.

With catlike grace, she glided around the table, setting out menus.

"They already know what they want." Jude removed his jacket and slung it over the spare chair of their table of four.

"Pan-a . . . pancakes, Miss Kabatay." Rebekah beamed up at Raven.

"Me, too." Noah drummed his fingers on the table. "Guess what? Guess what?"

"What?" Raven's dark eyes twinkled at him.

"Dad's coming with us next weekend to visit Mom." Noah's big smile stretched to his ears.

If only Jude could do a head-desk right now.

Raven grinned back, but her dark eyes lost their sparkle. "Your dad told me last night. I think it's great." Even her words were strained.

"Are you gonna come?" Rebekah asked innocently.

"No. I . . . I work on Saturdays. So, it's pancakes for both of you?"

The kids nodded and kept grinning.

"Oatmeal and toast on brown for me," Jude said. He tried

to smile, but his curving mouth held about as much enthusiasm as Raven's dead eyes.

CHAPTER SEVEN: NO CONTROL

Not wanting to dwell on Jude's upcoming weekend in Kenora, Raven did her best to keep busy by pouring another round of coffees for her regulars, even though the customers hadn't asked for refills. Jude's trip kept blinking in her brain like a red alert.

Tuesday morning. She'd spent Sunday and Monday, her days off, catching up on laundry, homework assignments, and helping Mrs. M clean out the closet in the spare room. Anything to make sure Raven's mind stayed blank.

The diner door opened. At Clayton strolling in, her stomach fluttered.

"How's Mom?" She turned over a mug at the counter, pushing it forward.

"Not good." Dark circles sat beneath Clayton's eyes. His normally lean face was drawn in, a true pinched expression. He flopped on the stool.

"Is Fawn still there?"

"Yep." He reached for the creamers and sugar.

"When'd you get back?"

"Yesterday afternoon." He covered his mouth, yawning. "So . . ."

"It's not good. And she's not good. They're trying to find out what stage the cancer's at."

"It is cancer?" A lump probably the size of Mom's tumor formed in Raven's stomach.

Clayton nodded.

"Why didn't you text me?"

60

"It was too crazy. Fawn's a mess. Lark's hysterical. Wren's in denial." Clayton set his hands on the counter. He tilted his head back and moved it to the right and left. "I'm waiting on a text. Mom might have to go into surgery right away. They're doing more tests this morning. They're also talking about chemotherapy and radiation to shrink it before the surgery. I'll know when Fawn texts me."

Ice seemed to grip Raven's spine. She placed the pot on the counter. "People do live through this — right?"

"I don't know." Clayton slowly shook his head.

Raven clacked her nails on the counter. Maybe she should see Mom. Fly out on the weekend. Cookie would give her time off. But Mom hated her. Fawn, Lark, and Wren hated her. Just Clayton was here, speaking to Raven.

"I'm gonna . . . I'm gonna go."

"T Bay?" Clayton glanced up.

Raven nodded.

"It might stress out Mom."

"She still hates me? She doesn't ask about me?"

"No," Clayton uttered.

Pain formed in Raven's chest.

He reached over the counter and clutched her hand. "Hey, we'll go. I'll talk to them. Okay?"

"I . . . I shouldn't have . . ." Why oh why had she sided with the Matawapits? They weren't her family.

"It's done. We gotta move forward."

"You're here. Why?" Raven choked out.

"Darryl's right. Right about what he said at the forum. We take care of our own. You're my sister."

Tears welled up in Raven's eyes. She dashed into the kitchen to not cry in front of everyone. At least someone from her family still loved her. And she'd betrayed the very man who'd never turn his back on her.

****

Alone in his office, Jude reread the text. He massaged his temples.

Gastroesophageal junction cancer.

He sat forward and texted Dad. In a few seconds, Dad responded, stating he was on his way over for coffee.

While waiting, Jude took care of some paperwork he needed to address. Fifteen minutes later, Dad came through the office door.

Jude glanced up. "Hey."

Dad headed for the coffee counter. "I'm very sorry to hear about this."

"So am I." Jude reached for his mug. "I'll know more tonight. I'll take Raven out after class."

Dad meandered to the desk and sank in the opposite chair, back hunched. This was very unlike a man who used correct posture and had an authoritative walk that matched his voice, traits Jude had inherited.

"Are you ever gonna tell Mom?"

"No." Dad cupped his mug. "It's in the past."

"Is it?" Jude's pulse pointed seemed to stand still.

"Yes." This time Dad's eyes reflected his usual probing stare. "I'd never lie to you. But I feel bad. Very bad." He glanced up at the ceiling. "Arlene's had a tough life. Now this . . ."

"You can't blame yourself. She had choices. You had choices. You two were teenagers."

"Did she?" Dad's words were almost echo-like. "Did she really? Did any of us who attended those schools sincerely have choices? Or did we grasp at whatever would stop the pain, stop the loneliness?"

Jude crossed his legs. Uncrossed his legs. And re-crossed

his legs. "I don't know. I never attended one."

Dad licked his lips. "Each of us left those schools completely defeated. And we all tried our hardest to hang on to anything. I hung on to a bottle, and Arlene hung on to me. And I . . . I let her go . . . let her run off."

"You told me she came back here."

"She did."

"And she chose a husband."

"But did she have a choice? You know how tight housing is. During our days, it was a hundred times worse. Fifteen people in a home, sometimes even more. She was stuck living with eleven people in a three-bedroom place no more than nine hundred square feet. Housing priority goes to families. Why do you think she married him? Why do you think she had children?"

As a principal, Jude ran into kids who weren't being properly fed here. It was why Dad, before he'd retired, had started the healthy meals lunch program. While Jude's own people had suffered up at the reserve, he'd been living the dream in Thunder Bay.

"I feel like at times I'm not qualified to work here. I'm not any different than the non-natives who come up to only get job experience." He tossed his pen on the desk.

"Don't say that . . ." Dad lifted his finger. " . . . or what I suffered and worked my ass off for means nothing. I sobered up, straightened up, and turned to God and gave my children and wife what I never had—so you wouldn't experience the suffering I did. I never, ever want my children to experience what I did. Ever.

"I know I sometimes upset Emery and Bridget. They think I'm interfering, but many times I can't help myself. I should leave their lives in the hands of God, but it's hard. Very difficult to undo the years I was in the school. Five to sixteen. That's a lot of years to spend mistrusting and hating."

"Dad . . ." Each time Jude heard about the Indian Residential School from his father's lips, pain gripped his heart. Dad never should've had to suffer like that—all for being the wrong skin color, the wrong culture, the wrong spiritual beliefs.

"It's why I don't blame Arlene for her bitterness. She has to turn it on someone, so if it's me, then I'll embrace it." Dad gazed at Jude. "I let her down. She looked to me for help, and I couldn't even help myself, let alone help her. I know sobering up and marrying your mother still bothers her. Understand, I didn't sober up completely for your mother."

Dad thrust his finger at his chest. "I did it for myself. I was tired of hating. Tired of being angry. Tired of being bitter. I wanted . . . I wanted to be happy like anyone else on this earth."

"Dad . . ."

Dad lifted his hand. "I'm telling you this for a reason. To comprehend why Arlene might—God help her if she can't fight off the cancer—die feeling the same way Annie did. Me? I'll more than understand and will pray for her."

Jude's stomach churned. Annie Keejik. Darryl's dead aunt, who'd passed on two summer ago, a woman Dad had admitted to cheating on Arlene with. A woman who'd raised Darryl from the age of four. A woman who'd raised Darryl the same way Arlene had raised her children.

"You told me once, after I signed my divorce papers, God has a plan for all of us—if we're willing to listen to Him. I know why I'm here. I couldn't understand it before. I was too angry. But I do now."

Dad's smile was quiet. "You're enjoying your new job? New home? New partner?"

"Yes. Yes. And yes. Okay, the house is a little small. Oh heck, too small." Jude chuckled. "It'll do until I have a new one built for us."

"Minister's Guarantee?"

"Yep. We'll see what the new chief and council say. I understand how housing works and why we have a housing shortage."

"Our options are very limited. If only the general public knew our housing doesn't work the way theirs does."

Yep, one either applied through the band and sat on the waiting list to see if they'd get one of the prepackaged houses constructed by the reserve. Or they applied for a minster's guarantee through the leadership table, since the reserve had to sign off on the loan, stating they'd pay for the mortgage if the owner defaulted. Even after the reserve approved their decision, the person had to again wait to see if the minister would approve. Those were Jude's two options. He didn't have the equity off the reserve the bank could snatch if he defaulted, because the bank could not come on the reserve to foreclose.

"We made do with our two-bedroom." Dad sipped his coffee.

"No way. Uh-uh. I want something at least nineteen-hundred and ninety-nine square feet. I'm used to an upstairs, a main floor, and a basement."

"You mean you're used to well over thirty-five hundred square feet." Dad's booming chuckle filled the office.

At least Dad was laughing now. Jude kneaded his thumb against the handle on his mug. But with the news of Mrs. Kabatay, there'd be little laughter over the next coming weeks.

"Are you sure this is what you want to do?" Jude rested his hands on the steering wheel. The engine hummed. The headlights captured a stand of poplar trees, since they were at the Treaty Grounds. Geoff had returned from Mexico and had opened his camp this weekend, readying for the spring season.

"Yes." Raven tucked a thick strand of hair behind her ear.

Jude had never witnessed her use this kind of gesture before. He reached over, setting his hand on the back of her seat. "When are you leaving?"

"Saturday morning. Cookie's giving me time off. I . . . I talked to Git. She's letting me stay at her place," Raven replied, referring to Bridget by the nickname she'd christened Jude's sister with when they'd become tight friends, much to his delight.

"Git told me she hasn't finished readying the baby's room yet, so it's available for me."

Medical services would only pay for one accompanying adult while Mrs. Kabatay was in the hospital, and that was Fawn, who, naturally, wouldn't let Raven stay in her hotel room.

"I'll be flying back on Monday."

Her day off. He'd be leaving with the kids on the Friday afternoon flight for Kenora.

"What about you?" she asked.

"I'm booked in at the *Holiday Haven*. Noah's bunking with me. Becky's in Charlene's room."

A weekend getaway, but with the wrong person.

Raven slowly nodded. She kept her eyes down. Even during class this evening she'd been quiet, when she normally fired a million questions his way.

"Hey . . ." He squeezed her fingers. "Need a vape?"

"Yeah." She dug inside her purse and left the truck.

Jude got out and followed her. Not even a wink tonight, or a sassy smile. He settled behind her, wrapping Raven's tiny waist.

When she leaned into his chest, her buttocks nestling against his crotch, a quiet breath left his lips. At least she was responding to him and not shutting him out. If she'd gone silent, he wasn't sure how he would've reacted.

"I love you . . ." He nuzzled her ear.

"I love you, too, Jude." She turned her head.

His lips brushed her silken mouth that was a silken invitation to explore. The kiss deepened, and he licked at her tongue.

Raven shifted, moving so they were face to face. Her nails raked his short hair. Shivers touched his skin and bumped down his spine. The supple kiss she returned, and her weakening in his arms, coaxed the natural protective instinct in him.

She broke the kiss. "I need you, Jude . . ." Her dark eyes searched his. "I . . ."

"C'mon." He tangled her fingers with his and led them to the truck.

They really ought to find a place to be alone that wasn't the back of his vehicle. But Mom and Dad's place was a big *no,* and he couldn't take Raven home while his two kids sat in the living room.

He opened the door and flipped up the seats so they could stretch out on the carpeted floor. Thank God he'd bought the top-of-the-line luxury edition for this model of truck.

She locked her arms around his waist while he readied their jackets as pillows they could rest on. Another praise God he wasn't over six feet like Emery, or this could get complicated. For once Jude appreciated being five-eleven.

They climbed inside, using a position of bent legs. Even though the back could easily fit three full-size adults, the automobile company forgot to take into consideration two adults needing to lie down.

Raven's lips searched out Jude's. They brushed his chin, offering a tiny peck, and then covered his mouth, her breath fanning his nose. The kisses were light puckers. He could've spent all night simply tasting the lush moistness of her mouth.

Was she wet for him? Did her pussy already possess the familiar musky aroma he enjoyed sniffing?

She ground her crotch against his hard-on. The heat from beneath her leggings saturated his groin. She moaned between his lips while sweetly licking his tongue. Her saliva filled his mouth, a lovely taste of peppermint from her flavored e-cigarette. The breaths of air came harder, moistening the dip below his nose.

He eased his hand up her sweater and traced the tiny goosebumps on her warm skin. Her tongue kept licking, deep strokes followed by satisfying sighs. He slid his hand up her rib cage where her chest rose and fell.

She broke the kiss. "I think it's time we got our clothes off."

"I think so, too." This was always a fun event. "You get the truck. I'll get most of mine off outside." Since it wasn't freezing cold anymore.

He sat up and opened the back door. While he removed his sweater and dress shirt, Raven's dark eyes drifted up and down, her gaze stroking his stomach and chest. He tossed the clothes in the front seat. At the same time, he unzipped his pants and she scooted out of her leggings. Much to his disappointment, he had to leave on his shoes and pants. It was easier for one of them to only be half undressed.

Raven waggled her finger in a *come on over here* gesture and then patted the tiny spot he'd have to squash in. Jude joined her on the floor. She moved on top, their usual position for maximum comfort. Boy, they were getting to be real pros at backseat sex.

Her breasts brushed his bare chest. Nipples erect. Her warmth coated his skin.

"You're so beautiful," he whispered. Never could he get enough of looking at her bronzed flesh and firm tits.

Her pussy draped his cock. She kept her eyes open while feathering her landing strip of cunt hair along the head of his erection. Her stroking was building a thick fire in his crotch. Each sassy stroke was a welcoming torture, arousing him enough that he thrust his hips in rhythm with her light rocking.

She swept her mouth across his lips. Her tongue swathed his in rich velvet, and he groaned. The caresses to his cock, her satin skin on his, and her deep kisses wrapped him in sensual bliss. He pushed against her pussy opening, and his cock was shrouded in wet, tight flesh. Saliva slid from the corner of his mouth from her deep gasps and heavy breaths.

He fucked slow and easy, savoring each delightful sensation her creamy snatch offered. And he reveled in her hungry kisses savaging his mouth. He massaged her flexing buttocks with his fingers, her ass rising and falling with her rhythm that matched his thrusts.

She was working him into a fever. The air was hot and thick in his lungs. He fucked harder, his cock demanding to get off. Her own moans and gasps between his lips fired electrical shots of ecstatic pleasure through his limbs. He was one with her again, moaning and telling her how much he loved her.

CHAPTER EIGHT: JUST NO GIVIN' UP

Located about four or maybe six kilometers outside of Kenora, the airport wasn't that big. Charlene was waiting at one of the seats. The kids scampered ahead, dashing for the door, shouting for their mother. Jude dragged his heels behind them. He'd brought his laptop and briefcase for work if Charlene took the kids somewhere.

"Mom! Mom!" Rebekah darted to her mother.

Noah swaggered up to them, grinning.

While they reunited, Jude waited for the luggage to be unloaded from the plane. He kept his back turned. Charlene had cost him a weekend with Raven. He could've accompanied her to Thunder Bay and been a shoulder of support.

Instead, he was in Kenora. Spaghetti town, because of its hills, sharp turns, and streets that twisted and wound everywhere, as if someone had come up with the road plan by tossing a plate of noodles into the air.

It'd be a snaking drive to Highway Seventeen A where most of the hotels were in the east end of town.

The luggage was set out with those of the other passengers. Jude lifted the handle for the suitcase he'd packed for him and the kids and strode over to where Charlene and the children stood.

A year and a half had passed since they'd last congregated this way. Foreign now, to join his ex-wife with their kids after growing accustomed to only the three of them.

Charlene kept her arm around Rebekah. "It's good to see you." Shyness lurked in her half-smile, but her blue eyes sparkled.

Jude nodded. "Ready?"

"Yes." Charlene motioned to the door. "I'm parked right outside."

She led the way, still holding Rebekah's hand. Noah walked beside them. Jude chose to bring up the rear. The sun was out, having followed them from Ottertail Lake.

"How's work going?" Charlene glanced over her shoulder at him.

"Good." Emery had insisted Jude and Charlene needed to have a good and final talk. What they would say was beyond him. His gut had turned black again. The tightness in his chest had reappeared.

"Here we are. Here we are." Rebekah pranced around Charlene's SUV, the one she'd driven from Thunder Bay to Kenora to begin her new life with Stephen Baker.

"Dad still won't let me sit in the front," Noah whined. "Are you gonna make me sit in the back?"

Charlene pointed. "It's for your own safety."

"Aww, geez." Noah climbed into the vehicle, and Rebekah joined him.

Jude's chest kept tightening.

While Charlene continued to talk to the kids, window open to the backseat, Jude loaded the suitcase, laptop, and briefcase into the hatchback. He shut the door and rounded the SUV, heart seeming to grind instead of beat. Tomorrow, Raven would leave for Thunder Bay. He'd text her tonight while Charlene took the kids out for supper.

"Is there a restaurant at the hotel?" Jude got in the front. Spotless as always. He drew the seat belt across his chest and lap.

"Yes." Charlene also buckled up. "There's a pool." She started the engine. "Thank you." Insecurity filled her words. Fragile. A bit jittery. "Thank you for coming."

"Not a problem." Jude slipped on his sunglasses and gazed out the passenger window. This would be a trying weekend. Come Sunday, they'd leave on the afternoon flight so the kids could first attend church.

Jude finished storing Noah's clothes in the dresser. He'd already opened his laptop and had set up a makeshift office on the table by the window.

"When are we gonna eat? I'm hungry." Noah flopped on the bed.

"I'm sure Mom'll take you out pretty quick. She's getting your sister settled."

"You're not coming?" Noah's head popped up in the mirror Jude faced.

Jude gazed at Noah's reflection and shook his head.

"Why?" Noah's dark eyes narrowed, and his lower lip turned down into a pout.

"I explained to you already this isn't a family weekend. Your mother asked me to come so she could speak to me."

Handing his eldest child the authoritative tone left a bitter taste in Jude's mouth, but his son must understand there wouldn't be a magical family reunion. Unfair? Yes. As if he wanted to be the cause of his children's unhappiness.

"I'll take you swimming when you get back."

"Are you gonna swim with me?" Noah's dark eyes brightened.

"Sure. I brought my bathing trunks." Jude swiveled on his heel. Each time he looked upon his son, he stared back in time at himself. Dad had said he'd felt the same way when Jude was eight going on nine.

His cell phone buzzed. He swiped it off the dresser. Charlene.

I'm freshening up me and Becky. Are you joining us for dinner?

Jude drew in his cheeks. He typed back.

Sorry. Got lots of work to tackle. You go on ahead.

He set down the phone and returned to finishing stuffing Noah's socks into the drawer. With that chore out of the way, he scooped up his phone and sat at the makeshift desk to get some work done before the kids returned from supper.

A swim in the pool would be nice. It'd been well over a year since he'd last joined them for a fun time in the water.

While Noah watched TV, Jude worked away on his laptop for about fifteen minutes when his phone buzzed again. Raven?

I don't know why you got to be this way. It's one simple dinner.

No big surprise there—his ex-wife had hemmed and hawed to herself before re-texting him. She'd probably paced the floor, rummaged around in the drawers and closet, and then huffed in and out of the bathroom first. Just as she'd said his mannerisms were as predictable as a January northwest wind, so were hers.

If I go for dinner, this may give the kids hope. They're children. It's why I told Noah no when he asked me to come fifteen minutes ago.

He hit *send*.

Fine!

He gritted his teeth and typed away on the phone.

I'm taking them swimming when they get back from dinner. Or did you have something else in mind for them?

Nothing came back. She was hemming and hawing again. He returned to working. Five minutes later, his phone dinged.

No other plans. I'll join you for swimming.

The dreary blackness loomed like a storm cloud above Jude's head. He glanced at Noah sitting cross-legged on the bed. Nope, there wasn't a chance Jude could bang the table. He'd have to put up with a family swim.

Jude slipped on his water shoes and slung the towel over his shoulder.

"I'm ready!" Noah bolted from the bathroom, swimsuit donned and clutching his goggles and towel.

"I texted your mom and sister. They're ready." He grabbed his key card and opened the door.

At the same time, Charlene's door opened beside them. At least they didn't have connecting rooms. A yellow coverup hugged her five-foot petite form. Her blonde wavy hair was secured in a ponytail. Her tiny feet were in flip-flops, and she carried a bag.

Rebekah pranced around her mother in a pink swimsuit. "Dad, we ate at *Burger World*."

Fast food was a rare treat for them, so the kids must've enjoyed themselves.

"Did you?" Jude strolled down the hall of the two-floor hotel.

"Yeah." Rebekah giggled. "C'mon, Mom."

"I'm coming," Charlene murmured.

They passed a few damp people, having come from the pool before heading out for dinner. To reach the swimming area, they had to go through another door and then down a set of stairs.

Noah bolted ahead, eyeing the signs pointing to the pool

area. "I get dibs on first dip." He threw open the door and darted inside.

"Hold up," Jude called out. The kids were excellent swimmers, having excelled at swimming lessons and having a pool of their own before the divorce, but they couldn't jump into strange water without adult supervision.

"Aww, Dad." Noah's grumbling carried into the hallway.

Jude held the door open. Charlene and Rebekah joined Noah, who stared at the pool where children were already swimming. A few adults sat in the hot tub.

Charlene claimed them a table and set down her bag.

"C'mon, Dad." Noah darted to the pool.

"I'm coming." Jude removed his water shoes and t-shirt.

Charlene folded her arms and quickly glanced away. "Let me help you," she said to Rebekah.

"But I'm already ready," Rebekah protested.

"Okay then. Go ahead. I'll wait here." Charlene pulled out a chair.

Jude wrapped his phone in his towel.

Charlene eyed it. "Are you expecting a call?"

"No, but I always have it on hand." He didn't need to explain he wanted to take a text if Raven needed him. Turning, he wandered off to join the kids.

He couldn't quite move in his usual authoritative steps, maybe because he sensed eyes on his backside.

Noah used the ladder to climb in, as instructed whenever testing new waters. So did Rebekah.

Jude eased into the pool. The water surrounded him. Warm. Refreshing. It'd been ages since he'd last swum. He was saturated in the scent of chlorine. He cut his arms through the water and paddled his feet, face in and then face out to take a breath. Swimming a few lengths would work off the sandwich and fries he'd ordered from room service while the kids had gone out to eat.

He tumble-turned and again cut through the water to reach the other end of the pool. Splashes of water hit him. He stopped. Rebekah grinned. She was treading beside him.

"Want a shoulder ride?" His baby girl might be seven going on eight, but she was as sweet as the toddler who used to wave at him to take her in to swim.

Rebekah climbed on his shoulders and they were off.

"Mom, c'mon!" Rebekah waved.

Jude stiffened.

"Yeah, Mom! C'mon." Noah plugged his nose and did somersaults.

Charlene gathered her hands together, nodding. She stood.

"Where'd you wanna go?" Jude glanced up at his daughter.

"The deep end where you were." Rebekah pointed.

A splash hit the water.

Jude turned just as Charlene popped up, blonde hair pushed back and droplets of water beading down her face. Tension lined his stomach.

This wasn't right. He was seeing someone. If Raven was present, she'd be hurt. But the kids were enjoying themselves. As their father, he had to seek neutral ground, one that didn't impede on his new relationship but allowed the kids to enjoy both their parents.

He'd chosen Charlene as the mother of his children. Nobody had held a gun to his head. And he'd gladly fed her with life to grow in her womb. He'd accompanied her to the prenatal classes, had coached her in the birthing room, and together, held their children after each had slipped from the spot where she'd nourished them for nine months.

His ex-wife was an excellent mother. This past year, she'd seen them one weekend a month and on holidays. She was hurting big-time. Yes, she'd cheated. Yes, she'd given up on their marriage. No matter how they felt about one another, they both loved Noah and Rebekah.

Maybe she needed time to mourn their marriage and that had been why she'd moved into a hotel.

Oh man, was the Lord ever testing him. Jude gritted his teeth.

"Dad?" Rebekah tapped him on the head.

"Yep. We're moving." He started through the water toward the deeper end.

When he finished swimming, he'd sit at the table and speak to Charlene.

Holding the towel, Charlene patted down her face and arms.

Jude did the same. He reached for his t-shirt. Normally, he didn't care about being half undressed poolside, but swim trunks while sitting with his ex-wife wasn't proper.

Charlene donned her coverup.

Jude glanced away. Fine, he could admit she had a great body. As a nurse practitioner, Charlene believed in setting an example of good health.

"Do you still jog?" he asked.

"Yes." Charlene tied her shoulder-length hair back into a ponytail. "How about you? Are you eating right? I know it's hard to do up there. It's so expensive."

She'd always consulted the dietician at the clinic where she'd previously worked about the best meals for their family and had made sure he and the children ate properly. "Yeah."

He stared out at the kids swimming. So did she.

Tension circled the table like a hawk searching out its next meal. Each second dragged on. Jude didn't move. Neither did she.

Then the dreaded, "How's Stephen?" "How's your . . . new girlfriend?" came out at the same time.

"Go ahead."

Her face reddened. "No, you go ahead."

Enough of looking at her from his peripheral vision. Jude adjusted his chair to meet Charlene head-on across the table. She kept staring at the kids, arms folded. Emery would say, based on her body language, she was drawing comfort. It was up to Jude to get her to relax, even if she'd been the one to initiate this weekend.

"Are you staying here for a while?" He did his best to keep his voice amiable.

"I'm . . . I'm not sure." Charlene rubbed her arms where flecks of goosebumps rested.

"Cold?"

"No." She wet her lips, still staring at the kids. "I . . . I told you. I needed time alone. To think."

"Is Stephen okay with everything?"

Charlene's delicate jawline tightened. Her throat moved, as if she'd swallowed. "He's doing his . . . best . . . to understand."

She was too much like Mom. Babbling about dirty dishes, dirty floors, being taken for granted—talking about everything but what was bothering her.

"You do the same thing," she muttered.

"Do what?"

"You're the same as your dad." She shrugged.

Great, not this argument again. "What do you mean exactly?"

"You don't talk either." She shrugged again.

"I wasn't judging—"

"Yes, you were. I can see you from the corner of my eye. You're giving me *the look*."

Tension seeped across his forehead. "What look?"

"The same narrow-eyed look your dad gives. Studying me. Picking me apart. But you won't say what you're thinking. And if you won't say what you're thinking, why should I?"

He palmed his knee. "Let's not argue. You wanted to talk. I'm here. Listening." Again, he did his best to keep his voice level, even though his forehead was ready to burst from the pressure pushing against his skin.

The pinched expression around her blue eyes softened. So did her mouth. "Thank you."

"I'll get us something to drink from the vending machine."

"Okay, I'd like that." Warmth appeared in her eyes.

He grabbed his wallet off the table and strolled over to the vending machine. Giving her a few moments to think was imperative. Once she had time to gather her bearings, and he offered a listening ear, she'd say what was on her mind.

A shriek came from the pool. Jude whipped around just as Noah swam by after Rebekah. At least the kids were having fun. The bottled waters were two dollars each, so he plunked two toonies into the machine. While here, he plunked in two more toonies and bought Rebekah and Noah something to drink.

The kids continued to laugh and splash about in the pool as Jude strolled back to the table, clutching the four bottles. Funny how he hadn't bought them pop. Those were considered treats in Charlene's eyes and a rule Jude had respected during their marriage and even to this day.

He sat and handed her the water while setting the other two bottles on the table and kept one for himself.

"Thank you." With trembling hands, Charlene uncapped the water and took an elegant sip. "You're doing . . . the kids are doing great."

Jude uncapped his own bottle. He rolled the cap between his thumb and index finger.

"I . . . I . . . I miss my sister," she said.

Charlene's parents had retired early and had moved to Victoria. Her brother resided in Calgary, and an older sister in Toronto. This left Charlene and her other sister in Thunder

Bay. During their marriage, they'd spent a lot of Saturday nights at Michelle and Shawn's place.

"We chat a lot on the laptop." Charlene stared out at the pool. "I ... I ... really miss the kids. I ... I ... I'm seriously considering moving back to Thunder Bay. No. Wait. I *am* moving back to Thunder Bay."

Chapter Nine: After this Love is Gone

Jude's heart almost fell into his stomach. "Wh-what? What about Stephen?"

"It's why we fought." Charlene picked at the label on the water bottle. "He . . . he thinks starting a new family will make everything right. He doesn't understand I already have two children and they are my life."

If this was about custody . . . Jude cleared his throat. "What are you saying exactly?"

"We both rushed," she huffed out under a small breath. Finally, she peeled her gaze from the kids and met his, her blue eyes deeper than usual, a rich shade of the midnight sky whenever she was dead serious.

"You and Stephen?"

"You and me."

"Us?" Jude choked down his gasp.

"Yes. The ink was barely dry on our divorce papers and you packed up and moved to the reserve." Her chin jutted out. "All I got was a text. Did you think that was fair to me?"

"I don't understand—"

"I'm not from the reserve. I know how reserves operate. I'm an outsider. An intruder. My children and my ex-husband are band members, but I don't belong. Do you think I can simply fly in to see them whenever I want to?" Her perfectly plucked brows narrowed.

Jude leaned into the table. "If you want, I can arrange for

you to visit. There's a motel—"

"Yes, another motel." Her answer was as exasperated as her flicking hand.

"You were the one who moved." He wasn't going to take all the responsibility. She had to take her fifty percent.

"Did I have a choice? You asked for a divorce. You wouldn't hear me out. You told me either I had to leave or you were leaving."

"You agreed to the terms of the divorce."

"Yes, I did . . . for . . ." She hunched over in the chair. "You don't think I . . . that I . . ." Her eyes took on the essence of rain streaking a window on a gloomy night. "You don't think guilt consumed me?" Her voice shrank. "Of course I agreed to the terms at the time.

"I know . . . I know what I . . ." She folded her arms across her stomach, bowering her head. "I know what I did to my family . . ."

Jude pulled at the scooped neckline of his shirt. The humidity in the pool area was intense. Thick and wet.

She glanced up at him.

He kept his mouth closed and held her stare.

"I . . . I wondered if . . . if . . . if I could have the kids for the summer." Pleading reflected in her gaze, as if she was ready to get on her knees and beg him for mercy.

The whole summer? But that was his time off. Every summer, before the move, he'd babysat Bridget's son Kyle during the break. He'd take the three kids golfing. Take them up to Mom and Dad's for a visit. Plan picnics at Sleeping Giant Park. Haul them to the midway that stopped in the city during the end of June.

The kids sure weren't sitting around at home either, staring at screens. Visits to the library. The recreation center. And proper lunches made from one of Charlene's numerous lists she'd leave on the fridge.

"You know I . . . Char, you know what I do each summer."

"I'm asking for one summer. One." She held up her index finger and then dropped it.

"You'll be in Thunder Bay?"

"I don't know." She adjusted her ponytail. Adjusted the water bottles on the table. Refolded her swimming towel. "Like I said, I told Stephen I need time. All I can say is I miss my children. I miss . . ."

She set the towel on her lap, limp eyes drifting back to the kids still splashing about in the pool.

The sympathy slowly building vanished. He stood.

"Where're you going?"

"Back to the room." He snatched up his wallet and towel. "I'll think on what you asked me."

"I'm not . . . I'm not done."

If she dared bring up anything else other than the kids . . . He sat.

"Can I say something?" he asked.

Charlene nodded.

"I think before we talk about if the kids can stay with you all summer, you gotta speak to Stephen. Please figure out what's going to happen between the two of you. Is he not living up to your expectations?"

She sighed. "Stephen's a good man."

Good man? A good man didn't screw another man's wife. "I'll think about it."

"Go ahead and think then," Charlene snapped. She shoved back her chair and stood. "They've been in the water for almost an hour. I'm going to get them." Her flouncing ponytail was as angry as her flouncing stride.

****

Raven sat cross-legged on the bed. She held her tea, one toe resting on the laptop. "Thank you. You got the best ear."

Bridget's red lips almost stretched across the screen. "I'm glad I was able to make you laugh. I'm so sorry to hear about your mom. Adam'll be there tomorrow, waiting. We already have the spare room fixed up."

Good ol' Adam, Bridget's husband, and Raven's recovery sponsor. "Thanks. When do you think you'll finish the nursery?"

"It's getting there, but work's kept me busy. I still have a million things to do before I go on leave. Adam did paint the walls. You'll see it tomorrow. I still have to buy furniture."

Raven touched her own lower stomach. Even though she'd done her best to accept Jude's vasectomy, deciding whether she wanted children or not hovered in her mind.

And Bridget was a glowing soon-to-be mother, face slightly rounder at eight months pregnant. Glossy black hair spilling down her back even thicker than usual.

"Is there something else?" Bridget's gaze was searching.

"No. I just wanted to talk about Mom." Raven picked at one of her electric-blue nails she'd painted earlier.

"You sure? C'mon, it's me. Y'know you can tell me anything."

How did a woman Raven had first loathed wind up becoming the one person she confided in and adored from the moon and back?

"You know, don't you." Raven didn't bother to end her inquiry on a questionable note.

Bridget nodded. "He told me."

"He tells you everything, doesn't he?" Those two were like fraternal twins.

"I know he wasn't happy about going."

"Yeah, I got that impression. We . . . it's when we get our *alone* time." Raven tried to giggle, but her chest ached too much.

"I think that's what bothered him the most." Bridget set her finger on her lower lip. "I know what you mean to him. And I know when he's a happy man. Sincerely happy."

"He's happy?" The tightness in Raven's chest lessened a smidgen. She glanced away. This Charlene, who Raven hadn't seen, had claimed Jude's life since he'd started university. She'd taken his virginity, and he'd taken hers.

"Hey." Bridget pointed her finger just as the deacon and Jude did when they meant business. "He divorced her. He loves you."

"I know. I know." Fuck, there was so much happening. "I'll see you tomorrow. Okay?"

"We'll talk some more then. Remember, he wasn't happy about going to see her this weekend." Bridget emphasized each word.

A text came in. "I gotta go. Someone texted. It might be Clayton."

"Okay, sweetie pie. Muah. Take care. I'm saying a Rosary tonight for your mom before I go to sleep."

"Thanks, Git." Raven's heart warmed.

"G'night."

Fawn called. They're gonna do chemo and radiation first. Then surgery.

Raven clutched the phone, rereading Clayton's message. Maybe the treatment would shrink the tumor or tumors enough that Mom wouldn't need surgery. Maybe they'd cure her.

The phone dinged again, and her heart soared.

Hey, beuutiful, what's up?

Raven quickly clacked away on the phone, using her nails.

Not too much, sexy. How goes the weekend so far?

Yeah, that LOL. A little trying. Discussion one ended at the pool, and it didn't go over well. Wish me luck. Round two's happening tomorrow.

Oh? What happened?

I'll tell you when I can sneak in a call. I can't right now. Noah's in the room. Maybe tomorrow when the kids go out somewhere with her. I'm going to stay here and work.

How about tomorrow evening? I'll be at Git's after seeing Mom. I can update you then on how it went.

Okay, but call me if you need me. Okay? I'm in bossy mode LOL. That's an order.

If Raven's heart grew any warmer, she'd turn into a puff of cotton balls.

I'll let you be the boss . . . tonight.

She bit her lower lip and giggled.

Oh? You got something in mind for when I get back?

Yes. It's a surprise.

If she dared to do the very naughty, for sure he'd be hers.

Yes. A big surprise. You're gonna love it. So make sure Emery babysits on Tuesday night after class.

Looking forward to it, beautiful. I'll talk to you tomorrow night.

Love you.

Love you, too.

Raven made sure to send lots of heart emojis.

****

At eleven in the morning, discussion number two awaited Jude in Charlene's hotel room. She and the kids had returned from the mall. Rebekah lolled on the bed, playing with her new doll, while Noah punched away on the screen of his latest hand-held game.

Jude packed away his work and stood. "Remember, I'm right next door, and I can hear everything."

"Yeah, yeah. We know, Dad." Noah kept staring at the screen.

"You can't leave the room for anything." He raised his finger.

"Dad, we know the rules." Noah slumped forward, setting his chin in his palm.

"Lock and chain the door after I leave." Jude handed Noah his cell phone. "Use this. Text Mom right away if you need us."

Noah's eyes lit. He set aside his game. "Cool. I get a phone?"

"No. I'm lending you *my* phone. And you're to only use it if you need us." Jude used the most threatening tone he could muster. "I already called up Mom's contact info."

Jude pointed at the screen. "Just hit *send*." He tapped where the message he'd typed in earlier was. "Got it?"

"*Mom, come quick?*" Noah grimaced. "You typed that?"

"Yes. This isn't funny. Remember the walk Auntie Bridget organized two falls ago? Remember why? Because a native girl went missing and she was found in the river, dead. This happens to native kids a lot. People can be cruel. Not all people. But there are people out there who don't like natives. I told you this over and over."

"Okay. Okay." Noah set the phone aside. "I'll lock the door as soon as you leave. I'll keep the phone beside me. I'll hit *send* if something weird happens."

"Good. C'mon. I'm going to see Mom." Jude started for the door.

Noah tagged after him.

"I wanna hear that deadbolt turn and the chain rattle." Jude opened the door. "Got it?"

"Yeah, yeah. Got it." Noah shut the door.

Jude stood outside. The deadbolt clicked, and the chain rattled. Excellent. He knocked on Charlene's door.

She opened it, having changed into leggings and a sweatshirt, what she'd always liked to relax in. "I ordered up some tea."

Another of her rituals while relaxing, since she limited herself to one cup of coffee per day.

"Thanks." He strolled to the table and chairs by the window and sat.

A carafe was on hand and two mugs. Even some honey in small containers. He did what he'd done in the past and readied their drinks.

"Thank you." She grasped the offered mug and sat in the opposite chair. "How're the kids?"

"Good. I gave them their instructions." He offered her one of the honey packets.

"They had a great time at the mall." Charlene stirred her tea.

The same tension from last night permeated the room. She spoke in barely a hush, what she did when unsure of herself.

"I know I already apologized, but I'm doing so again." She kept the mug near her lips, hands trembling.

Jude opened his mouth then clamped it shut. She was speaking. His days of interrupting were done. He wouldn't brush off her apology.

"I'm sorry. Very sorry." Sincerity, regret, and sorrow reflected in her eyes.

"Apology accepted." Raven would be proud. He was making excellent progress as a man who listened.

"I know . . . I know I hurt you terribly. The children terribly . . ." Her pain-filled gaze drifted across the carpet to the bathroom at the front of the room. "I'm doing my best to try and make up for—"

"Don't do this to yourself."

"Can you please let me finish? For once?"

Jude fictitiously smacked his big mouth. "I didn't mean to interrupt. I didn't. I just don't want you—"

"I understand. I do." Her gaze transformed to one of acceptance. "What I did was . . ." She sighed. "I hurt a lot of people—especially you and the kids. I never wanted to hurt anyone."

But you did. He sipped more tea.

" . . . and if I could go back in time and undo what I did, I would." This time her stare was solemn, one he'd witnessed many times in the past.

He drank more tea and refrained from asking, *What about Stephen?*

"I know . . . I know the church views us as still married. And the annulment will allow us to participate fully in the sacraments again. But . . ." She set down the shaking cup and glanced to the carpet. "Do we have grounds?"

A question he'd gladly answer. "Yes, we do. You didn't honor your vows to me."

Her face reddened. "I see . . ."

"May I ask something?"

She jumped a little.

"I didn't mean to surprise you. Don't think I'm not working on my fifty percent, because I am."

"Fifty percent?"

"Yeah, fifty-fifty. I had a lot of time to assess what I contributed to the end of our marriage." He crossed his legs and held the cup in one hand and pointed casually with the other. "I know I'm not an easy man to . . . I guess we'll use the word *bear*."

She nodded.

"And it's something I'm working on. I know now I did my share of . . ." His stomach lurched. "I had a contribution to what you did. The . . . affair."

"No." She held up her hands, giving a slight wave. "I don't want you blaming yourself."

"I have a right to." He kept his voice firm. "I spent a lot of time reflecting. And it's something I don't want to repeat."

Her lips moved into a straight line of annoyance. Her blue eyes narrowed. "I see . . . you're . . . you're going to . . . going to give *her* what you didn't give me."

"This is why we need an annulment." He tried his hardest to keep his suggestion light. "Because of the mistakes I made going into our marriage, too."

"Your mistakes?"

He brushed at his short hair. "Yeah, my mistakes. Too bullheaded. Too opinionated. Too bossy. Too busy trying to . . ." He pushed at the empty honey container. "Trying to live a dream I had no right asking of you. I didn't see it at the time but I do now."

"Dream?" She squinted. "What dream?"

"Trying to be like my father. Trying to create a marriage like my parents'. I was wrong. Very wrong."

Her eyes bulged, and her mouth fell open. She set her hand on her chest that moved up and down. "I never . . . Oh my goodness, I never heard you admit you were wrong before."

"I was wrong, Char." He cupped the mug. "Very wrong."

"So . . ." Her delicate shoulders curved. "So . . . you mean . . ."

"If I could go back in time and undo what I did, I would. I have no regrets about our marriage. I married you because I loved you. I wanted to spend my life with you. But we were young. Only twenty-two. We had a lot to learn."

He sat forward and clasped his hands together. "Unfortunately, we didn't make the hurdle. I was too late. And you were too late. What's done is done."

"Done . . ." Her lower lip quivered. "I can't believe it's done." Tears filled her eyes.

Emery was right. Just as Jude had to mourn, so did Charlene. Neither of them had a true chance at crying over what they'd lost.

"I'm sorry." He reached across the table and touched her shaking hand.

The tears streamed down her cheeks. She licked at one at the corner of her mouth.

"You have a new life now, and so do I. We can't un-ring the bell, Char." He squeezed her delicate hand.

She again licked at a tear.

"C'mere." He kept holding her hand while standing and making his way around the table.

She stood.

He drew her into his arms, and she cried into his chest. God-awful sobs he'd never heard before, sobs that shook her lithe body and dug into his heart like claws. At one time he used to hold her, kiss her, and reassure her. But he couldn't today.

She kept crying, and he tightened his grip, maybe more for himself than for her. Little tears pricked his own eyes, and a tiny lump invaded his throat. They'd done what they'd needed to do—truly shut the door on their marriage.

He stroked her lower back. Maybe they could finally move forward. They needed to think about the kids and the best way to parent them.

Chapter Ten: Nightmare

Now on her way to see Mom at the hospital, Raven sat in the passenger seat of the sporty black truck Bridget had retrieved her in. Too bad Raven couldn't spin back time and be in the truck again, heading for dinner at Bridget and Adam's with Jude instead.

"Remember what Adam said," Bridget reminded her.

He'd told Raven to leave everything in Creator's hands. She looked straight ahead at the expressway, having passed on stopping at the house to unpack her duffel bag. Going to the hospital from the airport was imperative, because she'd then finally know if Mom still hated her.

"Your brother could've caught a ride. He didn't have to take a taxi." Bridget also looked ahead, designer sunglasses perched on the bridge of her sleek nose.

"Clayton's Clayton." Just because her brother was speaking to Raven didn't mean he'd changed his mind about the Matawapits or anyone associated with the family.

"Did you talk to Jude?"

"Yeah. We texted last night. We couldn't video chat. Noah was sleeping by then."

"How's that going?" Bridget made a face.

Raven didn't make a face, but her chest burned. She set her elbow on the passenger door. Telling Bridget about Charlene asking to keep the kids for the summer was a no-no. Even though Jude had taken Raven into his confidence, it was up to him to inform his sister.

"How'd you feel spending a weekend with an ex who

cheated on you?" Raven couldn't help the dryness in her words.

"Gotcha. Not good then?"

"He didn't seem mad, more like he wished he was anywhere but there."

"Can't say I blame him," Bridget snapped. "She's such a . . ." Bridget turned to face Raven briefly, her cheeks drawn in.

"He's gonna call or text tonight."

"Awesome." This time Bridget smiled.

The closer they got to the hospital, the more Raven's stomach fluttered. She licked her dry lips.

Bridget made a right turn through a set of lights. There was the hospital. Cars snaked around the roads leading into different parking lots. She made another right and slowed the vehicle, glancing about to watch for anyone who might race across the intersection and more parking lots they were driving by.

The hospital wasn't tall but took up the length of two malls. Okay, Raven was exaggerating.

Bridget pulled up at the main gate.

Raven clutched her purse.

"Call me when you need a ride back."

"It's okay. If she boots me out, I'll take a taxi. I probably won't last more than fifteen minutes."

"It'll be fine." Bridget reached over and squeezed Raven's fingers.

Before seeing Mom, Raven would buy some water to relieve her dry mouth and lips. "I hope so." She glanced at Bridget. "Thanks." *Thanks for being a real friend, the first real girlfriend I ever had.*

"Call me. Promise?"

"I will." Raven slid from the truck. People kept coming and going. Vehicles kept coming and going. An amplified voice asked people not to smoke in front of the building.

She tapped the truck. Bridget waved, driving off.

With a deep breath, Raven proceeded for the main doors. Mom wasn't in the cancer unit yet, according to Clayton. It was the next building over, the one they'd passed to get to the main area of the hospital.

When she entered through the automatic doors, directions and information were written in English and Oji-Cree syllabics. She already had the room number. There was a *Reggie's Donuts* across from the main admitting area. She swerved through the crowd of people and into the small restaurant to buy a water and coffee.

Being late morning, about eleven-thirty, only two people stood in line. The lunch crowd wouldn't arrive for another half an hour.

Once Raven purchased her coffee and water, she made her way to the main area until she came to the stairs and climbed up to the second floor, meeting more people dashing by here and there.

How could she have lived in Winnipeg for so long? After being on the reserve, enclosed in the city was like being shoved into a colony of ants. And the walk to Mom's ward was a hefty jaunt.

After breezing by the surgery admittance area, she came upon the two wards. Clayton had said B. She located room two-seventeen.

Before entering, Raven stopped to take a few deep breaths. Clayton was already here, having left in the cab. He'd told her he'd warn Mom ahead of time.

Fawn's reassuring words carried from behind the farthest curtain. So did Clayton's. Nothing came from Mom.

Raven inched by the other privacy curtain. She stopped, her breathing growing thicker.

Mom moaned. "Goddammit, what next? Huh? What's next?"

Raven bowed her head. She pushed on the curtain.

Clayton glanced up.

Fawn scowled. She pointed at the door.

Raven lifted her quivering chin at her older sister's flashing black eyes.

"Nerve. A lot of nerve," Fawn mouthed.

Mom groaned and shifted. Her dark eyes settled on Raven.

Raven inched back a step, but her heart leaped to her mother, begging to snuggle against the woman who'd given her life and now suffered horrible pain.

"Mom?" Raven croaked out.

"Is that you?" Mom squinted.

"Yeah." Raven crept forward.

"What're you doing here?" Mom asked weakly, but a hint of anger lurked in her question. She didn't sit up. She didn't move.

"Clayton told me what happened."

"And who brought you here? A Matawapit?" There was a hint of the old mom stirring in the hissing question.

Raven squared her shoulders. "Did you want me to leave?"

"Go." Mom flicked her hand. "You won't understand. You won't until I finally tell you the truth." She seemed to search for her breath, moving her head on the pillow. "If I'm forced to tell you the truth, don't get upset. You asked for it."

Raven looked to Clayton. He shrugged. Confusion lined Fawn's narrow face.

Mom huffed and closed her eyes.

Fawn waggled her finger and stepped around the curtain. Raven trudged after her sister.

"I'll stay with Mom," Clayton said to them.

Raven followed Fawn out into the main hallway. She should've worn running shoes with all these jaunts happening, instead of heels. Her feet were already cramping.

"Why'd you come?" Like her animal namesake, Fawn

zipped down the hallway.

"I'm wearing heels. Slow down."

Fawn stopped and pivoted. She eyed Raven's ankle boots. "Did you bring running shoes?"

"No."

"You'd better buy a pair. There's only one elevator. And it's at the end of the hall." Fawn pointed.

Great. Raven fell in step with her sister. "Are they doing any more tests?"

"Monday morning."

"Monday?" Raven's heart pinched. "When're they gonna start the chemo and radiation?"

"They'll decide once they get back the results from all of the tests."

"How long will Mom be here?"

"I don't know." The frustration Fawn must've felt echoed in her reply.

They walked in silence, passing the operation admitting area, the line of windows overlooking a courtyard, and more doors with *hospital staff only* signs until they reached the main staircase.

Fawn led them down to the bottom floor to a vast, open area full of tables and chairs and plenty of windows. There was even a food court.

"Let's get a coffee." Fawn seemed to drag herself to the counter. "I need something to eat."

Raven still clutched her coffee and water. She waited at the end of the three various counters at the cashier stand.

While balancing a tray and her purse, Fawn motioned at an empty table where they could sit. Raven joined her sister.

Fawn uncapped her coffee. "Where're you staying?"

"Bridget Guimond offered me her spare room."

"Figures." Fawn rolled her eyes. "Just 'cause Mom's sick doesn't mean what you did is forgotten."

But Raven hadn't done anything other than reminding her family they hadn't conducted themselves fairly during the election campaign. As if they'd listen to her. She kept her mouth shut.

"And you're staying there. I won't say anything to Mom. She's suffering enough." Fawn drew out each word and packed them in ice.

Raven glanced away to the people meandering about the big eating area. She shouldn't have bothered to come.

"Spare me the pitiful look." Fawn snorted.

Heat pricked Raven's skin. "What pitiful look?"

"The one you were using a second ago. It's what you always do. Mom's right. Everything's gotta be about you. For once, put aside *yourself* and think about someone else."

"I wasn't—" Raven again clamped her mouth shut. Fuck it. She'd have better luck debating with a brick wall. Hopefully Jude was having better luck with his ex-wife.

"What's your problem?" Fawn snapped.

Fine, if big sister wanted to be a bitch, so could Raven. "I'm sick of this. No matter what I do, it's never good enough. Nothing's good enough for you guys. You wanna hate me? Go ahead. Call me a fuckup. Say I'm like Dad, since that's Mom's famous words. Hate me like she hates me."

Using her fingers, Fawn drew circles on her temples.

Big sister wasn't fighting back? She always got in the last word.

"Mom doesn't hate you," Fawn muttered.

"She does, too. It's like she's hated me since I was born." Raven seized the coffee and yanked back the tab. The cup wasn't hot to her fingers. Perfect, she'd probably get a gulp of lukewarm joe.

"What am I gonna do?" Fawn mumbled more to herself. She shoved away the toast, bacon, and panfries she'd bought, and lifted her coffee, hanging her head.

Big sister defeated? Seriously? "Wh-what's going on?" Raven reached across the table, but Fawn snatched her hand away.

She stared at Raven through hollowed, sunken eyes, and bags lined beneath them. Forever youthful looking, she now showed her forty-four years. "I need a smoke. Let's go."

Raven stood. "There's something you're not telling me." She scooted after Fawn, who'd already started away, dashing for the stairs.

On wobbly heels, Raven darted after her. "What's going on?"

Fawn raced up the stairs, bolted down the hallway, and sprinted out the main exit doors into the never-ending traffic of people being dropped off or being picked up. She didn't stop until she'd reached a flower garden, far on the other side of the main entrance.

Almost out of breath, and her toes pinching, Raven caught up. "Will you please stop? I can barely walk."

"I . . ." Fawn withdrew her cigarettes. She lit one, staring out at the numerous parking lots across the narrow, winding road that snaked all around the hospital. "I . . . Mom'll kill me."

Looming dread was a blanket ready to engulf Raven. She dug inside her purse for the e-cigarette. "What?"

"You don't understand how hard it's been for Mom." Fawn's lips clamped around the filter. The ember burned bright.

"Are you gonna tell me or not?"

Plopping on the edge of the cement pad of the flower bed, Fawn glanced up. "You know how old we were when you were born."

"Yessss." Raven also sat.

A cab pulled up and let out a man.

"Something happened. Something really awful." Fawn

also stared at the cab as the vehicle drove off.

"What?"

"Mom had booted Dad out by then. His drinking was way out of control." Fawn's normally husky voice was nails grinding on a chalkboard.

"Booted him out?" Nobody had told Raven there'd been a breakdown in the marriage.

Fawn trembled. "Dad . . . Dad was really drunk. He kicked in the door . . ." She took another drag. "Kicked in the door. We were scared. So scared." Her head bowed. "I took Wren. Clayton took Lark. We hid in his bedroom." She puffed again. "Hid under the bunkbed."

Something ominous crept up Raven's spine. Cold infiltrated her blood.

"He . . . he . . ." Fawn swiped at her eyes. "Are you sure you wanna know?"

Even though her heart screamed *no*, Raven's brain said she must unearth the answer—the answer to why Mom hated her so much. She forced her head to nod.

"He was shoving Mom around. Clayton . . . Clayton . . ." Fawn's teeth clacked. "I made Clayton stay under the bed."

Raven squeezed her eyes shut, trying to visualize her frightened brother and sisters cowering under a bed while a drunken monster tore apart their home and assaulted their mother. Her mother.

Fawn would've been eleven. Clayton ten. Lark nine. Wren eight.

Reality punched Raven's gut. She'd been born nine months later. "No . . ." She pressed her palms against her temples.

"Yes . . ." Fawn dug her fingers into Raven's hand. "Y-y-yes."

"He . . . he . . . he . . ."

"He kept hollering it was his right." Fawn cringed. She scooted closer to Raven and set her arm around Raven's waist.

"No . . . this can't be . . ." The words died in Raven's throat.

Chapter Eleven: Far Cry from a Heartache

"I'm sorry . . ." Charlene sniffled. "I didn't mean to wreck your shirt." Her smile was as weak as the pain lingering in her eyes.

"It's okay." Jude unwounded his arms from her waist. "You okay now?"

"Okay?" Charlene shivered, cupping her arms. "I . . ." She turned to the chair, sat, and picked up her tea. "I . . ."

Jude also sat. He couldn't let guilt lead him to an answer. He had rights, too. And Charlene must take some responsibility for putting them in this situation. "I told you I'll think good and hard on your request for the summer."

A limp smile tugged at the corners of Charlene's mouth. "I really messed up." She pushed at her hair tied back in a ponytail.

"We both did."

"If I could go back . . ."

"No . . . it's done." Jude also sat. He picked up his mug of lukewarm tea. "Need a refresher?"

"Please." She held out her cup.

He took both and went to the bathroom to rinse them. Raven should be at the hospital by now. Hopefully her family was accepting her presence. He rinsed the mugs and strolled back to the main area.

Charlene had drawn up her legs against her chest, looking tiny in the big chair.

He set down the empty mugs and refilled them. After fixing his coffee, he sat. "Have you heard from Stephen?" At least saying the man's name didn't blacken Jude's gut anymore.

"No." Charlene sipped. She set the cup on her knee. "I told him it'd be a busy weekend and we'd talk on Sunday night after the kids go . . . go to your house."

True. The kids had two homes now. Well, a home and a hotel.

"How long are you staying here?"

Charlene stared at her mug. Steam whispered upward. "I don't know." Her reply was barely audible. "I'm thinking . . . thinking of visiting my sister next weekend. But I . . . I've only been a year into my job. I can't ask for time off . . ."

"Time off?" Jude's brows drew together.

"I haven't had a break since everything went . . . pear-shaped. You at least get the summer off. Christmas holidays. The March break."

Jude wasn't going to feel guilty for his job allowing him those perks. The fact was, he spent that time alone, except the summer holidays. He drummed his fingers on the table. Two months without the kids? Impossible.

"We could work it out this summer like we did last year, but opposite." Charlene kept speaking quietly. "You could get them for the Canada Day holiday, the Civic Holiday in August, and a weekend at the end of each month. What do you think?"

She finally faced him. Eyes still red from crying. Face splotchy.

He didn't want to feel sorry for her. He tightened his grip on the mug. "Like I said, I'll think about it."

"I . . . I . . ." She huffed a breath. "I don't want us to go back to court."

"What?" He didn't mean to speak sharply. He set down the

coffee mug and straightened.

"About the kids. I'm telling you . . ." She also set aside her mug and twisted her fingers in her hands. "I'm telling you I miss them. I want more time with them."

"And if I don't comply, you'll haul me into court." Jude shoved the mug away and stood.

"Don't act like this. Please." She also stood, her pleading full of frustration.

Before he could move, she bolted in front of him. "Will you please hear me out?" Her eyes begged him to listen. "God . . ." She set her delicate fingers on his biceps.

He stiffened. The words *don't touch me* sat at the front of his mouth. Yes, he'd touched her earlier, but that had been to offer comfort. This time, having her fingers daring to smother his arms, a spot reserved for people who deserved to touch him, was a reminder she'd touched another man, had opened her legs for another man, had pursued this other man who'd been interested in Bridget at the time.

Jude stepped back, and Charlene's fingers slid from his biceps. "I said I'll think about it."

Before she could throw her usual, *you're not listening to me, it's always gotta be your way, for once can you please consider my feelings*, he drew in a breath to control his fierce tongue bordering on lashing out at her. "I'll seriously consider it."

The corner of Charlene's eyes pinched.

"Put yourself in my shoes. Okay? How would you feel if I turned this around on you and had an affair because you won't speak about your feelings? I can easily use your faults against you. But I'm not."

Charlene's shoulders sagged. She shook her head and looked to the window. "Fine. As always, you gotta get the last say."

He trounced for the door. "We'll finish this later — after I've had time to think."

"Go on. Go ahead." When he glanced back at her, she

flicked her hand in a dismissing manner. "It's always gotta be on your terms. I should've known better."

She gave him her back, folding her arms.

Jude threw open the door, and it slammed shut behind him.

****

Raven remained outside, Fawn having received a text from Clayton that Mom was asking for her. No wonder why big sister was Mom's top pick, and Raven was . . . She hugged herself, rocking slightly back and forth.

This couldn't be true, but everything added up. Why Mom hated her. Why Mom accused her of being like Dad. Every time Mom looked at Raven, she was reminded of the most horrible night of her life. Dad had died while Mom had been pregnant. Had he really died from alcohol poisoning or had . . .

Raven slapped her hand over her mouth.

Her sobriety birthday was coming up this summer. Three years. *But . . . I can't do this. I can't do this.*

She kept rocking back and forth. Fawn had forgotten to take her cigarettes. Raven fumbled for one. She stuck the smoke between her lips and flicked the lighter. The taste of tobacco curled into her mouth. She sucked in a massive drag, and the smoke raced down into her lungs.

Her skin tingled. Head buzzed. The panic thumping at the bottom of her spine, the anxiety rushing through her blood, the pain tightening around her heart settled a smidgen. She puffed on the cigarette and inhaled more nicotine and smoke.

She stood. Her legs threatened to give out from under her.

She sat. Her body kept buzzing. A rush of something thundered through her veins, something creepy, something damning.

She stood again and puffed more on the cigarette.

A man walked by, grinning.

She scowled and whipped her hard gaze on the flowers.

Life went on. Cars continued to crawl by. People kept coming and going from the hospital. The amplified voice never shut up about people smoking on hospital property.

But the skin of truth coiled around Raven's limbs. Squeezed her heart. Churned in her stomach.

Jude. She must call Jude. She whipped out her phone. Just as fast, she tucked it back into her pocket.

She took another drag off the cigarette. Adam. He was her sponsor. He'd stop her from running, from heading for *The Gator* to slam back a drink. She punched in his cell number.

The phone rang four times.

Please, please pick up.

"Hello," his low rumbled filled her ear.

"Adam . . ." She took another drag off the cigarette. "Adam . . . I'm a . . ." What could she say?

Another taxi pulled up.

She should get in. Get in the cab and go somewhere.

"Where're you? I'll come and get you?" Concern lingered in his question. Like a typical person in the recovery program, he came through for her.

"The hospital."

"I'm on my way."

"I'll . . . I'll be walking. Toward Oliver Road." She couldn't stay here and wait. Her feet itched. She had to do something.

"Gotcha." Adam hung up.

The air had grown warmer. Raven shrugged off her jacket. Her feet still pinched. Even burned. She had to get another pair of shoes. Her ankle boots were made for bipping here and bipping there, not enduring hikes all over Thunder Bay.

Traffic hummed to her and past her on Golf Links Road.

The flashy, sporty black truck appeared and slowed on the

other side of the road. Raven dropped the cigarette butt. She'd better get more smokes. Maybe Adam could drive her out to the reserve on the other side of the city, just over the Kaministiquia river. Cigarettes were much cheaper there.

Raven managed to find a break in the traffic and scooted across the road. She'd have blisters on her blisters soon, but at least her screaming feet had kept her mind off the truth.

"Where we going?" Adam sat with the seat almost in the back, his six-foot-five muscular body smothering the cab.

Raven scooped up his beige cowboy hat because he was too tall to wear it in the vehicle. She got in. "Anywhere. It doesn't matter."

"Gotcha." Adam glanced in the rearview mirror and merged the truck back into traffic.

"Smokes. I need to get Fawn more smokes. The rez."

Adam simply nodded. He turned the truck off Sunrise Boulevard and did a U-turn. In seconds they were back on Golf Links Road, heading south toward the mountain.

"You navigate this hood like a local." The panic had subsided now that Raven was with someone who understood her, someone she'd snorted cocaine with, drank with, ran the streets of Winnipeg with.

"The mountain's a big help. But yeah . . ." Adam nodded. "I'm getting used to this place. Got Fort William nailed. Port Arthur still buggers me up." Meaning the two split neighborhoods that had once been their own separate townships before amalgamating into the city of Thunder Bay.

He kept driving south until they reached Oliver Road. Here, he turned west off Golf Links Road.

In the distance, the mountain loomed over the city. The gigantic rolling hills of the Shield weren't even close to the Rockies. These mountains were much older. Steep but not pointed. And the big one on the reserve was wide and flat, made of rock. Bald on top and peppered with spruce trees around its middle and bottom.

They were leaving Port Arthur behind and heading to Fort William where the reserve was located. Adam finally got them on Highway Sixty-One. This would take them to Chippewa Road where the reserve was.

Raven sat back. It'd be a good fifteen minutes' jaunt. And naturally Adam hadn't pressed her for answers.

Out on the main expressway, there wasn't much to look at. There wouldn't be until they came closer to Arthur Street.

"Jude told me where he used to live."

"Yeah?"

"The last time he took me here. I asked him on the plane. I never did get to see his old house."

"Upper middle class." Adam's big hand almost consumed the steering wheel. "Got your bag at my crib. You need anything?"

They were almost in his neighborhood.

Raven shook her head. "Maybe some running shoes before I go back to the hospital. Fawn'll need her smokes. She's probably dying for one right now."

"Yup, like walking the Trans Canada from Kenora to the 'Peg to get around that hospital."

"I'm a product of rape." The words tumbled from her mouth. Raven toyed with one of the fringes on her purse.

"Aren't a lot of us." Adam shrugged.

Raven whipped her head in his direction. "That's all you can say?"

"What else can I say?" He glanced at her then back to the expressway. "Y'know what my homelife was like. If the ol' man wasn't cracking the ol' lady's skull, she was cracking his with a cast-iron pan. Left him on the kitchen floor one night, bleeding. My oldest sister called the ambulance."

"You weren't supposed to be born either?"

"I dunno." His replies were as nonchalant as someone

talking about what kind of toppings they wanted on their pizza.

But Raven knew his pain, although Adam didn't reveal his hurt. Or maybe he found a way to work past it. "It doesn't bother you?"

"Course it does." Adam kept staring straight ahead. "Thing is, there's nothing I can do about it. What's done is done."

"I'm sorry."

"Nothing to be sorry 'bout." Adam peeked in the rearview mirror and guided the truck into the other lane. "When'd you find out?"

"Just now. Today. Before I called you."

"You'll live."

"I guess so." Raven stared out the passenger window.

"You did the right thing by calling me. Betcha you wanted a drink."

She gasped and again whipped her head in his direction. "How'd you know?"

"Takes one to know one." Adam sort of flicked his thumb on the steering wheel. "There're meetings tonight. Four places."

What would Raven have done without this big lug who'd used to scare everyone out of his path? "I'm in."

"We'll get your smokes. Get you some walking shoes. Then get you back to the hospital. Once you're at our place, have a shower, fill your gut, and then we'll go to a meeting."

"Thanks." Raven reached over and patted his massive biceps.

"Just doing what we're s'posed to do—giving away the program to stay sober."

"I know but—"

"And make sure to level with your ol' man. Honesty is what makes our lives easier. Don't hide this from him."

Raven sputtered. "How'd you know I was gonna—"

Adam's low rumbling laugh filled the truck. "'Cause we're alcoholics. I told you already—it takes one to know one."

So, Adam would've reacted the same way. This comforted Raven like a big pillow. Nobody had said sobriety was going to be easy. At least she'd craved a glass of whiskey and cola instead of heroin.

"What am I gonna tell him about the smoking?"

Adam sort of crinkled his one eye. "Better than chasing the dragon, ain't it? Better than ending up on a barstool at *The Gator*, ain't it?"

"How goes your vaping?"

"Still at it."

"I'm going to try to stick it out. No more smoking."

"You do what you gotta do. First things first."

He was right. Her goal was to stay clean, not worry about falling off the smoking wagon. She could tackle quitting cigarettes another time, but not right now. Her shaking body needed another fix, something the nicotine in her vape couldn't satisfy. Maybe after tonight's meeting she'd feel better.

"Remember, if we work our program, we can handle anything."

"I know. I know. I just . . ."

"Easy. You're here. I'm here. We'll do this."

Raven sat in the big eating area at the hospital. Fawn and Clayton were still upstairs with Mom.

She sipped the coffee. Her feet thanked her for the pair of running shoes. Like a good sponsee in the recovery program, she'd listened to her sponsor and had bought a sandwich. But forcing down the egg salad on brown had been like pushing cardboard down her throat.

Five o'clock on a Saturday, and the area was quiet. Adam

would get her at six. She'd go back to the house, shower, eat, and they'd leave for the meeting. He'd said it was only fifteen minutes from their place.

She glanced up to Fawn and Clayton coming down the stairs, feet dragging, hands gripping the railing. They probably needed a shower and food, too.

"We're going for supper. Are you coming?" Fawn dabbed at her eyes. She stuffed the tissue paper in her pocket.

"I . . . I thought about . . . I was gonna see Mom before I head out."

"She's sleeping."

All the better. Raven stood. "I'll sit with her."

"Okay. We're gonna eat first. We'll be up in about a half an hour." Fawn's statement was as heavy as her sagging mouth and limp eyes.

Raven ascended the staircase to Mom's room. Each step she took, her stomach flipped upside down and then tumbled forward.

Chapter Twelve: Can't Go On

Raven stopped at the door to Mom's room. The curtain was open to the one lady's bed who was fast asleep.

She drew back Mom's curtain where all was quiet.

Through heavy lids, Mom stared back. "What're you doing here?"

Raven set down her purse and sat in the chair beside the bed. A tray held a glass and pitcher of water. "Do you need a drink?"

"What I need is to get the fuck outta here."

Before she fired back a *save it,* Raven clamped her mouth shut. She must remember what Mom had suffered. "How're you feeling?"

"How do you think I'm feeling?" Mom shifted and groaned. "You didn't answer me. What're you doing here? Where's Mr. Money Bags?"

How was Raven supposed to tolerate a half hour of this bullshit? "Clayton said I could come." She slumped in the chair and folded her arms.

"Bah." Mom waved her hand.

No matter how Raven brought up the horrible truth, this wasn't going to be pretty. She might as well spit it out. Either way, she'd earn more hate. More contempt.

"I know."

Mom mumbled.

"I know the truth." Raven drew her fisted hands over her chest.

"What're you talking about?" Using her elbow for support

and flinching, Mom slapped at the tray.

"I already asked if you needed water." Raven reached to grab the plastic glass.

"I don't need any help. I'm not an invalid." Mom winced. She coddled her stomach and settled back in the bed.

Raven held the water under Mom's chin. "Here."

Grunting, Mom lifted her head and clamped her wrinkled lips around the straw. The water kept lowering in the cup. She released her lips and rested against the pillow.

"Did you eat?" Raven set the cup back on the tray.

"How the hell am I supposed to eat?" Mom again coddled her stomach. "This is what I get for now." She held up her hand where the IV needle fed her fluid.

"You can't eat anything?"

"They brought me some cheese and crackers. And what are you blabbing about?"

Maybe this wasn't the best time to bring up the horrible truth. "We can talk later."

"No. Out with it. I'm sick and tired of everyone . . . quit walking on eggshells. That's all everyone's doing. If it isn't Fawn, it's Clayton. Now you." Mom threw out her hands. "I don't know why you're all here if you're gonna act this way. I'm not dead, am I?"

"No." Raven couldn't help the quietness in her answer. She glanced away.

"Or maybe that's what you're hoping for so you can have the house, huh?"

The accusing words punched Raven's heart. "Stop it."

"No. You're living with that family." Mom thrust her finger at Raven. "Why're you here? Why bother coming? I told you I don't want you around. Get outta here."

Raven stood. She grabbed her purse. Mom would go to the grave hating her for something she had no control over. She squeezed her eyes shut and hung on to the steel pole between the beds.

"Go." Mom raised her voice.

"I'm going." Raven forced her feet to move.

The old woman in the other bed was awake, glaring.

It figured everyone believed Raven was to blame, even a stranger. Instead of taking the stairs to the bottom floor, she used the elevator so Fawn and Clayton wouldn't see her.

Fuck all of this. Jude wasn't here. He was too busy in Kenora dealing with his cheating ex-wife. What did he see in Raven, anyway? She was a loser. Born from rape. Hated by her own mother. Earned nothing but disgust from everyone.

Talking to Bridget was pointless, too. She was born from a family who loved her. Jude was also loved. The witch of an ex-wife was probably trying to cajole him into giving her a second chance.

The elevator doors opened. Raven trounced down the main area. A cab waited outside by the curb. She stormed straight for the taxi and threw open the door.

"Where to?" The driver craned his neck.

"The Gator."

Raven opened the door to the cab. Two men lingered outside the bar. This area of town was pretty sketchy with a few run-down buildings and back alleys. In the past, she'd have thought nothing of strutting into this place or telling the two guys to *screw off and find a peep show if you wanna stare.*

She shut the cab door.

"Lady?" The cabbie turned, peering.

Raven gave him the address to Bridget and Adam's.

They drove off.

Tears built in the corners of her eyes. A lump formed in her throat. The *jumping off place,* the worst place for a recovering addict or alcoholic to be, was the precipice where Raven now stood—couldn't drink but unable to handle life without a drink.

She swiped at her eyes.

Ten minutes later, the cab pulled up at Adam and Bridget's bungalow. Raven shoved more money at the driver and got out.

Adam sat on the porch, vaping. He stood.

Raven wandered up the walkway.

"You didn't call." His low rumble wasn't accusing.

"No." She had to almost shout because the word wanted to remain in her mouth.

"'Sup?"

"Take me to a meeting." She wobbled up the steps.

He stuck the vape in his jeans and opened his arms.

She melted against his chest. The sob hurled from her throat. Closing her eyes didn't stop the rainfall of tears, so she let them spill down her cheeks. He cupped the back of her head.

The front door opened. A gasp. "Oh my God, what happened?"

Raven couldn't find a breath to acknowledge Bridget's question. The crying continued, filling her throat and wailing from her mouth.

"Her mother didn't—"

One of Adam's arms left Raven's waist.

"Oh geez."

Bridget's swollen stomach bumped against Raven's side, and her lengthy nails kneaded Raven's lower back.

During such a crisis, she was comforted and hugged by the enemy.

Raven sat in the living room, sipping the tea Adam had made. Before taking a shower to calm herself, she'd told him to go ahead and tell Bridget the truth. The only comfort, although she'd wished it wasn't so, was Adam sharing the same miserable life, and he'd gotten past the abuse he'd suffered at the hands of his drunken parents.

Adam flopped in the armchair.

Bridget scooted to the sofa and snuggled up beside Raven. "I'm so sorry, hon. Terribly sorry."

"It's okay, Git." Raven sniffled. She blew her nose. "There's nothing to be sorry about."

"Yes, there is. What happened to your mother is horrible. And what's even more horrible . . ." Bridget squeezed Raven's thigh.

" . . . is she's taking it out on me?" Raven wiped her eyes and set the tissue on the coffee table. "I'm used to it."

"No, you're not," Bridget said firmly. "If you were, you wouldn't be crying." She looked to Adam. "He's your sponsor. He went through it. I'm going to call Jude."

Raven cupped the bottom of the mug. "He's busy."

"It doesn't matter if he's busy. You're in a relationship. When shit hits the fan, you juggle it all."

"His ex-wife is being a—"

"I know what she's doing." Anger crept into Bridget's interruption. "Pulling out the waterworks and laying on the guilt."

Raven stiffened. This Charlene had better not be trying to win back Jude. "I should get dressed for the meeting."

"There's enough time." Adam spoke up. "Remember H.A.L.T.?"

"Yes." Raven sighed. "Hungry. Angry. Lonely. Tired."

"Then let's eat." He stood. "Kyle should be home pretty quick. He's over at Grayson's house."

Thank goodness Adam and Bridget's son wasn't present to witness Raven's meltdown. "I gotta get my act together. I don't want to upset Kyle."

"He's a big boy." Adam moseyed off to the kitchen.

Raven's phone rang. She glanced at the number. Jude.

****

Jude sat back in the chair. He held the phone. Maybe they could video chat. "What's up?"

Raven's swollen eyes, makeup-streaked face, and sunken shoulders pinched his heart.

"What's going on?" He pushed aside his bottled water and stood, clutching the phone. "I'm going to contact you on Bridget's laptop. Tell her to fire it up."

Raven nodded and disappeared from the screen.

Jude paced back and forth. Charlene had taken the kids to the movies. He had until nine o'clock to talk, and by God he'd find out what was going on. He kept pacing, glancing at his laptop screen. Five minutes later, the message popped up. He clicked *accept*.

The same swollen eyes, makeup-streaked face, and sunken shoulders appeared in front of him.

"What's going on?" He touched the screen, tracing the tear slipping down Raven's high cheekbone.

The corners of her mouth edged upward. "Th-thank you."

"No need to thank me."

Her finger appeared. It followed his movements on the screen. "I . . . I . . ." She lowered her head.

"It's okay. I'm here," he whispered.

Raven wiped her eyes. "Gimme a second. I'm gonna take the laptop to the porch."

"I'll be right here." He sipped water, gut tight, while glimpses of Bridget's house flashed on the laptop screen. The light-gray carpeted hallway. The same carpet flowing into the living room. A hint of the contemporary furniture she'd previously had at her condo. A peek at the front door. Then the laptop rested on the glass wicker table out on the porch. The brick wainscoting of the home's façade appeared.

Raven's slim knees filled the screen. As she adjusted the laptop, he got a view of her flat stomach, firm breasts, and finally settled on her shaky hand holding a cigarette, her cherry lips clamped around the filter.

Smoking? This wasn't good. She'd been proud of kicking the habit at the beginning of January.

"What's going on?" The words came out as light as a flickering flame.

"Adam . . . Adam and I are gonna hit a meeting tonight. Pretty quick." Raven took another drag and blew the smoke from her mouth. "I . . . I came close to drinking."

Whoa. Hold up. Time out. "Why?" Jude brought the laptop closer until his face was almost against it.

"I didn't. I . . . I split. It's not worth it." She swiped at her eyes and took another drag.

"What happened? Please tell me. I can't . . ." Dammit, he wasn't supposed to swoop in like a warrior in his canoe. He must lend an ear. Lend a shoulder.

"I . . . I . . . I found out today how I was . . . conceived." Raven's words came out small — small enough for Jude to adjust the speaker volume to the loudest level.

"I'm here. Keep talking," he said in his most reassuring voice.

"Fawn . . . Fawn t-told m-me." Raven's lower lip quivered. She grabbed her tea and sipped. Her tongue snaked out and licked the rim of her mouth.

"What'd she tell you?" To keep his mounting anger in check, Jude drew in a breath or he'd be boarding a plane to hunt down Raven's family to read them the riot act.

"I . . . I need a second." Raven stood. She disappeared from the screen.

"Wait," Jude called out. He banged the arm of his chair. Patience. He couldn't force someone to talk, either.

A few moments later, Adam sat in the wicker chair.

Finally, someone. "What's going on? Where's Raven?"

"In the kitchen. With Bridget." Adam removed his e-cigarette from his pocket.

After watching Adam vape and sip some of whatever he had in his mug, Jude said through clenched teeth, "Enough. What's going on?"

Adam arched a black brow.

Jude sagged in the chair. He used his thumb to rub his water bottle. "I can't help it. I'm worried."

"She found out today how she was conceived."

That again. "You mean her dad's not her real dad?"

"Oh, he's her dad. He made more than sure he's her dad, if you get my drift."

The saliva drained from Jude's mouth. There was only one way a man could guarantee he'd fathered a child. His heart slowed to an almost halt. "You mean . . . Mrs. Kabatay was . . ."

"Yep." Adam's nod was slow.

"Aww, geez." Jude pushed the chair away and stood. He slathered his palm across his face.

No wonder why Mrs. Kabatay had a hard-on of hate for her youngest child. But what had happened wasn't Raven's fault. Yet, she was a constant reminder of a terrorizing time in Mrs. Kabatay's life. And Dad didn't know the truth. Jude's conscience started a wrestling match. To tell Dad or not to tell Dad.

He sat in the chair. Adam waited on the screen.

"She said she almost drank today."

"Yup. Pretty close. She's been close all weekend."

"You mean there was another time?" Jude sputtered.

"It's been tough. That's why I'm taking her to a meeting."

Jude managed to nod.

"She's gotta accept what she can't change."

But could she?

"Gotta work hard on her recovery. She's only got three meetings a week up there. I'm gonna meet with her over the laptop on the other nights."

Raven didn't have a computer and was using Mom and Dad's. "I'll buy her one while I'm—"

"Don't be going all charity case on her," Adam warned.

"This isn't a charity case." Jude came half out of his chair.

"It ain't?" Adam continued to wear his perennial stone face.

A face Jude wanted to rattle and shake at this moment because his brother-in-law never gave away a flicker of his true emotions. "No, it's not. She'll need a laptop to meet with you—"

Adam removed the vape from his mouth. "I think it's up to Creator to play Creator. Right?"

Heat climbed onto Jude's face. He was doing it again—trying to take control and solve everything. He managed a weak *yes*, but damn, it galled him.

"I'd say her higher power's provided her with what she needs. She's got a laptop my in-laws loaned her."

In this day and age, everyone needed a laptop. "Fine. Where is she? Can she talk?"

"She's in the kitchen. It's been a . . ." Adam exhaled some vapor from his mouth. "It's been tough. Her mom booted her from the hospital room, too."

All Jude could do was trust his sister and brother-in-law to watch out for Raven while she was in Thunder Bay and make sure she didn't take off drinking.

As for Jude, all he could do was pray.

CHAPTER THIRTEEN: BACKTRACK

Jude pulled up at Mom and Dad's house where he wouldn't find Raven. She was spending her day off in Thunder Bay so she could attend another meeting with Adam this evening. Late tomorrow afternoon, Adam and Bridget would take Raven to the airport for her flight home. Then she'd be attending the meeting at the reserve's recovery center. They'd finally see each other Tuesday night after class.

No, he wasn't happy about this, but what Raven needed came first. Living by the twelve steps of the recovery program was what guided her through life. If not for Adam and the program, she might've uncorked the bottle this weekend, or God forbid, tried to score some heroin.

He shuddered.

At least he'd managed to get through his own trying weekend. The kids had arrived at the hotel around quarter after nine on Saturday, which meant straight to bed, so Jude didn't have to look at his ex-wife. Sunday morning, he'd packed up their belongings and taken them to church. Later, they'd had brunch before Charlene had driven them to the airport to catch their plane. She'd let him go with the understanding he'd seriously consider her request.

The stress of everything gripped his shoulders tight, almost nail-like spikes being driven into his muscles.

While Jude trudged up the walkway, Noah and Rebekah took off to play. They needed fresh air after being cooped up in hotel rooms, malls, movie theaters, and church. He hauled himself up the front steps and threw open the door.

Mom poked her head into the hallway from the kitchen. "I'm cleaning up. There're leftovers."

"It's okay. The kids are going to bed early. They got into junk on the plane ride."

"Chips?"

Jude nodded. He wandered into the living room and flopped on the couch.

Dad sat in the recliner. He set aside his newspaper. "How'd your visit pan out?"

"I need to talk to you." Jude wiped his face. "Alone."

"Sure." Dad rose from the chair. "I'll get your mother to make us some tea."

"Sounds good." Jude also stood. He wandered through the dining area and drew open the sliding door that led to the deck.

At the end of April, the air was growing warmer and the sun was still above the tree line. He rested his folded arms on the railing. The light breeze created ripples on the water. Squeals and shouts from the kids somewhere in the yard carried to the deck.

This was a beautiful spot. Maybe he could build somewhere around here. The children could simply go to their grandparents' after school.

The sliding door opened, then closed. "Here's your tea."

Jude pivoted.

Dad set the mugs on the table. He eased into his chair. Daily walks and proper eating kept him in good shape for a man pushing seventy. He still had a full head of black hair and probably wouldn't gray until his eighties.

"How'd your weekend go?" Dad lit a cigarette.

The stench of the smoke curled Jude's stomach. Because of this weekend, Raven had started smoking again. "Char wants the kids for the summer."

Thoughtfulness gathered in Dad's black eyes. "She's a

mother. I would expect no less."

Jude plopped in the opposite chair. "She agreed to our original terms. Now she wants to change them. It's . . . never mind." He picked up his tea.

"Of course she agreed to the previous terms. Guilt consumed her. She not only hurt her kids terribly, she hurt you."

"Yeah . . . well, I told her I'd consider it."

"Are you?"

"I dunno. I told her I'd consider it to . . . well . . ."

"Keep her quiet?" Dad asked gently.

"At first . . . but now?" Jude cupped his palms around the mug.

"You're thinking about what's best for them?" Dad pointed to where the shrieks and laughter came from.

"Yeah. I guess she wants to move back to T Bay."

"Really?" Dad's eyes rounded.

"Yep. She's unsure if she dove in too fast with Stephen."

"How do you feel about this?"

"Honestly? Nothing. Was I a bit smug at first? Yeah. Now? I'm more concerned about Raven."

"Is her visit not going as planned? I was a little surprised when Bridget called and said she wouldn't be taking Raven to the airport until tomorrow afternoon."

The frown tugging Jude's lips downward landed in his gut. "That's what I needed to talk to you about."

"Okay. I assumed this was about Charlene. I see I was wrong."

"Not wrong. Char concerns me. Raven, though . . ." Jude sat forward, legs parting, elbows on his knees. "She almost drank this weekend. Twice, according to Adam."

Dad winced. "They're many times an addict will face tests. Unfortunately, this won't be the last time she'll have to make this decision."

Jude looked out to the water. "I see . . ." He gazed back at

Dad. "I can't have my kids —" Dammit, he loved her so much.

"She did the right thing. She's doing the right thing. She's surrounded herself with people who'll support her sobriety."

"That's why she's not coming back until tomorrow. Adam's taking her to a meeting. And she'll go to her meeting here on Monday evening. She'll be using your laptop the other nights to meet with him."

"It's tough. Her mother's very sick. Her family's angry —"

"It's more than that." Jude stared at the table. "She found out something horrible, and she's devastated."

Dad edged forward. He also rested his elbows on his knees, gripping his mug. "What did she find out?"

"How she was conceived."

Concern flooded Dad's eyes. "Ernest isn't her father?"

"He's her father. He . . ." Jude's chest burned. He set aside the mug and stood. The water lapping at the rocks helped still the rapid beating of his heart. "He . . . Adam told me he . . . he forced himself on Mrs. Kabatay."

Dad's gasp echoed in Jude's ears. The chair scraped against the deck, followed by slow, methodical footsteps. Dad appeared in Jude's peripheral vision and also leaned on the deck railing.

"I see . . ." Dad bowed his head. Heavy breaths came from his mouth. "Sweet Jesus . . ."

"I didn't tell you this so you could blame yourself." Jude turned to Dad's chin resting on his chest. "Don't do this to yourself."

Dad blinked a few times. "Cancer. The residential school. Ernest. Now this . . ."

"Dad, don't . . ." Jude clamped his hand over his father's wound-tight shoulder.

"I . . ." Dad scrubbed his face. "I guess I know why she hates me so much now. If I'd been any kind of —"

"We've been over this already." Jude kept gripping Dad's

shoulder. "You were kids, for cripes sake. You were both suffering. She wanted you to take away her pain, and you were killing your pain in a bottle."

Dad faced him. Devastation still hovered in his dark eyes. "Raven doesn't know, does she?"

"No. I never told her. I don't think her mother did either. I don't think any of them know the truth."

"I hope . . . I just hope . . . I hope this doesn't . . ." Dad rested his elbow on the railing and cupped his forehead in his hand, covering his eyes. "I don't want you to pay for my sin."

"Your sin?" Jude gasped. "You didn't do anything wrong."

"I should've been there for her." Dad shook his head.

"Please. Think about Mom. She wouldn't want you feeling this way. You did your best. Doesn't that count?"

"And if Raven finds out? She'll . . . she'll leave. She won't want to stay here." Dad looked to the sky. His fingers grazed the railing. "And I've put your mother through enough already."

"If you're talking about your fall off the wagon when Bridget and I were babies, that's in the past." Bridget had told Jude about their father's lapse in sobriety when Mom had confessed the truth during the Healing the Spirit workshop two falls ago.

"I'm talking about what . . . you know what kind of man I'm like." Dad cleared his throat.

"We're not rapists, like Mr. Kabatay was."

"In no way am I excusing his behavior. Not a chance." Dad raised his finger. "But where do you think he learned it from? Why would he do that?"

Those damned Indian Residential Schools. Jude had heard one had used a freaking electric chair. The remnants of the tortuous device had been found in the school after it had closed. If those people had been crazy enough to shock innocent little kids, of course they'd done worse.

"Do you think Mr. Kabatay was . . ." Oh man, this was hard to say. " . . . sexually abused?"

"Many were." Dad strolled back to the chair and sat.

Jude followed, heart almost dragging the wooden floor of the deck. "I'm glad it didn't happen to you." Wait. "It didn't happen to you, did it?"

"No." Dad lit another cigarette.

"Raven told me her mother always hated her." Jude shivered. He should've worn a sweater.

"It sounds like Arlene's still suffering. Whenever she looks at her daughter . . ."

"They'll never reconcile, will they?" Jude moved his chair closer. "Adam told me Raven has to work on accepting what she can't change. He said it's her biggest problem."

"She's on the right track if she's dedicating herself to meetings," Dad said somberly.

"At the end of each month, the meeting's open to everyone. I'm . . ." What the heck did happen in those rooms? "I'm going. I'm going to support her."

"Smart idea. Bridget attends open meetings with Adam. It's good to understand the program they live by."

"How come you never went to meetings?"

"I found my recovery through the church. As they say, whatever works for you." Dad pursed his lips. "Perhaps I should attend one. I'll admit the last two years have been very trying."

"You mean with Emery and Bridget?"

"The way my faith's been tested." Dad slouched.

"I'll get her tomorrow. You don't have to go to the airport."

"Of course."

Jude picked up his tea. What if Raven wound up hating his family if she learned the truth? What if she wound up hating him? His worst nightmare might come true.

****

Raven looked through the haze of sand, her nose pressed against the airplane window, and her heart jumped when she saw Jude standing in the airport. He'd come to get her instead of the deacon. She squirmed as the small plane did a turn on the gravel runway.

After what he'd endured this weekend at his ex-wife's hands, Jude had shoved aside his own problems to be here for her. He must've come straight from work. A white dress shirt hugged his strong upper build. A loosened tie dangled around his collar.

A few minutes later, the plane came to a rest in front of the airport.

Raven threw off her seat belt and dashed down the aisle. The disembark door opened. At the same time, Jude bolted for the airport door.

"You came. I missed you so much." She threw her arms around his shoulders.

Jude wrapped Raven in a tight hug, almost lifting her off the ground. His lips brushed her ear. "I missed you," he murmured. "I missed you so much."

"I missed you, too." His cologne clung to her nostrils, a heavenly scent of the outdoors.

"I wish I coulda been there." He nuzzled her ear.

"It's okay. Your kids come first. I'm simply glad you're here."

"Listen to you." He let go of her waist and cupped her face. His dark eyes glittered, and a light smile tugged at his lips. "You're worse than Mom and Bridget. Putting everyone first over yourself. And that's why I love you so much."

"Oh, Jude . . ." She melted her lips on his.

He enveloped her in a sweet, tender kiss that shrank the enormous pain sitting beneath her skin.

****

With the kids at Mom and Dad's for the evening and Jude set to pick them up once he'd dropped Raven off for her meeting, he guided her into the house, duffel bag strap slung over his shoulder and his palm resting on her backside. After what she'd endured, he didn't want to let her go. Ever.

"Do you want something to eat? Are you hungry?"

Raven dragged her feet into the house, stopping at the kitchen table. She set her hands on the back of a chair.

Before following her into the kitchen, he set down her duffel bag next to the bathroom.

"I had a sandwich while I was waiting for my plane." Raven swiveled. "I . . . I want you."

Jude eased forward. He'd been ready to hold her, talk to her, comfort her. But same as the night she'd run to the nursing station to see her mother, she craved him inside her. His cock hardened.

"C'mere." He waggled his finger.

Her hips slightly swayed as she moved one leg over the other, gaze centered on him. Her crotch met his erection. Warmth invaded his pants. He held the back of her head and guided his mouth over hers. A moan came from her, and she locked her arms around his waist. Her hands climbed up his back, the tips of her fingers kneading his muscles. The silky caresses raised the goosebumps hiding under his flesh to the surface of his skin. He shivered.

She eased his shirt out from his pants, walked her fingers up his spine, and caressed the tips along each bump. His breaths grew heavier. Close to panting. He slipped his tongue between her lips. She returned his licks with a slow exploration of his mouth. Her sweet sighs teased his prick, and he grinded against the heat of her pussy buried under the leggings painted to her hips and thighs.

He laid his hand on her ass. Her buttock tightened beneath his touch. She wiggled her hips, massaging her cheek with his strokes and caressing his crotch with her cunt.

All this teasing, rubbing, and kissing heated Jude's blood. He steered them to his bedroom a mere three steps away, still licking and tasting her tongue.

Raven wormed from her leggings and unbuttoned her cardigan. Jude drew open his shirt. Her palm rested on his chest, right on his furiously beating heart. She nipped at his mouth and then flicked her tongue at his lower lip.

A growl rose in his throat. He unfastened her bra and claimed her breasts, crushing the nipples beneath his palms as he caressed her tits with hard strokes.

She wrenched on his pants, dragging the trousers down his hips with his underwear. The tepid air gathered around his bare butt. She lightly feathered the tip of her finger at the edge of his cleft, toying with this sensitive area. Each ticklish stroke produced shivers walking up his spine, and he pushed his cock at her pussy.

While still stroking his cleft and using her tongue to trace the outer edge of his mouth, she guided him down to the bed.

She spread her legs, keeping her free hand on his neck, gently forcing him to stay put. His chest heaved. His cock squashed between their lower stomachs.

She kept tickling his buttocks with her incessant rubbing of his cleft. He'd never been touched in such a personal spot. Each time her finger glided lower, almost hovering in his crack, the air was drained from his lungs, and his kisses became ravenous, an unquenchable hunger that his tongue couldn't get enough of, tasting every region of her mouth.

When Raven's finger left his crack, a sigh of disappointment escaped Jude's lips, but just as quickly his blood flowing through his veins escalated as she draped her legs around his hips and nestled her pussy against his throbbing cock.

She arched her back, her hard nipples melting into his chest. "Fuck me," she whispered, her order scratching at his skin. Her tongue flicked at his chin.

"Gladly," he panted.

He was going to ease into her, but her grinding hips captured his entire length and sucked him deep within her. She clenched her pussy, gripping his erection. Each time he thrust, her cunt clamped around his prick. Her tongue kept exploring his mouth, flicking at his chin, tracing his cheeks, leaving him heaving and groaning.

"Easy." His voice ached with the same amount of pain as his balls. "I wanna fuck you hard."

She moaned, scratching her lovely nails down his back. "Fuck me hard. Fuck me as hard as you can."

Her bold invitation was a sweet enticement beckoning him to move his cock in a circular motion inside her creamy cunt. He'd stretch her good and wide.

"Oh, Jude . . ." The grit in her husky whisper was music to his ears.

He thrust fast, raising his hips for leverage and slamming back down. Her legs tightened further around his hips. She was locked about his neck. Clinging to him.

When the fevered heat captured him, her own moans joined his heavy groans.

Chapter Fourteen: Love the Way You Love Me

The past two and a half weeks had been busy. Tonight, the new chief and band council would be installed into office. Jude didn't get to see much of Raven, since she was keen on attending her meetings every night, whether at the recovery center or on the laptop with Adam. They'd managed quick cups of coffee together at the diner on her breaks, or they sat out on the deck after enjoying a dinner cooked by Mom at his parents' house. Homework also kept Raven busy because she was *this close* to acquiring her grade ten math.

A light glow bathed Jude's chest a sunny shade of yellow. The kids bickered in the back of the truck. They were on their way to get Raven. The family was heading for the community center for supper and then the installation ceremony.

Jude pulled up at the house. Mom and Dad were already leaving. Raven brought up the rear.

"We wanna ride with Grandpa and Grandma," Noah called out from the back.

"Go ahead."

The kids darted from the truck and raced up the walkway to their grandparents.

There was a warm breeze this evening. Spring was fighting to show up, but old man winter still insisted on sticking around, so Jude wore his jacket.

He wandered up to Raven and pecked her warm mouth. "How'd work go?"

"Same ol' thing." She took his offered hand. "How about you?"

"I finished up two more reports and met with the education committee this afternoon."

"Jenny's portfolio is education. I wonder if she'll keep it."

They wandered to the truck.

"She'd . . . uh . . ." How could Jude speak ill about Raven's brother?

"She'd, uh, what?" Raven smirked.

"I wouldn't exactly call your brother and I BFFs." Jude grinned. He opened the truck door. "In you go."

"The kids are riding with your parents?"

"Any chance they get." He shut the door and rounded the vehicle.

The kids were already in the back of Dad's truck. Jude waved.

He got into his own vehicle. "Have you heard anything new?"

"No. Mom's almost done her chemo. When she's finished, she'll get to rest. They're gonna let her come home for a bit. Then she'll return for the surgery."

"After surgery?"

"They'll do more tests, I guess. Then she'll get to come home again. I think it'll be radiation after that." Raven scrolled through her phone. "Lemme double-check. Clayton sent me the last update."

They drove down the road.

Raven tucked the phone into her purse. "Wren's there right now. I guess Mom's upset she won't get to see Clayton installed."

"He's served a lot of terms."

"People believe in him." She glanced away.

Jude reached over and took her hand. He squeezed her fingers.

"How about you? It's the Victoria Day weekend. Did you make a decision?"

A sigh seemed to run through Jude's windpipe. "Not yet. Char's leaving for T Bay after work on Friday. The kids are flying there. I guess she's staying at her sister's, so that's where Noah and Becky will bunk."

"Is there enough room?"

"Yeah. Her sister's place is . . . it can accommodate guests." He'd almost said *it's like my old house,* but there was no point in talking about a home he'd once owned with another woman.

"They're close?"

Jude nodded. "Very close."

"Are they close in age?"

"A year apart. Michelle's one year older." Jude pulled into the packed parking lot at the community center.

They joined Mom, Dad, and the kids. Everyone piled inside to find a place to sit. Already, Darryl, Emery, Roy, Jenny, and Clayton were seated at the head table with the other councilors being installed.

After the prayer said by Basil and songs by the drum group, everyone ate supper. Next up was the opening ceremony.

The drum group sang a few more songs, followed by Basil leading another prayer. Each councilor stepped forward to receive a blessing by Basil and an eagle feather.

Jude glanced at Raven. She'd been quiet sitting amongst the Catholics during dinner and the ceremony. Across the big hall, her family had taken up three tables. Pride had filled Raven's dark eyes when Clayton had received his feather.

Darryl stood front and center. "*Meegwetch,*" he said into the microphone. "I want to thank everyone who voted for me. Your faith and belief in me as leader are humbling. I promise to work hard during my two-year term, and as I promised,

the self-governance project I worked on will be imple-
mented."

Clapping thundered through the center.

"I know many are anxious to hear our plans and when our
first meeting will be. I can tell you it'll happen Tuesday evening after the Victoria Day weekend. We have a lot of work to
do. The former chief and council started a lot of good projects
that will help the community. As your new leader, I will do
my best to see those through.

"It was Willie and his council from six years ago who first
proposed the self-governance project. With our beloved
chief's passing to the spirit world this January, I aim to make
him proud by restoring our system to our ancestors' original
governing model."

Again, everyone clapped, and this time the people rose
from their chairs.

The seven councilors stood on either side of their new
chief. Darryl would decide on the portfolios with input from
the new council. Clayton wanted education. And four of the
councilors supported him.

Raven slipped her arm through Jude's.

He glanced down at her. "You happy?"

"Yes." Her eyes lit. "Clayton said he'd do everything to
make sure I get the loan for the diner. I'm not sure now if it's
something I want, though."

"Really?"

"I did a lot of thinking on this. If I could manage it, that'd
be fine. It'd mean a higher wage. But if the band issues a BCR
guaranteeing profits are funneled to the recovery program,
that'd be better. After what I went through these last couple
of weeks . . ." Her teeth clattered. "Recovery's important. Darryl promised to focus on healing for this community. Healing
after all that happened to us because of those schools." Her
jawline tensed. "We have a profitable business to do it."

"I think it's a good idea." Jude patted her arm. "You always surprise me. And make me love you more."

Her dark skin brightened. "Me, too."

"Me, too, what?" He couldn't resist teasing her.

"Make me love you more," she whispered.

He set his arm around her waist. A sense of freedom seemed to rise from his chest — free to be himself, free to stand beside the woman he loved at a community event with his children at the table.

He wouldn't let Clayton take this from him. And if Clayton dared to go after his job at the school, the son of a bitch was asking for trouble.

After losing his beloved sanctuary in Thunder Bay, Jude had found a new one here. Nobody was going to stand in his way of continuing to build a wonderful life at Ottertail Lake.

****

Raven packed her duffel bag. Jude should arrive any second to get her. He was dropping off the kids at the airport so they could spend the Victoria Day weekend in Thunder Bay. Noah and Rebekah had been eager this time, instead of having to be dragged to the airport.

She slipped the teddy from her drawer, giggling. At the same time Mrs. M emerged from the bedroom across the hall. Raven quickly stuffed the sexy lingerie Jude had bought her into the duffel bag.

Too late.

Mrs. M's face reddened. "I . . . oh . . . uh . . . I hope you enjoy your weekend."

"I will." Raven moved to the dresser to retrieve the small plastic bag she used for her toiletries. "What are you and . . . ." Argh, it was hard calling him Norman. " . . . Mr. M doing?"

"Puttering around here. It'll be quiet."

"Are Emery and Darryl already gone?" They'd planned on taking out their boat, heading for an island to camp and fish, and wouldn't be back until late Monday afternoon.

"I believe so." Mrs. M motioned at the room.

"C'mon in." The manners Jude's mother possessed were impeccable. And she never crowded Raven's space. Too bad her own mother wasn't the same way. Wait, the program had taught Raven comparing two people was wrong. Mom was Mom.

"How's your mother doing? Have you received any updates?"

"I was telling Jude once she finishes chemo, she'll be coming home for a break. I guess she's pretty weak."

"When do you expect her?"

"End of May, or maybe sooner. They started her on chemo—When did I tell you?"

"The last week in April," Mrs. M replied.

The front door opening then closing carried into the bedroom.

"That must be Jude." Mrs. M turned. She'd pinned her blonde waves into a chignon. "I . . ." She stepped forward. "I want to . . ." Her blue eyes searched Raven's. "My grandchildren are so much more relaxed. My son is happy. Very happy. Thank you."

"Oh, uh, you don't have to thank me." *Your son and children have brought nothing but happiness to my life, too. I wish I could spend more time with them other than at your house. But I'm trying my best to understand Jude isn't ready for the four of us to be close yet.*

"Well, I am." Mrs. M smiled. "I'd better let you finish." She indicated the duffel bag. "See you Monday evening."

"See you then." Raven turned back to the duffel bag, clacking her nails against the zipper. These people were turning into a new family. She'd lost her own, but Creator had given her another.

Her stomach soured slightly. But they weren't *her* family. Her family would never become what she wished them to be—the very reason why she was attending many meetings. Like tonight. She'd walk over to the recovery center from Jude's.

Forget it. This was their weekend. They'd wake up to one another for three nights. She grabbed her duffel bag and left the room.

Raven washed another plate. They were cleaning up after Jude had cooked them a simple meal of spaghetti and meatballs, Caesar salad, and baked cheese bread.

"Full?"

"Full of food . . ." She bumped her hips against his. "Something else needs filling up."

"Oh?" Jude dried another plate, grinning. "And what would that be?"

"My cunt."

He threw back his head and laughed.

He had such a nice laugh, deep and sexy, just like him.

"I can arrange that." He set the tea towel over his shoulder and slid his hands around her waist.

He gathered her to his chest. Suds of soap sat in her palms. She couldn't resist and swiveled. His dark eyes twinkled. She flicked the suds onto his nose.

"Oh? Is that what you wanna do?" He released her waist and bulldozed his fingers through the suds.

"No. No. I was kidding." Raven darted around the kitchen table. He was quick on her heels.

She bolted for the living room mere steps away. Jude's breaths and laughter ran down the back of Raven's neck.

His strong arm captured her waist, and his palm of soap suds came at her face. Giggles raced up her throat. Warm wetness saturated her t-shirt from his palm lying across her belly.

His other hand smeared the suds over her face, and she gasped, fighting back the bubbles invading her mouth.

"You're gonna get it!" She wiggled from his grasp and darted back to the sink.

Again, Jude's breaths bore down on Raven's backside, and his deep chuckles.

She scooped a heaping of bubbles from the sink, whipped on her heel, and chucked them at him. The suds landed on Jude's cackling face. He locked his arms around her waist.

"You're going in headfirst." His laughter bordered on howling.

Raven's own laughter raced from her mouth. She was held by the nape of her neck, inches from the sink. The heat from the water moistened her face.

"No!" Her hair fell into the suds, swirling on top of the dish soap.

"Oh, yes you are." His teasing words were hot on her ear.

"If I'm going in, so are you." She tried to reach behind her to grab at him but couldn't. There was one way of beating him at this game. She submerged her hands into the sink and launched a palmful of suds and water into the air.

Jude kept laughing. "Bad girl. Now I have to mop up the kitchen." He grinded his hard prick against her ass, his lips near the nape of her neck.

Heat saturated the inner lips of Raven's pussy, stroking her clit with velvet caresses. She moaned.

"Mmm . . . you got that right," he whispered.

His sweet kisses pressed along the area between her shoulder blades. She cooed, arching her back.

"Oh yeah, that's it." He remained over her, his erection still pressed between her butt cheeks.

His fingers worked at the buttons of her jeans. For a moment, Raven's heart stilled. He tugged at the zipper. The click of each tooth being unlocked merged with her heavy gasps.

When the last of the zipper gave, his hands eased into each side of her jeans. He slid the denim material downward. Every tug allowed a whiff of air to caress her skin that he bared.

"So beautiful," he murmured. He pecked at her lobe, still lowering her jeans.

"Jude . . ." The moan sat in Raven's throat. She fought to work in some air. More heat saturated her flesh.

The sound of Jude unsnapping the button to his pants and the lowering of his zipper tickled her insides. Quivering. Shaking. She folded her lip over the other. He drew back her wet strands. Her knees threatened to give out from under her.

"Fuck me . . ." she managed to sputter through the thick coating of saliva in her mouth.

"I'm gonna do more than fuck you." He slapped her bare cheek.

"Fuck my ass?" she sultrily uttered.

"Oh? Is that what you want?" A hint of a growl lingered on his question.

"Yeah." While bracing the counter, she shifted and thrust her buttocks at him.

"Hmm . . . would love to. Would love to very much." He nibbled on her lobe. "I'm assuming you brought something. You're the expert at this, beautiful."

"Yes." Fevered. Heat coated her skin. Even clammy.

He kept grinding his cock between her ass cheeks.

She turned her head slightly to his pants around his ankles. He removed his shirt and tossed it on the table. "In my . . . in my duffel bag. The plastic bag. With my toiletries."

"Don't move." His order was as deep and authoritative as his natural voice that sent quivers down her spine.

She remained clutching the counter in front of the sink.

The heat of his breaths and warmth of his skin vanished. Her peripheral vison caught his pants being tossed over the chair.

So close. She couldn't remember the last time she'd gotten fucked up the ass. And that had been a tradeoff, a way to coax Sully into giving her more drugs, nothing more.

Footsteps brushed the floor.

She gulped. This, what she was about to do, was truly giving, and what she truly wanted.

"I take it you know what you're doing," he murmured. From the corner of her eye, she glimpsed the tube of lube he held. "And you're gonna guide me through this like the good girl that you are."

His sultry words seemed to fondle and lick her clit that filled to a hard nub, eager for his touch.

"Yes," she managed to say through clenched teeth.

He flipped up the cap and squirted a generous helping into his palm. "I wanna fuck you slow and easy. Very easy. I don't wanna hurt you, Raven. I only wanna make you feel good."

"You already do." And he did. The excitement wetting her pussy bordered on bursting. "Please, Jude."

He eased his hand around her waist and parted her cunt lips. He smeared the area with slippery warm lube, a silky massage that coaxed her to arch her back and raise her ass.

"Oh, lookit you, how ready you are for me." His words brushed her neck, and he kissed the nape. The head of his cock feathered her crack.

The massage he gifted her with, fondling her pussy from front to back created rippling waves of pleasure through her clit.

"Please," she begged. "Please."

The head of his hard prick pushed at her asshole. Raven bit her lip. There'd be discomfort, and she'd only done this while drunk or high. She concentrated on the silky sensations erupting between her legs the more he lavished her cunt with hot strokes that seemed to liquefy her insides.

The length of his erection squeezed into her, and lubricant filled her butt, massaging her hole. Jude's heavy panting was thick on her shoulder. His lips puckered and nibbled.

His cock edged in farther, stretching her asshole. The pleasure building within Raven bordered on exploding. He continued to stroke her clit while gliding his cock that was half in her back and forth. Her body shook. Her knees weakened. Her breaths came in deep puffs.

"How're you, baby?" His voice possessed the familiar gentle crackle when he was fully aroused. He nuzzled her hair.

"More," she whispered. "More."

His pumps were slow at first, satiny fucking, feeding her sweet pleasure. She rocked in rhythm with his thrusts, taking him in her and then gliding down his length until she reached the head and squeezed her buttocks.

He gasped. His moans were as thick and creamy as the wetness of her cunt.

He moved quicker, his plunges coaxing her to fully open to him. She clung to the sink, gasping and groaning. Her clit was on fire, tingles of excitement pricking her most sensitive area.

White lightning seemed to coast along her skin, and the pleasure climbed, gathering into an ecstatic burst of bliss that left her crying out his name.

Chapter Fifteen: She Takes My Breath Away

Jude lay in the bed, knee raised, cup of tea on his stomach, and Raven's head nestled in the pit of his arm. He'd never experienced this kind of sated before — so relaxed he could've melted into the cotton sheets.

Never did he believe a woman would give herself to him like this. And what floated through his thoughts had nothing to do with the anal sex Raven had asked for. He stroked her hair.

The way she gave up the diner. The way she embraced his family. The way she welcomed his children into her life. And the kids liked her. Probably because Raven didn't push herself on Noah and Rebekah. She was letting a relationship develop naturally by seeing them when they came over for dinner at Mom and Dad's, or when she ate over once a week with the three of them.

If Jude gave Charlene the kids for the summer, it'd stall the budding relationship he and Raven were creating with Noah and Rebekah. But if he told Charlene this, she'd become resentful, which was unfair, because he hadn't stopped her from having Stephen in the kids' lives before she'd moved into the hotel.

Already, Jude was losing out on Noah's birthday next weekend because the kids, again, would be in Thunder Bay or Kenora for the end-of-the-month visit.

"Mmm, so sleepy." Raven's words dusted his nipple. She

wound her leg over his calves.

"I guess you are. You did get your cunt licked, besides your ass fucked." A low chuckle built in Jude's chest.

"Mmm, you're so good to me." She pecked his nipple.

Her sweet touch created even sweeter tingles around his spine. "I could lie like this forever."

"Me, too." She traced her finger around his areola.

On the only night table in his bedroom, her phone buzzed. He reached over and grabbed it. "Here you go, beautiful."

Raven took the cell.

Jude sipped his tea. Maybe they could go out fishing after church on Sunday. Take Dad's skiff on the lake and catch some walleye to eat for dinner. But they'd go in the opposite direction of Darryl and Emery, who wanted privacy, which was why they'd probably gotten away from the reserve. Dad was checking in on the two cats they owned.

"Mom's coming back next weekend. With Lark."

"Lark's there now?"

Raven nodded. She handed him the phone. Her once relaxed body stiffened.

He set her cell next to his on the nightstand.

"How're you feeling?" He slipped his arm around her shoulder while leaning against the two pillows.

"I dunno . . ." She cozied up in the pit of his arm and resumed tracing his areola.

He pecked the top of her head. "Fishing'll get your mind off of everything."

"Fishing?" She shifted and peeked up at him.

"Yep. Fishing. Sunday morning. After Mass. What'd you say?"

"Sounds good. What're you doing tomorrow while I'm at work?"

"Cleaning." Not exactly what Jude wanted to do, but it had to get done. "The bathroom and the kids' rooms. And don't be thinking about your mother, please. We have the weekend to ourselves."

"Okay, I promise." Her sleepy reply said he'd worn her out.

"Get some rest. I'm going to stay up for a bit more." Her birthday was the first week of June. The big three-two. He had to do some online shopping, find her something special to show her how special she was to him.

****

Raven stood on the dock outside the Matawapits' house. She'd readied everything while Jude had been at church. Sandwiches to eat, something to drink, and Mrs. M had offered up fresh fruit.

The jeans, t-shirt, and pullover draping Jude's gorgeous body fit right into the rugged reserve surroundings. She wasn't sure what she liked better — Mr. Metrosexual or Mr. Outdoors. Perhaps both. He was gentlemanly outdoors. Pressed clothes. Clean hiking boots. Smooth hands.

The sun was out and not a cloud in the sky, which was a bit weird. This was the Victoria Day weekend, and the Great Mother loved to cleanse the earth on holidays.

"Ready?" Jude held out his hand.

Raven snickered. "I'm a bush girl. I've been in and out of boats my whole life." She eased into the skiff.

"You can probably drive this thing, too, huh?" The sun cast a blue hue to his jet-black hair.

"You betcha." Raven flipped up the seat in front of his. She set down the cooler and her small bag. "It's why I got everything ready while you were at church. Minnows. Gas. Hooked up the tank to the motor. We're all set."

"You always surprise me." Jude pulled on the cord. The motor roared to life.

"Want me to drive? I can take us to a great spot."

"Okay, you're on."

Raven handed Jude a travel mug full of coffee and switched places. She sat in the seat positioned at the stern.

"I'm assuming you know the lakes." With his designer sunglasses perched on his nose and a baseball cap he'd donned, he was every girl's dream.

"Silly man. Of course." She gripped the handle of the steering arm. Jude had earned major points in her book by letting her guide. Any other man's ego would've been pricked.

For the next half hour, she drove them from the bay, across the lake, and through the channel, heading southwest.

"Are you going to buy a boat?" Raven hollered.

"Say again." Jude swiveled.

"A boat. Now that you live here, are you gonna buy one?"

"Yep. But not this one." He laughed.

"Oh? Is it too bush for you?" Raven giggled.

"I want something with a steering wheel."

"Inboard or outboard?"

"Outboard. I got two kids. I want a spot where they can sit up front on plenty of seats and cushions so they can enjoy themselves. How're they supposed to have fun up there?" He pointed to the bow where another bench seat stretched across the width. Not too comfy at all.

Land awaited them. They were heading into Jones Bay, a full circle with hidden inlets.

She let back on the throttle. At least Mr. M had an electric trolling motor and she wouldn't have to use the outboard.

"What are we betting on?" Jude lifted his boots off the bench. He grabbed the minnow bag and removed a knife from his pocket.

"Betting?"

"Yep. If it's Emery and me out for the day, we always bet."

"Oh?" She couldn't help the amusement in her words.

"And who always wins?" *If he doesn't say Emery, he's bullshitting me.*

"Hah, hah. I see it in your eyes. Yep, Emery. Hey, he grew up here. He knows these waters." Jude motioned at the bay.

"I figured so, and I'm glad you were honest." She reached over and poked his knee.

"Moi? Honest?" Jude palmed his chest. "I'm always honest."

Raven cut the outboard and fired up the trolling motor.

"You worry about getting that ready. I got your bait." He poured the bag of minnows into the plastic bucket.

Like a true expert, he hooked their minnows to the jigs.

"You got a couple more sinkers than mine." He slyly grinned. "Is there something you're not telling me?" He handed Raven her rod.

"Never mind . . ." She took her rod. "You worry about yours and I'll worry about mine."

"Ooookay, girlie."

A few crows flew over them.

"Girlie?" She poked at his knee again. "Just for that, it's gonna be a tough bet. One full massage, and you get no sex afterward."

"Naked? Massage? And no sex?" He smirked. "If I win, I get a massage—and sex."

"You men are all the same. You think massages always gotta lead to sex."

"And you don't want sex?"

"Yes, I'll take sex, and a massage, please." She lowered her sunglasses a smidgen and fluttered her no-false-lashes his way.

"We don't gotta wager for me to give you a massage." He cast his line, snickering.

"The full massage. Feet. Calves."

"You got it." His rod moved as he jigged his line.

Raven cast out her own.

146

With no sound from the electric trolling motor, the only noise was the chirps from the birds. Raven reached into her bag and removed the pink e-cigarette.

She'd gotten Jude's full approval by the smile he bared in her direction, followed by a slow nod.

"I left my cigarettes at the house so I wouldn't smoke out here." She puffed on the vape.

"If it helps, it helps. I'm not gonna get on your case about smoking. It's nice to see you vaping, though."

"Oh? Did you hate having to kiss a dirty ashtray?" Raven puckered her lips.

"Hey, you're attached to the ashtray. I'll take your ashtray every single time." He lowered his sunglasses and winked.

He always left her walking on air. "Pour me a coffee?"

"Sure." Jude handed Raven his pole. He grabbed the thermos and fixed her up a coffee in a travel mug. "Here."

"Thanks." She returned his pole and took the coffee, which she set between her thighs.

"How do you think we'll do?" Jude continued to jig his line.

"I dunno. We're out pretty late. These guys like to feed early morning and in the evening."

"I guess we should've left earlier. The last time I fished was last summer. And I didn't have time to ice fish this winter."

"You had a lot going on. New job. New home. New life."

"Yes, a new life." Jude bared his pearly whites. "One I'm very much enjoying. We should make this our Sunday outing whenever the kids are in the city."

Raven's heart fluttered. "I'd love that. A great way to spend my day off."

"I know homework keeps you busy."

"That's 'cause you love dishing the stuff out."

They both laughed. The atmosphere coming from the boat was as relaxing and fresh as the warm spring air.

This wasn't the teacher Jude, the father Jude, the lover Jude. He was just Jude. The man she'd come to love and admire. "For someone very metrosexual, I'm surprised by how much you enjoy the outdoors."

"Hey, I'm from Thunder Bay," he said teasingly. "I enjoy the outdoors like any other boy growing up in Northwestern Ontario."

"How come you didn't have a boat?" Emery and Darryl had one. The deacon had one.

His jawline hardened. "We . . . did. Sold it. It was part of . . . the separation agreement. It's why our divorce was uncontested. We split everything down the middle. House. Snowmobile. The other toys." He wet his lips. "Some of the furniture I kept, but I had to pay out my share to Char. And what I didn't keep, I sold, and gave her half the money on it. I gave Bridget a bedroom set. The rest I put into storage."

"I'm sorry . . ." Gosh, he had really been starting over when he'd come up here in February.

"Don't be. It is what it is." He shrugged. "We earned everything together, so when we split, we divided everything in half. The only thing Char kept was her great-grandmother's dining room furniture. I bought a new set after she moved out."

"The one in your kitchen?"

"Yeah. I wasn't going to buy the cabinet, hutch, and everything else, though. At the time, I knew the house was selling, but we needed something to eat off." He chuckled. "We had a banquette in the breakfast nook. It's not like I could rip out the seating, so it sold with the house."

"What's a banquette?"

"A built-in eating area. We had it custom-made to fit the deep bay window in the kitchen."

"Oh . . ." Heat climbed onto her face. She was too bush.
"What?"

"Nothing."

"C'mon, fess up." His words were cajoling.

"Oh, never mind." She wiggled her nose at him impishly. "Big deal the bush girl doesn't know what a banquette is."

"Yeah, well, you're showing me a few things." Again, he lowered his sunglasses and winked. "I never got to be inside a beautiful ass before. You don't see me embarrassed about it, do you? I like it when you show me . . . something new."

"Ooh, you do?" A giggle fluttered up Raven's throat. "Then you'll have to let me tie you up and have my way with you."

"You can go on ahead and do *anything* you want to me."

"Oh? I can? And what would you do to me?"

"A gentleman always asks his lady what she wants." He grinned. "Unless you like surprises . . ."

"I love surprises."

"Then a surprise it is. Someone does have a birthday coming up."

"I wish I could have gotten you something nicer." Raven sighed. She'd made him moccasins for his birthday.

"Hey, I love 'em. And I brought them to get comfy and relax in out here today. They mean a lot to me, Raven." His smile lost its teasing and melted to warm, even cozy. "I really love that you went out of your way to make me and the kids something. Not too many people can say they have handmade deerskin moccasins."

"No, they can't."

"You should think about opening your own online business. Sell your crafts over the Internet. What you make are something else. Lookit these babies."

He held his rod in one hand and delved into the bag and presented the moccasins. Rich beading of various shades of blue and some white, because the color blue suited Jude — all shades of blue, especially the hue's darker shades.

"I'm glad you like them." For some strange reason her face warmed. She'd never been bashful about her work before. "Uh . . . so, when are you gonna get a new boat?"

"Not until winter." Jude returned to jigging his line. "I don't want to portage it over how many lakes to get it here."

They both chuckled.

Raven angled the boat closer to the rocks of the shoreline. Not even a nibble.

"You and the kids'll be the first to go for a ride in it," he assured her in a loving voice.

More warmth coated Raven's face. He was including her in his future by speaking about next summer. Twirls of excitement shivered in her stomach.

Chapter Sixteen: Gimme Some Water

Mom was flying in on the plane today for her end-of-the-month weekend pass. Everyone would be at the airport but Raven. At least Fawn had texted to give Raven the news. Now that everyone was home, she'd received perfunctory greetings all week whenever one of the family stopped in at the diner.

Tonight, Fawn was hosting a dinner Raven hadn't been invited to. Big deal. She was going to Jude's after work to spend the weekend. Already, she'd packed her duffel bag so she could simply walk over. Jude always picked her up at his parents' house but had suggested this time she go on over and watch the kids until he got home.

With her shift done, Raven retrieved her belongings. She'd prepped everything for the afternoon and evening crew.

"Heading out?" Cookie asked.

"Yep. What about you?"

"Super beat, beat. I need to put my feet up." Cookie wiped his brow. He wandered to the sink.

The bell tinkled above the door. The next shift was arriving.

Raven left the diner. Jude's place was only a road over. The days were averaging a warm fifteen degrees now. No need for a jacket. Last night, Mrs. M had cooked up a great dinner and made a special cake for Noah since he'd celebrate his birthday in Thunder Bay, which he was looking forward to because his old friends would be there.

This morning, Jude had dropped off his key for Raven at

the diner, slipping it from his neck strap.

A few older people sat out on their steps, rocking in their chairs. Raven waved. Pride lifted her shoulders upward and her back straighter. The kids would get home at ten after three. Jude had mentioned he'd packed their suitcases last night.

This was Raven's first time alone with his children. She skipped up the last step at his house and unlocked the back door. This was also her first time entering by herself, and she giggled with excitement. For a man, he sure was clean. Maybe it went with being a city boy metrosexual kind of guy.

She entered his bedroom and set the duffel bag on the duvet, seeming to take in his furnishings through fresh eyes. He'd downsized to a queen, and it fit perfect because of the room size. Instead of a dresser, he had a dark-oak chest of drawers to accommodate the clothing he didn't hang in the closet. The bland once-white walls needed a new coat of paint. The linoleum floors required a change-out.

Her gaze caressed the big pillow she always slept on, and where she'd sleep tonight.

She strolled back into the kitchen. The high-back cushioned chairs and rich wood table were meant for a dining room, but he'd done a nice job with a place in dire need of repair. Scuffed floors. Cabinets begging for a resurfacing. Bland laminate countertop. No wonder he wanted to build a new house.

A brown leather sofa, love seat, and matching recliner almost overpowered the small living room. He'd mentioned uprooting the family room furniture and selling everything in the formal living room and the rec room in the basement. Must've been nice to have three places to entertain.

Before the kids got home, Raven showered and unpacked her clothes and toiletries. At quarter after three, the back door opened then closed. Raven stood at the kitchen counter, fixing the kids an after-school snack. Mrs. M had mentioned

Rebekah liked cheese and crackers and Noah enjoyed munching on apple slices and peanut butter.

"Miss Kabatay," Rebekah called out. "Dad said you'd be watching us after school."

"Hey, Miss Kabatay." Noah entered, removing his backpack.

"You're just in time. I got your after-school snacks ready."

"Yeet!" Noah's face reddened. "I mean, thank you, Miss Kabatay."

Raven couldn't help the giggle. Jude had also said the kids couldn't eat in the living room.

"Here you go." She set the snacks on the table.

"We have to change first and put our stuff away," Noah announced. "I mean put away our belongings."

Goodness, Jude must have sat Noah down for a good lecture or had threatened to yank the birthday party if the boy didn't don a halo this afternoon. "Sure."

The kids disappeared inside their bedrooms. Sounds of drawers opening and closing, and closet doors opening and closing carried into the kitchen. They reappeared in their casual clothes. Both sat at the table.

"May we have milk, please?" The halo Noah had been forced to wear glowed.

"Sure." Raven chuckled to herself as she opened the fridge and grabbed the milk. She filled two glasses and placed one in front of Rebekah who quietly ate her snack, and the other in front of Noah, who dabbed at his mouth with one of the napkins available in the napkin tray on the table.

Raven would have to tease Jude afterward. She couldn't recall her nieces and nephews acting like this after school. Kids were full of energy after sitting in a classroom all day and needed to stretch their active muscles.

She pulled out a chair. "How's school go?"

Noah swallowed. "Good. I learned a lot."

Rebekah made sure and swallowed, too. "I had a good day."

Hmm, maybe Raven should switch out these Stepford kids for the real ones. "Did you wanna play outside?"

"I'd like to, please." Noah dipped his apple slice into more peanut butter. "I must finish my snack first."

"Yeah, we *have* to." Rebekah stressed each word.

"Your dad?" Raven gathered her fingers together, resting her elbows on the table.

They both nodded.

"He said if we don't behave properly, I don't get a birthday party." A smidgen of fear lingered in Noah's eyes. "I don't wanna miss my birthday party."

"I bet you're looking forward to seeing your old friends, hey?"

Noah dipped another apple slice into the peanut butter. "I get to sleep at my homeboy's. I mean, sleep at Auntie Bridget's. Me . . . I mean Kyle and I are going to game all night. Err, not game all night. We'll game until Auntie Bridget says we have to go to bed."

Raven was aware of the cap Jude had put on gaming. "You up for some road hockey?"

"Yep." He smirked.

Oh, he thought he could beat a mere girl? Raven also smirked. "Eat up. I'm going to braid my hair."

Ten minutes later, she was outside with the kids. They played on the road for maybe a half an hour, laughing and teasing each other, until Jude walked over from the school, carrying his briefcase.

Pride filled Jude's wide smile.

Raven leaned on her stick. "We need goalie nets."

"Those are back in T Bay. Storage. I guess I should arrange to ship them up here with the kids on their return flight. I'll ask Adam to pick them up at the storage facility and get them to the plane." Jude strolled up to them. "Who beat whom?"

"She's merciless, Dad." Noah's sprouting horns knocked aside his halo. "Totally trashed me. But I'm gonna get her back. I was only being nice 'cause you said I gotta be chill."

"She smoked you. Face it." Jude snickered.

"Aww, I only let her win 'cause she's a—"

Jude raised his finger. "What did I say about girls and women?"

"They are just as capable as us." Exasperation filled Noah's words.

"That's right. If your Auntie Bridget heard you . . ." Jude let out a low whistle. "C'mon, we have to get to the airport. The plane'll leave soon."

Much to Raven's delight, she was invited to ride to the airport to see the kids off. She waited inside with them and stood to the side while Jude gave his usual eight hundred rules and instructions. She followed him out to the plane as he led the kids to the steps to board. Then she stood at the window with him, waving, while the plane turned and headed for the runway. The kids waved back, their little hands at the windows.

Jude's jaw was harder looking than cement. He continued to wave. The plane raced down the runway and took off.

His chest matched his bowed head.

"You okay?"

"Yeah. I already texted Char. She'll be there to get them. We've done this too many times already." He stuffed his hand into his pocket. The other hand he wrapped around her waist.

"I'm sorry." Finally, Raven understood why Jude had given himself a vasectomy last Christmas. A painful twitch appeared at the back of her neck. He was a great father and deserved to watch his son turn nine tomorrow.

"We should go." He squeezed her shoulder.

Raven's cell phone dinged. "Sure." She reached into her purse and withdrew her cell. Fawn's message appeared.

Mom wants you to come tonight. She said she has something to say to everyone. Later.

"What is it? You went stiffer than a board." Jude leaned in.

"That was Fawn. I . . . uh . . . she wants me to go to the dinner she's holding at Mom's. She said Mom has something to tell us. I'm . . . they actually included me."

This was so strange. Part of Raven jumped full of anticipation at finally seeing Mom again. But the other half . . . this was another weekend alone with Jude. They'd planned on having dinner, she'd go to her meeting, and then they'd relax together on the couch and watch a movie before turning in.

"I guess you'd better go, then." Tension lingered in the enthusiasm Jude tried to show for Raven.

"Hey." She touched his stomach. "Look at me."

He held her gaze, dark eyes still full of sadness.

How could she leave him when he needed her? But if she didn't go, she'd be accused of choosing the Matawapits again. This was her time to finally reconcile with her family.

Instead of getting a ride, Raven chose to walk the ten minutes to reach her former nabe of Old Main. It'd taken every ounce of self-will to leave Jude's house when he needed her. She was twenty minutes late, Jude having finally forced her out the door.

The driveway was full of vehicles, but none were her siblings' — they must've also walked over.

Raven drew in a big breath and proceeded up the back steps. From inside, laugher, chatter, clanking dishes, and rattling silverware carried outside. She opened the back door. The bathroom kept her blocked for a few seconds. When she appeared around the corner, the house went silent. Everyone stared. Sisters. Clayton. Nieces. Nephews. Cousins. Uncle. Aunts.

There were so many people, they were bunched in like sardines.

Nobody said hello. Nobody smiled.

Raven squared her shoulders and wormed her way into the kitchen. Mom sat in the recliner, great-grandchild on her lap. Even she didn't smile.

Fawn leaned against the kitchen counter, arms folded. "You're late. Eat up. It's getting cold."

The chatter and laughter resumed. Raven squeezed her way through her relations who never stopped to ask how she was doing. She stood by Fawn. What was the purpose of inviting her here if she wasn't wanted?

"Give them time," Fawn said. Her reply wasn't welcoming, but it wasn't unwelcoming either.

"Mom seriously wants me here?" Raven muttered.

"Yeah, she does. So grab a plate." Fawn turned and busied herself with serving up dinner for the younger kids.

At least Clayton waved at Raven and also encouraged her to grab a dish. But they didn't get to eat together. Clayton was in the living room, sitting on a stool beside Mom, who failed to touch her plate of food. She'd lost more weight.

Raven didn't eat much either, which bothered her, because not only was she being disrespectful to those who'd cooked the meal, but also to the plant-based and animal-based life who'd offered themselves for this dinner.

To give herself something to do, Raven washed the numerous plates, never ending glasses, and constant silverware being dumped into the sink or set on the counter. Once she got those out of the way, she tackled the pots and pans. She was nothing more than a servant, meant to look after royalty who ate and drank. They may as well have held the party at the diner, since she did this all day.

There were hugs and kisses goodbye as everyone began leaving a couple of hours later. Nobody said goodbye to

Raven. She kept washing and drying.

All she had to clean was the serving bowls. There wasn't much food left.

While she stored the leftovers and put them in the fridge, Fawn set another water-filled kettle on the oven element.

Maybe Mom was finally going to make her announcement.

Once Raven put the last of the dishes in the cupboard, Fawn, Wren, Lark, Clayton, and Mom gathered around the kitchen table.

Fawn filled an extra mug. At least someone had done something for Raven.

"Thanks." Raven sat and fixed her tea.

Fawn said nothing.

"It's been tough. Very tough. At times I feel like I'm not going to make it," Mom murmured, staring at her mug of tea.

"You're gonna make it," Wren fired back. "Don't think that way."

"Enough." Mom held up her hand. "I asked to speak to you because I have something important to say." She pinned her bitter eyes on Clayton. "How's the new council progressing? Did you decide on your portfolios yet?"

"We're still going through the projects our previous council started." Clayton sat back.

Mom reached for her cigarettes.

Raven bit her tongue, or she'd scream *you have cancer*. But she'd be a hypocrite, having given in to her craving after quitting. At least she stuck to vaping now.

"When's the next meeting?" Mom took a drag.

"Next week. We've been having small meetings after our main one. Now that we reviewed all the projects and budgets, we're going to look at responsibilities." Clayton glanced around the table.

"What about those, them . . . Emery, Roy, and Jenny?" Deep frown lines appeared beneath Mom's grim mouth.

"So far they haven't done anything. We've agreed with what's gotta be done."

Mom nodded. Through hostile dark eyes, she focused on Raven.

Raven moved closer to the table but refrained from allowing the sneer to form that tugged at the corners of her lips.

"I want your brother to get the education portfolio." Mom's announcement was flat.

Heat burned beneath Raven's skin. "That's Jenny's portfolio. She's had it for—"

"See? There you go again. Siding with *that* family. And I've no doubt where you're spending the weekend, or where you walked from. Nobody saw that son of a bitch's truck pull up."

How could she speak so hatefully about the deacon? Raven kept holding Mom's hard stare.

"You'll be packing your bag after you listen up good to what I have to say." Mom's hands shook. She tapped the growing ash on the end of the cigarette into the ashtray.

"And what do you have to tell me that I don't already know?" Frustration gathered in Raven's chest.

"Your sister told me she told you the truth. You wanna know who started this bullshit?" Mom huffed. "You really wanna know?"

"Mom . . . easy." Fawn reached for their mother's hand, but Mom snatched it away.

"I'm not six years old. I don't need help," Mom snarled. She glared again at Raven and lifted her finger. "Norman Matawapit. That's who."

Chapter Seventeen: Died a Thousand Times

Jude's phone buzzed. The texter was Charlene. Great.

Do you have time to video chat?

He had all the time in the world, since he was waiting for Raven.

Sure.

Charlene's invitation popped up, and he pressed *accept.*

She appeared on the screen, her blue eyes bright for once, instead of misty. She held a glass of wine. She swirled the red liquid around. "I have something to ask. A big favor."

Now what? "Go ahead." He sank in the recliner.

"My baby girl turns eight pretty quick."

"I know. *My* baby boy turns nine tomorrow." He couldn't help the sarcasm in his words.

"All you had to do was ask, and I would've told you to come." Charlene peered at him curiously.

"I had no idea I was wanted." Jude reached for his lemonade.

"There's still time for you to fly in if you want to attend. The party's not starting until two tomorrow."

"Will Stephen be there?"

"Yes. He's visiting his mother for the weekend."

Jude bit back the disgusted breath of words ready to rush through his mouth. "We had a small party for Noah last night. I'll see him when he gets home."

"I . . . I have something to ask." Charlene tipped the glass and sipped.

"Ask away. The most I can say is yes or no."

Her mouth firmed. "I . . . I'd like to attend my baby girl's birthday party."

Rebekah's birthday was the following week after Raven's. Jude had planned on having cake at his parents' house on the Wednesday, but a full party on Saturday afternoon, also at his folks'. He'd already planned the activities of outdoor games with contests and prizes. Afterward, they'd barbecue hamburgers and hot dogs.

The word *no* sat on his tongue. "You aware you're more than welcome to see our daughter. I'd never keep Becky from seeing her mother on such a special day." *But I'd sure love to.* "Your visit would mean a lot to her."

Charlene's eyes brightened. "Thank you. I'll . . . I guess . . ." The brightness in her gaze dimmed. "I'll stay at the motel. I assume your . . . girlfriend will be there, since she's living at your parents'."

"Yes, she'll be there."

Charlene sipped more wine. "I'll see you then. I'll need a ride from the airport. I'll book my flight for Saturday morning and arrange to fly out Sunday after church."

Oh great, she'd be at Mass. "Sure."

"Have you thought about my . . . ah . . . summer vacation proposition?"

"I'm going to be honest . . ."

Charlene glanced away, shaking her head in the same manner she'd always shaken her head when she'd loathed what he had to say.

"They're having a hard time adjusting to Kenora. And if they go there for the summer, it means having to adjust to a new babysitter."

"I see . . . it's always—" The wine swished and swirled.

Not this again. "Hold up. Hear me out. Okay?"

"Fine." She sipped more wine.

"We gotta do what's best for them. Not what's best for us. Right?"

"Yes."

"And they're looking forward to spending the summer up here. They want to swim in the lake—"

"Kenora's on Lake of the Woods. There's nothing but lakes around here," she muttered.

"But it's not Ottertail Lake." Jude didn't care his voice was full-on authoritative mode. "If you want, I can take them in a few extra times besides their planned visits. During the day, I'll watch them, and when you get home after work, they can be with you. They can stay wherever you're staying."

"I'll be at Stephen's. We're working on . . . he's considering Thunder Bay. It's all up in the air, though. We might not move for a good year. But he knows how I feel about being closer to my sister, and he knows it's not negotiable."

"Okay. Sounds fine. Then we'll agree to a schedule when you're here for Becky's party. I'll start working on one. How many times did you want to see them?"

"As much as I can."

Great. He might end up spending most of the summer in Kenora.

"I'll talk to Stephen about . . . I'm gathering you won't want to stay at his house."

"Nope."

She flinched. "I'll talk to him about paying for your accommodations. It's only fair."

"Yep. Only fair." Jude wasn't forking out money on his ex-wife's behalf. If she wanted to break the custody agreement they had and cut into his personal time, she could dammed well get her *hero* to pay for it.

"Are you going ahead with the annulment then?"

"We've only been divorced since the beginning of January. Can I have a little more time to think?" Exasperation filled her question.

What was there to think on? And if he asked to file, he'd push Charlene into a further sulk. He cracked his knuckles. "Sure. We can talk about it when you come up for the party."

"Okay, I'll see you then. I should get going. The kids are in the family room."

"Sure. Bye." Jude switched off the phone. He sat forward in the chair, setting his face in his palms.

*****

"How's the deacon to blame for all this?" Raven refused to believe what Mom was saying.

"You wanna know how?" Mom thrust the finger that held the cigarette. "You ask him if he can deny what he did to me."

Something horrible seemed to squeeze Raven's rib cage. "Wh-what?"

"Wh-what?" Fawn almost jumped from her chair.

"What'd he do?" Clayton slowly rose.

"Sit. Sit." Mom used her hand to motion at everyone. She glanced away, murmuring, "He threw me over for a white woman."

"What do you mean?" Fawn's words came fast and loud. "You were seeing the deacon? Deacon Matawapit?"

Mom nodded.

"Just now?" Wren's mouth fell open.

"No." Mom sucked on the cigarette. She blew out some smoke. "He threw me over, leaving me no choice but to marry your father. And I wasn't the only woman he conned into bed using his lying mouth. My friend, Annie—"

"Darryl's aunt. *That* Annie?" Lark sputtered.

Raven folded her arms. "Not buying."

Mom's mouth fell open, and she almost clawed at the table to half stand. "How dare you!"

"Everyone knows everything on the rez. Why hasn't anyone said anything about this sooner?" Raven asked coolly.

"You don't think there was talk?" Mom's eyes narrowed. "You don't think people knew? We lived in Thunder Bay together until I came back here. And don't you ever again call me a liar. You go to your new home . . ." She banged the table. The sugar bowl and creamer rattled. " . . . go to your home and ask the deacon. See if he can deny it—if he can deny what he did to me. Ask him if he didn't fuck every woman he could get his drunken, using paws on. He's no deacon. He's a fucking lying son of a bitch who's got no right wearing that collar.

"Maybe he does? Lookit what those religious bastards did to us. So he does fit in with their kind." Mom buried her face in her hands.

Fawn reached over, hugging Mom. "You were in love with Deacon Matawapit?"

Mom's shoulders shook, and she nodded. "He . . . he . . . I trusted him. I never should've. How can a man treat his own kind that way?"

A fire flamed in Clayton's eyes. "I'm gonna—"

"No," Mom said quickly. "No. He's too old. The man is pushing seventy. You don't go fighting an old man."

Lark slammed her fist into her palm. "What did he do? Tell us. Please, Mom."

"He was just like those religious people." Mom sniffled and swiped at her eyes. "I was only a kid. You'll never understand how lonely the residential school was." Her mouth quivered. "I . . . I thought he loved me. He told me he loved

164

me . . ."

The blood drained from Raven's veins, and she forced herself to stay straight in the chair and not collapse from the feather-lightness in her head.

"He's a cold bastard," Mom huffed. With trembling hands, she butted out her cigarette and reached for another. "We . . . I thought we were in love. I followed him to Thunder Bay after I finished school. He'd stayed on in Sioux Lookout. He was attending the high school there. I made it one year but dropped out. We were too old for those grades. We didn't feel like we belonged after being isolated in the residential school for almost ten years.

"He promised . . . promised to take care of me . . . but he lied." Mom managed to get her cigarette lit. She took a drag, staring at the light above the table. "It never happened. He was drunk all the time. Staying out at night. Never around. Cheating with other women."

Mom hugged herself. "After the school, he put me through another nightmare. He used all the girls. Including Annie. They were both drinkers. They'd leave together for two to three days at a time. I was working. Trying to keep a roof over our heads. We lived in a slum, but it was better than the street."

Raven's heart bordered on cracking. She bowed her head.

"I . . . I put up with it until I was twenty. I had enough by then. Had enough of his lies, his cheating, his drinking, his temper . . ." Mom sniffled again. "I left. I came home. That's when your useless father and I got together. He always had a crush on me. He promised to treat me better than Norman did . . . but it was also a lie.

"Then . . . Norman . . . he straightened out a few years later. He straightened out for a white woman." Revulsion blazed in Mom's eyes. "He had the gall to become a deacon. And not once did he ever say he was sorry."

Mom blinked. She glared at Raven. "And you have the goddamn nerve to stay under his roof. Fuck his damn son. Do you really think Jude Matawapit's gonna marry you? He married a white woman just like his no-good-for-nothing father did. What do you really think you are to him? I told you before — I know the Matawapits better than you.

"You know nothing!" Mom shoved back her chair. She wobbled. "Nothing," she muttered. "You weren't around to witness what they did. You were too busy boozing it up in the city for how many damn years? Huh? While you were out tramping around, we bore the load."

Mom used her hand to make a circle, motioning at Wren, Lark, Fawn, and Clayton. "If you truly wanna be a part of this family, you'll walk away from Norman's son. You'll move out of that white woman's house. I've had enough." Her bony chest heaved. "Had enough."

She staggered and sank back into the chair, gripping the table for leverage. "I . . ." A sob left her mouth. "I . . . I can't do this anymore. I'm . . . tired. Tired of this life. Tired of what I had to live because of that son of a bitch."

Mom reached for her cigarettes, the one in the ashtray almost burning out to the filter. "After what Norman did, after what your father did, I wasn't going near another man again. All I got are my kids, my grandkids, and my great-grandchild. That's it.

"Are you going to be a daughter to me or not?" Mom puffed on the fresh cigarette. "I said my piece. I'm tired. I need to sleep."

She stood, resting her palm on her sunken stomach. "Help me."

Fawn scuttled to stand and took Mom's elbow. She shot Raven a dirty look and helped Mom off to the bedroom.

A cold sweat broke out down Raven's back. Her teeth clattered. She rocked in the chair. Mom was going to die — and two men had destroyed her in the process.

She forced herself to rise, but her shaking knees threatened to give out from under her.

"Where're you going?" Lark asked.

"I have something to do." Raven reached for her purse and shuffled from the house.

****

Jude checked the clock for the fifth time within a half an hour. Watching the hands move wasn't going to bring Raven back any faster. He'd best respect she'd been invited to a family dinner and be happy. Maybe she was having a great visit and planned on staying a couple more hours.

He settled back in the recliner to keep watching the golf tournament on TV. Earlier, he'd debated on popping in on Emery and Darryl, but he'd passed, because if Raven returned early, she'd need him if the dinner hadn't gone well.

Footsteps sounded on the back stairs.

Jude rose and hurried for the door.

Raven entered very slowly. She stood on the entry mat, staring.

He couldn't figure out her expression exactly. It wasn't accusing. Or angry. But something was off in her direct stance. "Did the dinner go okay?"

"I need to get my bag." Even her voice wasn't accusing or angry, but very direct like the way she stared at him.

"Your bag?" Was she staying at the house to help her mother? "Okay." He licked his lips. "Did you need any help?"

"Your family's done enough." She moved around him, making sure not to touch him, as if he was a leper from the Bible.

"Would you mind explaining what you mean?" He rested his hand against the doorway.

Raven opened the dresser drawer he'd specifically cleared for her, even though he needed the space, so whenever she stayed over, she had a spot to put her clothes.

He pushed his fingers hard on the doorway where they rested. "I asked you a question. Can you allow me the courtesy by answering?"

She whipped her dark gaze in his direction. "Your family's done enough," she hissed.

"May I ask what we've done?" His chest tightened. He'd expected her to come home either upset or happy, but not because of his family.

"You know what you did. Or did your dad forget to tell you? Is it his dirty little secret?" If she would've been a lynx, she'd have spit at him, fur standing on edge.

The heat seemed to drain from Jude's body, leaving a sheet of ice over his flesh. This couldn't be true, but somehow Raven knew the truth. He stepped backward.

"You know, don't you?" She yanked the clothing from the drawer and tossed them into the duffel bag.

What had Dad said? What had he warned Jude about? Now the nightmare was coming true, one he'd swept under the carpet, fingers silently crossed, hoping it'd remain in the dusty confines of the grave where it had rested. But it had risen from the dead, ready to haunt him, Raven, and their families.

"He told me back in March," Jude replied quietly. His breathing threatened to race like a windstorm from his lungs and onto the floor.

"March?" Raven slammed the drawer shut. She threw the last of her underwear into the duffel bag. "He told you about what he did to my mother, and you thought, *so what, big deal, I'll keep fucking her anyways*? Like your dad kept fucking and using my mom?"

"Whoa. Hold up." The ice washed away from Jude's skin,

and a hint of heat formed under his flesh. He straightened his hands into a T. "Time out. You're making a lot of assumptions and only hearing one side. Don't you think I deserve a say? That my dad deserves a say?"

"There's nothing to say. He can't deny he cheated on my mother and used a lot of women from here who went to the residential school with him." She zipped the bag shut. Disgust flared in her eyes. "Or that after he used a bunch of worthless *squaws*, he then straightened out for his precious white woman." Her mouth formed into a sneer.

Jude flinched at the *squaw* word. He'd never heard Raven demean her own kind before, much less herself. "They were never a bunch of *squaws* to him. None of our women are *squaws*."

"That's what every white man thinks, doesn't he?" She lifted her chin. "That's what they've been thinking ever since they sailed over here on their banana boats. And it's what you wannabe whites think, too. It's why *you* marry your precious white women. Because *squaws* are only good enough to fuck." She yanked up the duffel bag and slid the strap over her shoulder.

"What the . . ." His eyes almost popped from their sockets. "I can't believe you—"

Raven stormed straight for him. "Get outta my way." She elbowed Jude in the side and then shoved her way through the doorway, giving him a hard bump with her hip.

Jude swiveled on his heel and marched after her.

She stood in the bathroom, flinging toiletries into her bag.

"That's it? You're not gonna hear me out? Hear my dad out? You're gonna only listen to one side?" He didn't care his questions were demanding and fierce. Never had anyone dared to elbow him in the gut like a useless fly needing a swatting.

Chapter Eighteen: When You Took My Heart

With her bag zipped, Raven whipped on her heel, face stiller than stone and eyes as dead as rocks. She motioned at the bathroom door Jude blocked. "Get out of the way."

"That's it? You're not gonna talk to me?" He slapped his hand against his thigh.

"There's nothing to say." She shifted the duffel bag strap to her other shoulder. "My gut told me from the beginning what you were, and I should've listened to it. Get outta the way."

"Told you what I really am?" What nerve. "I see. Just because I married a woman who isn't Ojibway, I'm a bad guy. And what if I was white? Would you have gone out with me?"

"I only date *Anishinaabe* men." Her upper lip curled. "I don't go anywhere near using white men."

This was the old Raven talking, the woman Mrs. Kabatay had poisoned, the beautiful woman who'd stood outside of Healing the Spirit, holding a protest sign, the woman who believed traditionalists and Christians couldn't live in harmony. The woman who'd sauntered into his classroom with a va-va-voom wiggle from old Hollywood and had set Jude's blood on fire. The seductress. The vamp. The lynx with a fierce, teasing nip and sharp claws.

"To me, people are people." He raised his finger.

"Don't you dare give me your lecturing tone," Raven

snarled. She pushed at his finger. "Put that away, or I'll make sure you never point at another person in your condescending *Matawapit* way again."

"Matawapit way? And what's the Matawapit way?" He folded his arms, still standing in the bathroom doorway.

"You think you're too good to be an Indian. I bet you never wanted to be an Indian. You Matawapits are the truest apples of apples. You pay your taxes like upstanding *Canadian* citizens. You follow *their* religion. You live by *their* rules and *their* way. That's what you are. You even marry *their* kind." The words flew from her mouth with a vicious helping of spit.

"I see. That's what you really think I am?" Jude glanced her up and down. This wasn't the woman he'd fallen head over heels for.

"Think? Nope. Believe." Her husky voice was deeper, colder.

"You really wanna be a hater again? As racist as those out there?" He pointed toward the door.

"Racist?" She sneered.

"I'm not pointing at the reserve. I'm pointing at the people I met in Thunder Bay who didn't care I was a good little educated Indian. To them, red skin was red skin—no matter what. You don't think I faced the same remarks, the same taunts you did? The thing is, I'm not willing to lump an entire race into the *bad* category because of a good thirty percent who are truly cruel savages."

"It still doesn't excuse what your dad did to my mother."

"No, it doesn't, but it also doesn't mean my dad intentionally tried to hurt your mother."

"He's your apple dad who taught you to be an apple. Of course you're going to side with him. Get out of my way. I let your family destroy mine enough. Not anymore." Her eyes remained narrowed slits.

"So that's it?" Jude once more slapped his hand on his

thigh. "We're not gonna talk this out like two civilized adults?"

"There's nothing to talk about. You knew the truth and you hid it from me." She was too close to screaming.

"I was taken into another's confidence. I don't divulge other people's secrets, no matter what."

"Not buying. You kept your secret because you knew the consequences, and you were having too much fun getting some nasty sex your virginal, pure, Christian wife wasn't capable of giving you." She shoved her chin at him.

Jude swallowed his sputter. "That's what you believe? Truly believe? Seriously?"

"Isn't it true?" Raven tapped her foot. "It's pretty apparent she was so angelic she wouldn't even try anal."

"Okay, stop it." For the second time, he raised his finger. "We're not going into my former sex life. Do you comprehend? That stays between Charlene and me. And just because she's not on my good side, doesn't mean I'm going to break her confidence she trusted me with to another person."

"Whatever." Raven flicked her hand. "You don't gotta draw me a picture. I know exactly what you two were about. Get outta my way or I'm coming through . . ."

Jude had never forcefully touched a woman in the past, and it wasn't starting tonight, although his fingers itched to grab Raven's shoulders and shake the poison out of her.

Raven barreled out of the bathroom and threw open the back door. She stormed outside, and it slammed shut.

Heart banging and blood shivering, Jude leaned on the bathroom entranceway, his breaths coming fast and heavy. He curled his fingers into fists, fighting to get a bearing on the air racing in and out of his mouth and nostrils.

His Raven was gone. She'd turned into the vicious, angry, bitter, resentful Raven her mother had molded and shaped. He punched the wall.

The next morning, after tossing in his empty bed until four, Jude arrived at his parents' for coffee. All night his mind had played repeatedly the angry accusations coming from Raven's poisoned tongue.

She must've gone fleeing back to the woman responsible for injecting the venomous toxin into her children, because when he'd driven by the diner on his way to the Grassy District, Raven had stood at the big window, taking orders from a table of a few older women. At the sight of her, his heart had jumped and then curled into a wounded cut.

It was over. Fucking over. He whacked the steering wheel. Then he punched it, and the horn tooted.

He had to get his act together. He'd been hitting and kicking everything since last night.

Should he even go inside? He had no choice but to tell Dad what had happened, before Clayton's tongue started wagging.

Jude slammed the truck door shut and trudged up the walkway. At least the kids weren't here to witness this destruction and were safe in Thunder Bay.

He shoved open the front door and tossed his jacket on the coat tree hook.

Mom poked her head out from the kitchen. "I heard a horn. Was that you?"

Jude's heart almost crashed to the floor. Mom didn't deserve this. Dad had better fess up to the truth before Clayton or Raven or Raven's sisters told Mom out of spite.

"Um . . . yeah. I leaned on it by accident when I was getting out. Where'd Dad?" The black truck had been parked out front.

"On the deck reciting his Hours. He's having his cigarette and coffee."

Perfect. Jude hadn't even tasted a cup yet. "Sounds good."

He forced his feet to almost tiptoe across the hall floor, not stomp, even though he ached to pound his way to the kitchen and toss a few pots at the wall.

"Is everything okay? I wasn't expecting you ..." Mom peered, searching his face. "I thought, well . . . it is *your* weekend alone."

Jude snatched a mug from the cupboard and set it on the counter. "I'm fine. Raven's working, so I thought I'd come over."

"Okay." Mom's reply said she didn't believe him, probably because he'd never stopped over on Saturday if the kids were out of town, preferring to tackle his cleaning while Raven worked, marinate something for dinner before walking over to the diner to have a late breakfast, and then head home to wait for Raven's shift to end.

"Did you want anything to eat?" Mom removed a frying pan from the cupboard. "Your dad and I already ate, but I'll make you—"

"It's okay. I planned on stopping by the diner after." Hopefully, he sounded convincing. He fixed a coffee. Just as he was about to dash for the deck, Mom's trusting green eyes stopped Jude cold.

How could Raven had said those vicious words? Because her damned mother had raised her children to hate. He set aside his coffee.

"What is it?" Mom's gaze roamed his face.

He wrapped his arms around her slender waist. Her smell was the perennial sweet, summery fragrance that had always lulled him to sleep as a boy. This woman truly cared about others. She was a loving, kind person who shouldn't be spoken about so harshly. If not for Mom, Jude wouldn't be alive, because his father might still be suffering the pain the Indian Residential School had inflicted on him, might be still wandering around drunk, or even dead.

"I gotta talk to Dad."

"Okay." Mom's reply was quiet but understanding.

Funny, she never asked questions. She always waited for Jude to speak if he needed to talk.

He touched her face.

Worry filled her eyes, but Mom nodded.

Jude picked up his mug and went to the deck.

****

Using a high-strength industrial cleaning product, Raven scrubbed down the counter for the third time. The smell of oranges filled her nostrils. She swiped at a strand of hair having fallen from her braid.

The bell above the door tinkled.

Clayton strode in. "How you doing?" He slid onto a stool at the counter.

Raven forced a smile, but her heart continued to break like cracks of ice splitting on a frozen lake. Little cracks. Prickling cracks. Snapping cracks. Soon, the inevitable major break would open the lake and swallow her whole.

"It's gonna be okay." Clayton glanced around for a mug.

"Here." Raven scooped one up from the back counter. "I was cleaning. I haven't reset them out yet."

"Cleaning? Now? You don't do that until the end of your shift."

Great, he knew her routine. "I wasn't busy, so I thought I'd get it done now."

"Don't lie. Everything's cleaned during the night shift. You don't clean until the afternoon shift comes in." He motioned at the pot, creamers, and sugar Raven had to set out again.

She retrieved everything for him. "How's Mom?" She hefted the tray of coffee cups.

"What'd you mean? Didn't you stay there? I expected you

175

to after — "

"I stayed at the motel," Raven muttered.

"Oh . . ." Clayton's brow arched. "She's sleeping. The surgery and chemo really took a lot out of her." He fixed his coffee.

Raven set out the mugs. Eight-fifteen. She had six more hours to go. Even worse, she'd watched Jude's truck drive by about fifteen minutes ago. He was probably going to his parents'.

Sure, she'd done the right thing. The Matawapits had hurt her family too much, but dammit, she couldn't stop the knife-like pain piercing her insides. The hurt was in her blood, weakening her knees and slowing her steps.

"You did the right thing."

Raven set the last of the mugs in their spots and dragged her feet back to the other end of the counter where Clayton sat.

"Did what?"

"Dumping him." Clayton sipped. "He's a Matawapit. By the fall he'll be gone."

The blood didn't sputter through Raven's veins. It stopped. She gaped at Clayton. "What do you mean?"

"We're meeting on Wednesday about portfolios. I'm going to make sure I get education." Clayton snapped his fingers.

Something horrible shuddered through Raven's limbs.

"I'm doing this for Mom." Clayton tapped his finger on the counter. "We owe it to her."

"Yes, we do." Then why couldn't Raven believe her own words? Mom was hurting. Maybe even dying. She was a woman who'd known only suffering.

"The way to make the deacon pay, you hurt his own. His kids." Hate pooled around Clayton's dark irises.

"Uh . . . wh-what?"

"His children." Clayton emphasized the words. "We gotta

176

cut out his heart the way he cut out Mom's. But it's gotta be one of his kids. He'll feel it then. He'll feel every inch of pain Mom's feeling if we hurt his kids, or one of them. If we hurt him, he'll go on. He'll survive. But if we destroy his oldest child, his eldest son, his pride and joy, big boy Jude . . ."

"Hurt? How?" A blanket of apprehension swathed Raven's shoulders.

"I guarantee when the education portfolio's mine, Jude won't be here for the next school year. He'll be back on a plane for Thunder Bay."

"Th-thunder B-b-bay?" Raven gripped the counter before she stumbled backward.

"Yep."

She leaned in, taking a deep breath. There'd be no regrets. She'd meant what she'd said last night. This time her heart wouldn't betray her.

"After your shift, we'll get your stuff from the hotel. Then we'll get the rest of your stuff from Deacon Apple's place."

She stiffened. "I'm not ready to go there."

"Then I'll get your stuff. Mom needs you at home."

Raven trembled. "I . . . I can't." Let them call her selfish, but she wasn't ready to face anyone yet. "I'm gonna stay at the motel for a few days."

"Hey." Clayton rested his palm over hers. "I'm sorry, I really am, but it's all for the best. It wouldn't have worked out. He was coming between us. Your family. Your own mother."

"I know." Raven licked her dry lips, in dire need of water.

"I'll get your stuff once I get a chance. Then I'll bring it over to the motel."

"O-okay."

****

Jude sipped his coffee. The sun was out. The water sparkling.

Gentle waves lapped at the rocks. A slight warm breeze coated his arms. As peaceful as the morning was, meant to soothe, he shifted in the chair again.

Dad puffed on his cigarette, curiously peering.

There was no easy way to say this. "Raven knows the truth about you and Mrs. Kabatay."

A big sigh heaved from Dad's mouth. He wiped at his face. "I see . . ." He butted out the cigarette in the ashtray.

The only sound was the water continuing to lap against the rocks.

After a few more moments, and Dad staring off at the lake, he finally looked at Jude through weary eyes. "Then I best talk to your mother. Better she hears the truth from me than around the reserve."

"I think you're right. Clayton'll . . . considering the rumors he started about Darryl, I can imagine what he'll try say about you."

Dad nodded and grimaced.

A snort barreled from Jude's mouth. "Raven . . . she's . . ."

"Easy." Dad reached for his coffee, shoulders still sagging, gaze still weary. "It'll take her time to come around. She's had a lot to digest. A lot. Finding out how she was conceived was bad enough. As for this . . ." He shook his head.

"You weren't there. You didn't hear what she said." Jude's gut burned. "She . . . she's not the Raven I—"

"And she wasn't blessed with a good family who loves her simply for being herself. Arlene . . ." Dad sipped his coffee and made a face, as if he'd drunk moose pee. "The Kabatays have lived a hard life. Especially Arlene. I know she blames me for how her life turned out. And I know she resents your mother for . . . well, for being the woman I chose to marry."

"When are you gonna tell Mom?"

"The sooner the better. I'll speak to her this afternoon after she's done cleaning. She's storing away the winter clothes this morning." Dad's voice was as heavy as his heavy-looking shoulders.

"Did you need me there?"

"No." Dad let out another big breath. "They're some conversations a married couple need to speak about alone. I know she'll be . . . hurt. Hurt about who I . . . the women I hurt. She knows I wasn't the most faithful man in my day. She doesn't know who I was unfaithful to, or the woman I was unfaithful with."

"Do you think she'll be pissed?"

"I don't know." Dad rubbed his brow. "It's in the past. My past. But your mother's an understanding woman. Understanding enough to put up with me." He smiled weakly, but his eyes continued to wilt at the corners.

"I know after Bridget made us grandparents again, your mother wanted to stay in Thunder Bay to help her. She's only here because of me. Maybe I'll suggest she help Bridget for a couple of weeks until this all dies down."

Chapter Nineteen: Almost Like We Never Met

Accompanied by Emery, Jude forced his feet up the stairs of the church for a mass he'd observe but not participate in, as usual.

On Sunday, Mom sat with the choir, so they went to their usual spot in front of the confessional on the Epistle side of the nave, sans the kids, who wouldn't arrive in Ottertail Lake until the late afternoon flight.

Jude hadn't bothered to return to his parents' house on Saturday after leaving Dad on the deck once they'd finished their talk and had their coffees. A married couple needed privacy after such a revealing discussion, so he'd given Mom and Dad some space.

Mom sat on the Gospel aisle, surrounded by members of the Catholic Women's Association who also sang in the choir.

They were early enough to join in the Rosary said before Mass. Both knelt on the cushioned kneeler and withdrew their rosaries. Twenty minutes later, the opening hymn commenced. Throughout church, Dad's speech was as sunken as his chest that barely pushed out his dalmatic.

After Mass, everyone gathered in the basement for coffee. While Jude sat nursing his paper cup, barely hearing a word Emery said, their parents went through the motions of being friendly and talking to the other members of the congregation.

Later, they left for Mom and Dad's. When they all pulled

up in the driveway, the folks got out of their vehicle, didn't look at one another, and went inside. Jude trailed behind, hands stuffed in his pockets.

"What's going on?" Emery stopped Jude on the path leading up to the porch. "Something's not right."

Jude kept walking. "I'll talk to you about it later. A lot went down this weekend."

"Talk about what?" Emery's heels clicked against the wooden steps.

Jude opened the door and hung his jacket on the hook. "Shh . . ." He put his fingers to his lips.

Concern filled Emery's eyes. He also removed his shoes and hung his jacket.

They gathered in the dining room to silence after their parents had changed clothes. Dad stared out the sliding doors, rubbing his finger across his lower lip. Mom stood in the kitchen, readying brunch.

The silence was needles of torture pushing into Jude's ears. He cleared his throat. "What's Darryl up to?"

"He went out for the morning fish. He left before I woke up. He took the dogs." Emery pushed his spoon around in his mug.

"Walleye?"

"Yes." Emery glanced at Dad seated at the head of the table and then to Mom since the kitchen was across from the dining room and also faced the lake. "So, um, what're you to up to for the rest of the day?"

Dad shook his head, continuing to stare out the sliding doors.

"Darryl and I . . . we're going golfing this afternoon. Chump and his crew got the course ready. Did you want to come?"

Again, Dad shook his head.

Emery peeked at Jude. "Did you wanna come?"

"Sure." Jude needed something to get his mind off this mess, even if it meant golfing a par thirty with mowed-down greens instead of rolled and shaved to the quick. At least they had a golf course, even though it was hardly an architectural masterpiece.

"What time are the kids getting home?"

"Four. I got time for nine holes." Jude lifted his mug to force down another cup of coffee like he had at the church.

"Is Raven uh . . ." Emery glanced around.

Little brother was catching on, because Jude always bolted for his own house after church if the kids were away for the weekend to a delicious brunch cooked up by Raven while he was at Mass.

A knock came at the door. Everything on Dad stiffened—his face, his shoulders, his fingers on the coffee mug.

Emery rose.

"Let your brother get it," Dad whispered.

"Oh . . . okay." Emery sat, brows drawn together, staring at Jude.

Jude stood and took the living room to reach the hallway instead of cutting through the kitchen because Mom needed some space. He threw open the front door to Clayton Kabatay standing on the other side.

"I came to get my sister's stuff." Clayton's usual sneering, snake-like tenor was colder than a polar bear's butt during the dead of winter in the Arctic.

"I'll have to pack—"

"I already packed her possessions." Mom appeared in the hallway from the kitchen. Eyes full of pain. "It's on the guest bed."

Jude stiffly turned and headed down the other hall leading to the bathroom and bedrooms. Raven's boxed effects sat on the bed. Mom must've guessed someone would be by to collect them. He hefted the box, holding it tightly, his fingers almost digging into the cardboard, and trudged back to the front entryway.

Clayton held out his arms.

Jude still gripped the box. He forced himself to hand it over.

Without another word, Clayton accepted the box, turned on his heel, and marched down the stairs.

Jude shut the front door, strangling the knob.

"What do you think he'll do? They'll do?" Emery asked.

"I don't know." Jude practiced another swing. The sun from church this morning remained out, its rays warming his exposed skin.

Darryl stood on the tee box, contemplating where he'd hook his first drive of the season.

"I'll tell you what they'll do . . ." Darryl made a face as his ball drew into a big hook that landed somewhere in the bush. "Aww, shit." He teed up another ball.

"That's three off the tee." Emery was keeping score.

"Yeah, yeah, I know. But I might not use this one if I can find my other ball." Like he was swinging a baseball bat at the ground, Darryl again whacked the golf ball. It hooked but stayed clear of the bush and landed in the rough. Not too bad. If the course was groomed to professional standards, Darryl's ball would've hit what was known as the first cut.

"You're getting a bit better." Jude readied his ball. There wasn't any use in determining a shot because every fairway on this so-called golf course was straight and to the hole. "What do you think he has planned?"

"The education portfolio. What else?"

Jude took a few practice swings. Usually, he went to the driving range to get his game up to par, but he'd been too busy. Not that Ottertail Lake had a professional driving range. But there was a nice area of grass cut where a guy could hit some balls from his shag bag.

"I thought so." Jude moved around the ball and positioned himself.

Having already gone through the motions of what he must do, Jude let his body guide his swing. By the feel of the club-head meeting the ball, he'd nailed his drive. He held his hand a smidgen over his eyes. The ball sailed high and fast through the air and landed straight down the fairway.

Emery whistled. "Someone's been practicing."

"Nope. No time." Finally, a glow illuminated in Jude's chest after a weekend of gray clouds. "That is skill and talent. Pure and simple."

"Sure. Sure." Emery grinned and teed up his ball.

"You're meeting on Wednesday, right?" Jude opened his bottled water.

Darryl nodded while watching Emery. "Yep. About port-folios. We haven't had time yet. Too busy reviewing what the last council did. Well, what Jenny, Clayton, Roy, and I did, and the councilors who didn't get back in for this term. It didn't take the required time we anticipated because we had four returning councilors."

"You mean three. You're the chief."

Darryl grimaced. "Quit saying that. Everywhere I go, all I get is, *Hey, Chief, how's it going? Chief, hey, it's the chief.* I'm still me."

"So you have the final say in portfolios." This was promising.

"It doesn't always work that way." Darryl's eyes almost popped as he gaped open-mouthed at Emery's ball rocketing through the air and landing a good ten yards ahead of Jude's ball.

Jude snorted. "He can only outdrive me. And that's 'cause he's taller. But watch us around the greens. He's toast."

Darryl snickered. "It's all in the short game, huh?"

"Yep. A lot of great golfers weren't bombers on the deck. It's all in course management, short game, and putting. Driving, yeah, it counts, big-time, because you gotta stay on the fairway."

Three teenagers waited at the bench.

Jude wheeled his clubs to his ball with Emery in step. Darryl sauntered off toward the rough to begin his search for the missing ball.

"How you doing?" Emery asked.

"How do you think I'm doing?" Jude gripped the handle of his pushcart.

"I'm sorry. I really am. Maybe she needs some time —"

"Nope. Don't go there. I'm done. Women aren't worth it."

"Men then?" Emery said weakly.

Jude glanced at his brother, giving Emery a *great real* look. "Pass. Men are your department, not mine. It's my kids and me from now on." He moved his hand in a straight determined line. "I'm not putting myself through any more cheating or . . . I don't even know what to call what she did on Friday night."

"She was hurt. She reacted like anyone else would. But once she's alone, has an evening to think about —"

"Nope. Don't wanna hear it. I'm finished with her."

****

Raven flopped on the bed. No meeting to go to. No Adam to talk to. She didn't even have a girl friend to confide in, because Bridget, the only friend Raven had, was a Matawapit.

While standing behind the pine tree vaping outside the motel, she'd watched Jude drive by with his mom in the passenger seat. A half an hour later, he'd driven by in the opposite direction with the kids but no Mrs. M.

She should be glad Mrs. M had left. Maybe she'd left the

deacon for good. But Raven's bruised heart wouldn't let her forget the Matawapits' kindness and generosity.

She slammed her hand on the night table. She wouldn't feel sorry for *that* family—not after what the deacon had done to Mom.

Maybe she'd visit Mom, anything to escape the silence of the hotel room. She had two days off and had spent the morning in bed sleeping, trying to hide from her mind.

Yes, she'd go to Mom's, a reminder why she'd dumped Jude, and why she'd moved out of the Matawapits' house. A place to reharden her heart.

She snatched her purse and vape off the table and bolted.

****

With Emery watching the kids, Jude slung his briefcase and laptop case straps over his shoulder and walked the road over to the school. Everyone had eaten dinner at Dad's earlier, because Dad had refused to go to Emery and Darryl's and had also refused Jude's offer. Dad wouldn't say whether Mom had left him or if she'd gone to help Bridget and the baby.

Thursday was Raven's birthday, and next week was Rebekah's. The presents Jude ordered had arrived. But he'd be returning Raven's. Maybe she wouldn't show for tonight's class. As for the other students, hopefully they'd make an appearance. They were almost done for the summer. Three more weeks to go. Exams being the last week of the three.

He strode up the walkway to the adult education section and unlocked the door for the students. With a deep breath, he strolled inside. He could do this—treat Raven like a student if she showed up. As a teacher, his job was to instruct her so she could earn her grade twelve. Nothing more.

****

Just because Jude was Raven's adult education teacher didn't mean she'd stop going to class. She was *this close* to acquiring her grade ten math and finishing the last of her grade eleven subjects. Come the fall, she'd be in full grade twelve classes.

Jude always arrived ten minutes early before the students, so she didn't see him on the road as she walked from the motel to the school. Visiting Mom on Sunday and then going there to clean on Monday had left Raven's ears full of poison, because Mom's vicious tongue hadn't stopped jabbering about the deacon and how he was to blame for everything.

Raven trudged up the sidewalk. She nodded at the two students who'd, thank goodness, joined her, and followed them inside. While walking the hallway, Raven stayed behind them.

They reached the classroom. Since Raven brought up the rear, she inched over to the very last desk by the window, ignoring her usual spot in front of Jude.

"Verna. Lonn. Good to see you," Jude said, glancing up from his desk. His greeting lacked warmth.

Raven kept her head bowed but snuck a peek. She clutched the pencil and covered the books with her forearms. Jude typed on his laptop, eyes zeroed in on the screen.

True to form, Marvin scampered in at the last minute. "Mr. M, I got my last assignment finished."

"Great." Jude's voice was his professional one.

The continuous small talk was lost to Raven. She fired her stare out the window at two dogs playing in the parking lot.

"Okay, open your books to . . ." Jude's voice continued to remain professional.

Raven opened her textbook. Jude held his own and stood at the whiteboard, doing what he always did by reviewing what they'd work on for their homework assignments and giving his easy-to-comprehend examples.

The two hours seemed to drag on. Raven didn't want to glance up at Jude in his beige dress pants that fit his physique like the handsome Mr. Metrosexual he was. Or the light-blue, dress shirt hugging his strong chest. Or his slicked short hair accentuating his bold facial features. And she sure wasn't going to kick herself over losing a once-in-a-lifetime guy.

Throughout the lesson, Raven's heart kept doing funny things—folding in half when Jude spoke to everyone but refused to look at her, or growling when he'd use his know-it-all tone, or fluttering when he did lay his dark eyes on her briefly.

"That's it. We're almost there." Jude's gaze drifted to Marvin, Lonn, Verna, and then skimmed flatly on Raven. "You're welcome to stay and work on your assignments."

He peeped at the clock on the wall. "It's twenty to nine. I'll be here until nine if you need my help."

As usual, Marvin bolted.

Verna yawned and stretched. "I'm beat. I think I'll go home and work on this stuff tomorrow. Thanks, Mr. M."

"You're very welcome, Verna." Jude's dimples appeared.

"Say, maybe we can work together." Lonn hurried after Verna's departing figure, which wasn't a surprise because Lonn had done nothing but talk to, sit next to, and flirt with Verna during each class.

Raven itched to gather her books, rise, and leave, but someone must have put crazy glue on her chair. She screamed at her body to listen. Her feet remained under the desk, and she kept gripping the pencil.

This was a nightmare—her very own body refusing to cooperate. She'd make a fool of herself if she stayed.

Again, she tried to gather her books. Nothing. She attempted to turn in her seat. Her waist wouldn't make the three-quarter-degree shift.

Even worse, Jude still stood at the whiteboard, arms

folded.

Chapter Twenty: Forget About Love

Jude wet his lips that were drier than his empty water bottle sitting on the teacher's desk. He forced his shaking legs from the whiteboard. He set his trembling hand on the back of his chair and slowly pulled it out with as much casual finesse as he could muster. The wheels of the chair failed to roll smoothly across the floor and ran over his shoe. To stifle the yelp bursting to jump from his mouth, he bit down on his tongue.

He stopped his hand from shoving the chair in ferocious anger and sat.

Never mind Raven. He had a lot of work to prepare for the education committee meeting happening at the end of June. If Clayton was on the warpath, Jude had to snuff out the bastard's ammunition.

His fingers rested on the keyboard, but they wouldn't type. He snuck a peek. Raven remained seated, not writing, not reading. Jude's fingers kept sitting on the keyboard, refusing to push any of the keys.

Raven set her hands on the desk and dragged herself out of the seat.

Jude typed a D. Then forced his finger down on the E key.

A loud crash echoed through the classroom. He almost jumped from his chair. A red-faced Raven shot a vicious glare at the scattered textbooks, pens, and pencils rolling around, and binder flipped open on the floor. Even her purse and its contents were flung everywhere.

Jude growled under his breath. He shouldn't help, but his upbringing ordered him to stand, walk over, and assist Raven like a true gentleman assisted others. And without realizing how he got there, he stood amongst the mess, against his will.

He shifted to his haunches. Raven's scent of feminine soap and floral shampoo drifted under his nose.

"It's okay." Raven's hands fumbled with the bazillion items on the floor. She picked up her pen and dropped a textbook.

Jude retrieved the dropped textbook and placed it in her hands.

Her eyes narrowed. "I got it."

"Yeah, you got it, all right." He didn't mean for his answer to betray his anger, but her snotty look had released the tension riding up his backside straight from his mouth.

The silence pricked his ears as they continued to retrieve her belongings. The only noise was their gathering of books, grabbing pens, collecting her cell phone, and rescuing her makeup items.

Finally, she had her purse zipped, her textbooks and binder clutched in her hands, and her cell phone tucked safely away.

Just as Jude began to stand, Raven also straightened. At the same time, they slowly rose, facing each other. Their breaths carried back and forth, hers warm on his skin.

"You're all set." He motioned at her purse and books.

Her throat moved. "Yeah, I am."

"I'll . . ." He raised his arm halfway, hand flat out. "I'll let you get going." A ball had lodged in his throat, choking his words.

"I'll . . . get going . . ."

"Okay, then." Jude nodded.

"Yeah . . . okay then." She nodded.

His feet remained rooted to the floor.

She kept staring at him, dark eyes neither sparkling nor flashing.

Finally, he unpeeled his shoes from their spot and stepped backward. "I'll see you on Thursday again . . ."

"Yeah . . . Thursday." She moved one spiked heel backward, still staring at him.

He also moved another step back but couldn't strip his eyes off her.

"Mr. M!"

A rocket seemed to launch itself inside Jude, and he jumped. Marvin stood in the doorway.

"Uh . . . yes?"

"I need to ask you something." Marvin sauntered over.

Jude bolted for his desk. The sound of Raven's heels shimmying across the floor echoed through the classroom. Then her skittering steps bounced off the hallway walls.

Sucking in air to still his breathing, Jude braced his hands on the desk. He used his finger, indicating for Marvin to continue speaking.

****

The alarm buzzed and buzzed. Raven walked her fingers across the nightstand to switch off her phone. She yawned and hugged the pillow. Thursday morning. She was thirty-two today. Thirty-two and waking alone in a motel room. She'd celebrate her birthday by putting in a day at work and returning to the room at two-thirty to spend the afternoon alone until her class commenced at seven.

She dragged herself from the bed, started the small travel coffeemaker, and hauled herself into the shower. Once dressed, she retrieved her purse and phone and trudged to the diner. The sun was already up, rising around after five now.

"Happy birthday," Cookie called out from behind the counter.

Raven urged her mouth to curve upward. Hopefully this was the one and only person who'd wish her greetings. "Thanks."

"What'cha got planned?"

Already the coffee was brewing, and the diner smelled of freshly perked beans.

"Not much. Working. Going to class." She shrugged and made her way to the kitchen to put away her jacket and purse.

"I got something special planned. You wait and see." Cookie stood in the kitchen, wagging his finger and grinning.

"Thanks . . ." Her sagging heart managed a flutter. "You're awesome."

They went through their usual routine of readying the ingredients. Raven was amid cutting fresh potatoes when the bell overhead tinkled. She wiped her hands and strode out to the dining area.

Clayton strolled up to the counter, a cunning grin stretching to his ears.

"I take it last night's meeting went as planned." Raven turned over the mug the staff had set out the night before in preparation for the morning crew.

"Darryl got his way. He gave the education portfolio to Jenny, but I'm not worried." Clayton made a *pfft* sound. "As a member of band council, and a member of Ottertail Lake, I'll be at the education meeting at the end of the month. And by the time I'm done, the Matawapits are finished."

He waggled his finger. "The house is for the principal. Jude and his kids'll have no place to stay."

Joy should bubble inside Raven, but the same dreary cloud of doom had followed her from the motel and wouldn't leave.

"What're you planning?"

"It's simple. Look, I know how hard you're working for your diploma, but remember, this is for Mom." A dark cast seemed to hover about Clayton.

The dreary cloud looming over Raven's head formed into a thundercloud, carrying lightning, massive winds, and torrential rain. "Um . . . I don't get it."

"This is for Mom. You think it's right she suffered the way she did? Lookit what the deacon put her through. Dad . . ." Clayton's fingers curled. He bowed his head. "Lookit what you went through after finding out what Dad did. Lookit what we went through, having to . . ." He glanced away.

Raven shoved aside the dumb storm she'd let engulf her in pity and squared her shoulders. "What do you need me to do?"

When Clayton raised his gaze, pain filled his eyes. "Fail the math exam."

Raven hugged her books to her chest. She'd worked damned hard to finally understand math. If not for Jude's tender care, she'd still be swimming in a helpless mud pit of confusion, struggling to pass. Whereas she'd once been an F student and then squeaking by with a D, thanks to Jude, she was now pulling a C-plus. No, she'd never be an A student in math, but she could manage the lessons on her own now.

She trudged up the walkway leading to the school entrance for the adults. Ten after seven. Deciding to come had been the right decision. She'd worked too hard to prove she was responsible.

When she entered the school, Jude's lecturing carried into the hallway. Already, he'd begun the lesson. He was true to his upbringing and started at seven sharp, scoffing at the so-called *Indian time* of the reserve, and he ran the school the same way.

Jude stood in front of the class holding a marker, his

knuckles tapping on the whiteboard to get his point across. He didn't look in her direction when Raven beelined for the rear desk next to the window.

Marvin, Verna, and Lonn were present, casually spread out at their desks.

While Jude kept lecturing on Canadian history, Raven opened the textbook. This subject was the first conversation they'd had when Jude had arrived in Ottertail Lake. She'd insisted the Indian Residential Schools and every other conniving and cruel treatment her people had suffered at the hands of the government should be built into the curriculum, so kids understood *all* of Canada's history.

For the next hour and a half, she took notes.

About twenty to nine, right on the button, Jude stopped speaking. He moved away from the whiteboard and rested his buttocks against the top of his desk while crossing his leg over the other.

Raven's heart accelerated from barely thumping to rapidly pounding. It was his same casual stance as when they'd first met.

He slipped the end of the marker between his lips and sucked. Her pulse points fluttered. He'd done that, too, but he'd been nibbling on his pen cap back in February.

Jude placed his palm on the edge of the desk, his gaze traveling over each student. Finally, after what seemed like hours that left Raven jittery in her seat, his dark-eyed gaze settled on her. The blood quickened through Raven's veins, and she shifted at the desk. Tingles erupted between her legs. She ground her thighs together, and the friction generated sticky heat in her pink panties.

"Any questions?" he asked.

His deep voice caressed Raven's skin. She squeezed her pen and dropped her head to the notes in front of her.

"Okay. If they're no questions, you're free to leave, or stay and work on your assignments."

Just like on Tuesday night, everyone hurried off, and Raven was left sitting at her desk, unable to force her hands to close the books.

"Happy birthday." There wasn't a hint of warmth in Jude's well-wishing.

"Thanks," Raven mumbled. *Okay, hands, get busy.* She forced her fingers to close the textbook and binder.

One more week of Jude's presence and then exams. Raven's stomach soured. How could Clayton ask her to fail the math exam? She brushed at her hair falling over her shoulders.

The wiping of the cloth on the whiteboard hummed in Raven's ears. She picked up the books that seemed to weigh two tons and draped the purse strap over her shoulder.

She'd head for the motel and spend the rest of the evening working on the beaded buckskin purse for Rebekah's birthday, a project she'd started two weeks ago. Maybe she could leave the gift at the school.

Raven stood.

Jude swiveled, holding the cloth used to clean the whiteboard.

Chin held high and back straight, Raven strode from the classroom. She wouldn't run, even though her feet ached to flee.

He never called her name.

****

Jude remained at the whiteboard. He threw the cloth on the desk, but the light material didn't slam on the surface as he wished it would but fell like a whisper.

A classroom door shut. Emery had mentioned coming over to the adult education part of the building tonight to review a recorded lecture on the TV, since he was continuing to work on his master's through the summer, as he had the summer before.

Light footsteps echoed in the hall.

Emery poked his head in the classroom. "I thought I heard everyone leave."

"Hey." Jude packed up his briefcase and laptop case.

"Got time for a coffee?"

"What about Darryl? He's waiting for you." Darryl had offered to babysit tonight.

Emery shrugged. "He won't mind."

"Sure." A coffee was better than going home to sit by himself and brood while the kids slept. "Let me lock up first."

A few minutes later, Jude had the adult education wing secured.

They meandered down the walkway under a clear sky. Instead of taking a right, which led to Jude's house, they walked left to the main road that led to the diner. The smell of the spruce trees lingered in the warm air.

"We should've dropped this stuff off first." Jude patted his cases.

"What? Too heavy?"

It wasn't like Emery to tease, and Jude couldn't resist giving his little brother a poke in the side with his elbow. "Yeah, yeah."

"So how you're doing?"

"Okay."

"How're you really doing?"

"What do you think?" Jude kicked at a few pebbles on the dirt road. "It's her birthday today."

"I know. What'd you get her?"

"A laptop."

Emery stopped. His green eyes widened. "Really?"

"Yep." Jude scratched his cheek. "She needed one. She was

using Mom and Dad's. And when she wasn't living there, she was borrowing Clayton's."

"Do you still have it?"

Heat climbed onto Jude's face. "I . . . I planned on returning it, but . . . I haven't had the time."

"Huh?"

Okay, a lame excuse. All Jude had to do was go to the band office where Gina handled the mail as the post office employee. "I don't want to feel anything. Nothing at all."

"But you can't help feeling something?" Emery started walking again.

"Yeah." Jude fell in step.

"I'd expect to hear you say this. You cared a lot for her."

"After the way she reacted and the shit she said, I don't want to feel anything."

"It takes time."

"I don't need a counseling session. Save it."

"Do you think Mom's coming back?"

"I don't know. Dad's—"

" . . . being his tight-lipped self like you are?"

The motel appeared. Raven sat out on the picnic table, vaping.

Emery followed Jude's gaze. "Oh . . ."

They weren't in the classroom where Jude had to speak to her. Was he supposed to wave? Look away?

Emery waved.

Pricks of irritation appeared on Jude's skin. *He* was supposed to make the first move, not his little brother. So Jude also waved, but he didn't lift his arm like Emery did, but gave a half-hearted attempt to a woman who hated him, hated his father, hated his family. And God only knew what her family had planned for his family.

Chapter Twenty-One: Jealousies

Although Raven was supposed to fail her math exam, she continued to try study, which didn't come easy, not with her grade ten math credit in jeopardy. And enduring Jude's presence for the last official week of class on Tuesday and Thursday hadn't helped either.

She sat outside at the picnic table. With work complete for the day and the Friday night recovery meeting still hours away, she'd spent the afternoon starting a new project for Rebekah. Weird. Because Raven wouldn't see the sugary sweet little girl again.

Jude's truck appeared. The back windows were tinted, but she glimpsed two small heads. Two small heads she'd come to adore. Maybe even . . .

Raven sucked on the vape.

He turned off to Airport Road.

Strange. Rebekah's birthday party was tomorrow and was supposed to happen at the Matawapits' house, the reason why Raven had bought a new bathing suit before her life had gone pear-shaped. A high-cut, yellow, one-piece with spaghetti straps, because her teeny-weeny bikini might be a bit risqué around kids and families, but she'd wanted something sexy enough to make Jude's eyes pop.

Emery drove by in his truck. He also turned off to Airport Road.

She placed her finger on her lip. This was growing weird.

Ten minutes later, the sound of the approaching plane carried through the air. Raven gazed up at the bright-blue sky and the white plane. Mrs. M must be returning to attend the birthday party, but two vehicles weren't required to retrieve her.

Raven's curiosity refused to let her head inside the motel room. She stayed put until Emery's vehicle made another appearance. Adam rode up front, window down. Two adult heads occupied the backseat. Bridget had brought her family up for the weekend. Emery's truck went south to the Grassy District.

Jude's truck also reappeared. Waves of blonde hair flashed in the half-rolled down window.

The tip of a knife seemed to poke Raven's heart. Charlene was in his truck with Noah and Rebekah. And they didn't beeline their way to the motel or go south. They kept driving.

****

For the children's sake, Jude had let Charlene join them, although he'd rather she sit in the back of Emery's truck, since she'd bunk at little brother's for the weekend. Far away in Long River. Bridget, Adam, and baby Grace were sleeping at Mom and Dad's. As for Kyle, he'd share Noah's room.

Jude pulled up to Darryl sitting on the back steps of the log home. He stood. "Need any help?" he hollered.

"I got it." Jude headed for the rear of the truck and unlocked the tailgate where he'd stored Charlene's luggage beneath the bed cover.

"Got your room all made up." Darryl clapped his hands together, approaching them.

Begging filled Rebekah's blue eyes as she stared up at her mother. "I wish you'd stay with us."

Charlene, looking out of place in her wide-legged white pants, high-heeled sandals, sleeveless cream-colored polo shirt, and a scarf wrapped through her blonde waves, smoothed Rebekah's hair. "I told you already, sweetie. Kyle's staying there. Your uncles have more room."

Jude bit the side of his cheek to keep from blurting out the truth. He ascended the steps to dump off his ex-wife's luggage next to the bathroom door. Darryl could get her settled.

"Okay," Jude called out to the kids. "We gotta go. Uncle Emery will be dropping off Kyle, so if you wanna play, get in the truck. Pronto."

"I'm gonna stay with Mom," Rebekah announced.

Noah bolted for the vehicle.

"I'll drive Becky to the in-laws after," Darryl offered.

"Thanks." Jude trudged to his truck, got in, and drove off.

After leaving Long River and flexing and unflexing his fingers, he stole a peek in the rearview mirror at his son. "We're going to Grandpa and Grandma's for supper so everyone can visit once they get unpacked and showered."

"Is Mom coming?" Hope clung to Noah's question.

Something stole a smidgen of air from Jude's lungs. "No. It's just family. She'll be at the party tomorrow."

"Oh . . ." Noah's mouth turned downward. He placed his finger on his lip.

"What is it?" Jude kept stealing peeks in the rearview mirror.

"They always talk about fairness in church. And they talk about fairness at school. Is it fair to leave Mom by herself?"

Great. Not this talk. Jude drummed his fingers on the steering wheel. "Remember, Mom and I are divorced. And even though we're not married anymore doesn't mean our love for you and your sister has changed. Unfortunately, as I said before, Mom isn't a part of my family."

"Your family is Grandpa, Grandma, Uncle Emery, Auntie Bridget, Uncle Adam, and Uncle Darryl. Kyle and Grace. And Miss Kabatay."

Jude swiped at his hair. "Uh . . . yes."

Somehow, he must explain his breakup with Raven to the kids. He never should've brought her around them so soon.

"Are we going to get Miss Kabatay?"

"I already told you and your sister—her mom's very, very sick. She needs Raven right now. Raven has to be at the motel."

"Is that why she can't come tomorrow? She gave her present early to Becky."

"Present?" Shock surged through Jude's veins. "Uh, present? What present? She did?"

"Yeah, at school today. Mrs. Skunk gave it to Becky after class. She said it was from Miss Kabatay."

"Huh? Why didn't Becky say anything?"

"She said she has to wait until tomorrow 'cause tomorrow's her party. She wants to open it in front of Miss Kabatay—open it with her other presents. It's in her bedroom."

Jude guided the truck into the driveway. Great. Fucking great. What was he going to do? Rebekah would be majorly disappointed when Raven didn't show up, even though he'd already explained himself a bazillion times.

"I told Becky, twice, that Miss Kabatay can't come."

"Becky thinks she's coming now."

Jude sighed. He got out of the truck.

Noah hopped out. "Is she?"

"Is she what?"

"Coming?"

"No." Jude ought to slap his tongue for snapping. "No," he said more softly. He laid his hand on Noah's shoulder. "Her mother's very ill."

"What's wrong with her mom?"

"A bad disease. A bad disease that makes people very sick."

The debate in Jude's heart commenced. Originally, he'd

almost bloomed like a flower over Raven attending his daughter's birthday party. He tossed his keys on the kitchen table. But to ask Raven to reconsider attending for Rebekah's sake? She hated him. She hated his family. Well, at least she didn't hate his kids.

He didn't want his heart to warm from Raven giving Rebekah a present. His heart warmed anyway.

****

Raven sat at the polished black table at the recovery center in the meeting room. When Adam's big form filled the doorway, she almost fell out of her chair. He arched his straight black brow at her, lumbered around the table, and sat in the chair beside her.

"I . . . uh . . . what're you doing here?" She spoke quietly so the others seated around the table wouldn't hear.

"It's a twelve-step meeting. I'm a recovering alcoholic. Why wouldn't I be here?"

Goodness, he'd sure said a mouthful for a man of silence. "Coffee?" She motioned at the counter.

"Yep. Be a good sponsee and get your sponsor one." He placed his beige cowboy hat on the table.

Raven rose, her insides finally glowing after a week of lackluster stark. She fixed Adam's coffee and dashed back to sit with him.

"Thanks." Adam slurped away. He set down the mug, big hand almost covering the whole thing. "Y'know how the program works. You're s'posed to check in with me at least once a week. How come you haven't called or texted?"

"I . . ." She'd assumed Adam wasn't her sponsor anymore.

"Just 'cause you got a boulder-size resentment against my wife and her family don't mean I'm not your sponsor."

"I . . ." He didn't hate her?

"You been working your program? Seems to me you haven't," he said in his low rumble.

The chairperson joined the table.

"We'll do coffee after the meeting," Adam said.

They sat at the back diner table, far from the other couple who were in the booth up front. Adam stirred his coffee while Raven fixed her tea.

"I ain't gonna ask how ya been 'cause I know what resentment does to a person in recovery. Your life sucks right now, eh?"

A glimmer of rebellion reared its ugly head. Raven stiffened. "What makes you think I'm resentful."

"Welp, you had a good thing going with Jude. Had a roof over your head with two ace people. Were welcomed into an awesome family. But you let your family fuck it all up. This ain't analytic geometry." Adam shrugged and sat back. His once ruthless black eyes of the past, now thoughtful, studied her.

The scent of frying burgers cloyed at Raven. Her stomach churned. "You don't understand —"

"Why wouldn't I?" Adam's rose-colored mouth formed into a grimace. "You think you're the only person who comes from a fucked-up family? Whose family had it tough? Huh?"

She jutted out her chin, flames flickering up to her throat, ready to form her words into a growl. "Listen here —"

"Nope." Adam slowly shook his head. His menacing square jawline hardened. "You listen up, and you make sure to give me both ears."

Raven melted against the back of her chair. The last time she'd seen Adam take on such a cold countenance was during his gangbanging days.

"I know it's tough. You had to put up with a bitch of a mother your whole life, and now she's major sick." Adam kept his massive hand on his coffee mug. "I get that she taught you kids to hate. The thing is, if not the deacon, it would've been another man she'd blame for how her life turned out.

"Isn't that what we used to do? Every single one of us in recovery? Blame others for our misery? Blame others for coming from suck-ass homes? Blame others for the piss-ass jobs we have? Thing is, we got choices. Me and you." He pointed back and forth to her and himself, black eyes still colder than steel.

She swallowed.

"Welp, answer me." He tapped the table.

For a man who'd sat motionless his whole life, never giving away a hint of his feelings, Adam sure was letting her know exactly how he felt tonight.

Raven managed a nod.

"There's a little girl who talked about you at supper. She keeps insisting you'll be there tomorrow to watch her open her present. It's up to you if you come or don't. I know you're done work at two-thirty. Lots of time to be there. The party starts at two. Someone can come get you."

Raven leaned in, lips firm. "I . . . he brought his ex-wife—"

"She asked him if she could come. Nothing more. She's staying at Emery and Darryl's. Wasn't at supper tonight."

"Oh . . ." The word was as a surprise to Raven as it was to her mouth.

"Don't gotta be all jealous—"

"I'm not jealous!"

"You are, too. Heck, if Bridget had some ex-something sniffing around, and she stuck me in the doghouse, I'd be jealous, too. Takes one to know one." Adam sat back in the chair and folded his bulging-with-muscles arms.

"I doubt I'm welcome after—"

"You didn't cause any trouble. Your goddamn family did. I asked you a million times when you're gonna stand up to 'em."

"There's nothing to stand up—"

"I get it. You did them wrong. Drank. Drugged. Fucked. I get it. Y'know, Emery asked me a really good question when me and Bridget were going through that bullshit with Children and Family Services. He said to me, *Bridget forgave you, Kyle forgave you, when are you gonna forgive yourself?*

"So, I ask the same question to you—when are you gonna forgive yourself? Forgive yourself for not being there for your family? Putting them through misery 'cause of your addiction? When you gonna?"

"You don't understand . . ." Raven wet her lips. "It's more complicated than that."

"Nope. It is what it is." Adam picked up his mug and stood. "C'mon. I need a vape."

Raven grabbed her tea and followed him outside to the sun already behind the trees, but light still lit the reserve. "Clayton . . . Clayton's up to something."

"When isn't he up to something?" Adam withdrew his e-cigarette.

"He asked me to fail my math exam. He wouldn't say why."

"He . . ." The look on Adam's face was shock and complete disbelief, almost comical to see him crack his mask of stone. "What the hell? He's loonier than—"

"He's not loony."

"He is, too," Adam barked. "That's the most dumb-ass idea if I ever heard one. How's failing an exam s'posed to . . . shit, I dunno what the heck his plan is, but that's fucked up. Who the hell proclaims to love their family and then turns around and tries to rob the person they love of their dream?"

Raven shrugged. "I dunno."

"Do you think that's love?"

"No." Raven stuck the vape in her mouth.

"No, it ain't. So study for your test thing. Shit, if I can get my high school diploma, anyone can."

Adam was right.

"You coming tomorrow or not?"

"I'll . . . I'll text you."

"Think good and hard. Remember, your higher power's in charge. Not you. And you best listen to your higher power. If you would've, we wouldn't be standing out here right now. Am I right?"

He was right.

"C'mere." Adam crooked his big finger.

Raven melted against his brawny chest. For some reason a lump built in her throat. A big, thick lump threatening to choke her. Someone truly cared. The tears slid from her eyes because someone else had also cared. A whole family had cared.

Chapter Twenty-two: Maybe I'm a Fool

Raven left the diner and dragged her feet to the motel. She still hadn't texted Adam. And her body craved sleep after lying awake until four in the morning when she'd had to rise at quarter to six for her shift.

During her first cup of joe from the small travel coffee-maker, she'd read her daily meditations, had read pages eighty-three to eighty-eight in her big blue recovery book, and had smudged. Creator was pointing her to the Matawapit house. This was why she'd bought the yellow bathing suit.

She pushed on the door to her hotel room and flopped on the bed. The Matawapits were tolerating their ex-daughter-in-law today, after she'd cheated on their son. But Raven didn't want to be tolerated.

Damn Adam. He'd tell her one step at a time.

The phone rested on the bed beside her. She typed in the words . . .

Come get me in fifteen minutes.

Her heart stood still while she waited, waited, and waited. Five minutes later of sweat forming on her eyebrows and around her hairline, the text appeared.

On my way.

****

Out on the dock, Jude sat in the lawn chair beside his sister. Darryl and Emery were in the water, swimming with the twenty-five kids who'd come to the party. Charlene stood on the deck, fixing snacks and readying drinks.

Dad hid inside the screened-in deck, reading his newspaper.

Mom was in the kitchen.

"She didn't say anything?" Iced tea wasn't what Jude wanted. His taste buds demanded a cold beer with the hot sun baking down on him and the cloudless sky. A perfect day for Rebekah's eighth birthday party.

Adam approached them, muscles on display thanks to his black swimming shorts. He cradled Grace. "She's all yours. I gotta get."

"Go where?" Jude lowered his sunglasses.

"Raven. Gotta get her for the party."

A good coating of frost wrapped Jude's spine. "Wh-what?"

"You heard me," his brother-in-law said in a low rumble deep enough to shake the dock. "I'm getting my sponsee."

"Uh . . ." Jude glanced at Charlene and then back to Adam.

"Becky wants her here." Adam handed Grace over to Bridget. "So I'm getting her. Later." He lumbered away. "And Raven wants to be here for Becky."

It was Bridget's turn to lower her sunglasses. "This'll be interesting. Your ex-wife and ex-girlfriend."

"Don't go there." Jude thrust his finger at his sister. "This isn't funny."

"I'm not trying to be funny." Bridget coddled Grace. "I'd better get her inside. I don't want the sun on her."

"I'll . . . help." Jude stood.

"I think you'd better stay outside. It could get a bit uncomfortable."

"Yeah, for me." Jude aimed his finger at his bare chest. "I had no problem inviting Raven here when we were . . . before she dumped me."

"Like I said, this'll be interesting." Bridget walked off with Grace.

****

Raven had told Adam fifteen minutes, not right away. She scrambled to refresh her makeup, braid her hair, and pull on her shorts and tank top. Slides would suffice, since she'd be outside. All she had left to retrieve was a towel for swimming and her bathing suit.

When she opened the motel room door, Adam waited in Emery and Darryl's truck. She glanced around. There was no sign of her family. With a big breath, she darted for the vehicle and got in.

"Step on it."

"Step on it?" Adam shifted the gear and drove off.

"I'm not ready to deal."

"Oh. Your family."

Raven scrunched low in the seat. "If they see me in a Matawapit vehicle . . ."

Adam glanced down, nodding. "Gotcha."

"Who's all there?"

"Bunch of kids."

"Did you ever think we'd spend an afternoon with a Catholic family and a classroom full of kids?"

Adam's low rumble almost shook the truck. "Nope."

"Neither did I." A much-needed laugh bubbled up Raven's throat. What would she do without this big lug? Truly, Adam and Bridget were her besties. God, how could she have turned away from Bridget? And what if Bridget didn't want Raven there?

"Hey, um, how's Git?"

"Doing great. Wait'll you see my new rug rat. She's beautiful."

"I started working on some moccasins for her. Then I . . . stopped. But I'll get them finished."

Tires rolling over gravel carried into the truck. They hit small bumps now and then. The road needed grading again.

"Thanks. I mean that."

"Do you think . . ." Raven licked her lips. "Do you think Git will mind me being there?"

"Dunno. She knows I'm still your sponsor. She respects it. But you gotta remember how tight her and Jude are. Emery once described 'em as fraternal twins. You hurt Jude, you hurt Bridget."

"She's mad?"

"I wouldn't say she's mad. Upset? Yeah. I think she's more upset 'cause you didn't even text her, didn't let her know nothing."

"What was I supposed to say? I hated them at the time." Glumness steeped in Raven's chest. "I thought . . . I did a lot of thinking last night."

"What about?"

"About what you said. If I've forgiven myself. You know, how I treated my family during my addiction. About my mom blaming the deacon. And you're right—Mom was looking for someone to save her, because she had nobody. Or nothing."

"Yep. I couldn't keep blaming everyone. Neither can you."

"That's what I was doing. Blaming the Matawapits for Mom shitting all over me. It was easier than . . ." A big breath blew from Raven's lungs. "Easier than having to admit my mom's a total bitch. I can't change how I was born . . . because . . . Dad . . ." The truth stayed in Raven's throat, and she forced it outward. "My dad raped her."

"It's not your fault."

"I know it isn't." She toyed with the seat belt buckle because she couldn't see anything but Adam's bulging thigh. "It boils down to accepting what I can't change."

"Yep. You got no right telling your mom how to feel. And she's got no right telling you how to feel."

"No, she doesn't." Raven picked at the console. "I guess that means I should try and get my head together and finally study for my math exam."

"You haven't been studying?" Adam glanced down again.

"I've been trying, but it's hard. Every time I try, I see . . . blurred words."

"Maybe you should try to settle things with Jude. And the deacon."

"How're the deacon and Mrs. M.?"

"They're okay. It was the deacon who told Mrs. M to take a break and come visit. She needed it. She was pretty stressed when we got her at the airport."

"How's she now?"

"Doing better. She's having a good time looking after Grace."

"It sounds like she needed the break. She takes care of everyone but herself."

"Not really. She has her own program she follows. Her god and her church come first. And if they come first, like our program comes first, then you're in the right state of mind to face life. Y'know, what we're taught in the program."

"I'm glad she's doing better. I didn't mean to—"

"It ain't your fault. It's your family's fault."

"How's the deacon?"

"Dunno. He keeps it close to the chest."

Raven had counted the stops and turns to reach the house, and Adam had made the final turn onto Sucker Road.

"We're here, aren't we?"

The truck slowed. "Yep. Show time."

"Great," she muttered.

Adam patted the console. "Hang with me. We'll get you through this."

****

Jude remained on the dock, clutching his cup of iced tea. His head seemed to automatically keep turning to check for Raven. Through the shouts and screams coming from the water, the giggles and chatter erupting from the deck, and the squeals and laughter bursting from the badminton game set up on the lawn, he couldn't hear anything from the driveway.

Emery and Darryl were still in the water, swimming with the remaining four kids. Two being Noah and Kyle who should've been a couple of walleyes instead of children. Rebekah and her mother were on the deck. Bridget remained inside the house with Grace and Mom. A few other parents of the birthday party guests lounged about.

Jude used the corner of his eye to stalk the sliding door and somehow managed to keep his other eye on the water. His peripheral vision caught the corner of the house by the badminton game. His brother-in-law towered over everyone. Beside Adam was Raven.

She clutched a homemade beaded bag, her thick, black hair braided down her back. The silky-looking brown skin of her slim legs seemed to pop from the white shorts hugging her slim thighs. Sunglasses covered her eyes. Her head moved, as if she glanced about. Her sunglass-covered gaze settled on the dock.

Jude had ceased facing the swimmers. He stared outright.

Charlene stood and also stared outright. Rebekah jumped out of her chair and bolted for the lawn.

****

When someone poked Raven's side, she jumped.

"Miss Kabatay, I'm glad you came." Rebekah's blue eyes twinkled.

"Rebekah . . ." It'd been over two weeks since Raven had last seen this adorable little girl. "Happy birthday."

Rebekah blushed. "Thank you. C'mon, meet my mom." She took Raven's hand.

Panic juddered through Raven like a bolt of lightning. "Oh . . . um . . . I will. But first I need to go swimming. I promised Noah I would."

"I already went swimming. I'll go, too."

"Let me get changed first." Raven held up her bag.

"Okay. Hurry." Rebekah scampered to her mother.

Raven wasn't going up on the deck where Jude's ex-wife stood. She hurried around the house, the way she'd originally come, and darted through the front door to Bridget seated on the sofa, holding her new baby.

Stiffening, Raven shut the door. Why oh why did the hallway give a view of the living room?

Bridget said nothing and stared.

Raven said nothing and stared back, almost pushing the bag she held through her stomach. "Excuse me. I need to change into my swimsuit." With a shaky hand, she held up the bag.

"Go on ahead." Using her eyes, Bridget motioned at the wall of the living room, meaning to head down the other hallway.

There was a squeak on the floorboard. Mrs. M poked her head into the hallway from the kitchen.

Raven gulped.

"Hello. It's good to see you. How are you doing?" The question by Mrs. M was as soothing as cotton.

Licking her lips, Raven held up the bag. "I'm doing good. How are you? I was going to change so I could swim with Rebekah."

The sound of the sliding door opening then closing carried to where Raven remained rooted to her spot. While she kept gaping at Mrs. M, the corner of her eye caught Jude entering the living room from the dining room.

Raven could manage anything, but not this man in nothing but his swim trunks and bare skin, his muscles lightly popping beneath his bronzed flesh. The only place to escape was the front door that suddenly opened, much to Raven's surprise, then closed.

Adam cleared his throat.

A massive gush of relief spilled down Raven's spine, and she held up her bag for the millionth time. "As I said, I'm going to change."

The pat on her back from Adam's big hand was the bogeyman crawling out from under the bed, and Raven leaped. She ought to smack the big lug for making her almost bounce from her slides.

"Excuse me." Mrs. M pointed at the kitchen entranceway. "I should take the hamburgers and hot dogs outside."

"I'll start grilling 'em," Adam said.

To let him get by, Raven was forced to step into the dreaded living room. Adam lumbered down the hall.

Bridget stood. "I need to change Grace. Excuse me." She moved around Raven and disappeared down the hallway.

This left Raven and Jude in the living room, and everyone conveniently gone.

"Becky told me you're going swimming. I'll let you change." Jude held up his hand, indicating for her to leave.

Raven patted the bag. No matter how hard she tried, she couldn't stop her eyes from devouring Jude's bronzed legs she'd once caressed with her toes, well-defined pectorals she used to sample with her lips, flat stomach she'd previously ran her fingers over, and broad shoulders she'd formerly wrapped her arms around.

His eyes also moved up and down. Under his intense gaze, Raven's skin heated.

Jude stuffed his hands inside his shorts pockets. "Thanks for coming. It means a lot to Becky."

"Um . . . yeah . . ." Raven's gaze bobbed around the living room, resting on the deacon's brown recliner, then on the woodstove, over to the couch, and then bounced off the recliner rocker where Mrs. M liked to sit and work on her crafts.

She used to be a part of this room, occupying the couch, quietly talking with the deacon and his wife. "I . . . uh . . ."

"Make yourself comfortable. It's a party." Jude's greeting was a tad strained.

The sliding door opening almost rang Raven's ears.

"Give me a second. I put them in here," a woman with an adorable little-girl voice said.

Shivers shook Raven's limbs.

"Jude . . . where're the chips?" Charlene asked.

Raven backed up.

Jude turned his head to the dining room.

The wall of the living room kept Raven from seeing where Charlene probably stood.

"Oh . . ." The most stunning woman with wavy blonde hair piled high in a loose bun on top of her head, tiny shorts to match her petite, willowy limbs, and stunning blue eyes and a tiny waist appeared. Designer sunglasses were pushed up on her head. A pale-green spaghetti top enhanced her ivory complexion and slim arms.

"Hello . . ." Charlene glanced to Jude and then back to Raven. "Are you searching for the bathroom? Turn left to the other hall and it's the first door on your right."

She clasped her French manicured fingers together, a

delightful smile giving Charlene an adorable look of a popular cheerleader for the local high school. "Tell your children everything they need is on the deck. We have iced tea, lemonade, and pop. I'm getting more chips and dip. They're so hungry, they've already worked their way through the first batch."

Even Charlene's giggle was that of an adorable little girl. "Please forgive my lack of manners. I'm Charlene Matawapit." She extended her petite hand with probably a size one ring on her pinky finger.

Raven was a hideous giant, and her voice too deep, too scratchy, and just too damn un-girly compared to Jude's gorgeous ex-wife who was the miniature doll every child under twelve desired for Christmas.

She shuffled a few steps and extended her hand. "Raven Kabatay."

The smile faded from Charlene's peach-colored lips. The firm grip of her handshake limpened. "Oh . . ." Her gaze moved about, and she slipped her hand from Raven's. "I should get the chips. I think they're —"

"Mom put them in the box on the kitchen table. She was getting ready to take everything outside." Jude's reply was weaker than Raven's knees ready to give out from under her.

The corners of Charlene's mouth pinched. "I'll get them. It isn't often the children have treats." She nodded stiffly at Raven and vanished into the dining room. Her flip-flops squeakcd against the floor.

"I should . . ." Raven held up the bag again. "I should get changed."

"Um . . . yeah." Jude smacked his lips together. "See ya outside."

Raven tore off for the safety of the bathroom.

****

217

Talk about the most tense and awkward moment of Jude's life. Standing in the same room with his ex-wife and ex-girlfriend. He clambered for the dock, the safest spot at the house.

He snatched his sunglasses and plopped back in the lawn chair just as Emery hefted himself up on the dock from the water, dripping wet.

"You . . . you stay in there any . . . any longer, you'll turn into an orange." Dammit, Jude couldn't even get his voice under control.

"An orange?" Emery stared at Jude like he'd grown two heads. "Don't you mean a raisin . . . or a prune?"

"What?" Jude blinked.

"Your joke. Don't you mean a raisin or a prune? Why an orange?"

"What orange?" Jude shifted in the chair. This iced tea sucked bullshit. The dry reserve was going to drive him batshit crazy.

"If you keep scowling, the kids'll mistake you for a great white shark and you'll scare them out of the water." Emery chuckled. He bent and retrieved a towel.

"You should go in. It's refreshing." He plopped in the other lawn chair Bridget had previously occupied.

"I forgot I need something to drink. I'm beat. Can you do me a favor and get me one?" Emery asked ever so politely.

"Under any other circumstance I'd say yes, but not this afternoon, because with my luck, I'll find myself between my ex-wife and my ex-girlfriend again." Jude drained his glass of iced tea. "Get me a lemonade."

"Oh? Raven's here?" Emery wrapped the towel around his shoulders.

"Yep. And they just met."

"Oh . . ." Emery sat forward. "We're all adult here. I don't think —"

"Yeah, we are, but it means I have to sit here until six-thirty and try to get through this party. And it's only going on three. So do me a favor and get me another drink. If you can sneak over to the church and swipe me some wine from the cabinet in the sacristy, that'd be even better."

CHAPTER TWENTY-THREE: YOU'VE RE-ALLY GOT A HOLD ON ME

Normally, Jude took pictures during special events, but not today, which wasn't fair to Rebekah. Still, hiding on the dock was the safest option.

The sliding door opened. Raven emerged. From inside the screened-in deck, Dad said something to her. Raven shifted and squirmed. At least someone else felt as awkward as Jude. Charlene was in fast form, cutting watermelon and juggling drinks for five kids.

"It's Darryl's turn to morph into a prune if he doesn't get out of the water soon." Emery sauntered up the dock, carrying two drinks.

Jude held out his hand. "Thanks, man."

"Not a problem." Emery plopped in the chair. He slid on his sunglasses. "I'd better put on more sunscreen or I'll burn."

Jude should've made his usual joke about his little brother being a true pale-skinned Ojibway, but the sly remark sat somewhere in his tightening gut.

"Easy." Emery's reassurance was soothing. "You're in God's hands, aren't you?"

"God? More like the Devil's playing a joke on me."

"Not true." Emery patted Jude's shoulder. "There's nothing to worry about."

Raven sashayed to the waterfront.

There wasn't a beach. Only a big smooth rock to use for wading into the water. She set down her towel. The one-piece

bathing suit coated her bronzed skin like her own smooth
flesh. Hardly risqué, but subtly sexy with peek-a-boo cut to
give a glimpse of her beautiful breasts.

She dipped her toe in the water—the very toe she always
used to trace Jude's calf. He chugged back his lemonade. The
braid fell over Raven's shoulder and brushed her waist. She
wouldn't need sunscreen. Her dark skin kept her from burning. A woman made for the land and the outdoors.

"Hello. Hello." Emery's pale palm moved in front of Jude's
face.

He slapped at it. "What?"

"I guess you don't need my company, hey?" Emery asked,
amusement lingering in his question.

"What is it?" Irritation pricked Jude's skin. He turned his
head but kept the corner of his eye on Raven, who waded into
the lake, submerging her slim thighs she'd once locked tight
around his hips.

Darryl chugged through the water. "What's up? You ready
to get wet?"

Raven set her hands on her hips. "You splash me, and I'll
drown you."

Oh geez, she'd asked for it. Jude winced.

A big wave of water came at Raven, and Darryl's laugh
was loud enough to create a whirlpool. Water hit Raven at full
force, running down her sleek arms and legs, soaking her hair.
She curled away in retreat.

Wiping her eyes, Raven gasped. Then she swiveled and
came at Darryl, her hands pushing through the water.

"See?" Emery said. "Everyone's at ease. There's no need to
worry."

"I'm not worried." Jude sank back and crossed his legs at
the ankles.

Rebekah dashed from the deck to the shoreline, squealing,
"My turn. My turn." She ran down the rocks, aqua socks

giving her traction so she didn't slip.

Darryl held open his arms. Rebekah flung herself at his chest. He caught her and cradled her. "C'mon, birthday girl."

Pride filled Jude.

Raven swam over and hitched herself to Darryl's back. Off he went, one in his arms and the other clinging to him like a baboon.

The other children swam after them, hollering for piggyback rides. Darryl and Raven obliged. They'd sit the kids on their shoulders and then toss them into the water. This went on for at least fifteen minutes. By now, Jude was left alone on the dock, since Emery had dived back into the water to join the fun.

Jude drummed his fingers against his cup. Aww, screw it. He set aside the drink and dove into the lake. The refreshing liquid wrapped his body and hair, cooling his skin that had generated a huge amount of heat after sitting in a lawn chair for most of the afternoon. He came up through the surface, shaking back his hair.

Noah treaded in front of him, grinning. "My turn, Dad."

Jude dove underneath his son and grasped Noah's legs. He again broke through the surface with Noah on his shoulders. Rebekah was on Emery's. Kyle on Darryl's. And Rebekah's new BFF, a young girl named Michelle, sat on Raven's shoulders. The battle turned into who'd first topple into the water. The kids squealed and laughed, trying to tip one another over.

Jude struggled to hold Noah when they were both soaked and slippery. But his son fought back until he tipped Kyle off Darryl's shoulders. At the same time, Rebekah went down with a big splash.

"Let's get 'em, Dad!" Noah drummed on Jude's head and pointed at Michelle and Raven, the only opposition left.

"Not so easy, guys," Raven taunted. "Don't you know girls are tougher than boys?"

"Oh yeah?" Noah's little legs tightened around Jude's shoulders. "Watch and learn."

"Easy now," Jude warned. Noah was a chip off the old block—competitive.

Jude stood in front of Raven while the kids switched into battle-mode up above them.

Streams of water leaked down Raven's face while she wrestled to keep Michelle in the air.

Jude gripped Noah's wiggling legs. Circling them, Emery, Darryl, Rebekah, Kyle, and the other kids cheered, the boys naturally rooting for Noah and the girls egging on Michelle.

Eye to eye, wobbling in front of each other, Jude grinned at Raven. Her makeup had washed away, except for the mascara. She must've used the waterproof kind. Her breasts, molded against the snug wet swimsuit, bounced each time she jumped and staggered backward while Noah and Michelle fought up on top. Raven's nipples stood proud and perky, and goosebumps peppered her lean arms.

"No!" Michelle screeched. Her legs came up from under Raven's hands.

Raven fought to latch herself back to Michelle. This was Jude's opportunity, and he heaved one step through the water, then dug his feet into the sand and banged Raven's hip. Her eyes popped to the size of eggs, and her mouth formed into a big O.

In true *Terminator* style, Jude slyly shouted, "Hasta la vista, baby!" and howled with laughter.

"Jerk," Raven screamed, but her smile stretched to her ears.

The girls weaved and wobbled. They went over with a big splash that hit Jude's face and chest.

Noah pounded on Jude's head, yelling, "We did it, Dad. We kicked their butts."

"We sure did." Jude pushed on Noah's ankles and sent his son over backward. A big splash hit his back.

At the same time, Raven, Michelle, and Noah surfaced.

"What'd you do that for? We're partners." Noah giggled and climbed onto Jude's back.

Raven wound up her fists and whacked a good wall of water at Jude, capable of putting a rogue wave to shame. Michelle joined in, splashing them. Jude pushed against the water, thighs working hard from the pressure while Noah still clung to his back, cackling.

Rebekah jumped in Jude's arms. He struggled to hold his slippery daughter.

The fresh scent of the lake, the sun on him, his kids stuck to him, and Raven still tossing water on them seemed to lift Jude high up above the clouds. The puff of glee in his chest bordered on bursting.

He trudged up the rocks, daughter under his arm and son on his back, and Raven's giggles in his ears.

"Wet enough?" Raven jeered.

"Hey, we won." Jude set Rebekah down and lifted Noah off his back. "This deserves some food. Adam's cooking up burgers. Be good losers and feed the champions."

"Oh? A champion?" Raven set her wet hands on her wet hips.

The swimsuit coating her slim hips and perky breasts were an invitation for Jude to trace. Beads of moisture continued to run down her super-sharp cheekbones and dribble to her mouth that was a suggestion to kiss. The wave of water Jude had left behind in the lake seemed to hurl down his throat, halting his breathing.

"The food's almost done."

Jude blinked. His ex-wife had spoken. He turned to Charlene's folded arms and a smile not reaching her flat eyes.

"Mom. Mom. I won." Noah grabbed her hand.

"Yes, I saw . . . everything." Charlene's hard stare shifted from Jude to Raven. "C'mon, it's time to eat." She took

Rebekah's hand and led the children away.

"I . . . um . . ." Raven licked her wet lips where droplets of water lingered. "I'd better get dried off and changed."

Jude managed to choke out, "Yeah. I should change, too."

Raven grabbed her towel and left for the house.

Jude wouldn't look at her great ass or legs-to-her-neck thighs. He was a Matawapit, and she'd only come for Rebekah's sake. He turned and trudged to the dock to get his towel and shirt.

****

Raven stayed away from the main table where the Matawapits held court. Everyone else used the numerous lawn chairs available. She'd eaten a burger, coleslaw, and baked beans, and munched on some chips and dip.

Fifteen minutes ago, they'd sung happy birthday to Rebekah, with Charlene front and center, which was expected. She was the girl's mother, so she'd taken care of everything, from lighting the candles on the cake and handing out each serving with a scoop of ice cream to bringing over every present for Rebekah to unwrap while taking pictures.

This was Charlene and Jude's moment. And Raven couldn't dislike his ex-wife. The woman was friendly to everyone, making sure nobody ran out of refreshments or she'd ask if anyone needed more food. After the swimming adventure, Charlene had directed the kids to the bathroom, handed out extra towels, and poured the children more refreshments.

She even had Jude writing down each present Rebekah opened and who the present was from. Raven had seen this done at a couple of baby showers, and even at a wedding shower, but never at a birthday party. The purpose was to connect the gift to the giver to send a *thank you* card. Very thoughtful.

Yes, there was nothing to hate about Charlene. Jude had picked a beautiful and thoughtful wife who cared about others, which said a lot about him.

Raven tore a few pieces off the edge of her paper plate. Jude had also chosen her. A man who selected his partner carefully, ensuring the woman had traits he admired and approved of. He'd approved of her. He'd admired her. And she'd . . .

Rising to her feet, Raven withdrew her e-cigarette and walked away from the children and parents so she wouldn't rudely cast vapor everywhere. Her chest constricted. She'd gone and done the unthinkable. At the time, she'd only thought of Mom.

"Miss Kabatay. Miss Kabatay," Rebekah called out.

Raven turned.

Rebekah held up the purse, proudly fingering the fringes and beadwork. "Thank you so much. Thank you. I love it." She hugged the purse, beaming at her mother.

Since Jude was wearing sunglasses, Raven couldn't detect his feelings. As for Charlene, her smile did crinkle the corners of her eyes.

"Thank you," Charlene said gently, forcing Raven to strain to hear. "You're too kind."

Raven nodded. She motioned at the e-cigarette, so they'd understand she was heading off to vape. Hugging herself, she kept walking, alone, again.

"I'm tired. Can you give me a ride back to the motel?" Raven stood on the deck where Adam sat. It was quarter after five, and the children were back in the water with Emery and Darryl. Bunch of fish.

"Already?" Adam squinted.

"Yeah." Deflation threatened to haul Raven's shoulders downward. She'd had enough of pasting on a smile after the wonderful half hour in the lake. The rest of the afternoon had dragged.

"Sure." Adam stood. "Lemme find where they put the keys. Be right back."

While Adam lumbered off to the water, Raven wandered to the house to gather her stuff she'd left in the bag. Her swimsuit needed to be hung. She opened the screen door to the deacon sitting in his chair, reading a newspaper. As they'd done previously, they nodded briefly at each other. Raven disappeared inside through the sliding door.

Water running, chattering, and pots and pans being stored away came from the kitchen. Mrs. M and another woman were cleaning up.

Jude stood next to the counter, holding a can of pop. His gaze roamed to Raven and stayed there.

Raven managed to say, "It's time to head out. I'm getting my stuff."

"Sure. I'll give you a ride." Tenderness filled his offer.

"It's okay." Raven shuddered and attempted to point outside. "Adam . . . Adam's giving me a ride. He went to find the truck keys."

"Emery and Darryl are in the water. They'll never hear him over all the splashing. Go get your stuff. I'll meet you at my truck."

"Oh . . . uh . . . okay." Raven used the living room to vanish. She didn't dare go through the kitchen, which was the shorter route to reach the spare room where everyone had stored their things.

Her heart threatened to jump into her throat, and she scurried from the main hall to the secondary hallway. The talking continued. Jude even laughed. If he was relaxed, then Raven would also relax. She retrieved her bag and left the house. There was nothing to be nervous about. Like a true host, Jude was offering a ride back to the motel and nothing more.

The front door opened. As Jude started down the steps, the door reopened. Charlene appeared. She spoke quietly. Raven only caught " . . . and tell her I'll be right back," from Jude.

He strode down the walkway, tossing his keys up in the air and catching them.

Arms folded, Charlene turned and headed inside, delicate shoulders tight.

"Everything okay?" Raven asked.

"Yep. No worries." Jude approached the truck. He flashed his dimples.

Heat crept onto Raven's face. The locked doors opened. She got in.

Jude slid on his sunglasses. "Have a good time?"

"Yeah." During their swim, she'd forgotten about Mom, Clayton, and what had caused her to break up with Jude.

"Great." He backed up the truck, passing on the image screen mounted to the dashboard. His head moved to the right and left, using his rearview and side mirrors. He also glanced over his shoulder.

Raven wasn't sure if she'd be able to maneuver a truck this size through the tiny gaps allowed by the numerous parked vehicles or the narrowness of the driveway.

Once Jude had them backed out, they drove off. He peeped at her then back at the road. "How goes the studying?"

Shivers caressed Raven's spine. She rubbed her arms.

"Cold?"

"No. I'm fine."

He nodded. "Are you ready to kick math's butt?"

"Uh . . ." Her limbs squirmed on their own.

"Are you studying?"

Trying to.

"Yes or no?" He turned the truck onto the other road.

"Uh . . . I guess."

"Nope. Not *I guess.* Yes or no." He was in full-on teacher mode by the authority in his voice.

"I'm trying . . ." *It's not easy studying in a motel room with your brother demanding you fail the exam.*

Jude drummed his fingers on the steering wheel. "If you need help, I can help, but I need to know if you're having trouble. That's why I'm your teacher."

Even after all she'd done to him, he still wanted to help? And this was why she'd fallen madly in love with him. But if her family saw them together . . . Ack, where were her brains? He was giving her a ride back to the motel. Someone might see them.

"Are you having trouble or not?" He kept speaking like he stood in front of the class.

"I . . . uh . . . can't seem to keep my mind on studying."

"That makes two of us. I can't keep my mind on anything, either, and I have a big meeting coming up at the end of the month."

Raven stared out her window at the passing rolling tall grass found in the aptly christened Grassy District. "I . . ."

"Y'know, for a woman who spoke her mind when we first met, you keep a lot here." Jude tapped his chest. "Seems I had you pegged wrong, hey?"

She whipped her head to him. "Fine. Help me study."

Jude grinned. "Now there's the woman I first met."

"I see. You admired her?" She was treading water in a deep lake. If she didn't smarten up, she'd drown.

"Yep. I didn't see her as the kind of woman who'd let *anyone* tell her what to do."

Her face remained warm. "What are you insinuating?"

"Maybe she's not as tough as I thought she was. Anyone can be tough around strangers, even friends — but family . . ."

Oh, he was goading, was he? "I see. And you'd risk *everything* if your family didn't approve?"

"Didn't I already?" Jude lowered his sunglasses and peeked over them.

Raven's jaw almost plummeted to her lap. She straightened

and drew back her shoulders, giving her damp hair a shake. "Okay, teacher, teach me." Much to her shock, her words came out flirtatiously.

"What would you like to learn?" Jude lowered his sunglasses again, and this time he winked.

Gosh, he truly was a gentleman through and through. After all the hurtful things she'd said to him, after she'd walked out on his family generously offering her a place to stay . . .

"Stop the truck, please."

Jude pulled over to the side of the road. He engaged the gear to park. "What is it?"

"I . . . amends are important in the program. Very important. And I need to make a big amend."

"To who?"

"To you," she whispered, taking his hand.

"To me?" He placed his other hand on his chest. "Why?"

"For the things I said at your house." The words left her mouth calmly, courageously. "And I'm deeply sorry, Jude. I shouldn't have said what I said . . . or acted the way I did. It was wrong."

"Hey, I owe you an apology, too. I hid something from you. Something that I . . ." His lips formed into a straight line. "When I think about it, I used confidentiality as an excuse for not telling you. Honestly, part of me was pretty nervous you'd . . . well, I guessed correctly, given the way you reacted."

"Quit blaming yourself. You're not at fault. Your dad told you something, and I admire how you didn't out his secret to me."

He started to lean in, but she held up her free hand.

"There's something I must tell you." She fiddled with his fingers. Her loyalty was to this man, and now she'd divulge what Clayton had asked her to do.

Chapter Twenty-four: Let's Be Lovers Again

Mom would murder Raven. The same for Clayton. So what? She was *Raven* again—the old Raven who'd run off to Winnipeg to get away from her domineering family and live life on her terms. But this Raven was also responsible, even considerate, and could stand her ground even at the place she'd run from.

She packed up her textbooks and binder. All set. Sunday night, and she was ready to crush the exam with a good helping of studying from a super-awesome tutor.

When she left her motel room, all was quiet on the road, which was strange. Then again, it was ten to seven. Bingo had already started.

The weather cooperated. She savored the warm air as she made the jaunt to Jude's house a road over. If people wanted to *out* her for daring to go to a Matawapits home, let them.

Rebekah had gotten a new bicycle for her birthday. She pedaled down the road, accompanied by her best friend, Michelle. The girls rode up to Raven and stopped.

"Dad said you're studying tonight at my house," Rebekah announced. Beneath her white helmet, her black hair snaked down her back in a ponytail. Already as dark as Jude, the little girl had quite a deep tan going on after spending so much time outdoors.

"Your dad's helping me prepare for the math exam on Wednesday."

"The big test?"

"Yep. If I pass all my exams, I'll be a grade twelve student in the fall."

"That's the big grade. The really big grade," Rebekah said in awe.

"Next year at this time, thanks to your dad's help, I'll be a high school graduate. And you're starting grade three in September."

Rebekah and Michelle grinned.

"What time do you have to be back at the house?"

"Seven." Rebekah's little shoulders sagged. "Dad says I have to have my bath and get ready for bed. School's tomorrow."

"It's almost seven. Your dad told me to stop by at seven. C'mon."

"Okay. Bye, Michelle."

Michelle rode off in the opposite direction while Rebekah joined Raven.

"When did you learn how to ride a bike?"

"Last summer. Dad taught me."

"He's a good dad, isn't he?"

"He's the best." Rebekah's dark skin glowed.

Jude stood on the back steps, shouting, "Noah Abraham, get your butt home. Now!" His eyes widened slightly at them as they ambled in his direction. "I'm rounding up the last munchkin for the night. Go on in and make yourself comfortable."

"Okay." Raven headed up the steps while Rebekah handed over her bike and helmet to Jude.

"Can you start my bath?" Rebekah disappeared inside her bedroom.

"Sure." Goodness, the girl was a doll, a total opposite from cheeky Noah. When Raven had been Rebekah's age, she'd had to be hauled inside, stripped out of her clothes, and submerged into the old gray tub to wash up.

Once Raven set her books on the table, she ran the bath water. She checked the vanity and added a generous helping of liquid bubble soap to the tub.

Her heart warmed as she gazed around the small room while seated on the toilet lid. Small, yes, but cozy. She folded her arms across her chest. Maybe, just maybe she'd one day . . .

Screw it. She wasn't a coward but bold and honest. So, yes, maybe one day she'd sit here and help Rebekah bathe, because Raven did want this. She wanted the whole package. Jude and his kids. And she wouldn't play Mom. The kids had a mother—a very good mother. An excellent mother who'd instilled wonderful qualities into the kids.

But a stepmom would be awesome.

Rebekah appeared, wrapped in her pink robe. "Is it ready?"

"Almost. It's filling up."

"Did you wanna brush my hair? Mom always brushes my hair. So does Dad." Rebekah stood at the vanity.

"Sure." Giddy delight scooted up Raven's spine. She stood and grabbed the round brush Rebekah had pulled out from a drawer. "Are you excited about grade three?"

"No. I wanna swim and bike."

Kids didn't think that far ahead. Raven would make sure to remember children preferred the here and now.

Gently, she drew the bristles through Rebekah's flowing black hair. The girl was a true beauty with her bright-blue eyes, set off by reddish-brown dark skin. Her lashes and the bottoms and tops of her eyelids gave the same illusion Jude's did—as if rimmed with black liner and thick coats of ebony mascara. Even more adorable, Rebekah was tinier than girls her age. Small-boned and petite, like her mother.

"There." Raven set aside the brush. "The tub's done

filling."

The back door opened and shut. Noah whined while Jude barked quick orders.

"To your room. Now."

"Aww, Dad." A door banged shut.

"Don't you slam your door at me."

Raven sighed. She'd better get used to the fighting. "Let me know if you need any help."

"Dad washes my hair." Rebekah sat in the tub, surrounded by bubbles. "Mom said she had her hair washed until she was ten."

"Then holler when you need your hair washed."

"Okay. Thank you, Miss Kabatay."

"You're welcome." Raven started to shut the door.

"No. Dad leaves it open."

Rebekah mustn't be bothered about her older brother running about the house while she was undressed. Well, kids decided when they weren't comfortable around others of the opposite sex — siblings included.

Raven sat at the table and opened her books. Jude came out from his room, having changed into sweatpants and a t-shirt. Her heart warmed because he always donned this outfit when they were alone at his house together. "Got on your at-home outfit."

"Yep. You know I enjoy being comfortable as much as the next guy." He pulled out a chair and sat.

They spent the evening at the table, Raven listening to Jude's examples. Every now and then, he rose to assist one of the kids in the bathroom, and Raven washed Rebekah's hair, which was an absolute delight. She then fixed the children a before-bed-time snack. The kids watched TV while Jude continued to tutor like he had the first time he'd helped Raven understand analytic geometry back in February.

They also talked about their day off and what they'd done.

Jude had taken Charlene and the kids to church. Then they'd gone to the airport so the children could see their mother off before she'd boarded her plane. Afterwards, they'd stopped at his parents' for brunch.

Raven had spent her afternoon doing laundry at the laundromat, which was expensive, but she had no washing machine at the motel. It'd been a treat to dry her clothes in the dryer instead of hanging them on the line.

"If you need to do laundry, give it to me, and I'll take it to Mom's to wash." Jude sipped more tea from the pot he'd made for them earlier.

"You mean where your mother washes your clothes."

"Funny. Hey, I didn't ask her to wash, dry, and iron our clothes. She took that chore on herself."

The house was quiet, only the hum of the TV on low. Rebekah and Noah had been sent off to sleep over an hour ago. Their doors were closed, since they didn't need the heat from the woodstove to keep them warm in mid-June.

Jude set his chin in his palm, elbow resting on the table. "I think it's time we finish our conversation we started Saturday night."

The clock above the sink ticked away. Ten.

Raven glanced back at Jude. "There's nothing to finish. I'm here, aren't I?"

"Yeah, you are." His answer had a sweet *mmm* to it. He drew tiny circles on the table with his index finger while still gazing at her through heavy lids.

She squirmed, having seen *that* look in the bedroom many times, when his voice became hushed from arousal.

"Maybe tomorrow night we can study at your motel room?" His black brow lifted slightly, and a hint of his dimples surfaced. His eyes smoldered.

"If you promise to bring supper." She licked her lips. Her thighs heated from his gaze following her tongue.

"Should I bring anything else?" He winked.

"Your dick?" She giggled.

"It goes wherever I go." His dimples weren't a light hint but broad and full, matching his deep smile. "Trust me. If you need proof, I can show it to you."

A sultry laugh wound its way up Raven's throat. "I think you can keep your pants on—for now."

"I guess I'd better make sure and tell the cook to wrap our food. I guarantee we won't be eating right away or studying."

"Eat and study after . . ."

"After?" he asked coyly. "Okay. Then I'll see you tomorrow night."

"Tomorrow night." She re-wet her dried lips.

"You keep sticking that out, I'm gonna take it as an invitation to pull something out for you to lick." Jude snickered and walked his fingers across the table.

"You can wait until tomorrow night." Raven forced her hands to gather up the binder and textbook. "See you then."

She stood on wobbly legs.

He also stood.

As she sashayed to the door, she brushed up against Jude's side, whispering, "You're lucky your children are here to save you."

She managed to get her shaking hand to turn the doorknob and stepped out into the warm night with twinkling stars above.

The back light came on. She pivoted, ready to take the first step.

"Stay safe." His erection pushed against his loose sweatpants.

Delight shimmered between Raven's legs. "Is that a gun in your pocket, or are you glad to see me leaving?"

"Leaving?" He snickered. "Cock tease. You're gonna get it tomorrow night."

"What am I getting?"

"A licking."

"Ooh?" Her cunt pulsated. "One to my ass or one to my pussy?"

"Both?"

"I'd better get going or I'll be forced to rub one out before bed."

His gaze skimmed her belly and rested between her thighs. "Nope. If I gotta suffer, so do you. Keep your hands to yourself. I own that." He pointed at her cunt.

The *own* word sucked the air from Raven's lungs. Her thickening clit squirmed beneath her pussy lips. "You got that right. It's all yours."

****

"Studying, hmm?" Emery strolled into the kitchen, having arrived to babysit Noah and Rebekah.

"Zip it." Jude held his finger over his lips.

"Me? Zip it?" Emery motioned up and down at Jude's pants. "You're the one who should zip it."

"Very funny. Later. And thanks for watching the kids." Jude grabbed his textbook off the kitchen table.

"Y'know—"

Jude reached the back entranceway by the bathroom, stopped, but didn't turn. "Now what?"

"I'm saying this as a member of band council, not your brother. Okay?"

Oh great, this could take forever. Jude whirled and rested his hand on the wall. "Go ahead."

"You're a great teacher. One of the best teachers I know. But . . ." Emery moved a step closer. His fingers grazed the top of the kitchen chair. "You told me Clayton asked her to fail the exam, but he didn't say why. We both know he would've accused you of failing her because she stopped having . . . uh . . . relations with you."

Jude nodded.

"What if he does the opposite now? He's going to find out. And when he finds out, I guarantee it'll be on the agenda at the next band council meeting. Remember, he has the most votes at the table, not us."

"Which is why the math teacher's grading the math exams, and not me. He's the expert and teaches the elementary and high school students."

"I'm saying Clayton'll go for your throat." Emery clucked his tongue just like Mom always did.

"I know what I'm doing. I'm aware of the education policy. As the principal, I enforce it. I'm not breaking policy."

"Look . . . we're more lenient up here when it comes to nepotism. We have to be. Everyone's related to someone. It's a small reserve. Only two thousand people. Please. Be careful. Mrs. Kabatay's a very sick woman. I heard she went back to Thunder Bay today for more treatment. Her kids aren't going to let this go. The only one who can stop this is Mrs. Kabatay. They listen to her."

"Are you saying I should talk to Mrs. Kabatay?" If Jude became any more perplexed, he'd turn into one of Mom's jigsaw puzzles she enjoyed piecing together at the dining room table during the evening.

"No. That's something Dad'll have to do," Emery replied.

"I see." Jude checked the clock above the sink. Ten to seven. "Look, I gotta—"

"Can you please . . ." Emery frowned. He motioned at Jude's crotch. "Can you please put *it* on ice for a few more seconds?"

"Put it on ice? Whatever. What now?" Big deal, the exasperation tightening Jude's gut had rolled off his tongue.

"I'm saying be careful. If something comes to the council

table, policy states I must declare a conflict of interest, and so will Darryl." Warning lingered in Emery's words.

"Gotcha." Jude turned and threw open the door. Emery's frustrated sigh followed him outside.

****

Raven paced the motel room, and there wasn't much space to pace. She drummed her fingers on the dresser, picked at the matches on the small table, readjusted the two chairs, smoothed the bedspread, and plumped the pillows.

The clock on her cell phone read seven.

A knock.

In two strides she reached the door and opened it.

Jude held up the bag. "Tyrell double-wrapped our order. I said . . . ah . . . I wouldn't be eating until later."

She shut the door and locked her arms around Jude's broad shoulders.

"Mmm, now this is the kind of greeting I was anticipating." Jude set the bag on the table and drew her against his chest.

His lips brushed her mouth. Featherlike breaths from his nose skimmed her face. The kiss was light to start, which allowed her to savor having him back in her life again.

Jude steered them away from the door, his mouth still covering her lips, breaths growing quicker. His fingers dusted her back, silky touches urging her to explore his tongue. She opened her mouth slightly, and he gave her what she needed, what she'd missed terribly during their brief breakup.

Part of her yearned to beg him to hold her, but the other part urged her to open his shirt so she could explore his bare skin. She slipped Jude's shirt from his pants and massaged his muscles contracting beneath his smooth flesh. He shivered under her touch, his breaths heaving now and his tongue rougher, richer, devouring her mouth.

Heat budded between her legs. Creamy wetness slipped from her pussy and saturated her panties.

"Jude." She gasped. "Oh, Jude."

He broke the kiss. Hunger blazed in his dark eyes. "It seems like forever. I want you now."

She quickly shed her shorts and tank top and shimmied out of her panties under his watchful stare caressing her legs, landing strip, and breasts. He exposed his chest to her, and she groaned. His nipples stood erect to match his thick cock bursting with want for her.

"Then have me. Fuck me."

He gathered her in his arms and lavished kiss after kiss on her lips. His tongue searched every region of her mouth, licking and tasting. Her head lightened under his hungry exploration.

She was pushed to the bed, and he sank on top of her, his lips still claiming her mouth. His erection, slick with pre-cum, pressed on her crotch. She massaged his buttocks that flexed and thrust as he worked his cock along her pussy.

"Open them for me, Raven." His husky words, full of rich deepness from his arousal, sucked the breath from her lungs.

She spread her thighs and wrapped his hips. With one gliding pump he was inside her, panting and moaning. She raked her fingers through his short strands of hair and bit down on his shoulder so she wouldn't scream with pleasure. His prick was moving deep inside, stretching the flesh of her cunt, coaxing her to let him rut hard and fast.

He plunged quickly, his mouth still feasting on her lips. She held on, the pleasure already building and ready to burst.

CHAPTER TWENTY-FIVE: MY FRIENDS, MY FRIENDS

Raven twirled off to the bathroom, feet barely touching the floor. Jude had left five minutes ago, but their coming together reaffirmed she'd made the right decision. If others wanted to call her cold or selfish for daring to choose the love of a man over her family, over her mother's tragic past, so be it. *She* had to live this life, not Clayton, not Mom, not her sisters.

She switched on the taps to wash off her makeup. The dinging of her cell phone going off in the sleeping area carried into the bathroom. She skipped off to answer. Jude probably wanted to say goodnight.

Call me.

Nope. Not Jude. Clayton. Time for a showdown.

Raven pushed the contact number for her brother. She drew in a big breath and stood straighter.

"Hello." His greeting wasn't welcoming.

"Hey." She grabbed her bottled water off the dresser and sipped. Now was a good time to vape. With her e-cigarette and water, she padded outside while Clayton continued to say nothing.

Since bingo had finished over an hour ago, the road was quiet. No dust permeating the air. She sat on top of the picnic table beneath the pine tree and stuck the vape between her lips, still clutching the phone.

"Are you gonna talk?" She took another puff on the vape.

His hiss came through the phone. "He was there."

"Yeah, I know he was." Although Raven tried to keep her voice calm, her impatience came through.

"You're lucky Mom and Fawn went back. They woulda had a—"

"I made up my mind."

"Oh? You did, did you?" A hint of snarling invaded his words. "And it's the Matawapits, hey? After what that family did to Mom—"

"I can't help how I feel. If you'd listen—"

"There's nothing to listen to. I'm still doing this for Mom. It's the least we can do for her. Maybe if you'd stuck around, instead of the rest of us picking up the slack, you woulda seen what *he* did to her."

"I can't help what the deacon did." She threw out her palm. "And if it wasn't him, it woulda been someone else. Can't you see? Nobody's to blame."

Clayton's sharp breath almost pierced Raven's eardrum. "Not to blame? He's all to blame."

"I know he feels awful."

"He doesn't feel anything. He has his white woman. He has—"

"Please, listen to me." She searched her brain. "He hasn't been himself. He's—"

"Yeah, and you'd know it since you were at *his* house on Saturday. Had his son over at your room tonight. Were at his son's last night. After all I've done for you. If not for me, you'd be sleeping in the gutter on Main in the 'Peg."

Raven squeezed the vape. "I knew you'd do this. I knew you'd hold this against me. You don't think I appreciate all you've done for me?"

"No, you don't, 'cause if you did, we wouldn't be having

this conversation."

She hopped off the picnic table. "Not true. I chose you over them. Do you know how hard that was for me? I . . . finally . . . had something of my own. And I walked away from it—for you, for Mom, for the family."

"Yeah, and you went crawling back to him. To them. I don't give a shit how many excuses you give. Nothing's gonna justify what you did to me. To Mom. To your sisters. You wanna be a Matawapit? Go ahead. But it's not stopping me from what I'm doing for Mom. We owe it to her."

"Wait a second. You don't—" Fuck, the bastard had hung up. She switched off the phone and stomped inside her room and slammed the door shut.

Raven pushed away her exam paper. Finished. For two hours she'd endured a test that still scrambled her brain, but there'd been no guessing. She'd known the answers. Most of them.

She gathered her calculator and pencils.

"All done?" The teacher glanced up.

"Yes." She stood.

"Please bring me your paper."

At least the classroom was cool, although there wasn't any air-conditioning in the school because of the expense. But the janitor had gotten a nice breeze going through the rooms and hallways. Fans were set up everywhere.

She picked up her purse and test. Her legs moved with the confidence shimmering through her limbs. "Here you go."

"Thank you."

Eleven. Maybe Jude was around. A visit would be nice, but she was due at the diner. She'd promised Cookie she'd return as soon as the exam was finished.

Nobody walked the hall. Even the distant education class-room door was closed. Emery must be in a video session.

Oh heck, she'd go see Jude and finally get a look at his office.

To reach the main area of the building, Raven had to go through two other big doors. All was quiet. Only her heels meeting the floor echoed off the walls. This was the last week of classes for the elementary and high school students.

A door opened. Jude strolled out. His eyes lit. "Hey, how'd you do? You're ahead of time."

Delight filled Raven's chest. "Yes, I completed it a half an hour early. I'm due at the diner. Marsha's filling in for me. Got time for a quick cup of coffee?"

"Sure. Right this way." He made a gesture with his hand, just like a gentleman from the past escorting a lady.

Raven giggled and took his arm. "You're done on Friday."

"The kids are. I'm still preparing for my meeting."

The smoothness in Raven's shoulders vanished. "I wish you wouldn't underestimate my brother."

"Hey, I've done nothing wrong. He's not even on the committee and education's not his portfolio. What can he do?"

"I don't know, but he's cunning."

"Coyote?" Jude snickered. "Darryl likens him to one."

Raven snorted. "Coyote is a trickster. And maybe that's what Clayton is."

"That's how Darryl explained it to me. He said coyote confounds situations, but many times they are a blessing. He said if it wasn't for your brother, he and Emery wouldn't have reconciled."

"True. But what . . ." She stopped.

His gaze searched hers.

"I . . . I don't wanna end up like my mom," she whispered.

"Hey, you're not." His palm rested against her face.

"You don't think I'm . . ." Fretting wasn't her style. Jude had fallen in love with her honesty and boldness. "Your family's all I have now," she muttered.

"And we're glad to have you. Mom and Dad want you to move back to the house. They'd like to speak to you. I told them this week's too crazy since you're sitting exams, but I suggested dinner this weekend."

"Dinner?" The glumness of gray vanished. "Okay. Sounds good."

"I know the motel must be getting expensive, even with the discount they're giving you for an extended stay."

It was eating every dime in her purse. "Yup."

"I . . ." He licked his lips. His fingers caressed her hair. "It's gonna work out. Trust me?"

"Yeah, I do." She trusted him more than her own family.

"C'mon, you haven't checked out my office yet. Not that it's much . . ."

They both laughed.

Raven rode shotgun in Jude's truck. They were on their way to his parents' house. It'd been a great week so far. Besides killing her exams, she'd spent one evening apologizing to Bridget while they chatted on their phone screens. If only Raven could say the same about the Matawapits.

"Are they okay?" What if her family had destroyed the love between Mr. and Mrs. M?

"They're fine, or so Dad says." Jude's hand rested on the steering wheel.

"Your mom didn't seem quite herself at the birthday party."

"There's a lot going on, I'll admit. But they've been married for forty years. They'll work it out."

"Is it about my mom?"

"I think it's about everything." He turned the truck onto Sucker Road. "They know Char and I are trying to . . ." He huffed out a breath. "I'm just gonna come out and say it. You know before we split, she wanted the kids for the summer."

Raven nodded.

"I said no." He drummed his fingers. "I told her I'd be more than willing to let them visit a few times, besides on holidays and during the last weekend of the month. She works from eight to four-thirty, so I'm going with the kids. I'll watch them during the day and then she can come get them."

"Oh . . ."

"Don't worry." He took her hand. "I'm sure as hell not staying under Stephen's roof."

They both laughed.

"They're gonna pay for my hotel room. I'm considering a week in July and a week in August. Or . . . maybe a week and a half. I can't do two weeks. No way. I got stuff to do here. And I need a life of my own."

"That sounds fair. A week."

"I think so. They're moving to Thunder Bay within a year. Next summer . . ." He shook his head and let out a low whistle. "I don't want to think that far ahead."

"It's cool. It is." Yes, she'd miss Jude terribly if he left for a week, but she must accept he had children who came first. "Thank you."

"For what?" He pulled up at the house.

"For considering me."

His cherry lips spread into a big grin. "I always consider you. You and my kids."

"I know. It's what I love about you. And it's why I was so miserable without you." She leaned in and pecked his mouth.

He rubbed his nose against hers. "Northern kiss?"

"Northern kiss."

"C'mon." He pressed his lips on the back of her hand. "Let's go see Mom and Dad."

"Always such a gentleman." She giggled.

He held her hand as they started for the house.

The deacon opened the door, bright-eyed and smiling.

"C'mon in. It's good to see you two—alone."

"It's nice to be alone." Jude motioned at Raven to enter first.

She scooted inside.

Mrs. M stood in the hallway, green eyes twinkling. "I'm glad . . ." She stepped forward and wrapped her arms around Raven's shoulders.

Raven wasn't expecting a hug, but the smell of Mrs. M's fresh floral fragrance, her delicate hands as gentle as her fine bone structure, and her warm embrace as kind as her spring-grass-colored eyes almost brought forth tears. Why couldn't she have a mom like this?

No, she couldn't keep feeling pity about what she couldn't change, Adam would say. She had people who did care about her, and she'd be grateful for the Matawapits reopening their arms to her again, especially after the way she'd behaved.

"Thank you," she murmured. "I'm sorry I left without an explanation—"

"It's okay." Mrs. M lightly palmed Raven's cheeks. "Let's eat. I know Norman wants to talk to you after."

"Sure."

Raven followed the Matawapits to the dining room. Her wallet sang in approval over not having to buy another supper from the diner. She sat and glanced around. "Where'd Jude go?"

"Outside. He said he had to get something from his truck." The deacon sat at the head of the table.

"Oh, okay." Raven plucked her napkin from its spot and laid it over her lap

Jude returned carrying a wrapped gift with a big bow on top.

For a moment, Raven's heart stopped cold.

"Happy belated birthday, sweetie." Jude briefly kissed her cheek and set the gift on the table.

"I . . . uh . . . oh, wow."

"Go on and open it. Dinner can wait for a moment." Mrs. M set the platter of meat on the table.

Raven peeled back the wrapping paper to a big box with a picture of a laptop on the front. "Oh my God." Her eyes almost jumped from their sockets. She gaped at Jude. "Seriously?"

"Yeah. Everyone needs one." He folded his arms on the table, grinning.

"Very nice." The deacon pursed his lips, nodding.

"Thank you." Raven was about ready to burst.

"We can look at it later." Jude lifted the present from the table. "Okay?"

"Sure."

For the first time since they'd broken up, supper went down smoothly, even though Raven was anticipating checking out her new laptop. It was more than having her own computer. The gift came from Jude because he knew she needed one but couldn't afford one.

When Mrs. M began clearing the dishes, Raven stood to help.

"Do you have a moment then?" The deacon also rose. "I thought maybe we could take our teas outside. Jude can help Maria."

"Sure." Clayton's accusing words from last night rumbled through Raven's brain.

There wasn't a breeze outside. Only warm air. Not even the water lapped at the rocks. Just chirps from the birds, but no buzzing from the bugs.

The deacon lit a cigarette while Raven sucked on the vape.

"I understand your anger. I do." The deacon blew smoke from his mouth.

"I'm not angry anymore."

"I know." He frowned. "But you had every right to be. I

hurt your mother terribly. I never knew about what happened to her."

"Nobody knew. Only Clayton, Fawn, Wren, and Lark."

"Now she's battling cancer . . ."

"We . . ." Raven scratched her bare knee. "We learn in the recovery program life happens. Some of us get the worst hand dealt, but we have to decide how we're going to react to the horrible experiences. Nobody leaves this world without scars."

"No, nobody does."

"Am I angry about what my dad did? Yeah. I'm pissed. He not only hurt Mom, he hurt me." Raven rubbed her bare arms where gooseflesh had surfaced. "He hurt us all. My brother and sisters had to listen to . . . they were kids. Helpless."

"We were all helpless, and your generation is living with what happened to us."

Raven shivered. Maybe Dad had experienced something horrible in the residential school, which was why he'd behaved so cruelly.

"But we must look ahead. As much as the past hurts, we can't live in it. I know I can't live in it. If I kept living in it, it would have destroyed me." The deacon took another drag off the cigarette. "I'm proud of the progress you've made. Very proud. Kicking drugs isn't easy. And you did it without . . . well, your family didn't give you much support except for Clayton."

Raven's stomach tightened. "I know he's going to go after Jude to hurt you."

"I expected as much. He's your mother's son. And he's reacting as any son would."

"He is? Then what does that make me?"

"It makes you reasonable and understanding. You know nobody's to blame. Unfortunately, your brother can't see this. Neither can your sisters. And I don't fault them for it."

"I'm trying not to either, but it's hard. Really hard. They made me choose. And when I chose them, none of them were there for me. They . . . they didn't care that I was alone. They didn't even come around, except for Clayton."

"I'm sorry."

"Don't be." Raven squared her shoulders. "I made the right decision. If they want to hate me for it, I can't stop them. I can't make people like me. I can't make people believe me. I can't make people change their opinion about me. I can only accept it and move on. It's not easy. Not when my own brother's going to try to cut the throat of the man I . . . your son."

"If this is what Clayton must do, then it's what he must do. We can't stop him. We can only pray and have faith it'll work out for the best."

Raven's cell phone buzzed. "Sorry."

"It's okay. Take the call."

"It's a text." Holy hell, Clayton was actually messaging her.

Mom's test results came back. They didn't get all the cancer. Happy now?

CHAPTER TWENTY-SIX: BRING ON THE RAIN

Jude sipped more coffee. The education committee sat around the boardroom table, one yawning, another doodling on his package, and another rubbing her eyes. They were on the sixth agenda item. Clayton was present, having received approval from the chair, Kirsten, if he could address the committee about a concern he had, which was the last item.

When they finished up an hour later, Jude sat back, bracing himself for Clayton's attack. Once Raven's brother had stated his piece, Jude would let Raven know what had happened, since she was watching the kids during his meeting.

Clayton moved from the chair he'd occupied against the wall and joined them at the table. He folded his hands, his dark, slit-like eyes on Jude.

"I have a concern."

"What would that be?" Kirsten asked.

The other four committee members sat straighter, staring at Clayton, one half-smirking.

"About people in positions that impact those who aren't."

Kirsten's brows tweaked. "Can you be more specific?"

Jude gripped his pen.

"I'm talking about power and control." Clayton assessed everyone at the table. "My sister for example."

"Which sister?" Kirsten's voice remained even.

"Raven. She aced her math exam."

"That's wonderful." This came from Nancy, one of the committee members. "She's worked really hard to turn her life around."

"Yes, she did." Clayton tapped on the table. "I was there in Winnipeg when she called me, asking for help. My sister's the kind of woman who requires help from others. She's never been strong enough to handle anything on her own."

Before Jude could spit out the angry words in his throat, he swallowed them.

"I understand how policy works. We're a small community. Only two thousand band members. Much bigger than most of the reserves in our Treaty Area, but two thousand isn't a lot of people." Clayton cleared his throat. "Anyway, as I said, my sister's always seeking help from others. Whether it's me, the Matawapit family, others in the community."

"And . . ." Kirsten's lips straightened into a grim line.

"I know our principal was tutoring her for the exam, which I feel is a conflict of interest, even though our policy doesn't pertain to adult students and employees of the school."

"May I speak?" Jude raised his pen that he continued to strangle.

Kirsten nodded. "Go ahead."

"I've been an educator since I was twenty-three, after I earned my teaching degree and license. I've worked with many students over the years, and not all are made for classroom learning."

"Are you saying my sister's stupid?" Clayton rose half out of his chair.

"No. I'm not." Jude motioned at Clayton to sit. "Your sister's highly intelligent."

"Oh . . ." Clayton dropped back in the chair.

"However, she requires different teaching methods to help her learn. She explained to me the first time we met in the adult education classroom that math is not an area where she excels. Different teachers tried to help her but failed. I simply used a different method to teach her, and, well, she passed, didn't she? She earned her grade. That's all I'll say on this. Her file is confidential." Jude sat back and tugged at his shirt.

"Mmm-hmm, kept failing math, and then you showed up, and she started passing." Clayton's lips tilted at the corners. He glanced around at the committee members. "This is my concern about people in certain positions of power and other people in those of . . . lesser power."

"What are you insinuating exactly?" Oh, Jude knew exactly what Clayton's game was.

"She told me she was having a hard time studying. Then you . . . offered to help her study. Now she passed."

"My offer of assistance extends to all my students enrolled in the adult education classes. And I didn't supervise or grade the exams. I didn't supervise or grade any of Raven's exams, either."

The education committees' heads kept moving back and forth like watching a ball at a tennis match.

"But you saw the math exam, didn't you?" Clayton leaned in closer.

"No, I did not. Why would I?"

"So . . . we're supposed to believe you?"

Jude's internal temperature rose a few degrees. "Yes. If you think I'd lie, think again. I take my job seriously."

"Clayton, maybe you could get straight to the point," Kirsten suggested.

"Okay. I will. I believe this man seduced my sister by promising to give her good grades if she slept with him. She was having a tough time in math before this. Now she magically passed. I think he's using his position to receive sexual favors."

Jude sucked in his cheeks. "If this is how you feel, a formal letter should be forwarded to the committee, stating your complaint. This is not the time or place to address your accusation."

"It's a meeting, isn't it?" Clayton asked politely.

"Yes, a meeting, but you never stated on the agenda what your concern was, and now you expect the committee to address it. We have a policy in place. If you, as a band member, have a complaint, you send a formal letter to the chair, who will decide how to address your concern."

"I was allowed to sit here and speak on my issue, wasn't I?"

Jude looked to Kirsten.

A wrinkle appeared between her eyebrows. "I suggest you put your grievance in writing to the education committee. We can address your concern once we readjourn at the end of August."

"No. I want it addressed now." Clayton banged his finger on the table. "We're not some bureaucratic government who keeps adjourning everything and tying it up with red tape. We're *Anishinaabeg*."

Kirsten's face reddened. "Clayton—"

"I'll take this matter to band council, and they'll settle it." Clayton stood. "They have the final say."

Jude pushed aside his meeting package. The education committee had played right into the weasel's hands. "There's a process we follow. Band council knows they must first hear a report from the committee."

"And if the committee fails to address the grievance in a timely manner, it goes to band council. Don't you dare tell me how our reserve functions, not after I've lived here my whole life and you only showed up . . . four months ago." Spit almost flew from Clayton's mouth.

"I'm not telling you how our reserve functions. I'm telling you what's in the policy manual. And I have a right to speak as much as you do. I've been a band member of this reserve since I was born." Heat shot through Jude's veins.

"Then why didn't you ever live here? Why not work at the school after you received your degree?"

"I don't need to answer because your question doesn't pertain to your grievance. I'm not going to get into personal—"

"But part of this is personal, isn't it? You used my sister for your own personal gain." Again, Clayton banged his finger on the table.

"That's your opinion, not mine. To reiterate, there is a process the education committee follows."

The education director, Larry, gray hair coiled into two braids, sighed. "Jude . . ." He lifted his hand. "Let the committee do their job." He looked to the members of the committee. "Kirsten?"

Kirsten's gaze darted back and forth. "Jude, as principal of the school . . . Larry, as director of education, your roles are to serve as technical advisors to us and provide reports on the administration of the school and the reserve's education system. We have the final say in this matter. Jenny's band council portfolio is education, and she's here to provide counsel.

"I believe we'll adjourn until next week. This way Clayton can prepare his grievance according to policy and we can address it as a committee." She glanced around the table. "All in favor?"

Jude tossed aside his pen and flopped back in the chair.

Everyone on the committee raised their hands.

"Motion passed."

****

" . . . so that was the committee's decision." Jude sat at the kitchen table, kneading his temples.

"I'm sorry." Raven curled her fingers into a fist. She stood. After spending a wonderful evening with the children cooking popcorn and watching a movie, she'd looked forward to telling Jude how much she'd enjoyed herself, going through his cupboards like she lived here, getting the kids ready for their baths, washing Rebekah's hair and then sending them off to bed. She'd even kissed Rebekah goodnight, who'd insisted.

"You've been nothing but professional." There was one way to handle this. "I'm going to write a letter refuting Clayton's grievance."

"You don't have to go up against your brother—"

"Nope. If this is what I gotta do, then I'll do it." She brushed her fingers through his hair. "He's trying to get you fired. I won't let him."

He held her hand. "You've been through enough already—"

"No. I want to do this. He said I'm helpless, I'm always going around begging others for assistance. What kind of crap is that?" The nerve of her brother.

"I'm sorry," he muttered. His lips brushed the back of her hand. "The last thing I want is another battle between your family and mine. I know how tough it is on you—"

"Forget it." Raven's chest burned. "He's got no right. None. This is outright slander, because he knows damned well his accusations are lies. And I'm gonna call him out. I'm gonna tell the committee the truth—he asked me to fail the exam. Now I know what his original plan was. He wanted to accuse you of failing me because I broke up with you."

Jude squeezed her fingers, gazing up at her through gentle eyes. "Then that's what we'll do."

Shivers galloped down Raven's spine. *We* was the most beautiful word in the English language. The special word coming from Jude's lips enveloped Raven in white cotton. She leaned down and kissed him.

"I'm just sorry you're dragged into this again," he

murmured. "They didn't get all of your mother's cancer, and this is what he does during a crisis when she needs him."

Raven snorted. "She wants this to happen."

"Wants?" Jude squinted.

"Yes. Wants. She doesn't care if Clayton's by her side. She wants him to go after you to hurt your dad. She wants to see your dad suffer before she . . ."

Dies.

Her blood ceased flowing for a moment. "She's gonna go like Annie did . . ."

"Darryl's aunt?"

"Yes." Annie Keejik had died hating and resenting, bitter until the end.

Raven nestled on Jude's lap. At least she wouldn't die a woman full of hate and anger.

Raven was heading for the kitchen to put in another order she'd taken from her morning regulars when the bell above the door tinkled. She glanced over her shoulder at Clayton strolling into the diner. Something darkened in her stomach. She huffed to the kitchen and slapped the order on the board.

"Here."

Cookie took the order.

She marched back into the main area where Clayton sat at the counter, having the gall to show his face after what he'd said about her at the education committee meeting.

"Coffee." Her words were colder than the restaurant's deep freezer.

Clayton clasped his fingers together. "I know he told you. I want you to hear me out."

"What? Like you heard me out?" So what if she'd growled her answer? "After what you said about me?" She leaned in. "You're lying. Outright lying. That is not the traditional way."

His black eyes narrowed. "I'm not lying. I know what he's up to."

She flipped over his mug with a bang. "You're lying, and you know it."

"Like hell I am." His lips crooked. "He's a Matawapit. Do you really think after marrying his pretty little white woman he's gonna marry a redskin? Seriously? A woman from the bush? Quit kidding yourself. I know what he's about."

The insult slapped Raven across the face. "Oh. I see." She doused his mug with coffee that leaked over the rim and seeped onto the counter. "You're saying a good man can't love a woman like me. A former skank, hey? A girl from the bush? A girl who can haul a deer out of the woods after taking it down to feed my family? Or go out on the trapline and gather rabbits for stew and trim for my crafts? Is that what you're saying?"

"Yes." His stare was harder than his stony eyes.

"You're wrong. Dead wrong. And I'm not letting you plant any doubts in my mind. I know what I am to him."

She slammed the pot back on the coffee machine burner and faced her brother, arms folded. "You might think I'm helpless. But you didn't undertake twelve steps to become sober. You didn't sit every Tuesday and Thursday night in a classroom to earn your high school credits. You didn't show up at the diner at quarter to seven from Tuesday to Saturday to put in an eight-hour shift. I did."

She thrust her finger at her chest. "I'm also starting my crafting business. Jude bought me a laptop, and I used it to create an account at World Crafting where I'm selling my—"

"There you go," he said flatly. "Someone again helping you out."

"In the recovery program, we learn to ask for help so we can stand independently on our own two feet. I'm not afraid to ask for help. It takes a big person to hold out their hand and ask for someone to take it. And it takes an even bigger person to take what's offered and make good use of it, something everyone can benefit from, not only me.

"Do you see me still going after the diner? Nope. If it happens, it happens. If it doesn't, then it doesn't. I'm grateful I have a job when jobs are scarce around here. I'm grateful I have a roof over my head, thanks to the Matawapits.

"Most of all, I'm happy. Really happy. I learned happiness comes from what you can give, not from what you can get . . . or take from others, or by hurting others. Can you say you're sincerely and truly happy?"

A scowl seeped across Clayton's face.

"Mom's sick. The cancer is aggressive. She might not make it. Do you want her leaving this world knowing what you did? That you hurt someone else, all for revenge?"

"I don't need to listen to this." He shoved the mug aside.

"Maybe you don't want to listen because what I'm saying is true," she fired out.

Clayton stood and stormed for the door. When he left, the door banged shut, and the bell overhead tinkled faster than it usually did.

Chapter Twenty-seven: When You Gonna Satisfy Me?

Raven pushed the food around on her plate. How could Jude shovel back pork chops with the meeting happening at seven? She glanced at Rebekah, who was watching her dad. Noah dug into his pork and potatoes, but his vegetables remained untouched.

"Veggies." Jude pointed at Noah's dish.

"Aww, Dad . . ."

"Eat." Another helping of potatoes went into Jude's mouth. He glanced at her. "Eat yours, too, or no . . . *dessert.*" Teasing lingered on his words.

The gloom and doom sitting over Raven's head like a thundercloud drifted away. He was right. They were eating as a blended family. Her third dinner like this — the four of them at the house. No parents. No brother. No brother-in-law. And there was the promise of her kind of *dessert.*

"You never told me yes or no yet," Noah reminded his dad.

The kids, with school done, had adopted a stray dog just out of puppyhood. They'd been sneaking the hungry little furball food, and Jude had caught them today because he was officially done with work and home full-time.

"I told you we're going to be spending more time in Kenora than usual." Jude wiped his mouth, gazing at his son.

"But Rav — I mean Miss Kabatay, sorry, will be here to watch him." Noah pasted on an angelic smile to match his halo.

"I don't mind." Raven forked a bite of pork chop. "If a dog makes them happy, why not let them have one?"

"See? See? She doesn't mind." Noah gleamed. Little horns seemed to sprout on his head—the master manipulator had used her to cajole his dad into saying yes.

Raven didn't mind. Being a part of the conversation and helping Jude decide, well, this meant she was a part of the family now. Or was she? She chewed on the pork chop, not swallowing the piece.

Jude pierced another bite of pork. His lips tugged at the corners. "We'll discuss it. Okay? Because there are rules you'll have to follow."

"Oh . . ." Noah drew in a big breath. "Here we go."

"I'm serious." Warning lingered on Jude's reply.

"I know. I know." With a devilish smile, Noah scooped up a big helping of brussels sprouts and munched away, grinning at his dad.

"If it means you'll eat your veggies every night, I might consider saying yes." Jude waggled his brows at Raven. His grin seemed to say *I've played this game before and I always win.*

Biting down on her lip so she wouldn't laugh, Raven glanced at Rebekah. "You're quiet."

Rebekah lowered her head but couldn't hide her cute dimpled smile.

Kids. So, Noah had told Rebekah to let him do the talking as the true mastermind, and Rebekah was letting Noah handle their request because she wanted the puppy, too.

"I'll eat them every night. I promise." Noah's declaration was begging. His dark eyes, the same almond shape as Jude's, filled with pleading.

Jude snickered. "I want that in writing."

"I'll . . . I'll write it down." Noah pushed back his chair.

"Sit."

"Please, Dad? Please?" Noah plopped on the cushion.

"You realize how much work dogs are, don't you? Uncle Emery spends a lot of time caring for his zoo. Feeding. Walks."

"I'll walk him. Please, Dad. Please."

Jude clasped his fingers together, elbows resting on the table. His gorgeous dark eyes shifted from his son to Raven. "You don't mind watching the dog?"

"Not at all. I always wanted a dog, but Mom would never let any in the house."

"Our mom won't either." Noah frowned. "She says animals are messy."

To say animals were gifts from Creator might be disrespectful to Charlene's viewpoint. Raven kept her opinion to herself. "Well, it's the three of you living here."

"Yeah. Can we then, Dad?"

"Oh, please, Daddy." Rebekah's sweet begging could have given a bowl of sugar a toothache.

"Okay. We'll get the dog."

"Yes!" Noah jumped from his chair. "He's outside. I'll go get him!"

Rebekah also scrambled from her chair.

"Sit."

Mouths almost sagging to the floor, the kids sat.

"I have a very important meeting tonight. A very important one. Miss Kabatay is accompanying me. Grandma will be here pretty quick, and you know she's allergic to animals. It's why I never had a pet. You have to wait until I get home."

"But we'll be in bed by then," Noah whined.

"True, you will, but there might be someone to wake up to in the morning."

Gosh, Raven could have sat here and watched Jude parent his kids all night. He was firm but understanding. Tough, yet empathetic to his kids' desires.

"I'd better get the dishes done. The meeting starts soon, and I still have to freshen up." Raven wiped her mouth.

While the kids ran outside to play, Raven and Jude washed the dishes and cleaned the kitchen. They both freshened up for the meeting. Mrs. M arrived at twenty minutes to seven. They chatted for a bit and then left the house to walk to the education building. Jude carried his briefcase.

"You okay?" He glanced at her.

Gravel crunched beneath Raven's clogs. As they approached the section of the school where the education administration was located, her heartbeat accelerated.

"You okay?" Jude asked again.

"I'm pumping myself up. I never thought I'd go up against my brother."

"Don't be scared." He reached over and took her hand.

A truck rumbled by. People sat outside on their steps. Kids played on the road. Birds chirped in the trees.

"I'm not scared. What I'm . . . I never thought he'd do this."

"You mean go up against you?"

"Lie." Raven huffed out a breath. "I can't believe he'd lie. Oh, he says he's not, that he believes you're using me for sex, but I know deep down he doesn't believe himself."

Jude snorted. "Unfortunately, beautiful, your brother, well, he's not the fairest person around the reserve."

"I always thought he was fair. I believed his heart was in the right place. But this . . ." Raven shook her head as they walked up the path to the two doors.

Jude removed a golden key from his neck strap to unlock the door.

They entered the building. The windows were closed, and fans were running, which kept the heat out and the hallway cool. He opened the door to the meeting room. Raven scooted inside.

The sound of the door banging open, then closing, carried

to the room. Flip-flops squeaked against the floor. Sonya, the secretary, appeared.

"I'm not late, am I?" she asked. "I'll get the coffee started."

"Nope. It's only ten to seven." Jude checked his phone.

Raven sat so she wouldn't be in the way while Jude and Sonya set out spiral-bound packages, pens, pencils, a recorder for taking minutes, and paper for the committee members to write on.

She'd never seen Jude prepare for a meeting before. He didn't bring his laptop, but he had set out notes to refer to, and a couple of bound manuals.

The door opened then banged closed again. Jenny, Larry, and Kirsten entered. They pulled out chairs at the table. A few moments later, the rest of the committee arrived.

Clayton stood in the doorway. His eyes widened at Raven.

Raven folded her arms and stared back. Had he seriously not expected her to attend after what he'd said?

The elder was the last to arrive. He always said a prayer before the meeting began and was also on hand for spiritual guidance, since one of the mandates of the Education Committee was to nurture learning traditionally.

During the prayer, Raven snuck a peek. Everyone kept their heads bowed. Clayton sat beside the elder, hands bracing the edge of the table and knuckles white. Her thumping heartbeat slowed.

When the prayer finished, Kristen opened her meeting package and assessed the committee members. "We only have one agenda item tonight. You'll find the letter inside. We'll take five minutes to review Clayton's complaint."

There was no meeting package or letter for Raven to read, so she sipped her coffee while waiting on the committee.

The elder's heavy breathing through his nose and papers shuffling were the only sounds present. Sage burning in the abalone bowl soothed the knots in Raven's shoulders, and so did the scent of tobacco from the elder's pipe.

"Sooo . . . you're saying you think the principal is requesting a certain kind of favor for passing grades, huh?" The question came from David, an older man who'd always been involved in education.

"I sure do." Clayton sat straight, but his white-knuckled hands remained on the table. "My sister's in recovery. Vulnerable. She's trying to prove herself by earning her grade twelve."

Raven's ribs seemed to tighten around her heart. "May I speak?"

Kirsten nodded.

"Whatever's in that letter, since I wasn't supplied with a copy, is false. Jude has never ever asked me to have sex with him for better grades."

"Just remember something . . ." Clayton waggled his finger. "You haven't been in a real relationship before, so you don't know how one functions—"

"Okay, the conversation stops here." Kirsten tapped her meeting package. "Raven refuted your complaint. Besides Jude, she's also being accused of something she denies. Unless you have actual proof, I think this discussion's over." She slammed her meeting package shut.

"That's it?" A fire crackled in Clayton's eyes. He came half out of his chair. "I didn't get a chance to speak."

"There's nothing to speak about. You accused Jude of propositioning an adult female student for sexual relations and in return he'd give her a passing grade. If anyone should be bringing forth a complaint, it's the one being taken advantage of, but she has no problem with her grades, or Jude's teaching methods and classroom behavior."

"Welp, y'know, I gotta say Kirsten brought up a good point." David gently closed his meeting package. "There's nothing to discuss. You did your job as the male of the family, and your sister says she's fine. Unless she has a complaint of her own, which she doesn't, there's nothing to yap about."

"I'm going to take this matter to band council." Clayton banged the table.

"You go on ahead and do it. Thing is, you got no proof." David smacked his lips. "Band council also promised to never go over our heads after we make decisions, y'know? They're only s'posed to get involved if we can't resolve something as a committee. Got it? Don'tcha be throwing your weight around here, eh."

"Throwing my weight around?" Clayton's blank-eyed stare was a display of his shock.

"You heard me," David continued in his true northern accent. "Whatcha gonna do next? Have another protest? Quit kicking your sixteenth hornet's nest."

"I expected some professionalism here—"

"We're being professional." David grimaced. "You're the one who storms off to pout and then start protests when you don't get your way."

Clayton stood, shaking his head at the committee members. Then he directed his glare at Raven. "This is what you want? Your mother's fighting for her life, and you—"

"I think she's more than aware of what's happening to her mother," Jude said, quietly, but authority lurked in his words.

"You let her down. You really let her down." Using his hip, Clayton shoved the chair against the table, which sent a bang through the boardroom. He whipped on his heel and huffed from the room.

The committee members glanced around at each other.

A loud boom echoed in the hallway from the door slamming shut.

"Do you guys think he'll have another protest?" David asked with a straight face.

They walked back to the house, sun still high, children playing on the road, a truck rumbling by.

Jude reached over and entwined their fingers. "You okay?"

Raven's thumb stroked his. "Quit asking that. I'm fine. Really."

"You sure? I know if Emery was sitting across the table from me, accusing someone I love of false, inappropriate behavior, I wouldn't be happy. I'd be pretty upset."

"Maybe I've gotten used to being kicked around by my family." Raven shrugged. "Honestly, as much as I wish this wasn't happening, it is, and there's nothing I can do about it. I can't force them to share my beliefs. The recovery program teaches me to accept what I can't change. And I can't change the minds of other people."

If only she could. "I don't like fighting with them. I really don't. It hurts me. But I can't let what they're doing ruin my day. Or my life. I almost let them when we . . . when we broke up." She grasped his hand tighter. "Wanna know something?"

"Sure."

Two kids pedaled by them, laughing.

Raven kicked at a few pebbles. "I can handle my family hating me. I can handle them not wanting me around. Yeah, it sucks. But what hurt the most was . . . well, when we weren't together."

"Hey . . ." He spoke softly.

She glanced up.

"You weren't the only one hurting big-time." Within his dark eyes was how much he'd also suffered.

"Is that why you didn't return my birthday present?"

Jude's other hand wrapped the strap of his briefcase. He let go and held his thumb and index finger a smidgen apart. "I came this close, I was so pissed . . ."

A smile tugged at her lips, and he flashed his dimples.

"I'm glad you didn't."

"So am I. Maybe deep down I had some faith."

"Faith?"

"That we'd work it out. We've come this far, haven't we? Most normal couples get to start off in a honeymoon stage. Dating. Flowers. All that stuff. Us? We got thrown into a family feud with lines drawn down the middle. And we made it. What does that say?"

"It says I wanna be with you." Oh, fuck the blushes and hesitation. That wasn't her style.

She stopped.

He also stopped.

Still holding his hand, she faced him. "I made the best decision, ever. No regrets."

"I don't want you to have any regrets." His hand slipped from hers. He brushed her face, his palm warm. "I love you. I want you to be happy."

"I'm happy with you . . . you and the kids." Her voice crackled, but not from sadness, but from the glow filling her chest.

"I love you." His declaration was a deep whisper.

"I love you, too, Jude."

His mouth came down on Raven's, and she was greeted with a sweet, loving kiss, tender enough to melt her knees.

"Look, they're kissing. Hahaha."

Raven couldn't help the smile, and Jude's lips stretched into a wide grin. They glanced at the two kids running by.

"It's the principal. Mr. Matawapit. He's kissing Raven Kabatay."

"Perhaps we'd better get going," Jude murmured, his palm still brushing her face.

"I think so."

He draped his arm over her shoulder and steered them down the road. She leaned her head on his shoulder, hugging his slim waist.

Kids played on the road, calling out a hello to their principal. Pride filled Raven's heart.

Too soon, their walk in the warm air came to an end. They ambled up the driveway. Mrs. M sat outside on the back steps, reading a book.

"Kids inside?" Jude called out.

"Yes." Mrs. M shut her book. "Becky's in the tub. She talked to her mother already. It's Noah's turn while she's bathing. He's on the laptop."

After kissing Jude goodbye, Raven joined Mrs. M in the truck, and they headed back to the house. During the drive, Jude's mom didn't ask how the meeting had gone, and Raven didn't offer up any information. Jude could tell her. Her own sticky skin needed a bath.

When they reached the house, Raven ran some water in the tub and soaked for a good twenty minutes. Once she was dressed, she joined the Matawapits in the living room to work on her crafts. She had another order to make, a customer in Italy requesting moccasins for her husband.

A truck rumbling up the driveway filled her with curiosity. Maybe the visitor was Emery. Three doors slammed shut.

The deacon stood, peering out the living room window. His mouth formed into a grave frown.

"Who is it?" Mrs. M asked.

"Clayton, Wren, and Lark."

Ice captured Raven's heart. She tossed aside her work.

The deacon actually hurried for the front door.

"I want a word with you." Clayton's hissing order carried into the living room.

Chapter Twenty-eight: Can't Keep a Good Man Down

On shaky knees, Raven stood. How could her brother do this to her? To come to the Matawapits' very own home to cause trouble? Her vantage point offered a view of Clayton shoving his way inside.

Raven dashed into the hall.

Steam almost swirled from Clayton's ears. "You think after what you did to my mom, you can go on with your life? Keep living your happily ever after? Brainwash my sister? I'm going to make you take some responsibility. If she dies, you got blood on your hands, because you killed her—killed her when you cheated on her, abused her, and tossed her aside for a white woman."

From behind Raven, Mrs. M gasped.

The deacon set his hands on his hips. "I never invited you into my house."

"Nope, you'd never do something like that. The only Indians you want around are the ones who buy into your religion, like my sister did." Clayton shoved his chin at Raven.

"Your sister didn't buy into anything," the deacon said calmly. "She has her beliefs and my son has his."

"Yeah, your son." The spittle of words flew from Clayton's mouth. "I'm not finished with him. We don't need apples teaching our kids. We had to put up with you as principal, but not your son."

"My son earned the position fairly. He has the credentials."

"He does not." Clayton banged his fist into his palm. "He's an apple. He's got no idea about traditionalism."

"And neither do you," the deacon replied simply.

"And you're no deacon." Foam almost dripped from Clayton's mouth. He was a rabid dog, ready to attack. "You're a goddamn drunk who cheated on the woman you declared to love. Cheated on my mom with Darryl's aunt, and every other drunken *squaw* you thought to use and abuse and then refuse. Am I right? That's how you thought of them, hey? Drunken squaws instead of *Anishinaabe-kweg*."

The deacon's broad shoulders stiffened.

When Raven tried to edge around him, the deacon held out his arm, stopping her.

"I never meant your mother any harm. And I tried to apologize to her during my discernment for the permanent diaconate, but she refused my phone call. I tried again through a letter. She never answered."

"Oh, wow, that's really trying, isn't it?" Mocking saturated Clayton's sarcastic words. He hurled his blazing glower at Mrs. M. "That's the kind of man you wanted to marry, hey? A man who cheated on his partner. A man who used other women for sex. Fucking anything with a vagina in Thunder Bay."

"That's enough." Harshness filled the deacon's order.

"If you don't leave, I'm calling the police." A mixture of pain and anger lingered on Mrs. M's threat.

"Call the cops?" Bitterness tinged Clayton's half-laugh. "Yeah, go ahead and call the cops. That's what white people do best. Get your government to toss us into residential schools and strip us of our language, our families, and our culture. Sign a useless Treaty with us, and then throw us out of our homes after you find something of value on our land and relocate us to swamps and bedrock. Haul us from our homeland and force us to live in the Arctic so you can claim the land as part of Canada. Scoop our children during the six-ties because we're supposedly horrible parents. Flood our land for your greedy hydro but leave us living in the dark with no food or heat. You go right ahead and call the damned cops!"

"Enough!" The deacon raised his hands.

"I'm not stopping. I won't ever stop." Clayton thrust his finger at the deacon's chest.

Raven's heart went cold.

Mrs. M let out a strangled cry.

"And you got no right asking me to stop. Why should I stop? You never stopped."

"Never stopped what?" The deacon had lowered his voice but kept his hands raised.

"Never stopped torturing my mother. Where the hell do you get off coming back here to preach about a religion that almost wiped us out, and bring your damned white woman? Huh?" Again, Clayton thrust his finger at the deacon's chest.

When he stepped in closer, almost a breath away from the deacon's face, Raven again tried to get around the deacon, but for the second time he held out his arm, stopping her.

Footsteps scampered off.

"The bishop requested I return here. I was only following his orders," the deacon murmured, as if trying to understand.

"Yeah. Like the apple you are—"

"Clayton, can you say you are happy being this level of an-gry?"

"And what if all I have is my anger? Is the government and church going to tell me to stop feeling this way, too? Are they going to tell me I'm a bad person because I'm piss fucking mad? Huh?"

"Nobody's going to tell you what you're feeling is wrong or tell you to stop feeling the way you feel. But can you tell me you're truly happy?" The deacon's voice remained quiet.

"Happy? After what you did to my mother? Y'know what'll make me happy?" Clayton hissed straight into the deacon's face. "When you and your family get the hell off this reserve and take your damned church with you. That's when I'll be happy. It was bad enough putting up with you, your white woman, and your half-breed son. But now the other one's here. What's next? Your half-breed daughter?"

"Part of traditionalism is accepting Creator's will —"

"This wasn't the will of Creator." Clayton made a swopping gesture with this hand. "No Creator would condone what the white man did to us. Ever."

"No, He isn't happy about what was, and still is, done to us. However, He gave us free will. We can make choices. To follow His path or another. Which path are you choosing?"

"I'm walking the red road, and walking the red road means fighting to take back what's rightfully ours."

"We can't move the entire non-Indigenous population back to where they immigrated from. That's impossible. Isn't it? And there are many who're born here."

"But that doesn't mean they belong here. They're simply the sons and daughters of invaders, nothing else."

"And I said it's impossible to send everyone back to where their ancestors originated from. You know this. I know this. So where does this leave us?"

Clayton fisted his hands. "I already said we gotta fight —"

Whistling sirens carried into the house.

A sneer full of hate contorted Clayton's face. "I see your white wife called the cops. Typical. Fine. We're leaving." He almost shouted. "Remember something, *white woman*, remember what your husband did to my mom. Now she's sick. And he doesn't give a damn what happens to her. Keep on believing you're married to a great man of the cloth. But he's really the Devil in disguise."

Clayton turned on his heel and snapped his fingers. "Let's

go. Seems the deacon's white woman is afraid of the savage Indians. She called in the cavalry just like her ancestors did."

Wren and Lark cast Raven vicious sneers and then followed their brother down the stairs.

The deacon closed the door.

****

Jude stormed up the stairs to the church. Christ preached turning the other cheek, but after what his parents had endured at their home last night, he was ready to tear off to Clayton's house and rip the piece of shit in half. Thank God the children were at the recreation center for activity day so they couldn't witness his hatred.

Emery's quiet footsteps followed behind. "Try to stay calm . . ."

"Calm?" Jude whipped around on the third to last step leading to the entrance of the church. Heat scorched his skin. "After what he said to Dad? After he made Mom cry? After he hurt Raven?"

"Raven's fine. Dad said she went to work."

"Fine my ass." Jude growled his words. "My mother, *our* mother, is in there upset." He pointed at the door. "Y'know, sometimes a man has to go to war."

"And how's a battle going to resolve this?" Emery folded his arms. A light breeze ruffled his wavy black hair. "Are you going to retaliate with anger as Clayton did, as he's always doing? Or are you going to have faith and listen to the Lord?"

"Oh, save it." Jude snorted and whipped on his heel. "I don't wanna hear your preaching."

"Maybe you should listen to me for once." Emery's voice remained calm. "We're about to attend church. Yes, it's weekday Mass and there'll be no homily, but listen carefully to the Gospel. The Lord's always speaking, constantly speaking to us, if we're willing to listen."

For crying out loud, his brother was the next coming of Jesus. Talk about the disposition of a saint. Jude huffed into the church. He dipped his fingers into the shell of holy water and signed the cross.

With Emery behind him, Jude trounced down the aisle to their usual spot. He genuflected and flipped down the kneeler to, well, try to pray. Prayer always worked for his brother. But Emery had studied for the priesthood. He possessed a direct line to God.

Jude bowed his head and clasped his fingers together. Emery was a man of peace. Christ had also been a man of peace. The only way to stop this damned feud that had been going on ever since Darryl had first instigated the trouble two summers ago was to attain resolution between the two families, but how was that possible if the Kabatays wouldn't give an inch?

Fine, Jude would start by praying for Arlene Kabatay, the woman responsible for this mess. Her cancer was back, aggressive and relentless.

God, I'm willing to listen. The man tried to get me fired. He invaded my parents' home last night and made my mother cry. What the heck am I supposed to do?

Something warmed Jude's heart. As if a little voice was saying *trust me.*

Wasn't failing to trust why he'd never gotten past the orientation for the permanent diaconate? He must learn how to trust God. Do what Raven was doing in her recovery program—leave everything in a higher power's hands.

Basil Skunk, the elder Darryl always consulted, forever spoke about living right, living in the day, and letting Creator take care of the problem.

Jude shifted on the kneeler. Maybe this was what he was supposed to do as his last bit of growth after he'd come so far ever since his arrival in Ottertail Lake back in February—let go and let God.

Jude sat out on the screened-in deck sipping coffee after Mass. "What did the cops say?"

"I told you, twice already, Clayton didn't utter threats. There's nothing they can do, however, even if he did, I wouldn't bring charges on him. A seat on band council is all he has, and I won't take that from him." Dad lit a cigarette.

"He doesn't deserve a seat." Jude tapped his foot on the floor.

"The people feel he does, otherwise they wouldn't have voted for him," Dad replied frankly.

The sliding door opened. Emery stepped outside.

Jude glanced up. "How's Mom?"

"She said she's going to lie down and take a nap." Emery sat in the chair beside Jude.

Nap? Mom never napped after Mass. She preferred to doze off for a half an hour after lunch while going through her Catholic Women's Association information.

"Dad, we gotta do something."

"Let it be." Dad's heavy sigh was as strong as the weight that probably sat on his shoulders.

"It's not your fault."

"I realize this." Dad took a drag off the cigarette. "However, Arlene has the right to feel the way she does. I can't tell her what she can feel. Nobody can."

"So everyone has to suffer, especially her daughter, because she can't let go of the past?"

Dad frowned. "Please. Let it be. You must learn sometimes you have to leave it in the hands of the Lord."

"And what about Mom?" Jude pointed at the house. "Why should she suffer?"

"She's not suffering. She's upset, yes, but trying her best to accept what happened last night. It shook her up."

"Of course it did. She thought Clayton was going to start a brawl—in her very own house. Are we going to wait around and see what he does next? Is that what choice we have left?" Jude used his hands to scrub at his face.

He was doing it again—controlling, solving, demanding, after a half an hour ago he'd learned he was supposed to have faith.

****

Raven made another fresh pot of coffee. What had happened at the Matawapits' last night was the talk of the diner, everyone chattering under their breaths while stealing glances at her.

The bell above the door tinkled. She swiveled. A hard ball formed in her stomach.

Lark and Wren flounced to the counter.

Raven let go of the coffee pot and stood in front of them, shoulders back and spine straight.

"When are you gonna let this go?" Lark whispered.

Wren folded her arms.

"Let what go?" They had a lot of nerve coming here after what they'd done.

"The Matawapits' son. Their family." Lark leaned in, elbows grazing the stainless-steel top. "Fawn texted me this morning. She is piss, piss mad."

Raven skimmed her nails on the counter's edge. "Why can't everyone accept I'm seeing him? Why's that so hard?"

"You know how Mom feels about this. Lookit what his dad did to her." Lark kept speaking quietly, stealing peeks at the patrons who had stopped talking and avidly watched. "He really hurt Mom. She came home because of him. She married Dad because of him."

"Nobody forced Mom to marry anyone."

"He didn't?" Lark clamped her lips together. "What choice did Mom have? She couldn't stay in Thunder Bay. A man she trusted and loved was hurting her. Drinking. Cheating. Being a total jerk. Where else did she have to go?"

Not this conversation again. Raven grabbed a dishrag and scrubbed at a small spot on the counter. "I've been over this a hundred times. You don't think I thought good and hard before getting back together with Jude?"

"And you don't care about how Mom feels?" Lark's gaze searched Raven's.

"I got my own life to live." Frustration seeped across Raven's chest. "I can't keep living my life for Mom."

"You've only been back here for three years." Lark's dark eyes widened.

"And before I left, I had to live with her . . ." Raven swiped at another spot on the counter. "You guys didn't see what she was like around me. Because of what happened, she hates me."

"She doesn't hate you." Lark gasped.

Wren also nodded, but she'd always followed Fawn's and Lark's lead.

"She does." Raven rested her hand on the counter. Her gaze bobbed about. "I'm a reminder . . . a reminder of what Dad did. Maybe I don't blame her?" She shrugged. "Who wants a baby they were forced to have?"

"That's not true."

"You guys weren't even living at home when I was growing up. You weren't there to see what Mom put me through. Nothing I did was good enough. I was in the way. I did everything wrong. I was a pain in the ass. That's all I heard from her. I couldn't take it anymore. I couldn't. I wanted to live my own life, and I did. She left me no choice but to split for the 'Peg."

"She seemed fine after you moved back."

"Fine?" Raven scoffed. "Nothing changed. It was the same bullshit after I moved back. When I broke up with Jude, why do you think I stayed at the motel? There wasn't a chance I was bunking at Mom's again. I woulda rather slept outside."

The bell overhead tinkled. Raven peered around her sisters. They gasped.

"What's going on?" Clayton slowly walked up to them, a swagger to his hips.

The diner got even quieter, if that was possible. A few customers grinned.

"We . . . uh . . . we thought we'd try to talk to her. See if we could change her mind." Lark trembled.

"There's nothing to discuss. She made her choice." Clayton raised his finger at Raven. "If anything happens to Mom, you're not welcome, so don't bother coming around."

Chapter Twenty-nine: Turn the Light Off

Raven walked down the road. The children's dog, Twinkles, pranced up ahead, sniffing at the grass in the ditches. Jude and the kids were in Kenora and wouldn't return until Friday's four o' clock flight. She had two more days to herself. Even though it was the second to last week of August, the days were still warm.

Any news she heard about Mom's health came from people at the diner, because her family refused to speak to her. There'd been a community fundraiser held during July to help pay travel medical expenses. Raven had passed on the big dinner. So had the Matawapits. But the rest of the reserve had gone. Lots of money had been made.

From what she'd heard, the chemo and radiation weren't working. The cancer was too aggressive.

Charlene was still stalling on the annulment. Jude had told Raven he was going to talk to his ex-wife about why she couldn't decide. If Charlene didn't file, Jude said he would.

Raven massaged her throbbing temples. The only wonderful thing about this summer was the time spent with Jude and the kids when they weren't in Kenora, and watching Jude's house while they were away. It was wonderful to climb into the queen-sized bed, Twinkles by her side, and fall asleep in a place she hoped to live someday.

Her craft business was growing, and she spent her evenings curled on the couch at Jude's every evening, processing orders while he watched the sports channel. Cozy. Quiet after the kids had gone to bed. Then she'd take his truck back to the Matawapits'. She'd drive it to work, then Jude would stop by to get his vehicle in the morning. After work, she'd head over to his house.

Next year, if she had more time, they should consider following the powwow trail. She could set up a booth to sell her crafts and make more money.

Jude had helped her build a website for the crafting business. Thanks to math, she was handling the financial side of it.

The dream of having the diner had vanished. Making crafts and selling them full-time was her new goal. Jude supported her. Each time he went to Kenora, he came back with more material she'd requested.

Her only wish left was to somehow put a stop to this ridiculous feud.

A truck chugged down the road and stopped. Roy Morrison rested his arm on the driver's-side door. His baseball cap was on backward. He flashed his yellow teeth and a few gaps.

"How ya doing, kiddo?"

"Great. What about you?" Raven removed the e-cigarette from her shorts pocket and settled her hand on the truck.

"Not too shabby. Just seeing how you're doing. The news about your mom must be bothering you."

"What news?" Dread coiled around Raven's skin.

"The doctors said they can't do any more for her." Roy's crow's-feet-littered eyes squinted.

"Wh-what?" Raven tightened her grip on the truck. Yes, she knew this was coming with how aggressive the cancer was, but hearing Roy confirm it, the doctors confirm it, the little girl inside her that had prayed and begged Creator to magically cure Mom—the magnitude of the reality was a huge weight crashing down on Raven, crushing her.

"Geez, I thought your brother or one of your sisters woulda told you. I'm really sorry to be the bearer of bad news." Regret reflected in Roy's gaze. "Really sorry."

"I . . . I . . ."

"C'mon, sweetie. Get in. This ain't no time to be alone. I'll take you to the Matawapits'."

"I . . . I have Jude's truck. I . . . I get them from the airport when they're in Kenora."

"Nope. Get in."

"I have to get Twinkles."

"Sure. Bring him."

Raven called out to the dog, who bounded over to the beat-up truck. The children's beloved pet could play outside like he always did because of Mrs. M's allergies.

When they got in, the scent of oil saturated Raven's nostrils. Twinkles sat in the middle, panting and glancing around, ears perked. She petted the dog's fur. Running her fingers through silk eased away the tension pulsating at her lower back.

As Roy drove, she kept petting Twinkles, but her heart wouldn't stop racing. "Did . . . did you hear anything else? Is she still in the city? Is she coming home?"

"I dunno. But I'll phone around and find out once we get to Norman's. Sound good?"

"Sure."

****

Jude palmed the ice-cold beer bottle. The hotel lounge was a perfect spot to talk on a Wednesday night, because only two people were present, seated over by the pool table. Charlene had ordered a gin and tonic.

"Thanks for sticking around. I'll get to the point," he said.

"Sure." Charlene lifted the drink and sipped.

"I won't keep you long. I know you wanna get back to Stephen." Jude's gut failed to blacken, nor did his neck pinch. The first couple of times he'd come to Kenora, his insides had burned ugly. Now, he simply wanted to get home to Raven. "When are you going to start the annulment proceedings?"

Charlene glanced toward the bar, clicking her nails on her glass.

Perhaps getting straight to the point had been the wrong idea. Well, his days of taking her feelings into consideration were done. That was Stephen's job. "When are you — ?"

"Can you give me a minute?" Her demand was as tight as the annoyed line of her mouth.

"Sure." Jude sat back and sipped his beer. The upcoming golf tournament he'd watch tomorrow evening was broadcasting the pro-am on the lounge TV screen. Yesterday, he'd picked his players for fantasy golf, since he liked going up against Emery to see who chose the winning golfers.

Jude called up the notes section on his cell phone and reviewed his list again. Emery had already texted his picks.

"Do you even care?"

"Hmm?" He glanced up.

"Nothing's changed." Charlene motioned at the phone. "I thought you were making progress, but you're back to being you."

"You asked me to give you a minute. I thought I'd use the time to double-check my fantasy picks." He set down the phone and picked up his beer.

"Whatever . . ." She flickered her hand.

Annoyance filtered through Jude's veins. "Look, in the past, I would've nudged you to speak right away. I was simply giving you some space to think."

"I bet you don't treat *her* this way," Charlene mumbled.

"Excuse me?" Jude sat straight and set down the beer bottle.

"You heard me." Charlene still spoke under her breath.

"Look . . ." He raised his finger. "I thought we ironed out our differences for the sake of our children. You don't see me taking jabs at Stephen, do you?"

"No, you wouldn't," she said dryly. "When have you ever cared enough?"

"Cared enough?" Jude swallowed down the sputter ready to burst from his lips. Aww, what was the use? "If that's what you want to think, go ahead. No matter what I say, you won't believe me anyway."

His cell phone dinged. He read the text. Although the kids were at Charlene and Stephen's house, they might need him.

I'm sorry to bug you. Bad news. It's confirmed. There's nothing more they can do for Mom.

His hand flew to his temple. He furiously typed . . .

I'll be out on tomorrow morning's flight. I'll tell Charlene we're leaving early.

You don't have to leave. I only wanted to let you know.

No. I'm coming home. I'm talking to Charlene right now. I'll call you when I get back to my room.

Okay.

Love you.

Love you, too.

He glanced up at his frowning ex-wife. "That was Raven."

"It figures. We can't even have a conversation without—"

"There's nothing more they can do for her mother. Mrs.

Kabatay's dying."

"And I suppose she wants you to cut the kids' visit short." The glare behind Charlene's eyes almost smacked him.

"No, she doesn't. I told her we're coming home. She told me to stay. If you want to get upset, get upset with me."

"I see . . . having drinks together . . . it was nothing more than talking about the annulment, wasn't it?" Charlene stood.

"What else would it be about?" Jude remained seated. "You have your life and I have mine. You have someone you love, and so do I."

The look Charlene cast him, he might as well have thrust a knife into her heart.

"You . . . you love her?" The rage had died in Charlene's eyes, and pain flooded her irises.

"Yes. You know she's been over at the house lots. You know she's been spending time with the kids. I wouldn't even consider bringing her over the way I have been if I wasn't serious about her."

"We're not even divorced a full year and already —"

"Excuse me?" Jude rapidly blinked. "You ran off with another man when I confronted you about the affair. I think that's some nerve, lady."

"Don't you *lady* me." Charlene's mouth twisted into a malicious snarl.

"Then if you don't want me to *lady* you, don't you patronize me. I spent over a year alone, by myself, after our split during our obligatory year of separation." *Unlike you.* "I didn't even consider seeing anyone after the way it ended between us."

"Oh, I see, and she magically appeared and fixed your heart." Charlene snatched her purse.

"Yes, she did. And don't be dragging Raven into our conversations anymore. She has nothing to do with what we can't resolve. Now are you or aren't you filing for the annulment?"

"Why? So you can get your dad to marry the two of you, like he married us?" Charlene's teeth gnashed together.

"Maybe I'm considering it." A bucket of ice seemed to race down Jude's back. Wasn't this why he was bringing Raven around more often? Wasn't this why he'd left her at his house while in Kenora instead of having Mom check on the place? Wasn't this why Raven was babysitting Twinkles? He was building a new life—a new life with her and the kids.

But he shouldn't be shocked. From the moment he'd laid eyes on Raven sashaying into his classroom like a vamp from an old-school movie, she'd laid out the trap like she did to snare rabbits. And she'd snared him good. Snared him willingly.

This was why they fought hard to overcome the hurdles placed in front of them that no brand-spanking-new couple should endure. And this was why they never gave up. They wanted this. He did. And Raven did.

"Your silence says everything." Charlene turned.

"What about the annulment?" Jude called out to her retreating figure.

"To hell with the annulment. You want an annulment, go file it yourself."

"I will."

She slapped at the swinging doors and stormed from the lounge.

Jude dashed from the plane, having left the kids with Charlene for the weekend to keep her bristling mouth shut. Now wasn't the time to deal with her aggravation.

Raven stood at the window. Her curled shoulders straightened, and she hurried for the door.

"Oh, geez," he murmured while sweeping her into his arms. "I'm so sorry, so sorry you had to face this alone."

"It's okay." She buried her face into his shoulder. "Your

mom . . . mom and dad were with me."

He kept his hand on her back while she remained glued to him, refusing to lift her face.

While he got his baggage, she continued to keep her face nuzzled in his shoulder, her arm around his waist. He struggled to use his free hand to lift the handle of his rolling suitcase, secure his laptop case, and carry-on bag. Thank God one of the attendants had grabbed his golf clubs.

"I'll get everything, Jude," Wayne said, one of the attendants. "Just get her to the truck."

"Thanks, man. I really appreciate it."

Jude urged Raven through the main doorway and to the truck with Wayne following. While Jude settled Raven in, Wayne loaded the luggage into the truck box. Jude insisted on tipping Wayne, who grudgingly accepted the offering but grinned because he probably needed the money.

As they drove off, Jude held Raven's hand. "We'll be home soon."

"Home?" Her voice cracked. She peered at him.

"Yeah . . . home."

He kept squeezing her fingers. A few minutes later, he pulled into the driveway. Twinkles waited on the steps, thumping his tail. He bounded for the truck.

"He missed you and the kids." Raven got out.

"Why don't you keep him occupied while I unload the truck."

"I'll unload it. He wants to see you." Raven shuffled to the back of the vehicle.

"Are you sure?"

"Yeah, I'm sure."

"Okay. I'll make you something to eat. Are you up to eating?"

"No." She blinked, wetting her lips.

How could he have forgotten when she was upset this way,

she wanted him inside her instead of hand holding, cuddles, or comforting?

"You can help me shower. Sound like a good idea?"

"Yeah," she whispered.

A few minutes later after they'd unpacked everything, he ran the shower while Raven stepped out of her shorts and tank top. For some reason guilt niggled at the back of Jude's neck over being turned on—and fully erect—during such a crisis. But Raven had trained him to react this way if she needed him, and this was how she needed him.

He let her get into the shower first. It'd been over a week since he'd last taken in her bare heart-shaped ass, small waist, her shoulder blades moving beneath her dark, smooth skin. The water from the showerhead soaked her hair and streamed down the cleft of her spine. He stepped in behind her to water swirling around his feet.

She turned, holding the loofah she'd lathered up. Her gaze drank in his body, feathering his calves, his thighs, and then rested on his cock. Suds dropped from the loofah to the bottom of the tub. She worked the mesh sponge into his crotch, the material scratching lightly at his skin.

Having his balls and cock washed eased away the tension rippling along his lower back after sitting in an airplane. His head lolled to the side, and he drew in a big deep breath that expelled as a contented sigh. She was the one hurting, yet thought to attend him. He stroked her wet hair. Beads of water streamed down her face, snaking to her lips and then creating a path to her neck. Her nipples glistened with moisture.

He lathered up the bar of soap while she kept massaging his groin. Using the loofah, she stroked his cock from the base to the tip. He clenched his teeth and groaned. She was teasing his erection with her languid jerks, the slippery suds and her tight grip as hot and wet as her pussy when he was deep inside her.

Steam twirled around him. Moisture gathered at his temples and hairline.

With his hand fully soaped, he set aside the bar. He cupped her pussy. A hiss seeped from between her clenched teeth, and she spread her legs. He parted her slit to folds of flesh hidden beneath her cunt lips. His fingertips met her engorged clit, hard and almost humming under his touch. He fingered her opening. All he had to do was thrust and he'd be inside her.

Raven dropped the loofah. Her fingers clamped around his cock. When her thumb rolled over the sensitive area at the tip, he jerked from the luscious sensations building in his crotch. She never shut her eyes while he slid his finger back and forth between her slit. A fire built in her pupils. Her tongue snaked out. She licked at the droplets of water around her mouth. What an invitation she presented to him.

He leaned in, tasting the water she attempted to lick away, and captured her tongue with his. She opened her mouth, and he feasted on her wet flesh.

Her jerks and the groans she rained on him taunted his cock and balls. A fever erupted beneath his skin, his body aching to be in her cunt, tasting her slippery pussy he kept fingering.

He broke the kiss. Through sleepy lids, she gazed at him.

"Turn around," he whispered.

They were under the stream of water. Her hands braced the wall. He palmed her gyrating hips, legs still spread and ass lifted to him. His cock feathered her crack. Her skin was smoother than silk, an invitation to fuck.

He worked his hand around her tiny waist and eased his fingers between her cunt lips. When the tips brushed her clit, she groaned and raised her ass higher. He massaged her folds of flesh and eased his cock into her opening. She was so ripe and ready he didn't have to push to get inside her. His prick slipped all the way in, to a taste of tight delight.

He didn't start slowly. He fucked her deep and quick while fingering her clit. Not only did he want to get off, he wanted her to come in the same rhythm as his fucking.

They were one. She was his. And he was hers.

CHAPTER THIRTY: SAVE A LITTLE ROOM IN YOUR HEART FOR ME

Jude pecked the top of Raven's head. They'd passed on dinner, choosing instead to while away the evening in bed. The last of the tension had left his stiff muscles after spending a week in Kenora.

Her head rested on his chest, her breaths dusting his nipple. "I can't let it end this way . . ."

He traced her slim arm. "Your mom?"

"Yep."

"Is she coming home?"

"Roy isn't sure, but he's going to keep me in the loop." She traced circles on his belly. "Or I could go into T Bay."

"That's an option. Whatever you do, I'm here for you." He kept rubbing her arm.

"Thanks."

"I know Bridget or Adam will get you at the airport. And they'll let you bunk in the spare room."

"I thought Gracie was in the spare room now? When I last video chatted with Git, she talked about finally setting up the nursery."

"No. She's still in the bassinet in their bedroom," Jude replied.

"Adam's not using any of the parental leave. He wants her to stay home. He says she works hard enough, and he wants her to concentrate on Gracie. It was awesome having them up here for a week."

Bridget, Kyle, and Grace had flown up the second to last week of July, since Noah and Rebekah had been around. They'd wanted to stay a couple more days, but Bridget had left after seven because Adam had remained in Thunder Bay for work.

"It sure was." This was what the Lord had wanted—for Jude to be unable to fix something. Only Mrs. Kabatay could make the change that was needed to end the hatred her children had for his family. And embrace Raven as a part of his family now.

"There's only one person who can help me," Raven murmured.

Maybe Jude was supposed to help. "Oh?"

"Your dad."

****

On Sunday evening, Raven shut the front door to the Matawapits' house. The children had returned from Kenora, and she'd left Jude and the kids at home so she could speak to the deacon and his wife alone. Thank goodness Jude had understood Raven's need for privacy. This was going to be a tough request, and she required Mrs. M's approval before propositioning the deacon.

"I wasn't expecting you. I thought you'd stay and have dinner." Mrs. M poked her head into the hallway from the kitchen.

"I thought I'd get my laundry done." Raven carried her soiled clothes in a brown bag.

"Sure." Mrs. M motioned at the small room housing the hot water tank.

"Do you have time for a coffee?" A little late for a cup of joe, but they should have something to drink while they talked.

"Tea?"

"Tea sounds great. Let me get this stuff sorted and in the wash. I'll meet you on the deck."

"Wonderful."

Once Raven had started the wash, she joined Mrs. M outside to a beautiful evening on the lake with birds chirping and a loon calling. From a spruce tree, a squirrel eyed them, chattering.

"Is everything okay?"

"Not really." Raven wet her lips and removed her vape.

"I'm so sorry about your mother." Mrs. M reached over and patted Raven's knee.

"That's what I wanted to talk to you about." Raven reached for the cup and sipped. "I . . . I . . . this is hard to ask." She puffed on the vape. "My family's hurt you enough."

Mrs. M's green eyes warmed. "I'm fine. There's nothing to feel bad about."

"Well, I do, because what I have to ask . . ." Raven fidgeted. "It's why I wanted to talk to you first. And I'm totally cool if you say no. I mean, I'll totally understand."

"Hmm . . ." Mrs. M tilted her head, peering. "What is it?"

"I . . . I . . . I want your husband to accompany me to Thunder Bay to visit my mom."

The shock in Mrs. M's eyes wasn't a surprise. Naturally, she hadn't expected such a question. Her delicate fingers tightened around the teacup. "You believe if Norman speaks to your mother, she might . . . might speak to you?"

"It's more than speaking to me. Or having her blessing." Raven scooted forward. "It's about my family and your family. I know yours doesn't have a problem. It's mine. I . . . if Mom . . . if Mom actually hears me out, maybe she'll . . . she'll tell Clayton and Fawn to let it go."

Mrs. M nodded. Her focus drifted to the lake.

Raven sipped her tea and puffed on the vape. "Look . . .

you don't have to answer me right away—"

"Please. Give me a moment. Okay?"

"Sure."

The sound of front door opening and closing carried to the deck. The deacon had been outside in the garden, weeding when Raven had arrived. His heavy footsteps sounded down the hall. A cupboard door opened and closed. He whistled away, the song making the squirrel chatter and stand on its hind legs.

"Maria?"

Mrs. M jumped. "On the deck."

"Is Jude here? I didn't see him pull up."

"It's Raven. Jude's at home."

The sliding door opened. The deacon held a teacup and a cookie. "I thought you'd be at the house with the kids. You haven't seen them for a week."

"I . . . I needed to talk to Mrs. M." Hopefully Raven's forced smiled reached her eyes.

"Oh?" The deacon shuffled to the door. "I'll leave you two—"

"Please. Stay." Mrs. M patted the cushioned wicker chair beside her. "Raven asked me something, and I was about to answer."

The deacon nodded and sat, but curiosity filled his intense stare.

"She asked if you'd accompany her to Thunder Bay to see her mother. I was about to tell her yes." A smidgen of hesitation filled Mrs. M's reply that was a lullaby capable of easing Raven off to sleep.

"Thunder Bay?" The deacon set the teacup on the wicker table with the glass top.

"I . . . I thought it'd help. Help my mom and I . . . well, see if she'd finally . . . at least try . . . something."

The deacon fingered his chin. "You know there's a good

chance she won't see me."

"Yeah. But she's in a hospital bed. It's not like she can walk away."

"Raven . . ." The deacon leaned forward, elbows on his knees. "I understand how rough this has been for you. Your mother's sick, and the two of you are estranged. I also more than understand why you called it off with Jude in May. And I don't blame you. You're stuck between a rock and a hard place. Your family or my son. Your mother tries. She does. However . . ."

"She was never happy, ever, was she?"

"No." The deacon's voice was hushed. "At the school, she was very unhappy. The nuns weren't kind to her. I think it was because your mother was popular. The boys liked her very much. And the nuns felt she was . . . ah, your mother never asked for attention. Being very attractive, she had a tough time making friends. The girls were jealous of her."

Raven's heart sank. Mom had never told her this. From the start, she'd been lonely, the same kind of loneliness Raven had experienced. Shunned by other women, and too many men to pick from.

"I get it. I guess that's why my sisters are tight. They never had a circle of friends, from what I can remember."

"The women of your family are extremely attractive." The deacon patted Mrs. M's hand. "Your mother . . . I was her only friend. So what happened between us as kids . . . it's taken root in your mother. It's so deep, I don't think she's capable of letting go of the past. In her eyes, I was the only person she had, and I let her down."

"It sure didn't help what my dad did to her." Raven's chest burned, and so did her throat.

"No woman should have to endure that. No woman on this earth." The deacon shook his head. "However, you're innocent in this. An innocent soul who shouldn't have suffered because of what happened. But it's hard for your mother to comprehend and accept after what she'd already experienced. She was simply looking for someone to love her. Remember, we couldn't go home during the summer or Christmas. A plane in those days was considered a luxury.

"I'm concerned, though, about how seeing me will impact your mother's already poor health. My intention isn't to put her life in jeopardy."

"You know what Mom's like. Seeing you or me isn't going to bother her physically. She's a great screamer. She'll tell us to get out."

"Ah . . . true." He patted Mrs. M's hand again and then squeezed her fingers. "It wouldn't hurt to try. I'm sure you'd like to see your grandchildren again, hmm?"

"Bridget still has the double bed in the spare room. I'm sure she'd want us to visit." Mrs. M glanced at Raven. "When did you want to go?"

"I know Sundays are out of the question. You're needed here at the church. Maybe we could leave next Monday? I could switch shifts, work the Sunday so I can have Tuesday off. I planned on coming back the next day."

"Then that's what we'll do," the deacon said.

The deacon drove Bridget's truck. They'd arrived in Thunder Bay over an hour ago, leaving Mrs. M at the house with Bridget, Kyle, and Grace. Adam was at work.

They were on Oliver Road, heading for the hospital.

The week had gone by fast. With school starting quickly, Jude had returned to work, so Emery was watching the kids.

Raven's heart never stopped thundering the closer they got to the hospital. When the deacon turned into one of the many parking lots, her breathing increased. As they walked to the main entrance, she snuck drags from her vape. Finally, they were inside the massive hall where people roamed everywhere.

Too soon they were up on the ward where Mom was staying. During their trek, they'd failed to meet any of Raven's family. The deacon motioned at Raven to follow him. They passed rooms until they reached the one the attendant at the main desk had given them.

The deacon's heels clicked against the floor. He stopped at the second curtained-off area. Raven tugged at the fringes on her purse. He pushed aside the curtain.

Mom lay on her side, her bony form barely filling out the blankets. Her bald head rested against the pillow.

When her sallow dark eyes flickered at the deacon, the irises brightened for a second and her chafed lips spread into a warm smile. It was the first true tender, happy look Raven had seen Mom give anyone, the exception being her grandchildren and great-grandchild.

Then Mom blinked. Her lips parted. She struggled to sit up.

"No. Keep resting," the deacon said, his suggestion a hush. He pulled up a chair.

Raven remained by the curtain, gripping the edge of the fabric.

"You need your rest."

"Are . . . are we almost there?" Mom managed to croak out.

"Yes, almost there, Arlene." Silk coated the deacon's words.

"I thought . . . thought we'd never get to Thunder Bay." Mom's lids started to close.

Raven's heart almost jumped to her throat. She was in the past, witnessing her mother as a seventeen-year-old girl leaving a brutal school full of brutal, strict, religious people with the one person who could save Mom from a tragic fate set by the Canadian government.

"Norman . . ." Mom's bony hand slid out from beneath the

covers. "Norman . . . please don't let go."

Grief flooded the deacon's rich, dark eyes. He curled his strong fingers around Mom's gnarled, skinny hand.

"I . . . I don't want her to beat me again." Tears rolled from Mom's eyes and seeped across her sunken face. "Not my fault. Not my fault," she murmured. "I'm not bad. I'm not a whore."

"No, you're not, Arlene. You're a good woman." Using his free hand, the deacon petted Mom's head, stroking her back and forth.

"She . . . she . . . they . . ." Mom shivered. She curled into a tiny ball, still trying to grasp at the deacon. "They're ugly. So ugly. I hate them. I don't want you to see them."

"I've seen them, Arlene. I've seen them, touched them, kissed them. They're a part of you as they're a part of me." He kept stroking her head and kneading her gnarled knuckles.

The lump in Raven's throat grew. Scars. The nuns had lashed Mom. Had beaten her for daring to fall in love and sneak off with a boy. She covered her mouth, stifling her gasp.

"I wanna go home." The tears kept streaming down Mom's face.

"You'll be home soon enough."

"I . . . I . . ."

Footsteps stormed across the floor. The curtain was yanked back.

Raven jumped and whipped on her heel.

"What's going on?" Clayton hissed. His angry glare fired from Raven to the deacon. "You." He thrust his finger. "Get away from her. Get away from her. Now!"

"Clayton . . ." The deacon stood slowly, hands raised.

"Norman . . ." Mom's voice rattled. "Norman . . . where are you?"

"Get away from her!" Clayton bellowed. "Get away from her! This is all your fault. Your goddamned fault."

Raven pressed against the wall. The woman in the other bed screamed for help.

Fawn, Lark, and Wren scampered into the room.

"What're you doing here? How could you do this to her?" Fawn strode straight up to Raven, hate flaming behind her dark eyes.

"You don't understand." Raven inched toward the window.

Fawn bore down, fingers curled, nostrils flared. "This is all your fault. Get out of here. Now."

Clayton kept yelling at the deacon, Fawn kept screaming, the woman in the other bed bellowed for the nurse again.

Through the animosity and rage permeating the room, Raven's gaze locked on to Mom's, who stared back, recognition flaring in her sleepy eyes that widened to saucers. She struggled to sit up.

"Help me," Mom shrieked at Clayton. She clung to the bed bar, trying to pull herself to a sitting position.

"Lie down. Mom, please lie down. I'm getting them out of here. Get the hell out of here!"

"Mom?" Raven's breathing rattled. "Mom, is this really how you want to go? Like Annie did?"

"What the hell?" Clayton spun around on his heel, snarling. "How can you say that about Annie? Where do you get off? She was a true traditionalist."

"I'm talking about how she drank herself to death from the hate and misery sitting in her heart," Raven pleaded. "Do you want Mom to go the same way? Hating? Mad? Resentful?"

The nurse tore into the room. "What's going on? Security," she called out.

"No . . ." Raven shook her head sadly. "You don't have to call security."

"They snuck in here." Clayton thrust his finger at Raven and the deacon. "They snuck in here and upset her. My mother's dying, and they came in here to torment her."

"I'm asking you to leave." The nurse stared coldly at Raven and then the deacon.

"We're leaving. If he'd just let me move around him." The deacon was trapped between the chair, the table stand, and the bed, with Clayton in front of him, almost chest to chest.

A blue uniformed guard appeared. "How can I help?"

"Please escort these two from the hospital. They're not supposed to be in here," the nurse said. "Mr. Kabatay specifically said family only."

"Let's go." The guard curled his finger into a *come here* motion.

As Raven inched around Fawn, her sister nastily bumped Raven's hip. An ache inside Raven clawed to bump her sister right back, but she maintained her composure and moved around her family and the guard.

The deacon's footsteps followed.

The guard led them out of the room and down the ward while speaking on his walkie-talkie.

They were escorted from the hospital, left standing at the main entrance outside.

Raven hugged herself and bowed her head.

CHAPTER THIRTY-ONE: THERE WILL NEVER BE ANOTHER YOU

Jude stoked the woodstove. The October nights were cool, but the days still carrying warmth. Attempting to build a fire that wasn't too hot but warm enough to heat the house was a trying task. If he didn't get this right, he'd have to call Emery, because there wasn't a chance he'd endure the get-naked heat like he had in the spring while trying to get a correct temperature in a slightly chilled house not icy enough for a roaring fire.

"Did you need any help?" Raven sidled up behind him, holding a mug of hot chocolate.

Help. It was what the Lord had asked of Jude since his divorce. Fine, he'd suck it up. "Yeah. Show me how to get this fire right. In May, I almost roasted us alive."

Raven giggled. "What kind of wood are you using?"

"Poplar."

"You should be good then. What's your fire like?"

"What do you mean, what is it like? It's a fire."

"I know, but that's a lot of wood you have. You don't need to burn so much. And it's all in the fan placements, too."

Jude sighed and held up the lighter. "Okay. You're in charge."

"Silly man." She pecked the top of his head. "You showed me how to conquer analytic geometry. I'll show you how to conquer fire."

She had a good point. His one knee rested on the floor. He

set his hand on his thigh. "Okay, teacher. Teach away."

Raven knelt in front of the woodstove and crushed up the newspaper. "The key is burning only a couple of logs. Let them almost get down to ash. Then place one small log in. You don't want to build up the fire too much as you maintain it."

"You're such a bush girl." He nuzzled her cheek.

"Aren't you lucky, hmm?"

His cell phone buzzed. "Gimme a sec." He meandered to the kitchen table and read the text.

Roy called. He said Arlene's calling out for me. I'm going to Thunder Bay. It's best Raven comes, too. I don't think Arlene's going to last another day.

For a moment, Jude's pulse stopped beating. Raven continued to build the fire at the woodstove. The kids and Twinkles were out in the yard. He texted back.

Book me a flight, too. I'm going with her.

Okay. We'll handle everything. It's best we stay at the hotel next to the hospital.

Perfect. Bye.

Jude clutched the phone and rubbed the back of its smooth edge against his forehead.

The glimmer in Raven's eyes died. She dumped the wood into the stove. "Wh-what's going on?"

"That was Dad . . . ." Jude swallowed. He straightened tall and strode over to her, stuffing the phone into his pocket. "He said you're accompanying him to Thunder Bay."

"It's Mom, isn't it?" Raven asked shakily.

Jude nodded. He wouldn't elaborate. Dad could find a way to explain that Mrs. Kabatay hadn't asked for her daughter, but the man who was once her lover, instead.

"C'mon. We'd better get packed. Mom's booking us on the next flight out. Hopefully we can leave early tomorrow."

"Will she make it through the night?" Raven's eyes filled.

"I don't know." He drew her into his arms.

****

They sat in the living room at the Matawapits' house. Raven clutched a tea in one hand and gripped Jude's fingers with the other. The deacon sat in his recliner and Mrs. M in her usual stuffed rocking chair.

"Did Roy say if he'd text again?" Raven asked.

"He's going to keep us informed."

If Raven texted Clayton, she'd probably get no reply—that was if her text got through, because he might have blocked her.

"What did Mom say exactly?"

The deacon sighed. "Remember, she's on heavy painkillers because their goal is to keep her as comfortable as possible."

"She's dying now?"

The deacon frowned. "Your brother and sister flew out yesterday, so yes, I believe so."

Only Clayton and Lark had been home for the past two weeks after Mom had returned to Thunder Bay, having come home to celebrate Thanksgiving, probably her last family dinner, and one Raven hadn't been invited to.

From what she'd heard, Fawn had accompanied Mom back to Thunder Bay, while Wren had flown back a week ago.

Raven squeezed her eyes shut. She tightened her grip on Jude's fingers. Thirty-two years of being unwanted. Thirty-two years of experiencing nothing but snarling words from a woman who'd loathed carrying and birthing her. Thirty-two fucking years, and this was how it'd all end.

"C'mere." Jude drew his arm around her shoulder, pulling Raven against his chest.

The pain seeped up from somewhere deep in her heart. When had she given up trying to coax love from a hateful, vindictive woman? Probably when she'd left for Winnipeg, creating a new life lost in drugs and men.

"No matter . . . no matter what I do, she's still there, poisoning me," Raven croaked out from the lump buried in her throat.

"Hey . . ." Jude's lips brushed at Raven's ear. He nuzzled her face.

Nobody would ever understand what it was like being raised by a mother who didn't want to be a mother to a daughter.

"You're here. We're gonna take care of you. We're your family," he whispered.

"I . . . I . . . I don't know what to feel," Raven gasped through the sob filling her mouth.

"You don't have to figure out what to feel. Just feel."

His soothing words calmed the tornado of emotions whirling through Raven's insides.

"You'll stay with me tonight. You'll stay at the house with me."

"Stay . . . at your house?" The tears became a flood breaking through the dam.

She hadn't expected Jude to take her to his place with the kids there. And at the same time, her heart hurt terribly from the confusion over Mom's death.

Part of her grieved for the relationship they'd never had, and the other part wanted to let out a big exhale that the woman wouldn't be able to hurt her anymore.

Jude parked his truck beside Emery's vehicle.

A thick weight pushed down on Raven. She forced her

arms to shove open the passenger door and then forced her legs to swing to the side and sit on the running board. Everything weighed a ton. Her thighs hurt, but she made them move until her feet touched gravel.

She put one foot in front of the other, making her way to the back door where Jude waited.

"Do you need help?"

"I'm fine." Raven set her hand on the railing. "I feel . . . thick. Heavy."

"C'mon." Jude took her arm and led her up the four stairs.

The back door flew open. "Dad! What's going on?"

Emery also appeared. Rebekah stood behind him.

"We'll talk once I get Raven settled," Jude told the kids.

"Is Miss Kabatay okay?" Noah peered.

"Remember how I told you her mother's very sick?" Jude asked.

The kids nodded.

"That's what we'll talk about. I want her to lie down for a bit." Jude led Raven to his bedroom only a couple of footsteps away. He shut the door behind them.

He drew back the duvet but not the sheets. "I'll call you when dinner's ready."

Raven curled up on Jude's pillow since his side was closest to the door.

He drew the duvet over her. "I'll get your duffel bag."

"Thank you." Everyone was so helpful. Before leaving the Matawapits', Mrs. M had packed Raven's stuff for tomorrow.

"Get some sleep." He stroked her arm beneath the duvet.

"I'll try." It was a fight to even keep her heavy eyelids open. She closed them.

What seemed like only minutes later, voices woke Raven. The bedroom was dark.

"Will her mom go to Heaven?" Noah asked.

"There are different places we go. Mrs. Kabatay will go to

the spirit world."

"What's the spirit world?" Rebekah's question was full of inquisitiveness.

"It's where the Ojibway people go when they die." Tiredness dragged on Jude's words.

"Will we go to Heaven or the spirit world, Dad?" This came from Noah.

"We'll go to Heaven, because that's what we believe."

"B-but, b-but what about Uncle Darryl and Uncle Emery?" Fright filled Rebekah's voice. "They won't be together after they die. Uncle Emery is like us. He goes to church. And Uncle Darryl doesn't. He's Ojibway."

"Honey, I don't think there'll be a problem. God and the Creator will make sure your uncles are together. Remember, God and the Creator are the most powerful beings in the universe. They can do anything."

"Will Miss Kabatay to go the spirit world then?" Noah spoke through a mouthful of food.

"Yes."

Raven could almost see Jude folding his hands on the table since he was speaking directly and seriously.

"I think it's time you started calling her Raven. I'd say we should lose the formality, hmm?"

"Really?" Shock peppered Noah's reply.

"Yes, but she must be addressed with respect. I'm letting you do this because she's a very close part of our family now. And she needs us. Her mother's going to the spirit world, and this makes Raven very sad. To help her, she's staying here tonight. Okay?"

"Okay. I can sleep on the couch. She can have my bed." Tender benevolence filled Noah's words, instead of his perennial mischief, cheeky teasing.

Raven's heart almost cried.

"You can sleep in your bed. Raven will stay in my room."

"Like Mr . . .. I mean Stephen does with Mom?"

"Yes."

"Uh . . ."

"It's okay. Remember, I told you I love Raven very much. She's already sleeping. I'm going to bring her some food once we're done. Then I'll let her keep sleeping. We have a big day tomorrow. That means you have to be quiet tonight."

"Dad?"

"Yes?"

"Is she going to be all right?" Concern crept into Noah's voice.

"She'll be fine. That's why she's here. She needs us. She needs me. She needs you. She needs Becky."

"We'll be here for her, Dad." Noah's promise was a puffed-up little boy's chest. "I'll make sure she doesn't cry."

"That's my big guy."

The chill peppering Raven's skin vanished. She was wrapped in warmth. Warmth from finally finding her family, people who loved her for who she was.

"You hungry?"

The concern in Jude's question penetrated Raven's dream, a safe place at her favorite fishing hole, the two of them in the boat while the kids played on the beach with the deacon and Mrs. M watching over them.

She peeled open one eye.

Jude sat on the side of the bed, his hand massaging her hip.

"What time is it?"

"Nine."

"Nine?" She sat up, pushing aside the duvet. "Why didn't you wake me?"

"Considering you never stirred while I was packing, I'd say you needed sleep." He motioned at the suitcase on the floor containing his clothes.

"Are the kids up?"

"No. I just got them off to bed."

Jude stood. Raven followed him out to the kitchen, rubbing the sleep from her eyes.

"Let me wash my face first. I have makeup everywhere."

"Go on ahead. I'll dish you up the food I set aside for you."

Raven padded to the bathroom and washed her face. When she returned to the kitchen, Jude had a plate set on the table. A chicken breast, baked potato, and carrots. She sat.

"What time are we leaving?"

"Mom got us booked for the early flight. The pilot's staying overnight. We'll be heading out at eight."

Now if this wasn't Creator at work, Raven didn't know what was. The odd time the pilots stayed overnight at the motel and flew out early with passengers if they came in on a late flight.

"What time did the plane get in today?"

"Not sure. But I'm guessing it was a late one, since the pilot's here." Jude stood at the sink, readying the coffee for tomorrow morning.

"I have to call Cookie."

"Already taken care of." He added coffee to the reusable filter.

"I can't . . ." She rose and circled the table to where he stood. "Thank you."

"You don't have to thank me. I'm doing this because I love you." He touched her cheek.

His warm palm was silk on her skin. She leaned in, hugging his slim waist. "I know, but I wanna thank you anyway. What you said to the kids before I fell asleep means everything to me."

He kept stroking her cheek. "That's because you mean everything to me."

"You're so sweet. Always offering your big shoulder when

I need you most."

"Maybe I'm making up for lost time." Pain lingered in his eyes. "Before . . . I woulda . . ."

" . . . tried to fix everything?" She couldn't help the smile.

"Yep." He grinned.

She rubbed his nose. "Northern kiss."

He rubbed back. "Northern kiss."

****

Jude unpacked his suitcase and Raven's duffel bag. Mom and Dad were in the next room. They were staying at the hotel only a twenty-minute walk from the hospital for easier access. Roy had mentioned the Kabatays were also staying at the hotel. Although there wasn't a restaurant, the hospital had a huge cafeteria with all kinds of food available, not the gross hospital stuff patients were forced to eat.

To keep the drama to a minimum, he'd order in food or take Mom to a nearby restaurant, steering clear of the hospital, because Bridget had loaned them her truck. She'd wanted them to stay at the house, but Jude had explained this was a crucial time and they must be minutes away.

Raven emerged from the bathroom, having freshened up, jeans melted to her slim hips and a turtleneck hugging her upper body. She'd brushed out her braid, and her thick, black hair hung loose down her back.

"You look great." He cast aside the shirt he was about to hang and drew her into his arms.

She licked at her mouth. Her dark eyes danced about, shifting this way and that way.

"It's gonna be okay," he said softly. "I wish I could be there, but Dad's right. Under the circumstance, it's best only the two of you go."

"We've . . . we've been through so much together already."

Her voice crackled. "Thank you."

"Why're you thanking me? You're always thanking me. Stop it."

"Because I never had anyone care for me this way before. Clayton did, at one time, but this is different. You only met me last February. It's been . . . eight months, and I dragged you through hell."

"Maybe I hung in there because I know a good thing when I see it." He again stroked her hair. "Yeah, most couples get to enjoy a stress-free first year, but fate didn't allow us that. And y'know something? I'm glad we did this together. Doesn't it tell you how bad we want this? Us?"

"Yes, it does. And I've never been happier." She rested her head on his shoulder.

Using small circles, he worked at her lower back where a ball of tightness had knotted her muscles. He kneaded away, hoping he could loosen some of her anxiety.

"I'm happy, too. Having you wake up next to me this morning with the kids there . . . it felt so good. You don't know how good it felt for the four of us to . . . dress together . . . eat together . . . say goodbye to the kids together."

Chapter Thirty-two: One Love

Raven clutched the bottle of water. On their way up to Mom's room, she hadn't seen her brother or sisters, but they were here—somewhere. They'd never leave Mom's side during such a crucial time. Maybe they were in the bright open cafeteria on the lower floor, having something to eat and sipping a coffee.

The deacon also held a bottle of water. He'd passed on his *holy* suit, the black outfit with the collar Raven had seen him wear many times around the reserve after church, or while making special visits to people who were Catholic.

She'd asked him if he'd send off Mom, but he'd shaken his head, telling her even though Mom was a lapsed Catholic, whatever that was, he could not anoint the sick. Only a priest could. But he could pray over her.

Clayton, Fawn, Lark, and Wren had probably arranged for an elder to come up and give Mom a final blessing to the spirit world anyway.

The deacon led the way.

Mom was in a room by herself this time. The curtains were pulled back. She lay on her side, staring instead of sleeping. Her lids flickered, resting on the deacon.

Wisps of black hair covered her head. She was maybe below a hundred pounds now, not good for a woman who stood five foot nine, and Raven shivered at her mother's gaunt, sickly, skeletal frame.

"You . . . you came," Mom croaked out, her voice scratchier than usual. "I dreamt about you."

"Arlene . . ." The deacon pulled up a chair. He gathered Mom's bony hand in his palm, gently rubbing.

This was the second time Raven had witnessed the deacon not asking the perfunctory, *how are you?* Emery was the same way. People always asked, whether to initiate a conversation, relieve awkwardness, or to break the silence. And those two always spoke the person's name during crises.

Mom kept staring at the deacon, and he kept rubbing her hand.

Raven's mouth dried. She uncapped her bottled water. Perhaps she should leave. Maybe they needed a moment alone. Mom was only aware of the deacon's presence.

Just as Raven was about to tiptoe off, the deacon motioned at the other chair at the foot of the bed. Raven inched to it and sat, her bottom barley touching the cushion. Mom still didn't look her way but faced the deacon.

"I . . . I missed you." A muffled sob came from Mom's throat.

The deacon simply stroked her hand.

"I . . . I . . . I can't let it end this way." The words heaved from Mom's mouth.

"What do you mean, Arlene?" Even whispering, the deacon's question remained deep and firm.

"The hate . . . the anger . . . the . . ." Mom sniffled. "I'm dying, Norman. Dying."

He lifted her raggedy hand and pressed his lips against the back, still staring at her with eyes as soothing as cotton balls.

Raven clenched her rolling stomach. This was it, after thirty-two angry years. She covered her mouth to stop her own sob from escaping.

"I . . . I've always loved you, Norman. You . . . you were my first love." Mom's quiet declaration was full of pain. "I always hoped you'd love me back."

"Arlene . . ." The deacon caressed her wisps of hair. "I

asked you twice to forgive me. And I'm asking again. I'm not making excuses for my behavior. You didn't deserve it, no matter what kind of pain I was experiencing at the time. I had no right to take out on you what the residential school did to me."

He sighed while Mom continued to stare at him with a gaze a seventeen-year-old fresh-faced innocent girl would gift on the boy she hoped to marry.

"That's what I did for too long, Arlene. I was making the wrong people pay for what was done to me. My story is about how I hurt others because of the school, not how the school hurt me. It took me some time to realize and accept this. And you — you above everyone else — didn't deserve the hurt and pain I caused you."

"Oh . . . Norman." Weak cries wheezed from her throat.

The deacon cuddled closer to the bed, still stroking Mom's hair as she sobbed into his forearm, since that was as close as he could get to her.

"What am I . . . what am I gonna do, Norman?" Her words trembled. "I can't stop saying your name. I used to hate saying it. Now, when I say it . . . it feels right." Mom quietly wept

"What the hell's going on?" Clayton stormed into the room, flanked by Wren, Fawn, and Lark.

Mom raised her limp hand. "Enough . . ."

"Get out. Now. Or I'm calling security," Clayton snarled.

"You got a lot of nerve coming here again." Fawn stared down hate-filled daggers at the deacon.

"Your mother's speaking," the deacon said quietly.

Clayton scowled and rounded the hospital bed. He bumped Raven's chair in the process. "She's delirious. She has no idea what's —"

"Shut up." Mom tried to yell from her wide-open mouth, but her order came out crackly and hushed.

The color drained from Clayton's face. "Mom, let me —"

"Please . . ." Mom waved her hand. "Leave us."

"Leave?" Clayton sputtered and stumbled backward.

"Yes, leave." Mom sagged back against the pillow. Her hand fumbled across the mattress until she found the deacon's resting on the edge. She clasped his fingers.

Clayton's eyes rounded and then narrowed. He motioned at Fawn, Lark, and Wren to follow as he huffed from the room. Raven remained half in and half out of her chair. When her brother curled his finger at her in the doorway, she rose and followed them.

****

"Are you okay with everything?" Jude flopped in the chair by the window where Mom sat at the round table in the hotel room.

"What do you mean?" Mom had brought her crafting and was working on her knitting. Her quick fingers drew yarn over a needle, and she twisted and turned the needles before starting the process all over again.

There was something soothing about watching Mom knit, the same soothing feeling Jude experienced watching Raven craft. Her legs to the side on the sofa, gaze pinned on what she was doing while glancing at the TV because she enjoyed binging on those *Wives* reality shows. Her current fave was *The Real Wives of Hip-Hops Hunks*.

"Dad being at the hospital. Mrs. Kabatay asking for him."

A tiny smile tugged at Mom's lips. She threaded the yarn over the needle. "Charlene was at Becky's party, wasn't she?"

"Yeah."

"And she'll be at Becky's grade eight graduation, her high school graduation, her wedding, her first baby . . ." Mom glanced up. "Does Raven mind? Even understand?"

"She knows whether I like it or not, Charlene'll be a part of

314

my life because of the kids."

"And you make an effort to be civil to your ex-wife even though she did you wrong, don't you?"

"For the kids' sake, I'm trying."

"It's the same for me. For the sake of her kids, I don't mind your father visiting Arlene during a sad time in their lives."

"Even after all the trouble they caused? And she's to blame."

"Nobody is to blame but the school. It had a devastating impact on Arlene. Something she never recovered from. Some do, some don't. I'm not going to judge her for not being able to overcome the trauma she experienced. Some of us never get over our pain. Arlene's one of them. Her asking for your father surprised me, but I know this is a very important chapter of his life that your dad must close. He always knew why the Kabatays wanted to . . . hurt us."

"You mean destroy us. They were relentless."

"For some time, Raven shared in their vengeance. She doesn't anymore. What does this tell you?"

Jude shifted. "That Dad went there to end . . . well, end whatever Mrs. Kabatay had started."

"It's so much more than that. He's burying the past, and so is she."

"They might, but I can't see Clayton burying his tomahawk. Wait, he wants to bury it all right—in the back of my head."

****

"He's got no right," Clayton spat out. He stepped aside in the hallway to let the nurse wheeling a cart pass by.

Raven leaned against the wall, clutching the bottled water.

"No, he doesn't." Fawn paced the floor, pushing her hair one way and then the other. She pointed at Raven. "Just because she called him here doesn't mean we're going to forgive him."

"I don't care what you think or feel." Mom was dying, and all they gave a shit about was continuing to inflict the poison Mom had injected into them on others.

Fawn stopped. She spun on her heel and barreled straight to Raven, who didn't shrink away, but stood straighter and forward in her stance. She met Fawn's black eyes an inch from her face, since they were the same height. The breaths from her sister's nostrils were a moose's ready to charge.

"She wanted to see *him*. She asked for *him*. Not you. Why're you even here?" A sneer formed in the corners of Fawn's mouth.

"Because Mr. M asked me to come." Although Raven's heartbeat accelerated to the speed of an outboard motor at full throttle, she clutched the bottle and kept staring down Fawn.

"Oh, I see. And we're supposed to forget who you chose?" Fire flared in Fawn's irises.

"I didn't choose anyone." Raven gripped the water bottle tighter.

"You did, too. Mom wanted something done about *him* working at the school, and Clayton tried, but you refuted everything he said."

"No, I didn't. I told the truth. Nobody seduced me. Do I look like I can be seduced?" Raven snorted. "Get real."

"I see. Got your way to get a passing grade, huh?" Fawn's eyebrow twitched.

The insult slapped Raven's cheek. She forced her hands to remain where they were and not leap through the air to punch Fawn square in the face. "Fuck off."

"No, you fuck off." Fawn was a breath from Raven's nose, hands on hips. "You're not wanted here. Go."

"Mom's in there dying, and this is what your priority is. Fighting with me."

"Again, it's all about Raven." Fawn's eyes almost rolled out of their sockets. "Wrong. I want you out of here because Mom doesn't want you here. Get it? When she needed you most, you thought with your clit, like you always do."

"What's going on?" A nurse scurried down the hall to them. "If you don't lower your voices, I'll have to ask you to leave. You're disturbing the other patients."

Raven swiveled on her heel and went to the one place where she wouldn't be slapped around by vicious words. She stomped to the cafeteria.

Third cup of coffee planted in front of her, Raven stared upward. Was the deacon still with Mom? He must be. She would've seen him leave from her vantage point below the main open spiraling wide stairs that were three floors high.

The corner of her eye caught the message popping up on her phone from Jude. She'd turned off the sound to escape the badgering of messages she might receive from her siblings. It was a good thing she'd caught his message by chance.

Where are you? Dad called.

I have my phone off. Long story about my sisters and brother. I'm at the hospital. In the cafeteria.

He called me from outside your mom's room. He said she's asking for you. Get up there. Now.

Okay.

Raven grabbed her coffee and raced up the stairs to Mom's room. Fawn, Wren, and Lark sat in the chairs surrounding the bed. Clayton leaned against the window. The deacon remained in his same spot on Mom's right, and she still clasped his hand. Well, more like the deacon was keeping Mom's hand afloat.

Raven inched over to the deacon's chair. He stood, motioning at her to use his seat.

"Norman . . ." Mom moaned.

"I'm right here, Arlene." The deacon shifted so he still held Mom's hand and motioned again for Raven to sit.

She drew up the chair beside Mom's bedside.

Through sleepy lids, Mom gazed at Raven. "I'm not doing well."

Raven set her coffee on the small table. She brushed her mother's wisps of hair. "It's okay."

"No, it's not okay." Mom's words came out thick and slow. "I'm . . . I . . . I won't see you graduate."

Pain smothered Raven's chest. Smothered her heart. Smothered her breathing. Thirty-two years, and they were finally speaking the way she'd dreamed about. "You . . . you already have. You're looking at a high school graduate. The . . . the first in our family. I'll get my grade twelve for sure next year."

"I know you will." More thickness coated Mom's words, slowing her speech. Her chest failed to rise and fall normally. It was a languid breath up and down. "I told your brother and sisters they have to accept you. Accept what you're doing with your life."

Raven's insides quaked. "You . . . you . . . did . . . did?"

Mom nodded and winced. "Hurts . . . I . . . I wanted to go home and die. Your brother and sisters convinced me I'd be better here. Better care. Better medication for the pain. I . . . I want the pain to stop."

"Then sleep. Rest." A sob formed in Raven's throat. This was truly goodbye.

"I won't see you marry." Mom's dark eyes moistened.

"Marry?"

"You'll marry him. You're doing what I always wanted to

do." Mom heaved a breath.

"Marry a Matawapit?"

"No. Silly. Marry the man of your dreams. Living your dreams. Reaching for your dreams. I'm . . . I'm proud of you. And was . . . was jealous." A tear slid down Mom's cheek. "You're doing what I didn't have the courage to do. Keep doing it."

Mom shifted and cried out in agony, torture filling her face.

Raven scampered from the chair. "Did you need me to adjust the bed."

"No," Mom whispered. "No. I need . . . need to rest."

"Okay." Raven sat back. She squirmed. This was her mother's toughest time, and she had no idea how to offer comfort or what to say. They were truly two strangers.

Like the coward she was, Raven bit her lip to stop herself from asking Fawn or the deacon to say something to help Mom.

Fawn stood. She sat on the other side of the bed beside Mom. She fixed the pillow and tightened the blankets around Mom's skinny, sickly body. Then she kissed Mom's forehead. "Rest. Okay? I love you." She pressed her cheek against Mom's.

Mom's lips were a half-smile, and she closed her eyes.

Raven hadn't experienced death before. Not someone she loved. She'd expected death to be dramatic, like on TV or in the movies, last words spoken, a pledge of love. Anything. But all that had happened was Mom's chest ceased to rise and fall. The monitor had stopped beeping.

In the middle of the night, during perhaps round number eight of coffees they'd kept purchasing from *Reggie's Donuts* downstairs, the numbers had dropped to zero on the screen.

Fawn buried her head in Mom's chest. Her sobs cut into the distressing silence haunting the room. Lark covered her face and cried. Wren wobbled to Clayton, and he wrapped her in his embrace, his own black eyes moist. The deacon didn't weep. Through hollow eyes, he stared at Mom, jaw slack.

Raven clutched his hand. His warm palm and strong fingers fed something to her that vanquished the horrible blackness dragging her into a dark hole. Roses and fluffy cotton seemed to surround her chilled skin. A crackling fire appeared in her chest, warming her.

Mom was gone.

CHAPTER THIRTY-THREE: PASSING BY THE GRAVEYARD

Raven sat at the restaurant table with her brother and sisters. They'd invited her to join them after they'd left Mom behind at the hospital, who'd be taken to the morgue and then flown up to the reserve for the funeral. With the exception of an old man at the counter, they were the only people present in the wee hours of the morning.

Wren stared blankly into her coffee. "She told the deacon she wants him to say her funeral."

Shock hit Raven's spine. "Um . . . what?"

"Those were her wishes. She told him while we were in the room. You were somewhere else," Wren muttered.

"She also told the deacon to . . . love us and take care of us. She made him promise to be a father to us the way Dad never was." Lark sipped her coffee.

Clayton fiddled with some empty creamer containers on the table.

"Wh-what?" Raven gasped. "How long were they alone?"

"A couple of hours," Fawn whispered. She kept dunking her teabag into her paper cup. "The deacon came out and said we were welcome to come back into the room."

The weight sitting on Raven's skin and limbs rolled away. She sat up. Mom hadn't died like Annie Keejik had. Mom had died peacefully. Content. Maybe even happy.

"She . . . she really loved him." This came from Lark.

Clayton crushed one of the empty creamer containers in his

palm.

"Don't . . ." Fawn tapped the table. "Don't start. This is what Mom wanted. We've always listened to Mom."

Clayton threw back his chair and strode outside.

Raven bolted after him into the coolness of the misty October night. Her brother stood under a streetlamp. She scampered over to him. His arm was draped across his stomach. He held the cigarette with his free hand. Smoke swirled upward.

"Got one for me?"

His gaze flicked over her. Jawline hard. Eyes cold. He slipped the packet from his jacket and handed one over.

"I'm sorry." She took his offered lighter and lit the cigarette.

"About what?" His question was colder than his eyes. He slipped the lighter back into his jacket pocket.

"Everything . . ." She puffed on the cigarette.

"I thought you quit?" Disdain flared in his eyes.

"I did." Raven's taste buds and lungs welcomed the palate of tobacco, but her stomach remained tight.

"Where's Tanya?"

"At the hotel with Tyrell."

"Tyrell also came?"

Clayton nodded.

A car drove by. They weren't on one of the main streets, so most of the area was quiet, and, well, it was four in the morning. Thunder Bay wasn't a big city that never slept, more like a big town.

"Are you okay with, um, with the deacon saying her funeral?"

Clayton took another drag. "If you don't mind, I came out here to be alone. Go back inside."

"I can't stand that you hate me," Raven murmured.

"Save it. You made your pick."

"Mom doesn't want us to fight." She pushed away her hair

the breeze kept blowing around.

"It's a little too late, isn't it? She started this. Started it from day one. And now she wants us to change because she said so?" Clayton shook his head.

"I think Mom realized holding her hurt and anger inside wasn't how she wanted to die, or even how she wanted to live. She wants us to be happy. She wants us to be what she never was. What she couldn't let herself become."

"I want nothing to do with any of this." Clayton took another drag.

"Do with what?"

"Her funeral. Everything." Clayton turned and walked off down the sidewalk.

"Please let it go," Raven called out. "Please remember what she wanted."

The funeral would be later this morning. Everyone had been gathering at Fawn's house to pay their respects and drop off food.

At Jude's, Raven stood in front of the bathroom mirror applying her makeup. She'd been staying here after they'd flown back to the reserve the morning Mom had passed.

As for Mom's place, Bryan, Yolanda, and their baby were still living there. Raven had told them to keep the house. They needed a place for their growing family. They'd mentioned she could stay in her old bedroom, but since a cousin needed a place to live, she'd offered him the room.

That was where the fire burned. Uncle Jack had started the fire when he'd received word Mom had passed. Today was the last day the fire would burn.

While dressing, Raven packed up her makeup and other clothing, because she'd return to the Matawapits' tonight.

To honor Mom, although the funeral wouldn't be traditional, Raven had donned the ribbon skirt Lark had made as a present a couple of years ago. She slipped on her ankle-length moccasins.

All she had left to do was plait her hair. The two beaded discs she'd attach to the ends of the braids remained on the vanity. As for earrings, because the discs were so big, a simple small set would do.

Jude poked his head in the bathroom. "I got the kids dressed. You almost ready?"

"Almost." Raven secured the discs.

His dark eyes flickered with love, his gaze traveling from her moccasins to her satin shirt. "You look absolutely beautiful."

"Thank you. So do you." And he did, in his black suit hugging his broad shoulders and tapering to his slim waist. The red tie brought out the copper undertones of his dark skin.

He took her hand. "Dad's already at the church. So's Emery. He'll altar serve."

The Catholic Women's Association was preparing the luncheon downstairs for after the funeral. As the president, Mrs. M was overseeing everything.

"Darryl's there, too?" Her voice shook. It was imperative the drum be present.

"Yep. Him and the drum group. Emery already laid the deerskin over the altar. There's nothing to worry about. Darryl knows what he's doing."

"Thank you." Raven and her sisters had decided they'd wanted traditional songs sung instead of the Catholic ones, and some elements of traditionalism at the church.

"They're set up in front of the main pew on the Gospel aisle."

"The what?"

"Never mind. You'll see them." Jude drew his arm around her waist. "Let's get going. The cars are already leaving."

They'd all meet downstairs at the church basement. Uncle

Jack was bringing Mom in the back of his pickup truck. They'd chosen traditional birch for her casket. Some young local boys had already dug the grave early this morning.

Before dressing, Raven had gone with her sisters to lay food in the casket. They'd also placed Mom's favorite moccasins on her feet. The funeral director had dressed Mom in her jingle dress, braided her hair, and decorated her wrists, neckline, and earlobes with traditional beaded jewelry.

They entered the kitchen, where Rebekah and Noah quietly waited. Jude must have uttered some big threats to get Noah to keep his mouth shut. Like his Dad, Noah was done up in his Sunday finest. Black shirt and black dress pants. Rebekah had slipped on a frilly black dress. Their faces were scrubbed to a shine, since Jude had allowed Raven to rub charcoal on their faces each night, so Mom's lonely spirit wouldn't inadvertently take a child with her for her journey to the spirit world.

The scent of cedar permeated the home, Raven having hung some over each doorway. Black sheets covered the windows.

She slipped her arm around Noah's little-boy shoulders. "C'mon. Walk with me."

"Okay." Noah gazed up at her.

She led them out of the house, down the stairs, and to the truck. A flower seemed to bloom in Raven's heart. Before Mom had died, she'd instructed the deacon to make sure Jude and the children accompanied Raven to the funeral as her family.

The kids got in the back. Raven joined Jude in the front. Wren's vehicle rolled by, coming from Old Main.

"Everyone's leaving at the same time," Raven murmured. She fingered the ribbon work on her skirt. "Lark and I should join our businesses. She makes the most beautiful ribbon skirts and shirts. Way better than I can. She was always the seamstress of us. I'm the crafter."

"Have you heard from Clayton?" Jude backed the truck out of the driveway.

"Nope." Raven looked out the passenger window to the neatly trimmed ditch Jude had taken the weed-eater to before putting away the lawn equipment for the fall.

"He's upset. Give him some time," Jude said.

They drove off, following Lark, her husband, and her teen-aged children.

"I hoped it would end after Mom . . . Mom and your dad made up. But I guess it hasn't." Raven folded her arms. There was a lot to see from the passenger window. Trees. Houses. The band office. The road to the airport.

Jude reached over and held her hand. "Hey, I'm here for you."

She turned. The glow in her chest forced her lips upward.

"Are you two holding hands?"

Raven glanced in the backseat.

Noah slapped his hand over his mouth. "Oops. Dad said —
"

"And I won't say it again." Jude raised his finger, hard stare positioned at the rearview mirror.

"I know." Noah's reply carried a hint of a pout. "Sorry, Raven. Dad says this is a really sad day for you."

"It's okay." The boy was only nine. In Raven's mind, Noah was handling himself wonderfully.

When they started onto Church Road, vehicles lined both sides, tires almost grazing the ditches. The parking lot was full, but spots had been saved for the family. Uncle Jack's truck was already present. Mom's casket rested in the box.

Raven's heart tightened. She lowered the visor and checked her makeup. Maybe she should have passed on the false eyelashes. She might lose one if she dared to cry.

Jude guided the truck behind Fawn's vehicle.

The family was gathered outside. The sun was out and there wasn't a cloud in the sky. It was as if Mom was shining down on them, although she traveled somewhere to the spirit world.

Someone had built a fire on the lawn next to the church. Traditionalist always carried the fire from the home to the funeral or wake.

"Did you bring the fire?" Raven asked as she sidled up to Fawn.

"No. Darryl probably did." Fawn dabbed at her eyes, where tears seeped.

Raven slipped her arm around her sister. Fawn had been Mom's favorite. Besties. This was going to be a tough day.

"I . . . I thought Clayton would come." Fawn squeezed the handkerchief. "I can't believe he'd do this."

"He'll . . . he needs time."

"Tanya and Tyrell are here." Fawn scowled.

Raven gazed at Clayton's wife and his stepnephew.

"Let's line up." Uncle Jack raised his arms.

Fawn's family went second, even though she was the oldest, because Clayton, as the only and eldest son, was head of the family, which meant Tanya and Tyrell stood front and center in his absence. Raven piled in behind her sisters' families. Jude, Noah, and Rebekah accompanied her.

From the path Darryl had previously cleared that led to the water a good one hundred feet away, Clayton emerged from the bush and poplar trees.

Raven's beating heart held still for a moment. He'd brought the fire. Her brother had come earlier to ready everything for the funeral. His moccasins dragged the grass, hair bound in braids and wrapped in rabbit fur. A ribbon shirt covered his slim upper body, and the legs of his black pants brushed together as he walked.

Throat burning, Raven clutched Jude's hand. Her brother

had come when they'd needed him most. Fawn broke from the line and threw her arms around Clayton's shoulders. Wren joined them, followed by Lark.

Raven hurried over and also joined the massive hug. Her heart wept. Her biggest dream had come true—her family was together after so much turmoil and fighting.

Through tears and sobs, Clayton led them to Uncle Jack's truck. They gathered around Mom's casket, just as they'd gathered around her as kids, for one last time.

****

The pallbearers carried the casket to lay Arlene Kabatay to rest. Clayton held the family's clan staff.

Jude kept his arm around Raven's waist. She'd never sobbed during the funeral and hadn't cried when they'd descended the church steps. He'd instructed the kids while in the pew to join Mom in the basement once the funeral concluded, because Raven would need his undivided attention at the burial.

Dad led the procession. Emery walked beside him, waving the incense-filled censure back and forth. The drum group was assembled around the grave, holding their hand drums. They'd sing the traveling song, Darryl had told Jude earlier.

With everyone gathered at the grave, Dad held the small book to say a final prayer over Mrs. Kabatay. He spoke in his deep, authoritative voice while Emery continued to swing the censure.

Jude squeezed Raven's shoulder. Her chest was heaving up and down, and she kept blinking.

"Almighty and ever-living God, remember the mercy with which you graced your servant, Arlene, in life. Receive her, we pray, into the mansions of the Saints. As we make ready our sister's resting place, look also with favor on those who mourn and comfort them in their loss. Through Christ our Lord." Dad lowered his hand.

"Amen," Jude said under his breath.

Darryl beat on his hand drum. The singers joined in, their powerful wails filling the air.

The boys lowered the casket into the grave.

Raven stared blankly. The casket went down farther into the earth. Tears filled her eyes. She turned to Jude, burying her face into his chest. Her slim body rattled and shook.

He clutched her, his heart breaking for the woman he loved, and there was nothing he could do to make everything right. All he could do was hold Raven and comfort her, as God simply wanted from him.

They stood at the graveyard fence. Raven puffed on a cigarette and clutched a cup of coffee. She'd removed her false eyelashes because she'd lost one during her crying at the grave.

Jude didn't care that her eyes were swollen, her makeup streaked, and black rivulets streaming down her face. His hand was in its ever-present spot—around her waist.

She sipped more coffee. "It was a nice Mass."

Technically, it wasn't a Mass. Dad could conduct a funeral but not recite Mass during one. But now wasn't the time to inform Raven of the two differences. Just as she had a lot to learn about his beliefs, he had a lot to learn about hers.

"Yes, it was."

She nodded, still puffing on the smoke.

"You hungry?"

"Yeah. I s'pose we should go inside and get something to eat."

"C'mon." He kept his hand on the small of her back as he led her beneath the carport and down the basement stairs where the kitchen was located.

The crowd hadn't let up. The buffet table had been restocked. Mom was serving. So was her BFF, Jenny, and another lady.

"Ready to eat?" A full apron with the Catholic Women's Association emblazoned on the front covered Mom.

"Yeah. Where's Bridget and Adam?" They'd arrived last night and were staying at Emery and Darryl's.

"Over by the door." Mom used her chin to motion.

Accompanied by Darryl, Clayton entered through the front door that faced the lake. They threaded their way through the crowd, stopping now and then to speak to people who offered condolences.

Jude filled both plates while Raven stared blankly around at the crowd.

Noah, Rebekah, Michelle, and Kyle tore by, heading for the back staircase to play now that they'd eaten and had behaved themselves.

With their plates loaded, Jude led Raven through the crowd to where Adam and Bridget sat. Dad and Emery had joined them. Baby Grace was much bigger now at five months old. She even managed to keep her head up on her own.

"Sit." Dad patted the chair beside him.

Jude motioned at Raven to take the seat, and he plopped down beside her.

"It was a nice eulogy," Raven said to Dad.

"Thank you." Dad picked up his coffee.

"I'm glad Mom wanted you to speak about her."

"It was an honor," Dad replied.

Clayton came down the aisle, holding his plate of food. Darryl was walking in front of him.

Jude's stomach tightened. He kept his hand on the back of Raven's chair.

"May we join you?" Darryl asked.

"Of course." Emery peered at his husband.

Clayton shifted his plate from one hand to the next, his gaze moving around.

Darryl pulled out a chair for Clayton.

Clayton set down his plate and sat.

The knots in Jude's stomach uncoiled. It was a start. The first Kabatay had joined them to break bread together.

Chapter Thirty-four: Two Tickets to Paradise

"The same hotel room? Seriously?" Raven giggled. She glanced about the room they'd shared during their first weekend getaway to the city a year ago. Queen-sized bed on the main floor and a sunken living room with sliding doors leading outside.

"Of course. A special room for a special lady." Jude wheeled their luggage inside.

Raven patted the designer suitcase he'd bought her for Christmas. A whole set, but she'd only brought the small one and her makeup case.

"We have a lot to discuss."

"Discuss? It's our Valentine's Day getaway. I say we should hit the sheets first." She fingered the plush beige comforter.

"Oh, we'll be doing that." Jude snickered. "But first we need to talk."

"About what?" She retrieved her makeup case to set in the bathroom. There'd be no storing away the many products, because the pink case served as her place of storage for brushes, lipsticks, and everything else to do up her face. One of the best gifts Jude could have given her.

Jude unzipped his own suitcase. He started removing his clothing to hang. "About us. What else?"

"What about us?" Raven called out from the bathroom.

Everything was going superbly. They'd celebrated

Christmas together, since the kids had been in Kenora for two weeks with their mother. Raven had enjoyed decorating the tree at Jude's house. After they'd left his parents' home on Christmas Eve, they'd made love before falling asleep. In the morning, they'd unwrapped the gifts they'd bought each other. Then they'd gone back to the Matawapits' for dinner, joined by Emery and Darryl. Bridget and Adam and their children had stayed for a couple of days before Adam had to return to work at the restaurant.

Even better, Jude had joined Raven at Fawn's house for Boxing Day to gather with her family. In his true bold style, he'd taken the time to speak to everyone.

For New Year's Eve, they'd flown to Thunder Bay to celebrate with Adam and Bridget by dining at The Bistro, the Matawapit family's favorite restaurant.

The day after New Year's Day, Jude had started the annulment proceedings for his marriage, which was still valid in the Catholic Church, even though he was divorced.

"There's my vasectomy we need to talk about." The sound of hangers sliding across the bar carried into the bathroom.

"What about your vasectomy?" Raven wandered back into the bedroom area and sat.

"You don't think about children?"

"No." She shrugged.

"Not at all?" He hung his last shirt and faced her.

"Nope." Her heart glowed. "I'm fine. Not every woman wants children. I mean . . . yeah, I wondered about it now and then." She patted her womb. "But honestly, I'm okay with being a stepmom."

The word had a nice ring to it. Stepmom. This was a serious conversation. She clasped the edge of the bed and leaned forward. "Why? Do you wanna try make one?"

Jude chuckled and joined her on the bed. He patted her knee. "We can practice, but I simply wanted to make sure you're okay with how we stand as a couple right now."

"Y'know, I love you so damn much." Raven touched his square jawline. "None of my other boyfriends ever took the time to ask me how I'm feeling. Well, probably because it wasn't about . . . love. More like drugs."

His dark eyes twinkled. "I love you, too. And I want to make you happy. It's why I asked about children. I'm asking because . . ." He pressed his lips together. "I meant to save this for dinner, but I'll . . ."

He rose and meandered to his parka hanging on the hanger.

Ice seemed to flood Raven's veins.

He dug around inside the inner pocket. "There wasn't a chance I was packing this in my suitcase and then having my luggage end up in Peru." He produced a small wrapped box with a purple bow on top.

"Oh my God . . ." Every muscle constricted.

When Jude shifted to one knee, Raven's breaths became trapped in her lungs. "Are you . . . Are you . . . Oh my God."

"Open it," he said quietly, studying her.

She tore at the wrapping paper. In her palms, she held a pink velvet box. Her hands trembled as she cracked open the lid to a massive solitaire diamond surrounded by smaller diamonds.

"Oh my God." Her heart shifted upward, and she could barely breathe again.

"Is that all you can say?" Amusement flecked Jude's question. He took her left hand.

Tears burned in Raven's eyes. Her chest swelled.

"Raven Dawn Kabatay . . ." His voice was the serious, quiet one he used when teaching a class. " . . . will you make me the happiest man in the world and do me the honor of marrying me?"

"Oh my God . . ." She used her free hand to cover her

mouth. Her vision blurred from the tears.

Jude winked. "I was hoping for a *yes*, sweetheart."

"Y-y-yes. Y-y-yes, I'll . . . I'll marry you." She leapt from the bed and threw her arms around his shoulders.

"Whoa . . . easy." Jude chuckled. "Let me finish."

"But . . . but . . ." She drew back, staring at him.

He slipped the ring on the finger of her left hand. The cool gold wrapped her flesh and her heart.

"Jude . . . Jude . . . Oh my God . . . you don't know . . . Oh my God, I've never been so happy." The sob left her throat, and she again squeezed him tightly. "Oh God, Jude."

She laid her head on his shoulder, the sobs continuing to leave her throat.

****

Jude snickered, since Raven was still on her phone texting away. So much for a romantic dinner alone tonight. His new fiancée had insisted on inviting Adam and Bridget to celebrate. Naturally, he'd let Raven get her way. If dining with his sister and brother-in-law made Raven happy, Jude was happy.

Already, he'd spoken to the kids about what he'd intended on doing this weekend. Their approval was important, and Noah and Rebekah had given their blessing, since they understood the marriage wouldn't happen until the annulment went through. They could look at a wedding not this summer, but the following summer.

He'd told Raven how they'd be married was her decision. And she'd agreed to his one and only request — that Dad bless their marriage in the church afterward.

From the amount of texting she was doing with Lark, it sounded like Raven was already working on her wedding dress.

He stood in front of the mirror to tie his tie. "Sweetheart, you'd better finish dressing. Bridget and Adam will be here soon."

Raven set aside the phone, giggling. She'd giggled while they'd made love. Giggled while they'd showered and dressed. And had giggled while applying her makeup and styling her hair.

Still in her bathrobe, she jumped from the couch and pranced up the two steps to her clothing hanging on the rack.

"Which one?" Raven held up a slinky black number and a va-va-voom siren red dress.

"The red. I'm in black. And red is for Valentine's Day. Plus, you'll match my tie." He waggled the tie at her.

"Matching now?" She wiggle-walked up to him, teeth bared, lips curled into a suggestive smile.

"Why not? We're officially engaged." Her drew her slim body against his chest and pecked her red-painted lips. "I'm not wearing lipstick, am I?"

She flicked the handkerchief from his pocket and dabbed at his mouth. "Better?"

"Better."

"I should slip into something."

"No rush." His gaze caressed her calves, brushed her legs, massaged her stomach, and then stroked her breasts. "You're my kind of dressed."

"Keep looking at me that way and you'll have to eat my cunt instead of steak." She turned and lifted the red dress off the rack.

"I'll gladly pass on steak for beaver." He couldn't resist teasing.

"Gosh, you men and the *beaver* word." She slipped her legs into the dress and pulled the stretchy, tight material up over her hips and chest. "Zip me."

He clasped the zipper. "Hmm . . . I'm not sure if I like you better dressed or undressed." He pecked the nape of her neck.

Goosebumps covered her smooth skin. She turned. "I am looking forward to having you fuck me for the rest of my life."

"Yeah? Well, I'm looking forward to having you fuck me."

She grinded her crotch against his. "Ooh, does this mean I get to take you for a ride after dinner?"

"You sure can." He clasped her shoulders and eased her away. "Enough of that, or we'll miss dinner. I think Adam and Bridget are here by now."

"Oookay, you're the boss." She retrieved her coat off the rack, the very leather coat with the faux fur trim he'd bought her last year as a present.

"Allow me." Jude took the coat.

Raven slid her arms into the sleeves. She then bent down and pulled on her fave spike-heeled boots, perfect for keeping her bare legs away from the chill of the February wind.

When she straightened, Jude again held her arms. He rubbed his nose against hers.

"Northern kiss," she murmured.

"Northern kiss for my northern girl," he said softly.

Epilogue: Life for the Taking

"If you get any whiter, you'll match your dress. Take it easy." Clayton patted Raven's arm.

"Easy? I'm about to get married." Raven ran her tongue along her mouth ever so lightly so she wouldn't smudge her lipstick. She clutched her brother's arm. In a few moments they'd leave for the Matawapits' house.

Everything had to be perfect for today. She'd worked too hard all winter for this magical moment.

The bedroom door opened. Fawn scooted inside. Her deer hide dress was the same style as Raven's, but instead of a soft doe-white, Fawn's was a light-tan brown. The blending of the two cultures was to honor the joining of the two families, something very important to Raven, and she'd received approval from Clayton and Fawn.

Jude had done his part when he'd gone out hunting last fall with Darryl and had taken down the doe to present to Raven's family. The material for her wedding dress came from the four-legged, beautiful deer Jude had slain and then had offered tobacco to while Darryl had said a prayer over the eternally sleeping animal, thanking their furry friend for its life, nourishment, and hide for this special day.

"Lookit you . . ." Fawn gripped Raven's fingers and raised their arms, her gaze running up and down the dress.

In the mirror, Raven caught their reflections. She and her sisters had done a gorgeous job on both dresses. The A-line skirts fell to their ankles with thin, wispy fringes dragging the floor. Loose tops with reversed V-shaped hems and sleeves to their elbows were decorated with more wispy fringes that also ran up the sides of the skirts to hide where the seams met. Matching beaded turquoise moccasins covered their feet. And Raven's veil—made by Lark—was a wonderful creation of the same beaded turquoise sewn into the doeskin headband and an eagle feather, gifted by Clayton, fastened to the back. For something borrowed, Lark had used the white transparent lace from Fawn's wedding veil for Raven's train.

Wren burst into the bedroom. "You are too beautiful. I think I'm going to cry." She gasped at Fawn. "Oh geez, and lookit you. You're both so beautiful. And lookit your hair!"

Pride glowed in Raven's chest. She'd braided two plaits bound in rabbit fur and beading.

"Let's get going. We don't want to keep your groom waiting." Lark looped her arm through Raven's.

****

Tonight, the vanity's second sink in the master bathroom would become occupied by Raven's toiletries once she became Jude's wife. The his-and-her walk-in closets were already filled. Together, he and Raven, with the kids, had designed and furnished their new forever home.

There were still a few places in the house that required finishing, and Jude let out a breath of relief because he and the kids had been able to move in at the end of May—two weeks before the wedding.

The window over the soaker tub allowed a clear view of the main grassy area where the wedding was being held. Guests had already begun arriving. All he had to do was walk over to Mom and Dad's.

Darryl was outside, supervising last-minute details to the skeletons for the fire circle. Basil had already selected the seven different types of wood to burn for the ceremony. Last night, he'd blessed the wood and the circle with a song. Only the two families had been present.

The drum group sat to the right, and the flute player off to the side of the circle. The guests were seated in the numerous chairs.

They'd gone through the rehearsal last night so Jude would understand protocol.

"How're you doing?" Emery poked his head in the bathroom.

Their black tuxedos matched, except for the cummerbunds, vests, and bow ties. Little brother's hair was gelled off his face, something new, and very different to see his forehead for once.

"Great." Jude smacked his hands together and strode forward. "I'm ready to head over and become a married man."

"You're not nervous?" Emery strode into the master bedroom that also overlooked the great lawn.

"Not at all." Jude did a light spin, taking in the tray ceiling, a quaint sitting area for Raven to work on a craft while he watched TV, both snuggling together later in front of the woodstove. Perfect. Wait until she saw the bonus room over the garage. She'd die twice. He snickered, since he hadn't let her near it.

Just under two thousand feet, the craftsman style nest wasn't as elaborate as Jude's previous residence in Thunder Bay, but his skin continued to tingle over sharing this beautiful place with his children and new wife.

He wandered from the master bedroom and into the mudroom, where he could enter the house from the two-stall garage. A utility room with a washer and dryer. Yikes at the hydro bill he'd have to pay. A full walk-in pantry. And a locker area where everyone could hang their coats and store their boots. The staircase went up to Raven's surprise room over the garage.

Jude wandered into the main living area, taking in the open kitchen and full eating bar, great room, and dining nook. The children's suites occupied the other side of the house. It was important to keep them close to the great room where the fireplace was so they stayed warm and toasty.

"Ready?" As best man, Emery held one of the woven baskets, made by Raven, which Jude would present to her during the ceremony.

"As ready as I'll ever be."

They left through the front door. The jaunt down the road wasn't far, since Jude had built next to his parents' house. Vehicles lined the road. Instead of going to Mom and Dad's, they went to the fire circle where Mom, Bridget, Grace, Adam, Noah, Rebekah, and Kyle were already seated. On the opposite side sat the Kabatays, except for Raven, Clayton, and Fawn, who were probably inside the house.

Basil and Dad came down the stairs from the deck. They made their way across the lawn, Basil done up in a ribbon shirt Lark had fashioned, and moccasins sewn by Raven. Dad wore his dalmatic.

The sun was out. A light breeze off the lake kept the heat at bay. For sure God was smiling down in approval. Jude glanced at the clear blue sky. Even his annulment had gone well, and he'd received his papers at the beginning of February, the exact time he'd first met Raven two years earlier.

Darryl and Tyrell were working on the kindling for the fire. Flames flickered. By the time Dad and Basil reached the circle of stones, the flames had curled and stretched around the seven different stacked woods in the middle.

This might get a little hot. Jude yearned to draw back slightly, but doing so might be perceived as disrespectful. He should have asked if using his handkerchief was permitted.

Darryl stalked off then stalked back. He handed the blue blanket to Emery.

The flames were climbing higher, the heat from the fire washing over Jude. His brother draped the blue blanket around Jude's shoulders. He tugged on it to bundle himself in the interlaced cotton Mom had spent all winter knitting.

Basil nodded at the flute player.

As the beautiful music sweetened the air, Fawn appeared, slowly making her way across the lawn, blanket draped over her forearm and clutching the basket. Then Raven, her arm through Clayton's, made her entrance.

The breath was sucked from Jude. With her braided hair, white headband swathing her forehead, the veil dangling down her backside, and the long, wispy fringes of her dress swaying as she walked, she was never more beautiful to him. His heart swelled.

This wasn't her va-va-voom walk. She was as graceful as the wedding dress she'd made from the doe he'd shot last fall. The closer she got, the more his heart rattled and banged. He had to steady his deep breathing, or he'd run out of air.

The melody of the flute wrapped him in silk, and so did Raven's languid approach, her moccasins seeming to skim the grass instead of crushing the green blades.

Her dark eyes held his gaze, red lips forming into a demure smile which was so unlike her. Truly, she was a shy Indian maiden of the past, readying to meet her brave to join as one.

He had so much to thank her for. She'd helped him become the man he was meant to be. Helped him find his culture. Helped him build them a new home. And most of all, helped him believe in love again. Thanks to her, he was fully re-newed.

Clayton let go of her arm. He turned and faced Raven, whispering something into her ear. Raven nodded. Fawn came forward, draping the blue blanket over Raven's shoul-ders. Raven hugged it tight and shyly fluttered her false lashes at Jude as she took his arm.

Her touch was tender, even slightly hesitant. The warmth and love flooding Jude's insides lit something silky in his eyes and compelled the corners of his mouth to move upward.

Basil stepped forward. The flute music subsided, and the drum group began beating a song. The old man sang the prayer while Darryl sprinkled medicine over the fire.

The beat of the drum reverberated in Jude's throat. There was something about the sacred songs that always called to his spirit, almost seeming to invite it from his body to dance with the rhythm of the beat and lose itself in the singing.

After a few minutes, the music stopped. Basil shuffled in front of them. He spoke in Ojibway, so Jude couldn't understand what the old man was saying, but last night Darryl had told him the prayer was about new beginnings, new life, and thanking the Creator.

The old man pointed to the south and north of the fire where kindling rested, ready to start the two smaller fires.

Jude moved to the north one and Raven to the south one.

With Emery's assistance holding Jude's blanket in place, he lit the small fire. He looked up to Fawn and Clayton assisting Raven, who started the other fire.

Emery handed Jude the shovel. Clayton handed Raven her shovel.

At the same time, his heart almost bursting, and Emery still holding the blanket in place, Jude pushed the tiny fire to the main fire, and Raven did the same. She maintained his stare, using the shovel to guide her small fire while Clayton and Fawn helped so Raven's dress wouldn't be scorched by accident.

Basil raised his arms and began singing again.

Slightly breathless, Jude met Raven halfway around the fire. Sweat dribbled down his back and coated his forehead. When Emery stepped forward and dabbed at Jude's face with a handkerchief, he'd never been so grateful.

They took one step together to honor humility in their marriage, stopping then to face each other.

"I humbly take you as my husband," she whispered.

"And I humbly take you as my wife."

They took another step to honor bravery in their marriage.

"For better or worse, and in sickness and in health, I will show bravery in our union," Raven said tenderly.

Gazing into her eyes, Jude repeated the words.

They took the last five steps that represented honesty, wisdom, truth, respect, and finally love.

"I promise to love you forever, Raven Dawn." The words came smoothly from Jude's heart where they beat. He touched her braid.

"And I promise to love you forever, Jude Norman." Raven's declaration was firm yet soft as she gazed deep into his eyes.

Emery removed the blue blanket from Jude, and Fawn removed Raven's blanket. Together, their best man and matron of honor swathed them in the white blanket Mom had made that represented their new life together.

Jude took the basket from Emery and handed the meat and skins over to Raven, a representation to always feed and clothe her.

Smiling, Raven took the basket and gave Jude his, filled with bread and corn, to always nurture and support him.

They set aside their baskets. Darryl stepped forward, holding the two-spouted jar filled with herbal tea. Raven drank from one side. Jude then sipped from the other. His heart almost stood still since they'd now drink together. He silently crossed his fingers they wouldn't spill any, because this wasn't an easy feat. Drinking together represented teamwork, cooperation, the ability to work together as a true couple — the first test of their marriage.

Following Raven's lead, Jude sipped, carefully studying

the gestures his new wife made with her eyes, telling him what to do. The tea slid into his mouth and down his throat.

Joy filled his chest. They'd done it. As explained to him, their sharing of the drink sealed their future life together of when to lead and when to follow to defeat the challenge at hand.

And he'd done so. A man who'd always had to lead had let his bride show him how to drink from the spouts as one, as she'd shown him from the first time they'd met.

****

Raven held tight to Jude's and Noah's hands, and Jude held Rebekah's. As a blended family, they rushed up the church stairs. In the world of the *Anishinaabeg*, they were husband and wife, but now they must marry in front of Jude's Catholic god and sign their marriage certificate to make it binding in the eyes of their government.

Adam and Darryl held the doors open.

Behind Jude, Raven, Noah, and Rebekah, were Emery and Fawn, followed by their families with the deacon already waiting up the aisle in front of the big altar and cross.

Raven couldn't help but almost stop for a moment to look around, because she'd never gotten a true glimpse during Mom's funeral.

Jude tugged on her hand, as did Noah, and they raced Raven up the aisle. It was a little snug, enough for three people to comfortably walk, but four was asking a tall order.

Still, they squashed themselves between the big lines of glossy stained wooden benches facing the altar and the big cross. The deacon waited on the first step, book in hand and outfitted in the fancy cover he'd worn at their wedding a good ten minutes ago.

Jude motioned at Raven to stop two feet in front of the four stairs. Emery placed his hands on Noah's shoulders, and Fawn did the same to Rebekah.

The deacon smiled. "Greetings."

This wedding was as formal as their traditional joining. The deacon gazed at them both, asking them to repeat to one another the words he spoke.

Jude's caring eyes while they recited to honor, love, cherish, and obey one another, forsake all others, and love one another in sickness and in health, till death do they part were enough to sweeten Raven's heart.

Emery and Fawn placed the rings on the pillow Noah and Rebekah both held. The deacon blessed them.

When Jude took the ring from the pillow, Raven's hand shook. He slid the beautiful wedding band that matched her engagement ring along the ring finger of her left hand. She then accepted the band from Fawn and slipped the beautiful gold ring onto his finger.

"By the powers vested in me, I now pronounce you husband and wife." The deacon smiled and leaned in slightly to his eldest son. "You may kiss the bride."

"For sure. You don't gotta tell me twice." Jude winked at Raven.

Everyone laughed, even the kids.

The kiss he offered Raven wasn't the sensual or sweet ones she was used to. It was affectionate, full of promise to cherish and love her for the rest of her life.

****

Jude carried Raven over the threshold and into the foyer. "It's your first official night living here."

The creamy texture of her doeskin wedding dress was as smooth as her bronzed skin. As he spun her around the hardwood floor, the fringes of her dress swayed in rhythm with their movements.

All he had to do was cross the rounded archway.

Raven pointed at the door to their right where his office was. "How'd it turn out? Did they do exactly what you wanted?"

"Never mind that for now. What I have for you is upstairs."

"Yes, the upstairs . . ." She coyly flashed a smile. "Why wasn't I allowed up there?"

"Because your wedding present's up there. You have a great designer eye, but this was all my doing — with the help of Lark and Wren."

"Oh? They had a hand in it but didn't tell me?" She grinned.

"C'mon." He carried her through the living area, straight through the kitchen, where the garage entry was located.

"Are you carrying me up the stairs?" She snickered.

"I'd love to, but if you want me to consummate our marriage tonight, we risk throwing out my back," Jude said teasingly.

He held her hand and led her up the staircase to the bonus room over the garage. "Stop here." He placed his palms over her eyes in front of the door that he opened. "Okay, move slowly."

She did as ordered.

Jude's chest swelled at the lovely crafting room he'd created just for her. Lark, of course, would be here lots, since the two sisters worked together on their new business. He removed his palms. "Okay, you can open them."

"Oh my God." Raven's mouth fell open, and her eyes bulged as she surveyed her new home business.

She'd ached for a beautiful, bright, white room with rich dark floors and a big window to let in the sun, which was exactly what Jude had the construction crew build.

Everything was new, shipped in with the furniture on the

ice road during the winter. There were drawers to store fabric and shelving to accommodate bolts of material to roll out as needed. Two sewing machines. A desk and computer for the business aspect of crafting. And an island to cut or measure. A deep closet to store more crafting essentials.

"Lark said this is what you needed."

"Oh my God." Raven kept gasping, hand on her chest and the other over her mouth.

"There's even a bathroom." He pointed. "The sofa unfolds into a bed so we can have guests."

"You did? It is? Oh wow." She leaned into his chest, her own heaving. "I love you. I love you so much. I don't know what to say."

"How about—you're officially open for business?" He snickered.

"Your parents will be grateful. And so will John," she replied, referring to Lark's husband, where the women had also crafted.

"Anything to make you happy," he murmured, nuzzling the nape of her neck.

She wiggled, turning to face him. Her dark eyes glittered. "And anything to make you happy, husband. I'd say it's time we tested out our new bathtub."

"Then what are we waiting for? Let's go downstairs." He draped his arm around his new bride's waist and shut off the light to the room.

It was time to begin spending the rest of their lives together.

YOU MAY ALSO ENJOY THE FOLLOWING FROM EXTASY BOOKS INC:

Dressed for Success
Maggie Blackbird

Excerpt

Bebe did a twirl as she shut the door to her condo. She tossed her keys on the side table and set down her purse.

Simba strolled out from the master bedroom, meowing like a male lion strolling the perimeter in the Serengeti since he was almost the size of one and possessed the same tawny coat as his bigger feline counterparts.

"Guess what happened to Mommy today?" She danced off to her bedroom with Simba on her clicking heels, still yowling.

She'd text her sister and mother back at the reserve right away. They'd be excited for her. Starting over in the city had been the best thing she'd done for herself. But a week with Alden Campbell was enough to throw her stomach into knots.

No, she wasn't going there. Alden was the consummate professional. Office affairs did nobody any good, other than forcing someone to leave a job they loved and to begin anew. Plus, Alden was fifteen years older with two kids in university. He'd given her a chance when she'd taken the real estate course and had earned her license. Everything she did was not only for herself, but to not let down a man who trusted her to work hard for his company.

So she'd send his sexy salt-and-pepper hair, his ice-water blue eyes, his black brows sloping almost upon his lids, and his right amount of stubble groomed into a moustache and barely there beard to the recycle bin of her brain.

The problem of why he kept sneaking out of the bin was that she enjoyed gazing at his waves of gray hair and his neatly trimmed sideburns way too freaking much. The same for the three embedded creases in his forehead and the crinkles around his eyes. He was in superb shape, too. Over the three years she'd worked for him, she'd learned he indulged in golfing, racquetball, swimming, cross-county skiing, and cycling.

Bebe hung the clothes in her walk-in closet and changed into her yoga pants and t-shirt. When she scooped up Simba who purred, she almost groaned from his sheer size and weight.

"Milk for you? Wine for Mommy. Where's Sly?"

As if hearing his name, Sylvester trotted out from his perch underneath the kitchen island. He flicked his black tail with the white end.

"There you are. We're having wine and milk." She set Simba on top of the island's granite countertop.

Sylvester yowled and jumped up, joining his kitty partner.

Rescuing them from the shelter in Thunder Bay upon first moving to the city had been the best decision on her part. Just as they'd been abandoned, so had she, and in her eyes, she needed them as much as they needed her.

"It's salmon tonight. Salmon steak for me. Salmon in the can for you guys." She opened the fridge and retrieved the fresh cream she kept on hand for them, and also grabbed the wine.

Once she got the kitties served, she sipped her wine and called up her sister's contact info on the laptop.

Gigi's glowing face appeared on the screen. "Well, what's up?" her big sister asked.

"It happened. It happened." Bebe plopped on the stool at the island. "He asked me to attend the conference."

"See. I told you so." Gigi grinned slyly. "I knew it. I knew it. Don't you ever underestimate yourself again. He believes in you. And so do I."

"You think so?" It wasn't easy being an Ojibway woman trying to build a new career in real estate.

"I know so." Gigi winked. "By the way, has anything happened on the romantic front?"

Heat scorched Bebe's cheeks. She made a face at the laptop screen. Why oh why had she told Big Sis about the hotness factor of her super-babe boss? "No. And nothing will happen. He's a true professional, as am I."

"It's been three years . . ." Gigi knowingly eyed the screen.

Taking such a big risk again was out of the question. There wasn't a chance Bebe would put her job in jeopardy for a second time. "Not going there. My days of office romances are done."

"You can't make all men pay for what Brad did," Gigi fired back, but a hint of sympathy lurked in her words. "You're single. He's single. You said you caught him looking at you a few times. You said there's enough sizzle to fry a pan of bacon—"

"No." Bebe raised her hand. "Pack it away. I called to talk about the conference."

"And . . ."

"I think it's time I stepped out of hibernation. There are bars there . . ." Bebe sipped more wine.

"Oh? Going dick hunting?" Gigi giggled.

"Don't be crass. Let's simply say I'm tired of my vibrator."

"But you won't let any men at the conference get a peek at your panties?"

"Nope. They're colleagues and business acquaintances. My personal life is staying far away from real estate. And you know how men talk. I won't be fodder for the water cooler."

"Y'mean men at the conference talking?"

"Yep. I aim to be strictly professional." Sure, it was okay for men to screw around on business trips with colleagues and acquaintances, but the double standard of a woman having some fun within the circle still applied, which was pure bullshit.

"But if there's a gorgeous stud in one of the bars who has nothing to do with real estate . . ." Bebe couldn't help her grin.

"What are you gonna pack?"

"Oh, I'll be dressed for success." Bebe waggled her finger. "My kind of success."

"A knock-'em-out killer mini-skirt? Fuck-me heels? Fishnets?" Gigi giggled again.

"Don't forget killer lingerie," Bebe added in a purring voice. "Once I say goodbye to you, I'm going shopping at Chest of Drawers."

"Ooh, that's the bad girl shop. Go you. It's about time."

"I'll talk to you later." More than a chuckle sat in Bebe's tummy. Flutters of excitement danced straight across her lower abdomen.

"Sure, sweetie. Muah. Muah."

Bebe closed the window and pulled up a new tab. She clicked the mouse and opened the website to the most daring lingerie store in North America for some well-deserved naughty retail therapy.

The Matawapit Family Series

Blessed (Book One)
Redeemed (Book Two)
Sanctified (Book Three)
Renewed (Book Four)

Other Titles:

Thanks to You (Short Story)
Tied Up with a Bow (Short Story)

ABOUT THE AUTHOR

An Ojibway from Northwestern Ontario, Maggie resides in the country with her husband and their fur babies, two beautiful Alaskan Malamutes. When she's not writing, she can be found pulling weeds in the flower beds, mowing the huge lawn, walking the Mals deep in the bush, teeing up a ball at the golf course, fishing in the boat for walleye, or sitting on the deck at her sister's house, making more wonderful memories with the people she loves most.

https://maggieblackbird.com/
https://www.facebook.com/maggieblackbirdauthor/
https://twitter.com/BlackbirdMaggie/
https://www.goodreads.com/author/show/18176196.Maggie_Blackbird

Sign up for Maggie's newsletter: https://yahoo.us20.list-manage.com/sub-scribe?u=92959d27295c47605a8325906&id=d83ed57ebd

www.ingramcontent.com/pod-product-compliance
Lightning Source LLC
Chambersburg PA
CBHW062009170626
46813CB00001B/89